A BOTANIST'S GUIDE TO RITUALS AND REVENGE

Center Point
Large Print

Also by Kate Khavari and available from
Center Point Large Print:

A Botanist's Guide to Parties and Poison
A Botanist's Guide to Flowers and Fatalities
A Botanist's Guide to Society and Secrets

A BOTANIST'S GUIDE
TO RITUALS AND REVENGE

A SAFFRON EVERLEIGH MYSTERY

Kate Khavari

CENTER POINT LARGE PRINT
THORNDIKE, MAINE

This Center Point Large Print edition
is published in the year 2025 by arrangement with
Crooked Lane Books, an imprint of
The Quick Brown Fox and Company, LLC.

Copyright © 2025 by Kate Khavari.

All rights reserved.

This is a work of fiction. All of the names, characters,
organizations, places, and events portrayed in this novel
are either products of the author's imagination or are
used fictitiously. Any resemblance to real or
actual events, locales, or persons, living
or dead, is entirely coincidental.

The text of this Large Print edition is unabridged.
In other aspects, this book may vary
from the original edition.
Printed in the United States of America
on permanent paper sourced using
environmentally responsible foresting methods.
Set in 16-point Times New Roman type.

ISBN: 979-8-89164-621-6

The Library of Congress has cataloged this record
under Library of Congress Control Number: 2025936645

For Erin

CHAPTER 1

February 1924

The motorcar was late.

Saffron Everleigh rocked on her heels on the pavement outside the train station, biting her lip. Bedford's Midland Road was a steady stream of motorcars and horse-drawn carts, drifting in and out of the cold violet haze of a late winter's evening. The old motorcar belonging to the Ellington estate wouldn't be easy to spot, but if memory served, its noisy engine would announce itself well before the battered green motorcar became visible.

Next to her, Alexander Ashton checked his wristwatch.

"I don't know what could be keeping them." Saffron internally winced at how high and nervous her voice sounded. She bit her tongue on further excuses or suppositions as to why their promised transportation was taking so long to arrive. She turned back to the station and saw Elizabeth glaring through the condensation coating the window. Her best friend hadn't bothered to come outside with them to wait.

She also hadn't bothered to make an effort to be pleasant company during their journey.

Saffron hadn't expected Elizabeth to be thrilled to accept the invitation back to their childhood home of Bedford, but knowing as she must how anxious Saffron was to be returning under the current circumstances, Saffron might have hoped Elizabeth would put on a better show of support.

One of those circumstances stood steady as a rock at her side. Alexander's olive-toned skin was tinged pink beneath his dark fedora, but he appeared otherwise unperturbed by the cold. She could only hope that his stoic demeanor was truly how he felt; she didn't want her beau to be even a fraction as anxious as she felt.

It was one thing to visit one's estranged family, and another to be bringing along an unexpected boyfriend likely to be unacceptable to said estranged family. But it was truly outrageous to add the inexplicable presence of a man who'd claimed murderous and treasonous acts without blinking an eye.

A white cloud plumed from her mouth as she sighed. And now they were late, not only to arrive at Ellington, but for dinner, which was a mortal sin to Lady Easting, Saffron's grandmother. If only the train hadn't been late! Delays caused by poor weather, though there were only scant snowflakes falling, had put them so far behind it was nearly eight in the evening.

Alexander stirred next to her. "A green motor-car, you said?"

She followed his gaze down the street. A dark green motorcar chugged along, inciting the ire of the drivers of several other vehicles that swerved around its slow progress. It made enough of a racket to cut through the buzz of the street.

Saffron bit her lip. "I believe that's our lift."

She signaled to Elizabeth, who emerged from the station with her fur stole wrapped tightly under her chin. A porter followed with their luggage.

The green motorcar came to a halt with a worrisome grinding sound. The driver bounded from the cab. He removed his cap, revealing a cheerful, middle-aged face. "Miss Everleigh?"

"Yes," Saffron said, stepping forward.

He offered her a quick bow, the Ellington livery of green and gray peeking from under his coat collar. "I'm Perry, Lord Easting's driver. I'll just load up the luggage and we can be on our way."

If he was surprised to see her with additional companions, he didn't show it. She smiled back at him. "Thank you, Perry."

The driver didn't bat an eye at the luggage overflowing the back, instead lashing Alexander's battered suitcase to the roof. He began a commentary on Bedford's noteworthy sights as they pulled away from the station. Most of the description of the importance of River Ouse and St. Peter's Church was lost to the noise of the engine, but Saffron didn't need to be reminded of Bedford's few claims to fame. Alexander, sitting next to Perry, nodded occasionally, though Saffron couldn't be sure he could hear him—or see, for that matter. It was quite dark, even with the mauve snow-laden clouds low overhead.

Bedford abruptly ended, replaced by open country. She knew there were frosty fields frilled with trees spread on either side of the road, yet she could see nothing but dark shapes.

Perry continued his lecture on nearby Goldington Hall and assorted points of interest, but his voice faded from Saffron's attention, replaced by nauseating anticipation.

Soon, the driver slowed and turned to cross the stone bridge over the River Ouse, and then they were on Ellington land.

A thrill of nerves had Saffron weaving her gloved fingers together in her lap. Nearly three years had lapsed since she'd last set foot on the property. Three years since she'd last seen her mother and grandmother. She communicated with her mother often, and now that her family home had been outfitted with a telephone, it would be easy to speak to her daily if she wished.

Her grandmother was another story. But her mother had assured her in their brief telephone calls to coordinate Saffron's travel that her grandfather had insisted she return to Ellington, and Lord Easting, even ailing as he was after a heart attack, could be as stubborn as a bull. He'd have to be to get her grandmother to agree to hosting their wayward granddaughter after the way they'd last parted.

The harsh words and subsequent pleading echoed in Saffron's mind as the motorcar passed under the elegant iron and stone arch and onto a gravel drive. Saffron resisted the urge to press her suddenly hot face against the cold glass window.

That window now showed something other than vague shadows; lights shone in the distance, growing larger.

The car came to a crunching stop, and silence rung in her ears in the absence of the cacophony of the engine. They'd arrived.

Perry hopped out and busied himself opening doors. Saffron peered around Elizabeth to see that the double doors of the front entry were closed. Her stomach twisted with an unexpected jolt of disappointment that no one was there to greet them.

Elizabeth, who'd more or less ignored her since they'd entered the motorcar, cast her a sardonic look. "Should we just turn around and go back home?"

London had been their home for a while now. But Saffron still held Ellington, and those within it, in her heart. And she could not let an unpredictable and dangerous person slither his way in like some venomous vine.

"No," Saffron said firmly. "Let's go inside."

Just as Saffron exited the motorcar, the double doors flung open.

"Finally!" cried the man who strode out onto the steps, pulling an overcoat on over a dinner jacket. "Lady Easting is going to have a bloody conniption if we don't get on our way—"

Saffron broke into a grin and stepped forward. "Grandmama having a conniption is just what I expected, actually."

Her cousin John stopped abruptly, blinking down at the trio arrayed before the car. "By gad, Saffron, what the devil are you doing here?"

Saffron's face fell. "What do you mean, what am I doing here? I was called to come back here, just as you were."

John waved a dismissive hand. "I know *that,* but what are you doing here now? I thought you were coming tomorrow since the train schedule was mucked up." He clambered down the steps and bent to give her a peck on the cheek before chucking her chin and grinning at her. His face was still boyish, soft around the cheeks and chin with mischievous blue eyes. Only his slightly receding dark brown hair hinted he wasn't a lad of fifteen rather than twice that. His attention shifted behind her and his smile broadened still further. "And you've brought Eliza! And a person whom I think I recognize from your letters."

"John," Elizabeth said, coming forward. "Still married to that French witch, are you?"

"Happily so, my dear," John said with a laugh, giving her a brief hug. "Don't let's fight over my very fine self. There's enough drama afoot as it is."

"Drama already?" Elizabeth snorted. "Excellent."

"This is Alexander Ashton," Saffron said, waving Alexander forward. He'd stopped just outside the motorcar. "Alexander, my cousin, John. I stayed with him and his wife and son when I was in France in November."

They shook hands.

"You haven't much time to change for dinner," John said, frowning at Saffron. "We were meant to leave twenty minutes ago, but the car was nowhere to be seen."

"I telephoned from the station," Saffron said, frowning. "Did Kirby not mention we were on our way?"

"That old rascal," muttered John before brightening. "This is far better. You'll be a surprise, and you know how Grandmama will *cherish* that."

They passed through the thick double doors and into the entry. The lofty space was bracketed by two matching staircases leading to the second floor. The familiar scent of beeswax polish and her grandmother's favored potpourri filled her senses. Immediately, she was set back in time when she'd stood in this same spot, memorizing her childhood home before leaving it for what she'd hoped was not forever.

A deep voice interrupted her recollection. "Miss Saffron, welcome back."

Saffron turned to the right hand staircase, where she found Kirby, the butler. He stood slightly more stooped than last she'd seen him. His head lacked more silver hair than before, too. She smiled politely at him. "How good to see you, Kirby."

"Thank you, miss. I see Miss Elizabeth has accompanied you." He bowed to Elizabeth, who rolled her eyes while his eyes were cast downward. This show of civility was a far cry from how he'd dealt with them as unruly youth. Elizabeth, in particular, had taken great pride in her ability to break the butler's sedate facade.

Kirby then cast his somber gaze on Alexander. "Sir, welcome to Ellington Manor."

"This is Alexander Ashton," Saffron said. "My friend, and if Lady Easting will allow it, another guest."

Her confident speech didn't do much to convince Kirby. He gave her a long look before intoning, "I will inform Lady Easting. If you will be so good as to wait in the drawing room—"

John waved a hand. "We haven't got time for that. Send their luggage up so they can change for dinner; otherwise, Lady Easting will have all our heads for making us still later."

"Do not be ridiculous, John."

Saffron's head jerked up to see a petite woman coming down the steps. Her hair, now more white than blonde, was set with diamond barrettes and her neck adorned with matching strands of jewels. Lady Easting looked regal in her mauve evening gown, but nothing completed the impression more than the haughty expression icing over her features. Saffron's grandmother was not a physically impressive woman, standing a few inches shorter than Saffron's own average height, but her conviction of her own absolute rightness in all things did much to elevate her person.

"It is not Kirby's fault we shall be late," Lady Easting finished as she came to a stop on the landing a few steps above where the rest stood. She surveyed each of them, her light blue eyes resting on Alexander before turning to Saffron.

There was an uncomfortable beat before Saffron said, "Hello, Grandmama."

"Saffron," she said. Her attention flicked to Elizabeth. "Elizabeth."

"Your ladyship," Elizabeth said with an obnoxious smile. "How do you do?"

Lady Easting took the final few steps to stand before Saffron on the polished tile floor. "I will be much better when my granddaughter ceases her poor manners and introduces her . . . companion."

Swallowing, Saffron took a half step back so Alexander was at her side. "Lady Easting, may I present Alexander Ashton? My colleague at the university"—she dreaded saying it but she couldn't waver, else her grandmother would inevitably use it against her later—"and my beau."

Her grandmother didn't blink. "I see." She inclined her head toward Alexander. "How do you do, Mr. Ashton?"

Alexander nodded back. "Lady Easting."

"I'm afraid we haven't the time for conversation," Lady Easting said briskly. "As John has mentioned, we are already quite late for dinner. You must excuse us."

"Don't be daft, Grandmama," John said with a laugh. "We'll all go. If we're already late, a few more minutes won't make a difference."

Lady Easting's mouth pinched, but any response she might have fired back was waylaid by another entrance.

Violet Everleigh walked into the entry hall. And she wasn't alone.

Saffron scarcely heard her mother's quiet exclamation of pleasure at seeing her, or knew to lift her arms to return her mother's embrace. She was too busy staring at the man who'd followed her into the hall.

He wore a plain black suit of quality, and his dark hair was parted severely in the middle and slicked back. His eyes were partially obscured by a pair of round spectacles, and a thin beard lined his jaw.

But she knew him, had dreamed of him whispering threats in her ear in the months since their would-be confrontation.

"Oh, Dr. Wyatt," Violet said, breaking away from Saffron and seeing Saffron's eyes locked on him. "Saffron, this is Lord Easting's cardiologist, Dr. Wyatt."

Bill Wyatt came to a stop before her, and with a slight smile and slighter bow, said, "Miss Everleigh, how pleased I am you are here."

CHAPTER 2

Saffron managed to fumble through the rest of the necessary introductions. She saw only the perpetual smile on Bill's lips, and the way her mother had beamed at her and Alexander when they made each other's acquaintance. That, at least, had been a good thing.

That fleeting moment of positivity was swamped in anxiety and impatience, for her grandmother did her equivalent of throwing her hands in the air by suggesting she, John, and Dr. Wyatt leave ahead of the rest.

"Dr. Wyatt is going?" she murmured to her mother as her grandmother was helped into her fur coat by Kirby.

"He was invited, yes," her mother said. She turned slightly, putting her back to the room to murmur, "Will Elizabeth be alright, do you think? I know she hasn't seen her parents since the incident."

"I don't anticipate it being a problem," Saffron replied. She was sure Elizabeth had no intention of seeing her family while in Bedford, even if theirs was the property abutting Ellington land.

"Good," her mother said, smiling. "The house-keeper, Mrs. Sharnbrook, is likely supervising the dinner in the servants' hall, so I'll show everyone to their rooms."

Lady Easting had swept from the hall out the doors without a departing word, and John and "Dr. Wyatt" followed. Saffron regretted she had no opportunity to question Bill as she'd imagined she would upon seeing him here, but she required privacy for the confrontation, and there was certainly none to be had in the entry hall.

That point was proven as they mounted the steps behind Violet and Elizabeth, who'd fallen into step together.

Alexander's voice was low as he asked, "What was the *incident?*"

She hadn't missed the way Alexander had tensed upon meeting Bill, nor how he'd inched protectively before her. She doubted he really wanted to hear about Elizabeth's past rather than plot ways of ridding themselves of Bill now that they'd confirmed he was at Ellington. She thought it likely he was trying to distract her. She was willing to be distracted, at least until she could figure out what to do next. "You remember me telling you that Elizabeth came to London with me to escape an intolerable marriage arrangement?"

"I do," he replied.

How it was she'd never had cause to explain to Alexander the circumstances under which Elizabeth left Bedford? "When her parents told her that she was to marry Mr. Roddingham, it was at a party they were hosting. He was a ghoulish old man living a county over, and we'd known him since we were girls. He was at least seventy, if not older. My greatest impression of him was that his teeth were atrocious. The Hales had already agreed to the marriage and signed some papers promising Roddingham would fund Mr. Hale's latest business scheme. The party was actually their engagement celebration."

Not for the first time, Saffron wished she'd been there. She'd not been invited, no doubt because the Hales, who'd always tolerated Saffron by virtue of her family's nobility, believed it was Saffron's influence that had goaded Elizabeth into wanting more from life than carefully arranged domesticity. Saffron would have gladly put up with Mr. Hale's grumbling and Mrs. Hale's high-pitched nattering if it had meant she'd been there to help Elizabeth. Not to mention the spectacle of Elizabeth utilizing all her powers of speech and sass to reject Mr. Roddingham and her parents would have been sensational. It had, in fact, been reported on in the *Bedfordshire Times*, a fact she knew because Mrs. Hale had sent them the newspaper clipping in an effort to shame Elizabeth into changing her mind. That clipping currently resided in a little brass frame on Elizabeth's dressing table.

Alexander's brows rose. "They surprised her

with the engagement? I can imagine how that went."

"Elizabeth enumerated the flaws in this plan—and Mr. Roddingham—so all one hundred guests could hear," Saffron said, lowering her voice. "Then she, ah, *requisitioned* the first vehicle in the drive and got herself on the next train to London to come find me. I was quite glad she had the sense to leave the motorcar at the station. The owners chose not to press charges against her for theft. They were guests at the party, of course. I like to think they had sympathy for her."

Ahead, her mother and Elizabeth had come to a stop along the gallery that separated the family wing from the rooms reserved for guests. The entry hall lay open beyond the balustrade, empty and echoing.

"Eliza, you'll be next to Saffron," Violet was saying.

Saffron opened her mouth, then closed it. She didn't particularly want to stay in her old bedroom. It held memories she couldn't afford to get lost in.

She must stay in the present, and her present was a rapid preparation for dinner at a thus far unknown location. "Who has invited us for dinner? And won't they mind if three extra guests show up?"

There was a beat of silence before her mother said, "Some local friends are hosting a rather interesting guest who offers some unusual entertainment, I gather."

"At Goldington Hall?" Elizabeth asked. "We might have just pulled over there."

Violet cleared her throat, her gray eyes worried. "No, not Goldington Hall. The invitation came from next door."

Elizabeth's lips parted, then closed.

"When your train was delayed, Lady Easting accepted the invitation to dinner from your parents," Violet explained quickly. She lowered her already quiet voice. "I believe it was in part because Lord Easting is not well enough to come down to dinner this evening and she wished to spare him what he would consider an embarrassment. You may stay here, Eliza, if you prefer. I will be here with Lord Easting, should he need anything."

"I will do no such thing." Elizabeth softened her strident tone, but her look of determination remained. "I don't object to your company, Mrs. E, but I'll not be deemed a coward for avoiding my parents. Give me five minutes and I'll be ready." She bustled inside her bedroom and shut the door.

Saffron then found herself alone with Alexander and her mother. The urge to say something in explanation of his presence was strong, but she'd imagined explaining to her grandparents and mother at once and nothing she'd planned to say

22

felt right. She didn't want to lie to her mother any more than necessary.

Violet turned to Alexander. "Mr. Ashton, I believe Mrs. Sharnbrook will not mind if I offer you the room just here . . ."

Saffron and Alexander followed her down the gallery and into the guest wing.

"It was prepared for Mr. Everleigh and his wife," Violet explained as they came to a stop in front of the largest guest suite, "but they told us when they arrived they preferred to be closer to the nursery for their son's sake. They're in John's usual room."

"That is convenient." Saffron internally winced at the inane comment even as she said it. Fortunately, her mother did not seem put off by the inconvenience of an uninvited and unexpected guest.

"Surprise guests are never easy to accommodate. Thank you, Mrs. Everleigh," Alexander said.

Saffron sent him an apologetic look. She didn't miss that subtle jab; she hadn't told him that her family was unaware he was coming. There never seemed to be the right time to inform either party without causing a great deal of unnecessary turmoil.

Violet smiled. "I imagine your luggage will be brought up momentarily. There is a bathroom two doors down that is shared, and of course, you are welcome to request a basin of water or anything else you require."

He nodded and murmured his thanks again.

Before things could further devolve into awkwardness, Saffron quickly said, "Elizabeth and I will meet you in the entry in a few minutes."

Alexander nodded his agreement and entered his room. Saffron and her mother turned back down the hall toward the family wing.

Where familiar comfort ought to have been, Saffron felt awkwardness instead. She began, "I hope you don't mind—"

"How lovely to meet—" Her mother broke off with a sideways smile.

Saffron cleared her throat. "I'm sorry for springing Alexander and Elizabeth on you. And Grandmama, though I think she'd still be disagreeable if I'd shown up alone."

"It's no trouble." Violet opened Saffron's bedroom door for her, but she didn't step inside. Violet smiled, tension in the faint lines around her mouth. "There is so much to say, my darling girl, but I dare not keep you longer than necessary. Come to my room when you get home, won't you? No matter the hour."

"I will," Saffron promised.

CHAPTER 3

By the time they'd changed and piled into the motorcar, it had certainly been longer than five minutes. Saffron sat between Elizabeth and Alexander, not an unfamiliar arrangement. The last few months Saffron and Alexander had been all but inseparable, spending much of their waking hours together at the university or out and about in the city. Saffron had taken to dragging Elizabeth along when they went out to the pictures or dancing.

It was a strange reversal of their traditional roles; Elizabeth had always been the social butterfly prodding Saffron to abandon her studies and live a little. But since November, Elizabeth was more likely to be found draining a bottle of wine in her dressing gown rather than sipping a cocktail at her usual haunts.

Yet another wave of unease sunk through her. Elizabeth was likely to dive headlong into whatever bottle was within reach that evening. It was her duty as Elizabeth's closest friend to show the Hales what a mistake they'd made in betraying their daughter, but she'd also have to ensure Elizabeth didn't get too out of hand.

Her gloved hand was suddenly enclosed in

Alexander's large one. He squeezed gently. His presence was a comfort as much as another source of anxiety. She also had a duty to Alexander, which she'd thus far failed.

"I'm sorry," she whispered to him, hoping he alone could hear her over the grumbling of the engine.

His dark eyes regarded her steadily in the glow from the headlights reflecting off the snow-speckled road. "No more surprises, I hope?"

For some reason, her heart sank. "None of my making."

When they turned down a lane marked with two overgrown oak trees, Elizabeth's leg started bouncing against Saffron's. Not releasing Alexander's hand, Saffron took Elizabeth's in her other hand when the house, lit up like a theater set, came into view.

Perry the driver eased to a stop. Alexander was the first out, leaving Saffron and Elizabeth momentarily alone in the cab.

Elizabeth extracted her miniature flask from her handbag. She unscrewed it and took a swig before offering it to Saffron. Though she was not one for hard liquors, Saffron would have taken a sip for courage, but she didn't dare walk into a dinner party smelling like whiskey with her grandmother present.

Elizabeth didn't share her reluctance; she took another gulp before tucking the flask away.

"Once more unto the breach, dear friend, once more."

The Hale home was a smaller establishment than Ellington, a two-story rectangular house Saffron had always thought of as a brick made of bricks. Now it looked like a brick that had melted on one side. A new wall trickled from the main building, seeming to taper off into shadow.

Elizabeth stared at it. "What is that?"

"New construction?" Saffron squinted past the glare of lights emanating from each window.

"Or they've begun ripping apart the back of the house and those are the stacks of bricks they're preparing to sell off," Elizabeth muttered.

The footman who'd opened the motorcar's door, a young man in servant's black and white with overlong blond hair, gave Elizabeth a look of alarm he quickly schooled into neutrality before saying, "This way, sir, madams."

He escorted them to the door. It was not the same door Saffron had pushed through any number of times, but a new one with intricate carvings deep into the polished wood. She exchanged a confused look with Elizabeth.

The entry was largely untouched, but signs of change were everywhere, from the wallpaper samples pinned to the wall to the very young-looking maids ready to take their coats. Something odd was happening here.

Saffron withheld a groan when Elizabeth

slipped out of her coat. Beneath the second-hand fur coat was a dress even Elizabeth had deemed scandalous.

Elizabeth caught her look and grinned, her wine-colored lips stretching wide. She ran a hand down the crimson fabric. "I couldn't decide if a ritzy sophisticate or a bohemian sheba would be more off-putting for my parents, so I decided to do my best impression of a flapper and hope for the worst. How did I do?"

At first glance, the dress was elegant. But a longer look revealed rather more than Saffron would ever consider showing off in public, let alone at a family dinner. The sheer gauze caught by a small, jeweled clip on either shoulder flowed over a dangerously low-cut slip. Though Elizabeth's figure was far more curvaceous than was popular, she'd sworn off corsets and slimming contraptions of any kind. There was therefore a good bit of cleavage on display, not to mention her upper arms where her gloves did not reach, and a generous swath of her back.

Alexander surprised her by saying, "Very successful."

Elizabeth beamed at him.

It was no lie to say, "You look marvelous," for Elizabeth truly did, like a star straight out of a glamorous film. Saffron knew better than to venture any other comment.

It was too late, anyway, for Elizabeth was

strutting toward the drawing room, from which a low rumble of voices came. Alexander offered Saffron his arm, and she took it. He, too, looked marvelous in his black evening kit. He'd combed his dark hair back, taming the curls that precipitation always encouraged to misbehave, and had somehow managed to find time to give his strong jaw a close shave.

Saffron's own ablutions had allowed only powder and lipstick reapplication and ensuring her short curls hadn't been too badly squashed by her hat during the journey. Her dress was nothing special, a simple emerald-green art silk shift gathered at one side with a glittering brooch that she wore often. But it was something she'd bought in London with her own money, and it gave her a bit more confidence walking into the Hales' drawing room.

The entire party was on their feet, save for Lady Easting, who sat near the hearth, and every last person was turned toward the door. They looked not at Saffron and Alexander, but Elizabeth and her mother. It was no wonder, for Mrs. Hale was making a good deal of racket.

She tearfully embraced Elizabeth, crying, "My dearest Eliza! How I have missed you!"

"I'm sure you have, Mother," Elizabeth was saying. She refused to return her mother's affection, instead holding herself still and staring ahead with a bored look. That bored look was focused on her father, who looked frozen where he stood, crystal tumbler in hand, a few feet away.

Mr. Hale was in his middle years, with thinning light brown hair fading to gray and a heavy face creased with frown lines. His pinstripe suit, cut in the latest fashion, emphasized his height, though no amount of stripes could minimize his width. Paired with his ability to shout down the entire house, his size had always put to mind a touchy elephant, likely to trumpet his irritation at the slightest provocation.

Saffron hoped his temper wasn't about to erupt. She was sure he'd not spoken or written a word to Elizabeth in several years, but it likely wasn't out of apathy. Rather than slink away from the spotlight Mrs. Hale was placing on herself and Elizabeth, Saffron stayed where she was, prepared to stand at Elizabeth's side should things turn hostile.

The others in the room looked on with discomfort, like John, or with tactless interest, like the Harvey sisters. The elderly spinsters, residents of Goldington Hall and a staple of higher Bedford society, huddled together, all but gaping at the scene.

With them stood a man and a woman, the former in his thirties, perhaps, with gingery hair slicked back neatly from his handsome face. His companion drew Saffron's attention away almost instantly. The petite woman looked as if she'd stepped out of a photograph from 1880. She wore unrelieved black save for a frill of white lace at her throat, pinned with an ivory cameo. Her dark hair was draped with black lace, putting into stark relief her pale, lightly-lined face. A pale face that was immediately familiar.

Saffron's mouth fell open. *Surely* that wasn't—

"Just as Madame predicted," one of the Harvey sisters said.

The other sister nodded. "The one who was lost has returned!"

That seemed to awaken Mr. Hale from his frozen stupor. He blinked, then took a gulp from his tumbler. He cleared his throat before saying gruffly, "Of course, Madame was right. Welcome home, Elizabeth."

Mrs. Hale, blinking back tears Saffron could see were not actually filling her eyes, took in Elizabeth with a tremulous smile. "All this time, we thought it was Wesley who we would be reunited with—"

Elizabeth was clearly as taken aback as Saffron by that jarring statement. Her cool facade fell away. "What?"

Mrs. Hale took Elizabeth's hand and dragged her toward the Victorian woman. "Madame Martin, was this not what your spirits foresaw? Reunited with my daughter, oh!" She made to pinch Elizabeth's cheek.

Elizabeth shook her mother off before taking in Madame Martin. Confusion flitted over her face before recognition struck her just as it had Saffron. "Madame Martin? Madame *Martiné,* the medium?"

The man at Madame's side stepped forward with a sociable smile. "Indeed, Miss Hale. Allow me—"

Elizabeth raised a hand to stay him. "And what would the bogus medium that was performing séances in the 5th Arrondissement three months ago be doing here, in my family's home?"

Madame's lips tipped up in a dreamy smile. "I was drawn here by the spirits. Drawn to your family, to help heal wounds." Her eyes, dark as night, focused on Elizabeth. "It is what Wesley wants, Eliza."

Elizabeth's face turned nearly as scarlet as her dress. Saffron stepped forward, prepared to intervene, but the butler, a new one Saffron didn't know, announced dinner was served.

Alexander smoothly offered Elizabeth his arm, for which Saffron was immensely grateful. Elizabeth, still glaring daggers at the medium, took it, and they moved in the direction of the dining room where the rest of the party was headed. It left Saffron without an escort, which didn't bother her in the least.

The medium's companion, however, offered his arm with raised brows. He spoke with an English accent, unlike Madame. "Miss Everleigh, isn't it?"

She accepted his arm simply because she didn't wish to make more of a fuss. Madame Martin had already drifted away, trailing the rest of the guests like a particularly sedate specter. "Yes, I'm Lady Easting's granddaughter, Saffron Everleigh."

"Bernard Fischer, at your service," he said. He had a bright tenor voice and an easy smile. "I apologize for this unconventional meeting. But much that transpires in my line of work is unconventional."

"Are you also a psychic?" she asked.

"No, not at all," he said quickly. "I assist Madame Martin so she might help those who need her to connect to lost loved ones. I manage her travel and appointments, maintain her accounts, that sort of thing."

They entered the dining room, which Saffron was surprised to see had been painted a garish shade of yellow. The long table in the center of the well-lit room was also unfamiliar. It seemed the Hales had replaced half their furniture, but with what money? Surely, they would have heard if the Hales had regained their fortune.

Mr. Fischer guided her to an open seat and then settled next to her. Saffron guessed the usual name cards had been discarded as a result of her and her friends' last-minute arrival. From how Mrs. Hale was happily chattering to Elizabeth, she didn't think she minded additional people at her dinner table. "Do you truly believe in Madame Martin's ability to speak to spirits?" Saffron asked.

Mr. Fischer's auburn brows furrowed. "I understand your skepticism. I was a skeptic, too. But I have seen things in my time with Madame Martin that have defied—expanded, even—my understanding of the world and what lies beyond."

"Elizabeth and I saw Madame Martin perform in Paris."

Mr. Fischer gave her a sardonic smile that suited his sharp features better than his earnestness. "Yes, I gathered that. Did you glean anything from watching her commune with the spirits?"

"I did." It wouldn't do to point out she'd seen straight through Madame and her "spirits." She and Elizabeth had thought it would be a lark to see a séance, and they were not disappointed. The whole thing was well done. The ambiance was right, and Madame Martin was appropriately theatrical but not histrionic. The actors they'd placed in the audience to "choose at random" to participate played their parts well. Saffron and Elizabeth had delighted in pointing out all the little tricks Madame had used. For Saffron's part, her scientific mind wouldn't allow her to believe that a mere touch could enable someone to speak to the ghost of a person they'd never met. Not to mention the dearth of conclusive evidence supporting the existence of ghosts. Their amusement had quickly faded when they came to understand the entirety of Madame's show centered on communicating with dead servicemen. They'd suffered too much in the wake of the Great War to appreciate someone making a living on others' grief.

"Madame travelling across the Channel suggests business is good," Saffron said dryly.

Mr. Fischer paused in placing his napkin in his lap to give her a hurt look. "It is a service, Miss Everleigh, to ensure the wishes of the dead are respected, their last thoughts to those they longed to speak to as they took their final breaths."

Wesley would not have wanted a stranger pretending to speak in his voice, even if it was a voice of comfort. She knew it with certainty; they'd been sweethearts before his death on the fields of Flanders. The middle Hale child, for all his youthful antics, had been a peacemaker, especially between Elizabeth and her parents. He'd rather be at rest than stirring up his family's grief.

She said none of this, of course. It wasn't polite to question one's dinner companion's morally dubious career choices.

CHAPTER 4

The medium's assistant leaned closer to Saffron to murmur something. Alexander's knife sliced into his chicken a la rose, scraping against the china underneath with an inelegant screech.

At his side, John Everleigh chuckled. "No need to look so sour, Ashton. A little flirtation doesn't hurt, does it?"

Alexander glanced at him and forced a light voice. "Of course not. But I'm sure you'd object to a stranger leering at your wife."

John's amusement was obvious. It reminded Alexander forcefully of Saffron, for they shared the mischievous twinkle in their matching blue eyes that promised trouble and delight in equal measures. "I concede," John said. "Suzette would likely tell me off for making a fuss, too." He took a sip from his wine glass. "Strange, these people, don't you think?"

Alexander looked down the table to where Madame Martin sat next to Mr. Hale at the far end of the table. From what little Alexander could see of the medium, both seemed engrossed in their conversation. They were a mismatched pair: Madame dressed in a fashion decades out of style with skin so pale she could have been one of the

36

ghosts she claimed to channel, and Mr. Hale, no different from any businessman bustling down a city street. He wondered what they could have to speak so seriously about.

As for the psychic's assistant and the attention he paid Saffron, it wasn't flirtation Alexander was worried about. He found the timing suspicious. A psychic had just happened to come to the house next to Ellington just as Bill Wyatt appeared?

Bill sat a few seats down, conducting himself in an unobtrusive manner as he steadily ate his meal. Alexander's eye had been drawn to him just as often as Saffron and her dinner companion. Alexander observed the others around the table, attempting to take the measure of each.

At Mr. Hale's other side was Lady Easting, who conversed with the older, bespectacled man to her left who wore a dog collar. Alexander guessed he was the local vicar. Next to him sat Saffron, then Madame Martin's associate. On the other side of the red-haired man was another Harvey sister. She and the woman to Alexander's left were short and thin, both dressed in shabby evening wear. The one wore gray, the other wore a shade of purple that might as well have been gray. She was engrossed in her meal, cutting each bite into minute pieces before savoring each one with slow, thoughtful chewing.

"I take it you're not a believer?" John asked, interrupting his thoughts.

"In spiritualism? I can't say I am."

"Nor I." John patted his mouth with his napkin. "The community here is so close-knit, formalities are often dispensed with when in small gatherings like this." When Alexander lifted his brows in question, John added, "Seating arrangements, you know. Not the done thing, to put two men side by side, but Mrs. Hale has commandeered Elizabeth and who could argue?" He tilted his head to his right, where Elizabeth sat next to her mother at the foot of the table. "You showing up has evened things out a bit, actually. Suzette would have ruined the numbers further. She stayed behind with our son, Benjamin. He's only three, you know."

Saffron spoke about John often and thus Alexander knew a great deal about John and Saffron's childhood antics, his law practice in Montereau, and his marriage to a French nurse after a brief romance during John's recovery after being shot in the arm in the war. "It must be difficult for him to travel so far from home."

"It was not a pleasant journey, no," John said. He signaled for a footman to refill his wine glass. He sniffed the red appreciatively, and his eyes briefly dropped to Alexander's untouched glass. "Even with Nanny traveling with us, it didn't feel right for Suzette to leave Ben. Not to mention my poor wife was sick as a dog on the crossing. Good they both get the chance to recoup. I intend to show them every corner of Ellington, all my old haunts. I spent a good deal of time here as a boy, of course. Most holidays I was tramping around the fields and woods, getting Saffron into all sorts of trouble."

Saffron must have caught her name in conversation. "Don't go telling tales on me, John," she said mildly. "Or else I'll tell Suzette every naughty thing you did growing up and she'll abandon you for someone less silly."

"Less silly?" John scoffed. "That's the entire reason she married me, don't you know?"

Saffron rolled her eyes and returned to her conversation. Though Alexander might have preferred watching her to see if he could infer what they were speaking about, he needed to give a good impression to John. He was beginning to realize John was less a cousin and more like a brother to her.

That, and John was an important source of information, and influence on his grandparents. It was essential he and Saffron were united against Bill and his machinations.

"You said this little community often flouted decorum," Alexander said. "Does that include employees socializing with the family?"

"Hm?" John patted his mouth with his napkin and leaned back so the footmen could move around him to change courses. "Employees? Oh, you mean the medium? I don't know if she's strictly employed by the Hales, but yes, she's been an anchor of social life here for a few weeks, according to my aunt. Mr. Hale met her in London and he was apparently so impressed he insisted on bringing her here. Something about getting closer to the center of the family to better communicate with those lost." He dropped his voice, his gaiety ebbing. "They lost their second son, the middle child, you know. Wesley. He was just a boy at Flanders." John's eyes dropped to where Alexander's right hand rested on the table, a clear sign Saffron had told him about Alexander's own wartime trials. He resisted the urge to slip the scarred hand under the table. "I don't know if I ought to mention it, since it was ages ago, but Saffron and he were quite close. She was just a girl, though, so . . ."

"She's told me about Wesley," Alexander said, eager to put this awkwardness behind them. "Odd that Mr. Hale was the one inviting Madame here. I believe spiritualism usually gets its hooks in women first."

John shrugged. "Who is to say? Regardless of who instigated it, you can see Mrs. Hale is fond of Madame as well. Hard to dislike the woman who tells you your son loves you very much from beyond the grave."

John soon changed the subject to less super-natural topics, for which Alexander was grateful.

• • •

When Elizabeth raised a finger to indicate more drink yet again, Saffron attempted to lock eyes with the footman carrying the pitcher of chilled sweet wine. He approached her friend's side, and though he caught Saffron's stern gaze and no doubt saw her widen her eyes in warning, he filled Elizabeth's glass once again.

Saffron clenched her fingers together in her lap. Even from half the table away, she could see Elizabeth was flushed, and her expression more and more cynical. A sure sign trouble was on the way.

Fortunately, dinner was nearly at an end. The servants had just served ice cream in delicate little cups.

On the other side of Mr. Fischer, the older Harvey sister, Lillian, said, "Divine ice, absolutely divine. And such charming dishes."

"Oh, thank you. Nicolas brought them for Christmas," Mrs. Hale replied. Her own complexion was flushed and her eyes bright. She'd spent the entire meal in a one-sided conversation with Elizabeth, who'd ignored her or muttered things that made her mother laugh. Unless things had very much changed in the last few years, any unpleasant comment out of Elizabeth's mouth transformed into charming jokes in Mrs. Hale's ears.

"I believe he said these dishes were made in

Istanbul, of all places! That's in the Orient, you know," she went on, quite incorrectly, to Miss Harvey. "How thoughtful he is, to think of us amid all his extensive travels. The army keeps him so very busy, you know."

"Dearest Nicolas," drawled Elizabeth. "What a fellow, I tell you."

Down the table, Alexander sent Saffron a speaking look. Beyond him, Bill was looking at her with a placid sort of amusement that set her teeth on edge.

Elizabeth crowed, "We had an *ever* so lovely time with him just a few months ago, didn't we, Saff?"

"It was good to see Nick again." Unwillingly, her eyes darted back to Bill, half expecting him to say something suggestive about their recent experiences with Nick, but he remained silent.

"We thought he was in the Ottomans," tittered Mrs. Hale, "until he quite unexpectedly arrived just before Christmas."

Elizabeth tutted. "The *Ottomans*. Not 1918 any longer, Mother."

Mrs. Hale paid her no mind. "It was thrilling to see him. Dear Nick always tells such amusing tales."

"Of *manure,*" Elizabeth said, then let out a loose laugh. "All of it was manure, wasn't it!"

Saffron winced at her too-loud hoot of laughter. Elizabeth wasn't wrong; all of what her older brother had told them of his supposed employment in the Agricultural Ministry had been a lie, a cover to allow him to investigate a murder and conspiracy Saffron had helped him to resolve. Alexander and Elizabeth had done their bit, too, and all of them had come out of it worse than they began. Elizabeth's boyfriend, Colin, was revealed as the worst sort of man, Alexander had received a thorough beating, and Saffron . . . Saffron had come away from the business with Nick with a debt to Bill that she had no means or desire to repay.

"Eliza," her mother said with an embarrassed little laugh. Her eyes shot down the table to Lady Easting, who looked on with pursed lips. "Hardly appropriate, darling."

"I wonder what Nick would think of this lovely guest you have here." Elizabeth leaned around the others to look down the table at Madame Martin. "Or what Madame Martin thinks of my brother. What did the spirits tell you about my living brother, Madame? Do they know his secrets?"

"I doubt the spirits are much interested in piles of paperwork," Saffron said. "For that is all Nick said he gets up to, even in far-off places. Rather a pity. But John, you said when your work calls on you to travel, it's much the same, isn't it?"

John clearly understood her purpose, for he leaped into action with a long-winded story of a tedious trip to settle a dispute for one of his clients. It took up the rest of dessert, and Saffron breathed a sigh of relief when it was time for coffee.

When Saffron arrived in the drawing room, Elizabeth was already standing at the cabinet that housed liquors. Saffron snatched up a cup of coffee and beelined to her.

"Absolutely not," she whispered as she snatched a bottle of gin from her friend's hand. "You are drinking nothing but coffee for the rest of the night."

"Provided it's got a healthy dollop of whiskey, fine," Elizabeth shot back. She reached for another bottle.

"Oh dear," Saffron said loudly, glaring at Elizabeth. "My hem is coming undone. How very irritating."

"*You* are irritating," muttered Elizabeth.

From where she stood before the hearth, Mrs. Hale frowned over at them. "Would you like me to ring for a maid to fix it for you? I just hired the most darling girl, you know."

"If I could just have a sewing kit, Mrs. Hale, I would very much appreciate it," Saffron said quickly. "Elizabeth could assist me."

"You don't want me armed with anything sharp," Elizabeth said, but Saffron was already dragging her across the room as quickly as she could manage with her cup of black coffee in hand.

44

"The retiring room?" Saffron prompted Mrs. Hale, who was looking nonplussed.

"I—well—" Mrs. Hale stammered, but Saffron didn't wait. Elizabeth was likely to start muttering again.

Just as the drawing room door closed behind them, Mrs. Hale could be heard saying, "Absolutely indispensable to Saffron, my Eliza. I don't know what she'll do when . . ."

"What rot," Elizabeth said. "*Indispensable.* I'm the most dispensable. Ask Nick. Ask Colin."

"The only thing I'd ask Colin Smith is 'How do you like prison?' " Saffron nudged Elizabeth down the hall to the retiring room, but stopped short when she opened the door.

"Well," Elizabeth said with a snort of a laugh, "I believe we are seeing the proverbial sow's ear rather than the silk purse."

Saffron was too busy whisking dustcloths off the masses of furniture cluttering the retiring room to mind that strangely twisted idiom. This was where the Hales' old furniture had been dumped, along with a great quantity of wallpaper rolls and jars of glue to affix it, and boxes labelled announcing contents of textured glass. She quickly found a pair of chairs and breathed a sigh of relief when she could put her back to the rest of the ghostly white-clad furniture. She still didn't like the look of covered-up furniture. "Sit down and drink your coffee, Eliza."

"I will," Elizabeth said with a pout, "but only because I like coffee."

When the coffee was gone and Elizabeth had leaned her head against the back of the chair, eyes closed, Saffron rubbed her temples. A long day of work, travel, greeting her family and Bill, and now this dinner had her head in a vice. "You've got to pull yourself together, Eliza."

Without opening her eyes, Elizabeth asked, "Why bother?"

"Because you want to show your parents they were wrong for mistreating you."

"If they can't see they were wrong, good riddance."

Saffron couldn't disagree there. "Because you want to show everyone else you are thriving in London?"

"Again, good riddance to anyone who cares."

Saffron sighed. "At least keep your head until we return to Ellington, please. I've got to make sure . . ." She trailed off, wondering if now was the time to finally tell Elizabeth the truth about Bill.

All she'd told Elizabeth was that her grandfather was ill and she wanted her to come home with her to Bedford. She hadn't wanted to burden Elizabeth with what had happened with Bill after Colin's betrayal. He was now imprisoned for treason, but three months on, Elizabeth had not recovered her spirits. Saffron couldn't bear to give her another reason to worry.

"I want to make sure Alexander doesn't feel abandoned," Saffron finished.

"I doubt he'll find trouble with my father or John," Elizabeth said. "John talks enough for the two of them put together. And I doubt there was much Alexander could do to offend Father Leavenworth." She cracked open one of her eyelash black-heavy eyes. "He's not a Catholic, is he?"

"I don't think so, no." Saffron stood with a sigh. "But let's go make sure they're not fighting over sacraments."

CHAPTER 5

How long were we gone?" Elizabeth muttered when they reentered the drawing room.

No longer the brightly lit space they'd left, the room had been transformed. The few electric lamps had been turned off in favor of a pair of candelabras, one on the mantel and the other on the sideboard. The fire had been covered by a heavy iron screen that cast flickering patterns on the walls. The table usually reserved for whist and other card games was being moved to the center of the room by a pair of sturdy footmen. Madame hovered nearby, a brass object cradled in her hands and Mr. Fischer at her side. They were clearly preparing for Madame to make a show of calling on some spirit.

"Perhaps we ought to call it a day," Saffron said.

"Oh no, we are definitely staying," Elizabeth said. "I am eager to take in the talents of the great Madame Martin again. Perhaps her spirits will tell her to shove off."

Mrs. Hale's voice rose. "If you please, take your seats at the table. The séance will commence shortly."

The others moved slowly toward the table, now

being dusted off by Mr. Fischer. Madame placed the brass object at the center and opened the top to fiddle with something within.

Lady Easting rose from near the fire. "I'm afraid I must take my leave. It has been a pleasant evening, Mrs. Hale."

Father Leavenworth seconded her notion to leave the party.

Mrs. Hale, all but ignoring the vicar, sputtered, "But, my lady, surely you wish to avail yourself of Madame's talents! With such losses to your family and the ease that Madame has given us, I assure you—"

"I've no need to relive those losses," Lady Easting said curtly, "least of all in this public manner. If you would summon my car?"

"Of course." Even in the half light, it was clear Mrs. Hale was peeved by this turn of events. She nodded to a footman, then called to the rest of the room, "To your seats, if you please!" When she turned back to Lady Easting, she caught sight of the footman, who hadn't moved. Scowling, she hissed, "Lady Easting's motorcar! Now!"

Looking stricken, he hurried away.

"Grandmama, Elizabeth will accompany you back to Ellington," Saffron said quickly.

Lady Easting lifted a brow at Elizabeth. "Will she?"

It was time to brazen things out a bit. "Certainly.

Mama said Elizabeth ought to stay with us." She tilted her head in Alexander's direction with a meaningful look. In a hushed voice, she added, "For propriety's sake."

Unaware of the byplay, Mrs. Hale laughed. "But Eliza will be staying here with us, of course."

Elizabeth's teeth ground together. "I will not stay in this house. I came here tonight out of courtesy and curiosity, Mother, and now I daresay I have little reason to return."

Hurt flashed across her mother's face before she noticed their exchange had garnered the attention of a handful of people. She recovered to say brightly, "But you want to stay with your friend. Saffron relies on you so."

"A good companion is essential in these dissolute times," said Miss Eloise, nodding as she laboriously got to her feet from the couch. "A woman requires someone to safeguard her reputation."

Elizabeth's mouth fell open, and a choked sound came out. She was just as astonished as Saffron was at the notion that *Elizabeth* might protect Saffron's reputation. She looked at Saffron helplessly, and Saffron could only weakly smile back.

"Indeed," Lady Easting said crisply. To Elizabeth, she said, "Well?"

"I'll stay to enjoy the evening's entertainment," Elizabeth said too sweetly.

50

Lady Easting turned to the vicar. "Father Leavenworth, may I offer you a ride back to the vicarage?"

"Oh, I say," he wheezed, his bushy eyebrows nearly disappearing into his equally bushy white hair. "How very generous of you, Lady Easting."

Lady Easting nodded to the vicar, then Mrs. Hale. "Good evening."

She allowed Mrs. Hale to fawn over her for only a few seconds before she took her leave with the vicar, leaving Mrs. Hale looking rather crestfallen.

"Mrs. Hale," called Mr. Fischer, "we're ready."

Mrs. Hale recovered herself quickly. She clapped once, then clasped her hands to her bosom with an almost gleeful expression. "Excellent. Take your seats, everyone, and let us see what spirits will speak to us this evening."

In the same manner with which Saffron might examine a particularly ugly specimen under a microscope, so did Saffron watch Madame Martin orchestrate her séance: with attempted objectivity colored by prejudice she couldn't quite bring herself to discard.

The pair of candelabras on either side of the round table created a cocoon of soft light, making the room more intimate. This feeling was only increased by the fact that Mr. Fischer had instructed them where to sit and asked that they put their hands on the table with the sides touching one another. Saffron's pinkie finger rested against Alexander's on one side, and Miss Lillian's on the other. From the center of the table swirled lazy coils of scented smoke. Rose and jasmine, overpowering and heady, filled the darkness.

Saffron could just make out Elizabeth cracking open an eye to glare at the incense burner. It was a pretty thing, the size of one's cupped hands, with little legs that held up its round, intricately decorated body. Smoke twisted from curved slits among a motif of flowers and vines. Since the flowers were reminiscent of lotus flowers, Saffron guessed the incense burner had its origins in the East.

Madame sat with her shoulders hunched over, arms spread wide and hands splayed on the table, a pose that gave the impression of a vulture bent over a meal. The incense smoke twirled in front of her, partially obscuring her shadowed look of concentration. Brow furrowed and eyes pinched shut, her head tilted to one side as if listening for something.

The medium had instructed everyone to close their eyes, as it would be conducive to her reaching out into the Great Beyond. Everyone had done so, including Alexander, the good sport, except Saffron, Elizabeth, and oddly, Mr. Fischer. He sat at Madame's side, head tipped back as if in rapturous concentration, but his eyes were slightly open. Flickers of firelight caught on them. He looked a touch demonic, truth be told.

"A dark presence," intoned Madame, making half the party flinch in surprise. "A dark presence has joined us."

At least she wasn't pretending to conjure Wesley. He could never be described as a dark presence. She looked at the only person at the table who qualified, but Bill was obediently still and quiet, eyes shut behind his spectacles.

"Malice," said Madame, dragging out the sibilant syllable. "Malice and greed."

Around her, the others stirred. Miss Lillian opened her eyes and looked about warily, her eyes landing on Alexander.

Elizabeth coughed, and it sounded suspiciously like "idiot."

Saffron stifled a giggle. The smoke was so thick, it was making her light-headed.

"Another being emerges," whispered Madame. "Familiar spirit, come forth. Tell us what you wish to say."

She apparently struggled to decipher the spirit's thoughts, for silence fell again. Saffron shifted uncomfortably. Though the night was cold and the fire banked, she was restless in the stuffy room.

Elizabeth looked to be feeling the effects, too,

for she blew out a loud breath and put the back of her hand to her flushed cheeks.

"You mustn't break the connection," said Mr. Fischer. His voice was low but urgent.

Elizabeth made a point of putting her hand back into place as slowly as possible.

Across the room, the fire popped, sending a flare of brightness through the grate.

"Eliza."

Saffron nearly jerked her own hands off the table at the abrupt, harsh voice.

It was Madame. Her eyes still closed, frowning in concentration, she said, "Glad you're back."

The delicate French accent Madame usually spoke with was gone, replaced by the familiar vowels of middle England.

"And with whom do I have the pleasure of speaking?" Elizabeth drawled.

A rusty laugh came out of the medium, raising the hairs on Saffron's nape. "Knew you wouldn't be afraid," she rasped. "Not after all those books we read as kids."

Elizabeth drew back, blinking rapidly. "What's that supposed to mean?"

Another laugh drifted through the haze. "The penny dreadfuls, of course. Ghost stories never frightened you, so me coming back wouldn't, either."

"I see." Though Elizabeth did her best to seem ambivalent, Saffron could see her confusion.

"Don't worry, Eliza," Madame Martin murmured. "Now we're back, I'm not going anywhere. I won't leave you."

Elizabeth shoved her chair back, causing the legs to screech against the floor. She wavered on her feet, fear stretching her features into something grotesque in the shadows.

Saffron's stomach bottomed out, a gasp slipping from her lips. A hand closed over hers—Alexander, looking at her with concern.

"No—the connection!" someone cried from the table.

Elizabeth's arms rose, not to steady herself, but as if to ward off something. Her breath was audible, harsh and uneven. Her back hit the liquor cabinet with a rattle.

Saffron lurched to her feet just as Elizabeth flailed wildly, her hand crashing into the cabinet's glass front. It broke with a harsh crack that sent the others at the table exclaiming.

Saffron rushed forward, Alexander at her back, but Mr. Fischer was already attempting to calm Elizabeth by the time Saffron reached her.

Elizabeth's eyes were shut tight, her breathing labored. Her lips moved as if speaking, but no sound came from her throat. Saffron insinuated herself between Fischer and Elizabeth, catching just the end of what he was saying about not being afraid of Madame's great power. She shoved aside her own disequilibrium to gather Elizabeth into her arms.

Fischer eased away, looking innocently empathetic. "I'm afraid the spiritual power has overwhelmed her. I would suggest a glass of wine to calm her, but . . ." He looked chagrined, and Saffron bristled.

"What she needs is to be away from this—" She swallowed the less than flattering words to describe the farce they'd just experienced on the tip of her tongue. "She needs quiet, and fresh air."

"And a bandage," Alexander said.

A glance at Elizabeth's hand confirmed that it was bleeding freely. Bill got to his feet as if to offer his assistance. Throwing him a glare, Saffron drew her friend closer, and ignoring the muttering of Mr. Hale and the concerned jabbering of Mrs. Hale and the Harvey sisters, she took Elizabeth from the room, from the house, and from the ghosts Madame Martin claimed to have conjured.

CHAPTER 6

A noise jolted Saffron from sleep. She came fully awake in an instant, and was out of bed and wrapping her dressing gown about her in another.

Her vigil at Elizabeth's bedside had been short-lived. Elizabeth had been disoriented and spitting mad when they'd returned from the Hales' house and quite a trial to goad into bed. Once she'd capitulated, she'd fallen asleep in the manner of a great tall tree falling in a forest: slowly, and then all at once. Saffron had stayed in her bedroom for another hour to ensure she wasn't going to be sick or sneak out of Ellington to confront Madame Martin, as she'd threatened to do in the moments before she'd collapsed into sleep.

Saffron doubted that Elizabeth preparing to make a trek through the cold, misty rain was what had awoken her. There was a shifting about in the room next to hers, easily heard since she'd kept the adjoining doors propped open.

A cry from Elizabeth's room caused her to nearly drop the match she'd struck to light the candle on her dressing table. She rushed into the other bedroom, candle held aloft.

Elizabeth stood at the window. She looked ghostly in the flickering light of the candle, all pale limbs in white art silk camiknickers. She clutched one opened curtain as she stared in horror out the window.

"It can't be," she mumbled. "It *can't*."

Saffron made to drag her from the window, but Elizabeth refused to move. "Come on, Eliza. You'll catch a chill, come now—"

They struggled against each other. "It's Wesley," Elizabeth insisted.

"I know, darling, Madame was horrible to torment you with him—"

"Saffron!" Elizabeth snapped, and Saffron was so startled by the sharp, lucid tone that she paused in pulling Elizabeth's arm toward the bed. Their eyes met. "It. Is. *Wesley*." She pointed to the window.

A sense of foreboding stilled Saffron. She turned to the window.

She flinched. The candle's light caught on their faces, creating feeble golden reflections against the gray fog that pressed on the pane. There was nothing there, not that Saffron expected to see anything outside the third-story window.

"For heaven's sake, Eliza," Saffron grumbled. "If you don't get back into bed—"

And then fog shifted. Standing on the ground beneath the window was a figure.

Chills raced down Saffron's arms. It was not just the figure of a man, but a man in a dreadfully familiar uniform.

The drab khaki hardly made an impression, however. Saffron couldn't tear her eyes away from the pair of gaping holes where eyes ought to be, a tube slithering from the soldier's would-be mouth.

Saffron's gasp made it only halfway out of her mouth. The rest was caught somewhere between fear and disbelief at the impossible vision of the soldier staring up at her.

Another wave of mist drifted past, blanketing the soldier, and he was gone.

Saffron did not sleep the rest of the night. She huddled with Elizabeth in her bed, facing the window. The curtains stayed open, for though neither said it, they both seemed to want to know if the soldier returned.

By the time dawn broke, Saffron had come to several conclusions.

The first was that Madame Martin was a much better conjurer than Saffron had given her credit for. She'd created the perfect circumstances for someone to see something that was not truly there. Elizabeth had seen a ghostly Wesley, being drunk and frightened and open to being manipulated, and Saffron's half-asleep brain had followed Elizabeth's suggestion, causing her to see Wesley, too.

The second conclusion Saffron had reached was that Elizabeth was in a worse state than she'd realized. The last few months had been difficult, and while Elizabeth had always been fond of drink and didn't temper herself when it came to indulging, she'd never been so far gone that she'd started *seeing* things.

With light glowing in the window, chasing away the fear that had clutched at her chest all night, Saffron now felt overwhelming worry. What could she do to help Elizabeth when she had Bill to contend with?

Elizabeth stirred beside her.

"How are you feeling?" Saffron whispered.

Elizabeth attempted to speak, but all that came out was a hoarse groan. She peered through her disheveled curls and croaked, "Water?"

Saffron went to the dressing table and poured her a glass. Elizabeth drained it almost immediately. She attempted to sit up, and muttered, "Ouch," just as Saffron opened her mouth to warn her about her injured hand.

"You cut your hand, remember?" Saffron said. "It didn't need stitches, but it was quite deep. Apart from the cut, how do you feel?" She wasn't sure she wanted to address the ghostly soldier just yet. Better to give Elizabeth time to get her feet under her.

"My mouth is positively Saharan and my eyes feel like they've taken one too many turns over a spit." Elizabeth gingerly sat up again, shuffling over to rise from the bed with equal care. She paused, a thoughtful expression crossing her face. "But my stomach seems to have no interest in rebelling, which is quite a welcome change after so much wine last night." That seemed to trigger memories, for she gasped and rounded on Saffron. "Last night! That *woman*! If I could, I'd see her hanged for that horrid show she put on."

"Indeed," Saffron murmured cautiously. She wanted to see what Elizabeth would say about the soldier. "The séance was dreadful."

"It was. Ghastly woman in that *ridiculous* getup. The smoke was so heavy, I felt I couldn't breathe." Elizabeth winced as she ran a hand through her short curls, evidently catching on a knot. "I suppose that's the point. To distract people with the smoke and the smell and the darkness so they don't pay too much attention to the nonsense she's spouting. She must add in the smoke when working in close quarters. I don't recall her fumigating the theater."

She sat at the dressing table and reached for her hairbrush. Saffron picked it up instead and began to comb through the nest of dark blonde snarls. They were quiet a few moments, until Elizabeth said quietly, "I felt I was losing my mind. During the séance."

She said it so bitterly that Saffron felt compelled to reassure her. "With the lights low and the incense so thick, I think we all felt a bit off. Adding in a good deal of wine wouldn't have helped." She paused, eyeing Elizabeth's downcast reflection. The same uncertainty she'd felt for most of the night lingered in the corners of her tired eyes, her tense lips. "It wouldn't be outlandish to have imagined things, you know. During the séance, or even after, like a bad dream." A shadow passed over her face, and Saffron rather thought she shuddered. "Are you all right, Eliza?"

Elizabeth's eyes, ringed with eyelash black, didn't rise to meet Saffron's in the mirror. "Yes, darling. Don't mind me."

Saffron paused on the stairs, listening to the footsteps come down the hall. She half wanted to rush on, avoid whoever might be coming so she didn't have to make polite conversation just now, but it might be Bill, the one person she'd come to Ellington to speak to.

To her mixed disappointment and relief, the footsteps preceded Alexander's appearance at the top of the stairs.

"Good morning," she called to him.

He didn't return her smile. "Good morning. How is Elizabeth?"

She'd left Elizabeth moments ago at her insistence, saying she was going to have a bath. Saffron hoped her plans didn't include a tipple; she'd secreted Elizabeth's flask under the mattress in her own bedroom and disposed of the half bottle of gin Elizabeth had evidently brought with her from London.

"Fine, all things considered. The cut on her hand looks worse than it is," Saffron said, skirting the issue of her friend's behavior. Alexander took a dim view of drink, having sworn off it himself. Elizabeth wasn't fine, not really, but she would shake off most of her malaise once she wasn't so hung over. She'd forget about the séance, just as Saffron would forget the haunting image of the soldier in the fog.

"I'm glad she's feeling better," Alexander said, and they continued down the stairs in silence, their steps echoing through the cool entry.

Nobody was about, though Saffron could smell breakfast mixing with the scent of potpourri and old stone. Pearly white skies promised another cold, gloomy day. She squinted at the windows, wishing she had a pair of smoked lenses. Her eyes stung with lingering exhaustion.

She'd been too worried about Elizabeth upon returning to Ellington to say much to her mother last night or that morning when her mother came to check on Elizabeth. She didn't know what she or her grandmother had arranged for the day. Hopefully, they would spend it learning about Lord Easting's condition and discovering what Bill was up to.

She recalled how he'd cooly tended to Elizabeth's hand when they'd reached Ellington.

Violet had insisted when she'd caught sight of the bloodied hanky around Elizabeth's hand. Bill had cleaned and bandaged the cut without saying anything more than it didn't require stitches. She hadn't been able to tell if this was real medical skill or basic caretaking, but she'd had no opportunity to speak to him further. Elizabeth had needed her.

On the last step, Alexander touched her arm. "Could we speak for a moment?"

"So formal," she said. He looked terribly serious. In actuality, he looked pale, and the creases in his brow a little deeper, like he, too, had been awake most of the night. "What's the matter?"

His dark eyes flickered to where a maid had appeared, dust rag in hand, across the hall. He wanted privacy, which should be achievable, if only for a short time.

The receiving room was just off the entry. She opened the door and, seeing it was empty, ushered Alexander inside.

The curtains had not been drawn, nor a fire lit. Saffron flicked on the nearest lamp, illuminating the room with a warm glow. The elegant space was free from dust, but it had none of the lived-in feel of the rest of Ellington. The walls were hand painted with a chinoiserie pattern of cherry blossoms against a blue background. The empty, spotless hearth was decorated with more elaborate chinoiserie designs, and a pair of antique couches sat before it. They were deathly uncomfortable, Saffron recalled. The room was only used to greet unfamiliar, usually unwanted, visitors. Now, it also housed the telephone, which had been installed next to the window, where a much more comfortable chair had been placed.

"Would you like to sit down?" she asked Alexander.

He apparently did not, for he came near and took her hands in his. "I'm afraid I have to leave."

She blinked. "Leave? What, Ellington?"

He nodded solemnly.

Disappointment dropped in her stomach like a weight. "But why?"

His throat bobbed and his hands squeezed hers in the moment it took for him to reply. "I wish I could simply go without telling you. I am . . . I am ashamed, in truth. But we have resolved to be honest with each other." He swallowed again, and the turmoil in his expression deepened to something bordering on despair. "I believe I'm not mentally fit."

"Whatever do you mean?" She squeezed his hands back. "Alexander, you're the most mentally fit person I know. You care for your mind better than anyone."

She didn't know anyone who meditated

regularly, who was so very aware of the things that might tip him over the edge into being unwell.

"I don't remember last night," he said in the tone of a confession. "I don't remember coming back to Ellington, or anything once I returned to my room. I woke this morning unaware of where I was." He dropped her hands and turned away, taking a few paces. "That hasn't happened in years. Not since I stopped drinking."

Though he continued to be reticent about speaking much about his wartime injury or recovery, Alexander had shared with her a little about his difficult recovery from extensive burns and a severe concussion. It had taken him over a year to regain full physical function, and much longer to attain what he considered full mental function. Drinking had been his means of coping until he'd found something better.

The similarities between his experiences then and Elizabeth's now were not lost on her. Did Elizabeth remember last night, after they'd returned to Ellington?

"Did you . . ." Saffron bit her lip, not wanting to shame him. "Did you drink at all, last night? Perhaps with my cousin after we returned from the Hales'?"

He turned back, looking almost surprised at her question. "No."

She hesitated but could think of no more delicate way to ask. "Did you, er, partake in anything else?"

His fists clenched at his sides for the briefest of moments before he exhaled forcefully, flaring his nostrils. "No."

It wasn't relief, exactly, that made her feel better, for she hadn't believed for a moment he had taken any of the drugs he'd condemned so stridently before. She went to where he stood in the middle of the room to wrap her arms around his trim waist. He smelled like bergamot and sandalwood, the fragrance she'd gifted him for Christmas. "I don't think you have anything to worry about. We all felt a little off after the séance, myself included."

His brows furrowed as he gazed down at her. "Yourself included?" He stroked his thumb over the delicate skin beneath her eye. "Your eyes are red."

"They're very dry. The incense, I think."

"You didn't . . ." His eyes searched hers. "Did you see anything, during the séance?"

A nervous thrill caught her breath. "Not during the séance."

"But after?"

"Elizabeth . . . She woke in the early hours. When I found her, she was at the window, convinced Wesley was outside. And when I looked . . ." She swallowed, finding it hard to speak when the fear that had gripped her as she stared down at the vision of the masked soldier had reawakened in her heart. "I saw him."

Alexander's hands, which had found their way around her waist, tensed. She leaned back, looking up at him. "It was just a dream, really. I was half-asleep, and Elizabeth wasn't in her right mind. She said he was there, and I saw him."

"You saw Wesley last night," Alexander said slowly, stepping out of her embrace.

"Well, I suppose I did. He wore a mask. A respirator mask, you know."

Alexander took a step, tension pouring off him as he rubbed a hand over his jaw.

Worry clawed at her. She'd rarely seen him so disturbed. "What is it? Did you see something, too?"

"Not exactly," he said. "But I'd felt that way before. In hospital, years ago. A sort of disconnected feeling. And you felt strange, and you saw something that couldn't have been there." Both hands rubbed over his face and pushed his hair back again. Expression grave, he said, "Saffron, I think we might have been drugged."

CHAPTER 7

Though Alexander's worry that they'd been drugged during the séance made Saffron feel as if she needed to scrub every inch of her body, she was determined to get answers first. If Alexander, Elizabeth, and Saffron had possibly been drugged, then there was another person that might have been, too.

Luckily, John was easy to find. Saffron and Alexander found him browsing the sideboard in the breakfast room, dressed in dark tweeds with a bright yellow tie slightly askew.

"Morning," he said cheerfully as they entered. "Grandmama has been generous with breakfast. She must have planned some sort of back-breaking labor for us to require such a spread."

There was, indeed, a good deal of food on display. Between bowls of fruit, there were platters of kippers, kidneys, sausages, and bacon alongside fragrant fresh bread and pots of jewel-colored marmalades. Saffron took a bit of everything and sat down across from John.

His dark hair was neatly combed, and his eyes bright with enthusiasm for his heaping plate of food. He wore none of the tension Alexander carried, nor seemed weighed down by lingering tiredness.

"How does the country air suit you, John?" she asked him.

"Tremendously well. I slept like a baby. Didn't even notice when Benjamin woke at the crack of dawn. Did you hear him? Wails like a banshee, that one."

If John was having visions of ghosts, he likely wouldn't sleep well. Then again, Alexander said he had no memory of the previous evening, so perhaps there were differing effects. Perhaps it was something they'd consumed that the others had not?

John looked to Alexander, who'd settled next to Saffron. "I say, Ashton, should we go out for a ride? It's a bit wet, but I don't mind if you don't."

Alexander seemed to consider it. "Thank you, but no. I believe Saffron wanted to show me around the place herself."

And find Bill. She wondered how he spent his time here. It was unlikely he'd hover at her grandfather's side all day. "Where does Dr. Wyatt stay?"

"The heart doctor?" John chuckled. "Having heart troubles, Saffron? I thought yours was in rather good shape presently." He winked at Alexander.

Saffron rolled her eyes. "I simply wondered if he walked here every day, or—"

"Walked here? No," John said. "He stays in the room with that silly mounted badger on the wall, you know the one."

Saffron blinked. "He's staying *here?*"

"That's what Aunt Violet told me yesterday. You mustn't worry. Grandmama is merely being overcautious about Grandpapa's health. Though I am surprised he's not charging in here, demanding we tour the farms. But I suppose Grandmama won't allow it. We only saw him for a moment during tea yesterday before she was shuffling him back off to his sickbed." He shook his head with a laugh.

John's levity did nothing to comfort her. Bill was staying in the house, which meant there was even less opportunity to figure out why he was there and make him leave.

"I'm sure he'll be stomping around again before long," John said kindly, clearly interpreting her tense silence for worry over Lord Easting's health. "Especially when he hears you've brought a friend along."

Alexander gave her a slight smile when she glanced at him to observe his reaction. "I look forward to meeting Lord Easting."

"I think he'll do just perfectly." John craned his neck and summoned the footman with the teapot. "Well, if we're not to ride, I suppose I'll go see if I can interest Benjamin in a walk. Perhaps you'd join us, and we can tour the house together."

"In truth, I'm feeling a little tired," Saffron said. When the footman returned to his post at the sideboard, she added, "After last night, you know. It was quite a spectacle."

"Ah, yes. The medium." John played at shivering. "Whatever the Hales are paying that woman, they ought to double it simply for the sake of the entertainment. I could have sworn I actually saw something in the smoke!"

Saffron exchanged a look with Alexander. Did that mean John had been affected after all?

"Didn't care for it, I don't mind telling you. Gives me the creeps." John sighed. "Of course, Suzette is chomping at the bit to meet Madame Martin. I think it's because of the French connection, but she enjoys the macabre, as well. She reads Benjamin some ghastly stories, truly. Elizabeth would probably adore them."

That reminded Saffron of what "Wesley" had said last night. "How do you know Elizabeth likes ghost stories?"

John paused with a piece of toast loaded with marmalade halfway to his mouth. "She used to read them, didn't she? I saw you two giggling over that lurid one about a runaway bride who'd hid in a haunted castle. I confiscated that one for myself." He waggled his eyebrows and crunched into his toast.

Now he mentioned it, Elizabeth had enjoyed gothic novels as a girl. Wesley, too. How could

Madame Martin have known that? "Did you happen to mention that to Madame Martin?"

John cocked a brow. "No. I only met her last night. Barely spoke three words to her, didn't I?"

Mr. Fischer had said he'd seen extraordinary things during his time with the medium, and plucking that fine detail out of the past was extraordinary. Saffron couldn't imagine that information could have been found in an old letter she'd discovered tucked in a drawer, and she doubted Mr. or Mrs. Hale would have known about the novels to mention to Madame Martin. How had Madame known?

John seemed to be suffering no ill effects. Saffron was given to believe Elizabeth's reaction to the séance and conviction she'd seen Wesley had been the result of her generous helping of wine and spirits, and Saffron herself had imbibed, too. But Alexander hadn't and he was also affected. How?

Theories spun in her aching head for the rest of the meal, and when John got up to retrieve his son for their exploration, she found she was left with more questions than she'd started with.

Saffron found herself rather at loose ends after breakfast before she recalled she'd told Alexander she would show him around the house. In the absence of anything more productive to do, she led him across the short hall to the drawing room.

"Things are a bit topsy-turvy with my grandfather ill," she told Alexander in a hushed voice. "He and my grandmother usually begin the day bright and early at the breakfast table, so I'm not sure what we ought to be doing."

She opened the drawing room door and stepped inside. The room was empty though the hearth was warm with a fire. The icy blue brocade on the walls didn't diminish the room's figurative warmth, either. The room was large and elegant, and appointed far more comfortably than the formal receiving room. The ceilings were tall and topped with intricate moldings. The floor, polished hardwood, was covered in antique Axminster carpets. Landscapes in gilded frames depicted the same fields and river one could see through the massive windows. Saffron had rarely spent time in this room as a child, but as she progressed through adolescence into adulthood, she'd been told to sit on the low-backed couches with increasing frequency, sipping tea and engaging in tedious conversation.

She found herself smiling at Alexander, inexplicably glad to be in this room with him. "We use it as a morning room and usually entertain visitors in here, rather than that other receiving room." She nodded to the French doors opposite the hearth, opaque with condensation. "Through there is the conservatory, and yes, I am itching to get in there and see what's blooming."

She crossed the room and pushed through the second pair of double doors. When she heard Alexander's breath audibly catch behind her, she grinned.

The library at Ellington was not as large as the university's, nor as well stocked, of course, but it was beautiful. The coffered ceiling soared over heavily laden shelves of dark, polished wood. The warm, salmon-colored walls complemented the blues of the chairs and couches clustered through the long room. Best of all were the two alcoves on either side of the grand doors that opened to the main hall. They were as tall as the ceiling, heavily ornamented with plaster molding and inset with more shelves set in semicircles. She'd always imagined the walls were blocks of ice cream, and a giant had scooped out the cream and set shelves inside. As a girl she curled up in the comfortable curve of the bottom shelves, carelessly scattering the books that occupied them to form a little cave. At some point, the servants had given up replacing the books and had simply shelved them elsewhere.

A pang of nostalgia tugged at her when she saw the first alcove's bottom shelf was filled with volumes of the encyclopedia.

"This is the library," Saffron said, turning to Alexander.

"I see that," he said, his small smile widening to almost a grin. "It's wonderful."

"If you don't mind, I'll nip upstairs to see if my grandfather will see me. There's a chance he'll be available." But as she considered what she would tell him about Bill, her hope wilted. "Though there is only a slight chance he'll listen."

Alexander's hand found hers and squeezed it gently. He said nothing, but she felt encouraged, nevertheless.

"Ring for tea or coffee or anything. The bell's there." She pointed to the strand of blue velvet hanging near the door to the hall.

Alexander eyed it warily.

"It won't bite," she said, then impulsively went to his side and pressed a kiss to his cheek. "Thank you for being here. I know it's a lot to ask, coming into this mess—"

"There's nowhere I'd rather be." He lifted his eyes to the bookshelves, laden with books. "Come to me when you're finished. I won't go anywhere."

CHAPTER 8

Saffron's knocks on her grandfather's door went unanswered.

She released an impatient breath, rocking on her heels on the plush carpet lining the gallery as she tapped yet again. She might resort to seeking out her grandmother to inquire about an audience with her grandfather, though from what her mother had told her as she'd helped Saffron put Elizabeth to bed the previous evening, it was unlikely Lady Easting would be helpful.

"Lady Easting is quite worried about your grandfather," Violet had told Saffron. "Lord Easting has done his best to downplay his condition, but her actions speak to just how unwell he is. I hope you will forgive her for her lack of hospitality."

"Lack of hospitality" was one way of describing how Lady Easting had greeted and dismissed her nearly in the same breath the previous evening.

"Tell me about Dr. Wyatt," she'd said. "Why does Grandmama think it necessary for him to continue to attend my grandfather?"

"You can be sure your grandmother does not confide her reasoning to me, but your grandfather truly is not well. I saw real fear in him." Her gentle smile had done little to reassure Saffron.

"I can only hope this is just a bump in the road. I have no doubt he'll make a full recovery if only he'd give himself the chance."

A pair of scampering feet pattered down the hall. Saffron caught a flash of a dark-haired woman and the small figure of a little boy before they disappeared up the stairs leading to the nursery. Saffron's heart squeezed. John's wife, Suzette, and their little boy. What dreadful circumstances for their first visit to Ellington.

Thanks to the merciless tide of war that laid claim to Saffron's father and her uncle's lives, John was their grandfather's heir, and when their grandfather died, John would become Lord Easting. He would inherit all the Easting land and property—and responsibilities. She knew many lords had sold off their estates, unable to make a living in these modern times in the way generations before them had. Ellington was not such an estate. Her forebears had diversified at the first sign of industrialization, and her grandfather had followed in their tradition. John would find himself in possession of a healthy estate providing for dozens of families hundreds of miles from his true home.

Neither John nor his wife had any interest in being Viscount and Viscountess Easting, but that future was coming for them. Saffron only hoped it would be years before the change came about.

The soft snick of a door closing brought Saffron

back to the present. From where she stood in the middle of the gallery open to the entrance hall, she could just make out a tiny flash of light in the gloom of the guest hall. A dim shadow came forward.

A thrill of alarm raced through her as Bill materialized a dozen feet away. He paused at the top of the stairs. They stared at each other for long moments before his lips tilted into a slight smile and he nodded. Then he calmly went down the stairs.

The hairs on the back of her neck stood up, as if she was being watched rather than doing the watching herself. Bill did not look at her again before he crossed the entry and vanished from sight.

Was this an invitation to follow? Should she confront him now, before speaking to her grandfather?

She hurried down the stairs to find out.

The library door had scarcely closed behind Saffron when Alexander let out a long breath. The abbreviated tour of the house—"house" was a poor name for the immense, expensively decorated manor—had reminded Alexander of something he'd allowed himself to forget the past few months.

The winter, usually his least favorite season, had been remarkably pleasant, all thanks to his renewed romance with Saffron. The frosty morning walk to the U promised her smiles, and icy evenings had them cloistered in her flat's parlor, enjoying each other's company. As London fell into deep winter, Alexander found he, too, was falling deeply.

The intoxicating spell of a perfectly spent season had been broken with the telephone call a few days ago, requesting Saffron's immediate presence at Ellington and bringing the disturbing news of Bill's continued insinuation into her life. Even if she hadn't asked him to join her at her family's home, the latter would have had him following her to Bedford.

The distance in class between him and Saffron was minimal, if one took them as mere individuals. They both worked at a university as researchers. Alexander was her senior, both in years and education, which translated into his superiority in the eyes of others. But with Saffron's family taken into account as the granddaughter of a viscount, and a wealthy one if the well-maintained house full of servants was any indication, sent her rocketing high above him in social standing.

He didn't care. He didn't, at least not for himself. But he worried now, as he never had before, what that meant for their future. He had ideas, very nearly plans, for what that future would be.

He wanted reconciliation for Saffron because,

though she spoke of her grandparents with scorn, he saw the lingering sadness she thought she hid from sight. He knew her every look by now, and it was clear that she loved Ellington. She'd soaked in every inch of the place, her fingers tiptoeing across furniture and her eyes trailing reluctantly away from the pictures on the walls and the view from the windows.

And, of course, he couldn't have missed the way her shoulders fell when her grandmother had barely taken notice of her the previous evening. Or how her mother's presence caused her to light up.

And when Bill Wyatt had entered the entry hall last night . . .

Saffron's pale face fighting for composure filled his mind's eye.

As much as he worried over the gaps between his circumstances and that of the Everleigh family, it was Bill who required the majority of his attention. He'd told Saffron she owed him a debt after she destroyed a set of valuable research materials he'd planned to sell to the highest bidder.

It had been suggested repeatedly that Thomas Everleigh, Saffron's father, had been involved in research that others might find valuable. One of the criminals Saffron had foiled had even supposedly used that research to create a dangerous poison.

Alexander couldn't believe that Thomas Everleigh's research and Bill's interest in Saffron were unrelated, just as he couldn't shake the suspicion that Bill's presence and that of the medium next door were linked. A phony psychic, drugging her patrons so her rituals seemed more real, just as an anarchist with a desire for revenge showed up? It felt too coincidental.

At least he knew that his strange episode the night before was not a coincidence; it was a result of Madame Martin's scheming. Saffron and Elizabeth had also been affected. He was now convinced it was the medium's drugs rather than her prowess that had affected him so profoundly. He was damned glad to know his mind was not spinning out of control just when Saffron needed him to be in top form.

Since Saffron had no idea what her father had been researching outside the realm of phytopathology, Alexander would start by determining what Bill was after.

The library was an excellent place to start.

It took only a brief scan of the shelves' contents to see that science was heavily represented. Biology and its subsets took up most of the first alcove: Mendel's works on hybridization, several first editions of Darwin's works, and even a crusty copy of Carl Linnaeus's treatise on classification. Alexander ran a finger over the spine of that one fondly. He'd learned the rules of taxonomy as a boy without much interest, but upon returning to school after the war, he'd found them intriguing. Comforting, even. Adrian, his older brother, laughed long and hard at his love of order and need for organization. It was true; he did itch to put to rights messes, including the one the woman he loved was currently embroiled in.

He knelt to examine the books on the lower shelves, finding familiar volumes of *Biological Science*.

"You won't find anything here," a quiet voice said.

Alexander's muscles tensed with the immediacy of a lightning strike.

"Why not?" he asked, slowly rising from his crouch. It was petty, but he enjoyed the way his body unfolded to his full height to put him well above that of Bill Wyatt.

"Because I've examined Thomas Everleigh's books," Bill said.

His voice was calm and quiet, appropriate for a library and oddly accented. The slight Continental lilt tugged on Alexander's ear. He surmised that, alone as they were, he was not putting on his Dr. Wyatt persona, complete with posh Oxford accent. His dark hair was slicked back. Glasses and a beard obscured his face, making his expression inscrutable.

Alexander wasn't surprised Bill had already

plundered the public rooms for information. "I take it you were disappointed."

"Oh, I was. But I have hopes that'll soon change."

"What do you want, Mr. Wyatt?"

"*Doctor* Wyatt, thank you." A sly smile lifted his thin lips. "I worked for that title, and I'd appreciate it if you would use it."

"Lying hardly counts as work."

"I am a doctor," Bill said, the slightest hint of offense in his tone, "and I am well equipped to attend to the needs of his lordship. As I'm sure your policeman will discover."

Bill grinned when Alexander's fists clenched. "Oh, yes, Alexander. I know you've asked your pet detective inspector about me. I doubt he'll be able to find any more information about me than Nick Hale and his people have. That is to say, none." He cocked his head, and light glinted in the lenses of his glasses. "When will you tell Saffron about your request to Inspector Green? I do hope it won't upset her that you went behind her back to work out my identity."

"She wants you gone," Alexander said through gritted teeth. He found it difficult to counter Bill's calm with calm of his own. "Stop playing games and tell me why you're here."

Bill's laugh was as soft as his words. "I believe you know why I'm here, Alexander."

"She doesn't know anything about her father's

84

work apart from what is published and accessible to anyone with a library subscription."

"But she will if she wants me gone."

"So that is your requirement to leave Ellington? Saffron discovers what Thomas Everleigh was doing?"

Bill's slight smile grew. A moment later, Saffron appeared at the edge of the alcove. She was pale again, but her eyes flashed with anger rather than fear.

"I will never share my father's research with you," she said. "If that's what you're here for, you might as well leave now."

One of his brows arched. "You'd rather I extract your debt to me in another way?"

The word "extract" sent a shudder down Alexander's spine. "Saffron—"

She shot him a furious glare. He didn't know how much she'd overheard of their conversation, but it was plain she didn't like what she had heard.

"I think you'll find my request is quite reasonable. I want what Thomas Everleigh was researching before his untimely end. It's the least you can do after you ruined what would have been a lucrative sale in November." Bill took a step back out of the alcove. "The research is a far less painful sacrifice." He gave them a short bow, and left the room.

CHAPTER 9

My father was a prolific note-taker," Saffron said. She was proud of how little her voice shook. "We'll start by finding books he annotated."

Alexander stared at her for a long moment before nodding. He had clearly caught on that she didn't want to talk about Bill's threat, nor the seething frustration and fear threatening to upend her breakfast all over the antique carpet beneath their feet.

She dropped to her knees and began pulling out the old *Biological Science* tomes. She flipped through the pages, blind to text and diagrams. She saw Bill's smarmy satisfaction as he left the room. After threatening her family. There was no other possible meaning to his departing words.

Worse, the solution she'd counted on, the thing that had given her some comfort when the memory of Bill brought her to the point of paranoia, had apparently already proved itself useless. She'd put off contacting Detective Inspector Green about Bill, in part because she'd hoped that he'd never step back into her life, but also because she'd hoped that if he did, she could handle it herself. The inspector had saved her a

86

number of times, and she'd been reluctant to ask him to do it again, even as she'd counted on his ability to do so.

She blew out a frustrated breath and slammed the book shut. "Why didn't you tell me you'd told Inspector Green about Bill?"

Apparently, she did want to talk about it.

Alexander paused with a book hovering above one of two piles of books he'd made. "Why didn't *you* tell him?"

She scowled at him. "Answer the question, Alexander."

"I told the inspector because I was worried about your safety. Bill was able to enter your flat wearing a police officer's uniform with none of us the wiser. He implied he's been stalking you for months, possibly years." His frown, which hadn't left his face since she'd come into the library, deepened. "He frightened you, Saffron, but not enough."

"I am plenty afraid of Bill," she said, but her heart wasn't in challenging him. Her shoulders slumped, and she pressed her forehead on her hands where they rested on the shelf before her. "Find my father's research and turn it over to Bill. How does he know my father had anything of value?"

"He had someone in the Path Lab feeding him information. He could have had someone at the U giving him information about what

Thomas Everleigh was working on nearly ten years ago." Alexander shook his head. "It seems unlikely. Then again, Bill Wyatt holding your family hostage against you until you give him information about phytopathological research seems extremely unlikely, yet here we are. There's too much we don't know about Bill and how he operates. He could have gotten lucky and heard about Jeffery Wells and his debt and decided to take advantage to steal secrets from the Path Lab. We have no proof he's done this before, despite what he claims."

"He has a reputation. Alfie's men were afraid of him," Saffron said, recalling how the men who'd abducted her and Elizabeth had exchanged wary glances when Bill came up. "He had access to immigration records through Colin Smith. Demian Petrov might have been one of a dozen he'd targeted." She sighed at the way her head spun, flinging out possibilities about Bill's possible connections to the Russian émigré's death. "If Petrov was even one of his targets. I'm still not clear if Bill had anything to do with Petrov's death. He said he didn't. He seemed almost upset by it, but I can't trust anything he's said or done." Her throat tightened and her eyes stung. She closed them, wishing Bill's request was as easy and straightforward as he made it seem and not connected to a host of complicated implications and consequences.

Warmth touched the bare back of her neck.

"I'm sorry," Alexander murmured.

"You've done nothing wrong," she whispered. "You were trying to protect me, speaking to Inspector Green. I don't suppose he told you anything useful?" She couldn't help sounding hopeful.

"He said he would look into it," Alexander said with a sigh. He squeezed the nape of her neck gently before his hand slid away. "Without proof of Bill's stalking or of his involvement in the crimes at the Path Lab, he couldn't do anything more. I'm not sure what information he has access to since Petrov's and Wells's deaths became a government investigation. But Inspector Green took it seriously, Saffron. He wanted to help."

"Well, that's something." She let out a shaky breath and sat up, wiping her damp eyes. "I sometimes wondered if I'd made the whole thing up. A strange, terrible nightmare."

"Unfortunately," Alexander said, getting to his feet and offering her a hand, "Bill is very much real."

She nodded, and a watery smile formed on her lips as she looked at the two piles Alexander had made of the books she'd flung around. "How did you sort them?"

"With annotations and without. Bill might not have found anything useful in here, but you know your father far better," he replied, hefting the nearer stack into his arms. "We'll start with these."

Luncheon came upon them quickly, and Saffron was loath to abandon the stacks of books they had not yet examined in the library. But Bill himself had said there was nothing of value in them, so it was unlikely they'd disappear.

"I forgot to give you a tour of the house," Saffron recalled as she and Alexander left the library through the main doors.

"I've seen the library and the dining room, and that covers the two most essential rooms, doesn't it?"

"You've seen the breakfast room. The dining room is just across the hall."

The doors to the dining room were already open, so she led Alexander inside. Saffron paused, momentarily struck by how grand the room must seem to Alexander, seeing it for the first time. It was the most ostentatious in the house, decorated lavishly in green and gold. The fireplace was so large its marble mantle stretched across nearly half the wall. A glittering chandelier crowned a table long enough for two dozen, elegantly dressed in white linen and silver. What would Alexander make of this room? What did he think of her family home? She hadn't had a moment to ask.

John and Suzette stood at the window and looked to be having a tense conversation. Suzette's frown dissolved into a grin when she caught sight of Saffron, and she rushed across the room with girlish enthusiasm. "Saffron, how do you do! I am very glad to see you."

Saffron returned Suzette's embrace with true affection. Though they'd spent only a few days in each other's company, they'd become fast friends during Saffron's trip to France in the autumn. Suzette rather reminded Saffron of Elizabeth with her determined competence mixed with a tendency to say precisely what was on her mind. In appearance, they could have hardly been further apart. Elizabeth was rounded with curves, sandy-haired and usually flush with healthy color, while Suzette was dark-featured and olive-skinned, her figure more akin to the waifs one saw in fashion magazines.

They broke apart, and Suzette raised perfectly groomed brows at Saffron and murmured, "*Mon amour, qui est cette montagne d'homme?*"

"Bonjour, Madame Everleigh," Alexander said. "*Moi, c'est Alexander Ashton. Je suis heureux de faire votre connaissance.*"

Suzette blinked at him, then broke into a grin. In the same language, she gushed, "But your accent is flawless! I did not think to hear anyone speak my language without slaughtering it for some weeks."

Saffron let out an exasperated sigh. Of course, Alexander's French was perfect.

"You are too kind," Alexander replied.

Suzette's pretty face was alight with curiosity. "But tell me, *monsieur*, have you only learned the pleasantries, or can you converse?" Alexander opened his mouth for what would have surely been a perfectly pronounced reply, but Suzette pressed on eagerly. "Only my English is lacking, and I dread having only John and our nanny to speak to. I adore Saffron, of course"—she sent her an apologetic smile—"but she makes me want to close my ears when she speaks. And I despise having John translate for me, it makes me look an idiot."

At this, John sent Saffron an exaggerated look of hurt. "Did you hear that? My own wife, calling me an idiot."

When Suzette scowled and made to correct him, he winked at Saffron. It was then that Lady Easting entered the room, followed by Violet, and more polite greetings were passed around.

As the meal began, Lady Easting asked, "How does my grandson get on, Mrs. Everleigh? I hope he is settling in well."

"He does very well, my lady," Suzette replied. She looked as if she wanted to say more, but left it at that. Perhaps she felt self-conscious of her English.

If she was, she would soon get over it, Saffron

mused as her grandmother pelted Suzette with question after question about Benjamin. By the time luncheon came to an end, no other topic had been broached, and Suzette had spoken more than anyone at the table. Alexander had said not one word, in fact.

"I wish for Benjamin to join us at tea this afternoon," Lady Easting declared. "Do inform the nanny, so she will know to bring him down."

She rose from the table, and the rest of the party followed suit.

"I shall bring him myself," John said cheerfully. Saffron didn't think he minded his wife facing the brunt of the interrogation. "I plan to show him around the old pile. We made quite good progress this morning."

"I wish you would not refer to Ellington in such a way, John. Lord Easting has exerted every effort to make Ellington modern and efficient." She cast a beady look around the group. "Unless you mean to suggest the house is not comfortable, in which case I will certainly endeavor to appease you."

"Don't be silly, Grandmama," John said with a touch of condescension Saffron believed was calibrated to further annoy their grandmother. "I mean only the estate is quite large. I anticipate Benjamin will enjoy a good long ramble, even if it does look a bit like rain." He ducked his head slightly, squinting at the windows.

Lady Easting frowned at him. "I hope you don't intend to let your son run freely outdoors like you and Saffron did as children. He'll catch a chill, not to mention he could wander into the lake or the greenhouse or the ice cellar or some such dangerous place."

John's brows winged up. "The greenhouse is still standing? When last I was here, it looked like the neighborhood miscreants had gone at it with stones. That wreck will collapse on some poor, unsuspecting gardener, Grandmama, and you'll be summoning me to defend a suit against you."

As Lady Easting's eyes iced over, Violet interjected, "You're quite right, John. The place is in disrepair, to be sure." Her gaze flickered to Saffron before adding, "I believe Lord Easting has plans to demolish it in the spring or summer."

An ache tightened Saffron's throat. The property housed two greenhouses, the conservatory attached to the house, and another near the stables that had been built specifically for her father. She could hardly believe there was serious talk of tearing down her father's sanctuary.

Well, she would certainly be a loud voice in opposition. She might not be welcome at Ellington, but John would inherit eventually. He would be sympathetic to her plea to restore the greenhouse in her father's memory, and maybe in his own father's memory, too. After all, Uncle Wallace had spent time there, too.

But first, she needed to see how bad a state it was in. Three years couldn't have been long enough for the structure to have decomposed that badly, especially since it was made of glass and iron. Perhaps it merely required refurbishment.

The party dispersed for afternoon pursuits. Rather than return to the library, Saffron beelined for her grandmother. The pleasant meal with her family had only brought home just how much Bill was threatening.

"Grandmama, if I could have a moment," Saffron said, catching her just as she was leaving the dining room. The others passed by them, her mother giving her a brief, searching look.

Lady Easting's lips pursed. "Very well."

"Could we, er, go somewhere a bit more private?" Servants were clearing the dining table at their back, and the hall still contained their family. Alexander, she noted, was walking in the direction of the library, bless him.

"I haven't the time to fuss, Saffron," her grandmother said, rather more severely than was necessary. "What do you wish to speak about?"

"Well," Saffron said, drawing out the word as a footman skirted the table near them.

"Saffron!"

She flinched at the harsh tone. Her grandmother was glaring at her. "It's just, it's rather delicate, Grandmama. I wouldn't want anyone to overhear."

Her grandmother turned on her heel and strode to the drawing room. Saffron followed, wishing she could approach this all-important conversation without feeling like a child scurrying after their caretaker.

"What is it?" Lady Easting asked the moment the door was closed behind them.

"I don't wish to bring more hardship into the household," Saffron began, resisting the urge to clutch her hands together before her. Her grandmother looked down on fidgeting. "And I don't wish to alarm you."

From how her grandmother's pinched expression tightened further, she was already making a muck out of this conversation. "I have to tell you something."

"For heaven's sake, Saffron," her grandmother barked. Her posture was so stiff, she resembled a statue, standing in the middle of the drawing room. "If you and that man have gotten yourselves into trouble, I wish you'd own up to it without this tiresome prevarication!"

"Grandmama, it's the doctor—"

Lady Easting inhaled sharply, rearing back with a pale-faced mask of fury. She seemed to speak with barely contained disgust. "I forbid you from asking Dr. Wyatt to assist you with a vulgar solution to a problem you claim to be intelligent enough to avoid."

Saffron's mouth fell open. "Vulgar solution—?"

Her grandmother's meaning became clear, and a surge of shame scalded her cheeks. "Grandmama, that is not what—*No*."

Lady Easting sniffed, looking away.

Some of Saffron's embarrassment faded as she realized her grandmother was not just blustering, she was actually repulsed. "Even if it was the reason I came here, if I was in *trouble,* that is the response I should expect from you? If I were to come home pregnant—"

Her grandmother held up a staying hand, white-lipped with contempt.

"If I was pregnant and seeking your support," she pressed on, "you would look at me with such"—she struggled for a word—"disgust? I am your *granddaughter.*"

"And that man is a stranger," Lady Easting said. She'd regained some of her composure. "Your Mr. Ashton, your beau who you regard so seriously that you would bring him here, about whom I have heard nothing."

"Whose fault is that, Grandmama?" Saffron burst out. "You all but cast me out of the house, out of the family, last we saw each other. And your letters can hardly be considered reparatory to our relationship."

"I wrote to you in the hopes that some time and distance from our disagreement would show you the error of your ways."

"And that has clearly worked so very well.

No amount of time or distance will resign me to marrying a man of your choice and abandoning my studies." She blew out a breath, remembering why she'd subjected herself to this horrible conversation to begin with. "The doctor, Dr. Wyatt. He's not who he seems. I don't believe him to be a fully accredited physician."

This was the tactic she and Alexander had decided on prior to arriving in Bedford, a simple means of planting enough doubt toward Bill that he might be dismissed.

"My friend, Michael Lee," Saffron continued quickly, "the nephew of Mattias Lee, Grandpapa's friend, is a doctor in London. I asked him for some information about heart attacks and such, and he asked after Grandpapa's health, of course—"

"You were spreading around the news of your grandfather's illness?" her grandmother asked imperiously. "In London?"

As if London were the most offensive part of that line of questioning! "No, I asked a close friend to reassure me that my grandfather wasn't about to *die*."

"Don't be overdramatic."

"Good Lord!" Saffron burst out. "Can I not share a concern without you jumping down my throat? Dr. Lee looked into this Dr. Wyatt and told me he had heard some worrisome things about him. I don't think that he ought to be in the house, let alone in charge of Grandpapa's recovery."

Lady Easting drew herself up. "This conversation is at an end. I will not subject myself to further childish outbursts." She opened the door swiftly and took a step, but paused to give Saffron a withering look that cut her to the bone. "You will say nothing of this nonsense to Lord Easting. If I hear that you have been needlessly upsetting his"—she exhaled, nostrils flaring—"If I hear that you are telling him anything of these baseless doubts, I will ask you to leave Ellington." She swept from the room, leaving Saffron gaping after her.

CHAPTER 10

As she had since before she was able to read, Saffron sought respite from her argument with her grandmother in the library. She found Alexander at their table, book in hand. Rather than sitting down in her previous seat, she stood at his back, arms wrapping about his shoulders as she sunk down against him. She sighed into his neck.

"It was a disaster," she whispered after a long moment.

He gently pulled her arms around so she stood at his side. The look he gave her was tender but serious. "I'm sorry."

"Me, too." She sighed again as the pile of books caught her eye. She really didn't want to look through a stack of books just now. An alternative arose in her mind.

"You have that expression," Alexander said, eyes narrowing, "that suggests you're forming a plan of some kind."

She couldn't help but smile a little at that. "Would you be willing to be uncomfortable for a half hour?"

By the time Saffron and Alexander made it out of doors, John's predicted rain had begun to fall. It was cold enough it felt like it ought to have been snow. Even equipped with galoshes and a borrowed mac, Saffron was miserably cold walking through the evergreen maze of the formal gardens. Piles of snow caught in shadowed corners became slush, and a biting wind cut through the waist-high box hedges.

Every so often, Saffron shot a glance over her shoulder. The sodden grounds appeared empty, but they didn't feel that way. She shivered and closed her umbrella in favor of huddling next to Alexander beneath his.

He cleared his throat. "That may not be a good idea."

"Using you for warmth? A very good idea, if my frozen fingers have anything to say about it." When he didn't reply, she looked up at him and saw his heavy brows had lowered over his eyes. His dark features suited the dark look, but she preferred him smiling. "I'm sorry things haven't gotten off to a better start. I would like to say that it's merely the stress of my grandfather's illness sending my family into turmoil, but . . ."

Alexander's look of understanding only worsened her discontent. She ought to have made more of an effort to acquaint him with her grandmother at luncheon. That would have made him feel less like the uninvited guest she'd made of him and it might have improved her grandmother's opinion of him, rather than seeing him as "that man."

It was her fault her grandmother saw him that way, and her fault that he felt unwelcome.

Guilt and disappointment twisted her insides. This was not the way she'd hoped to introduce Alexander to her family, in a rushed, haphazard manner with so many layers of complication separating them. She didn't know if there was a way to remedy it, especially after that dreadful row.

She realized when they passed by the barren arbor that, come spring, would be filled with the green shoots of roses, that Alexander was guiding them the wrong way. "The greenhouse is around by the stables."

"Yes," he said. "Just admiring the grounds."

She shot him a disbelieving look but followed Alexander around to the front of the house, pausing when he asked her to point out her bedroom window. She doubted he was keen to play Romeo and climb to it on some amorous errand, however. They eventually made their way through the stone arch separating them from the neat rows of cabbage and broccoli in the kitchen garden. They stepped through the gate of the low stone wall that separated the kitchen garden from the wood, and continued around to the stables.

A slender pillar of smoke drifted from one end of the low stone building, where the grooms were likely huddled around a fire. Saffron wished she hadn't decided to drag Alexander out into the cold rain. Really, she longed to be curled up with him on the couch in her flat's parlor, with the radiator on and tea steeping and his warmth pressed on her side, alone and content. They had been just that way not two days ago, happily ensconced in the small, comfortable world she'd created for herself in London. If not for Bill, they likely would have been there now. Then again, if not for Bill, perhaps she would have come to see her grandfather anyway. This might have gone differently, had it not been for Bill.

She stomped around the stables and stopped abruptly to stare at the glasshouse two dozen feet away.

"The rain must be making it look worse than it actually is, mustn't it?" she asked Alexander faintly.

"Do you want me to answer honestly?"

She sighed. "Yes."

"I think the rain might be helping. It's cleaning the remaining glass."

Her mother's comment that the greenhouse was in disrepair was a gross understatement. John's description of a wreck likely to fall down any moment seemed far more accurate.

Saffron approached the ruined greenhouse slowly, not out of caution, though it did look like the delicate raindrops might dislodge whatever it was that kept the building still standing. She could hardly reconcile the shell of a building with the last memories she had of the place.

When last she'd been at Ellington, it had been winter. She'd come to personally invite her grandparents to her graduation ceremony, hoping the olive branch would be accepted and the uneasiness between them over her decision to remain in London forgotten.

What followed was the worst row of Saffron's life. Her grandmother had voiced every cruel criticism and insidious doubt that lurked in the corners of Saffron's mind: she was wasting her time at university and could never hope to contribute anything meaningful, her unnatural obsession with science would push away any man of quality and she'd end up alone and impoverished, and worst of all—her father would be ashamed of her selfish decision to live far from her tortured mother.

Saffron had left just after the argument, but she'd walked the grounds during that visit as she always did. The greenhouse's glass had been mostly intact then, with the odd panel cracked or missing. Now, jagged shards littered the facade. The once elegant dome was pockmarked with broken panes. Here and there, the arm of a rogue plant poked through, dead leaves clinging to the tips.

A blast of icy wind sent the leaves fluttering. The iron structure gave an ominous creak. The rain picked up, pelting Saffron's stockinged legs. She shivered.

"Did you want to go inside?" Alexander

sounded doubtful of the wisdom in doing so.

Saffron couldn't exactly argue. "I'm not sure if that's a good idea."

Nevertheless, she moved forward. Her galoshes squelched in the mud ringing the greenhouse.

What would she find inside? With dirt streaking the glass at face level, it was hard to tell the state of the interior. Her chest ached imagining the condition of the raised beds and seeding stations her father had tended so carefully.

But as her hand rose to push open the door, it faltered. She leaned toward it, squinting through the icy rain. The patina of rust and grime on the lock above the door handle had been nicked by a trio of thin scratches revealing bright brass.

Someone had tried to get into the greenhouse.

"It might be nothing," Saffron whispered as she and Alexander discarded their wet coats in the boot room next to the kitchen.

Alexander's look told her he didn't believe someone attempting to get into her father's greenhouse was nothing, nor that he believed it was a mere *someone*.

"Very well, it was clearly Bill," grumbled Saffron. She shivered as she waited for Alexander to finish wiping mud from his boots. "All that tells us is that he is after my father's research, but we already knew that."

"It also tells us that he was likely unsuccessful

getting in," Alexander said, straightening up.

"Why do you think so?"

"Because he wouldn't have been so impatient as to scratch the lock if he'd managed to get in easily."

"It was always locked, and none of the panels were broken enough for someone to slip inside without shredding themselves to ribbons."

They'd circled the building several times to make sure that was the case before retreating to the house. Unless Bill had employed an exceptionally small person to get in and out of the building—

"Or," she said with defeat flattening her voice, "he has the key and was so eager he wasn't careful of the lock."

Alexander looked thoughtful. "Who kept it?"

"My father, when he was alive. Because of the sorts of things he worked with, no one else was allowed in unless in his company. I don't know if there was ever a second copy of the key, though it'd be easy enough to have a copy made."

"Would Lord Easting have taken the key after your father died?"

"I doubt my grandfather would have bothered personally about the greenhouse. He likely only mentioned it to my mother now because he wanted to prepare her for when he tore it down." Her mind conjured a heartbreaking vision of her mother, standing at an upstairs window, watching as her husband's beloved glasshouse was pulled to the ground. She sighed, pushing the image away. "The steward likely has the key. I don't know if Mr. Mathers is still the steward, though. I can find out now."

The kitchen bustled with servants, none of which paid them much notice outside of a curious glance and the bob of a quick curtsy. Saffron recognized several of them, whom she smiled at, including the girl who'd been assigned to tend to her and Elizabeth.

She sat with a trio of other maids at one end of the long table where the servants dined. She looked to be doing some mending while they chatted. Saffron's maid looked to be in the midst of a riveting story, for the other girls watched her speak with parted lips and wide eyes. The girl startled upon recognizing Saffron, and laid down her mending to rush over.

"Oh, miss, you ought to have rang if you needed something!" she chided good-naturedly. "What can I do for you?"

"It's Martha, isn't it?" Saffron asked.

She nodded, smiling broadly. "Yes, miss, Martha Garrett." She eyed Alexander, looking uncertain if she ought to address him, too.

"I wanted to know if Mr. Mathers was still employed here as steward."

"Oh, yes, miss, but he's not here. He went to see to his father in Corby, who'd taken ill." Brightly, she added, "He was laid up with the cancer, you see, and they thought a surgery would help. Mrs. Sharnbrook had a cousin with the same ailment and went on just fine after." Her brow puckered. "But poor Mr. Mathers died—senior, I mean, not our Mr. Mathers—and so Mr. Mathers stayed there to settle things for his family. I believe Mr. Kirby said that he'll be gone another few weeks yet."

"I see," Saffron said, repressing a smile at the avalanche of information. "Thank you, Martha."

"Miss." She curtsied once more before all but skipping back to the other maids. They'd been watching the interaction curiously, and immediately put their heads together when Martha returned to her seat.

Saffron led Alexander up the stairs, dodging servants as they came and went. She guided him back to the library, which she ensured was empty by quickly walking the room and peering into the alcoves. She didn't resettle at their table, however, but paced uneasily as Alexander watched her in silence.

"Mr. Mathers's office might contain the key to the greenhouse," Saffron said, half to herself. "It could also be in my grandfather's possession, though doubtful, or it might have been mixed up in my father's things, most likely in his study." Her lips pursed as she considered the possibilities. She didn't want to ask her grandfather; he wasn't likely to give her the key, and it would only provoke an argument between them.

Her father's rooms, his bedroom, study, and bathroom, connected to her mother's rooms to create a suite. Saffron would need to be absolutely certain her mother was not there when she looked through her father's things. It was a breach of her father's privacy, for one thing, but it would also hurt her mother to be reminded of her late husband. She would have to get into her father's rooms eventually, she had no doubt. But she could put it off until she'd exhausted the easier options.

"I should be able to pick the lock of Mathers's office and check for the key." Another thought occurred to her, and her pacing slowed. "But this is assuming that Bill didn't already figure that out."

"Do we need to get into the greenhouse?" Alexander asked.

"Yes." She stopped her pacing, and frowned. "Maybe. I don't know if there's anything useful in the greenhouse. But if Bill's been poking around in there, I want to see what he might have found."

CHAPTER 11

I don't know why you insist on making me lookout," Alexander muttered, "if you do nothing but doubt my abilities."

Saffron glanced up from where she knelt before the door whose lock she was attempting to pick. "I'm encouraging you to do your best."

"Encouraging?" he repeated, keeping his incredulity to a minimum so as not to draw attention. He glanced over his shoulder, the one not being casually leaned against the wall so as to block Saffron from view. The cavernous main hall was empty at present, which Saffron attributed to the servants preparing for afternoon tea, but that didn't mean there was no one else about who might catch them. "Did I not prove I was able to pick a lock in a timely manner during your last foray into breaking and entering?"

"It was *our* foray, thank you very much." She wiggled her hairpin aggressively into the lock, face screwed up. She jiggled the handle as she cranked her pin around. Triumph spread in a grin across her face. She pushed the door open. "And I've been practicing, too."

Despite the circumstances, he smiled. She winked at him and slipped into the room, leaving

110

him feeling a little off balance and not in a bad way.

He carefully closed the door and positioned himself so it wouldn't be readily apparent to anyone passing by that it wasn't quite latched. He blew out a breath, willing the momentary peace and quiet of the hall to soothe the headache that lingered from whatever Madame had slipped him the previous evening.

John Everleigh's hearty voice hailed him, and Alexander managed not to flinch. He turned to see John striding down the hall with a young boy at his side.

"How are you getting on, Ashton?" John asked. "Lost Saffron, have you?"

"She wanted something from the library and asked me to wait here. We've yet to finish our tour."

"I see." John rocked on his heels. "You've not met my son, have you?" He hoisted the boy up and said proudly, "Benjamin, my boy, this is Aunt Saffron's beau, Mr. Ashton."

Benjamin looked more like his mother than his father, with dark hair and eyes fringed with thick, curling eyelashes. He had John's—and Saffron's—eyes, though. Looking at the little boy did a strange thing to his heart.

The boy stuck out his hand, making his whole body sway against his father. "I am very glad to meet you. How do you do?"

Alexander blinked at the very formal words coming from such a small child. He'd mispronounced a good number of them, but the meaning came across perfectly. He accepted the tiny hand and shook.

John guffawed, replacing the little boy on his feet. "Been practicing that for Great-Grandmama, have you? *Bien joué*."

Benjamin smiled, his smooth cheeks dimpling. Alexander could see why Benjamin had captured Saffron's affections so quickly.

"So," John said, crossing his arms over his chest and leaning a shoulder on the wall. "What's Saffron looking for in there?"

"In the library? I'm not sure."

John chuckled. "I admire your loyalty, if not your skills of observation. Our little walk outside was ruined by the rain. We quite nearly drowned in the lake, so we sheltered in the library from the rain."

"And Nanny," Benjamin added solemnly.

John beamed down at him. "Quite so, my boy. No one likes practicing their letters on such a dreary day, do they?"

The boy nodded, plainly attempting to hide a smile. He scurried away, stopping abruptly to stare in fascination at a painting of a knight on a horse on the opposite wall.

"So we know Aunt Saffron isn't in the library at present." John cleared his throat, his voice dropping. "And this is the exact sort of thing she gets up to these days, isn't it? Picking locks and sneaking around while searching out murderers?"

"That doesn't seem to bother you." He didn't know if he should admit it was precisely as he said or not, so stalling seemed a good idea. Not to mention he'd had no idea John knew of Saffron's habit of getting involved with investigations.

"The crime-solving bit, no. Good for her, I say. The frequency with which she seems to find danger . . . Well, let's just say I've been worried for her more in this last year than I have all her life." John's eyes searched his, a familiar expression of curiosity in his blue eyes. "It bothers you, though, I'd wager."

The guess caught Alexander off guard, the intent and meaning behind it so clear and yet unexpected coming from someone who seemed to laugh off any problem, whether it be inconvenient weather or his grandfather's failing health.

Alexander didn't need to consider the implied question. He had realized things in the aftermath of Saffron's mysteries. First, he cared for her more than he'd realized. Second, he feared losing her. And third, if he was to ever have a chance of winning and keeping her love, he would have to reshape the sort of man that fear had made of him.

"It did," Alexander replied.

"Benji?" A feminine voice floated down from the gallery. *"Où es-tu?"*

"Ah," said John, turning to his son, who looked chagrined. "Bad luck, old boy. Nanny's calling."

"Papa," whined Benjamin, but John was shaking his head. "I liberated you once today already. Besides, you need to get scrubbed up to see your great-grandmama. Must be in good looks to charm the old dragon." He knelt down before the boy and whispered loudly, "Otherwise she might eat you!" He attacked the boy with tickles.

Benjamin giggled helplessly in his father's arms. The nanny, a young blonde woman in a plain gray dress, came down the hall and scooped him up. She did so with ease, and took off back down the hall, murmuring to Benjamin in French as they went.

"She's a good girl, Nanny," John said, rising to his feet, "for all that she sulks a bit. I prefer her to our last one, that's for certain. Been with us since Benjamin was born, then about a month ago up and leaves the moment she catches wind that her great-aunt or some such had died, thinking she'll get a bit of money. She barely gives notice before she leaves and—can you believe?—she comes back not a week later, saying there'd been some mistake and there was no money and could she please have her position back?" He snorted and fell back into place leaning on the wall next to the estate manager's office door.

"Suzette had already hired Nanny Badeaux and was satisfied. And who'd bring a woman like that back in, anyway? I'll not have someone caring for my son running away at the slightest enticement."

"Quite so," Alexander said.

An awkward silence was poised to fall, and John prevented it. "Well, shall we just stand around out here pretending Saffron isn't inside, or shall we join her?"

Alexander was saved from answering.

"Oh, you are so *very* bothersome," Saffron's muffled voice said from behind the door. "Very well, get in here. But quickly, before anyone sees you."

Saffron scowled at them as he and John filed into the steward's office. It was plainer than the other rooms he'd seen thus far, with white walls adorned with only a single—albeit large and likely quality—painting of a hunt. Shelves with books relating to horticulture and animal husbandry mirrored each other with a curtained window in between.

John flopped onto one of the worn leather chairs before the desk and looked at Saffron with smug anticipation.

Saffron perched on the large desk tidily arranged with lamp, blotter, and a stack of massive square books that could only be ledgers. "You've caught me snooping. Are you happy now?"

115

"Very much so," John replied. "What exactly are you snooping for?"

Irritation, put on or genuine, faded from Saffron's face. There was a pregnant pause that left Alexander's nerves dancing. What would John's reaction be to learning Lord Easting's doctor was an impostor? He was a lawyer, a former soldier, a father, not to mention his grandfather's heir, but thus far he'd proven an exceptionally easy-going man. He rather reminded Alexander of his brother, Adrian. But Adrian, for all his joviality, would brook no offense to his family, often to his detriment. Would John prove the same?

After a drawn-out moment, Saffron wet her lips and shrugged. "Nothing. I'm not looking for anything in particular. I was just . . . curious."

CHAPTER 12

Tea time proved to be Saffron's salvation, for just after John rolled his eyes at her dishonest explanation, he noticed the time and sprung to his feet.

"Got to summon the troops," he said, heading for the door. "Nearly time for tea."

Saffron swallowed hard, but it didn't help the feeling that her tongue had swollen twice its size. She gave John a tight smile, and he left the room.

"Just curious?" Alexander asked as the door closed.

The entire story had been poised to unravel so it might stop twisting around her insides. But though she'd planned to tell John about Bill and what he threatened, she found it would not come out. John thought her investigations were good fun touched with danger. She had only herself to blame for that; he knew only what she'd told him. He didn't know how her head had ached for weeks after being struck or that nightmares still plagued her. That she was being blackmailed and the entire family was more or less hostage. She found she couldn't bear to tell him of her failure to foresee the consequences of her actions and how that failure now meant his wife and son were in danger.

She shrugged helplessly. "I didn't know what to say."

Alexander nodded, his dark eyes watchful. "Did you find the key?"

"No." She'd have to pursue one of the less appealing options for recovering the greenhouse key. "Shall we go to tea?"

In deep winter, the trio of windows in the saloon provided a lovely view of the lake in late afternoon. Sunset would paint the lake in cool pastels, frosted branches of the wood beyond would be illumined by the slant of the setting sun, and the world went quiet and still. Though the sun had yet to dip below the trees, evening had crept in early. Without the whimsical colors of twilight, rain bled color from the landscape, rendering the view a dreary watercolor of blurred brown and gray.

The saloon itself was cozy and bright. The fire fairly roared in the hearth, and it seemed that every available light in the room had been ignited to chase away the gloom outside. Light glinted off dozens of frames on the walls: photographs, paintings, drawings, and maps covered so much of the wall that the burgundy paint beneath looked like a shared border. The couches and chairs, the same worn gold paisley she'd grown up jumping on, were arranged so tea could be served from the heavily laden cart set at the center.

Elizabeth, Saffron was pleased to see, was

ensconced in the center of the Everleighs, though she looked rather worse for wear. Pale and quiet, she sipped tea while staring into the crackling fire. When she caught Saffron's eye, her lips only quirked to one side in a sad imitation of a smile.

Saffron had no chance to greet her or anyone else, for Lady Easting immediately asked, "What kept you, Saffron?"

She was rather surprised her grandmother was speaking to her. "I was showing Alexander around." Alexander was already in conversation with John, but he nodded in acknowledgment to her and Lady Easting.

"John said you were showing your friend this house this morning," her grandmother shot back.

"There is quite a bit of house to see, Grandmama. And we went to see the grounds, too."

Her grandmother gave the windows a pointed look, where the worsening storm ate up murky dregs of daylight.

Saffron forced lightness into her voice. "We're both used to working in the field under uncomfortable conditions. A little rain would hardly keep me from seeing the gardens and greenhouse."

Lady Easting didn't reply, merely pursing her lips before addressing Suzette with another inquiry about Benjamin, who sat next to Suzette in an adorable little suit.

Rather than sit awkwardly in the way of their conversation, Saffron fixed herself a cup of tea and went to sit next to Elizabeth.

"What have you gotten up to today?" Saffron asked her.

"Nothing worth mentioning," Elizabeth said sourly.

Saffron didn't reply, unsure of what she could say that would improve matters.

"I might just return home," Elizabeth muttered. "I doubt I'll be of any use to anyone here."

It was so patently unlike Elizabeth that Saffron swung around in her seat to stare at her. "Why ever would you say that?"

Elizabeth shrugged.

All at once, Saffron realized what the problem was. "Eliza—are you feeling quite yourself? Have you been feeling strange today? Tired, with aching eyes?"

"Considering you watched me drink a bathtub's worth of wine last night, I think you already know how I'm feeling."

"No, this is something else. Alexander had an idea . . ." In a near whisper, she explained about Alexander's suspicions about Madame Martin drugging the attendees of her séances. As she spoke, she realized that she ought to have planned this better, for telling Elizabeth something like this would lead to a bombastic reaction better not on exhibit before her family.

120

But when she was finished, rather than anger, Elizabeth's eyes betrayed hurt.

"You let me believe," she said slowly, quietly, "that woman had some sort of real power over me and my family for a *whole day?*"

Saffron was so taken aback she only managed to say, "I—I'm sorry. I ought to have told you right away." She wished she could explain about being shaken by the ghostly soldier, then overwhelmed by her family and Bill's demands, but how could she add yet another burden on top of how upset the séance had made Elizabeth? "I didn't—"

Elizabeth stood, set her teacup in its saucer on the nearest table, and strode from the room.

"More tea?"

Her mother was already gently taking Saffron's cup and saucer from her hands.

"Oh, yes, thank you." Saffron rallied a smile, though it felt rubbery on her lips. How badly had she mucked things up with Elizabeth that she wouldn't even shout at her when she deserved it?

"I take it Elizabeth is not quite recovered from last night," Violet said. "Your father used to make a wonderful concoction to help with the aftereffects of too much drink. Fresh mint, chamomile, a raw egg, and myrrh."

"Myrrh?" Saffron repeated. She associated the fragrant resin with the smoky scent of churches.

She would have guessed it was toxic to consume. "What on earth for?"

"It's actually quite useful," Violet said. "It's an astringent and has all sorts of applications."

"I can't quite tell if you're poking fun at me or not."

Her mother's eyes twinkled in response. She sat next to Saffron with a sigh, but it wasn't an unhappy sound. "I have missed you, my darling. Speaking through letters and even over the telephone isn't the same, is it? And how nice it is to have the house full again."

"You and Grandmama host the neighbors often, I imagine."

"Oh, yes. I see a good deal of Miss Lillian and Miss Eloise, and Mrs. Hale has visited frequently these last few months. She has come often to ask my opinions about their home's refurbishment."

Saffron wondered if her mother knew anything of the Hales' turn in fortunes, but asked instead, "Have you met the psychic they are hosting?" She knew the answer; her mother hadn't left the house in years, not even to go next door. But she wanted to hear her mother's opinion on Madame Martin's presence in the neighborhood.

"No." Her mother sipped her tea. "I don't imagine Lady Easting would take kindly to entertaining her." She smiled slightly. "I wouldn't mind meeting so interesting a person, but I don't believe I would wish her to conjure spirits here. I shouldn't like to see who has been lurking in the house."

Saffron laughed. "Nor I. They would likely tell tales on me and get me into trouble." She sipped her own tea, stalling. Should she ask about the greenhouse key?

"Do you know if your Mr. Ashton is interested in children?"

Hot tea caught in Saffron's throat and she sputtered, drawing the eyes of everyone around the room.

Her mother patted her back gently. "I take it my question took you off guard."

"I—Why, no," Saffron said sheepishly.

"I ask only because he seems to get on well with Benjamin." Violet nodded to where Benjamin knelt on a cushion in the window seat and pointed out the glass. He was speaking animatedly to Alexander, who sat next to him, listening with an expression of serious interest.

Butterflies fluttered in her stomach. "He speaks French very well. Benjamin must enjoy having someone new who is fluent."

"He speaks English very well," her mother said, a slight frown puckering her brow.

"Alexander *is* English."

"You know I meant Benjamin. Benjamin is English, too. He'll only become more English, I'm afraid," her mother said with a sigh.

"What do you mean?"

Her mother sent her a look. "Despite John's protests, he and Suzette will have to move here eventually. John isn't at all the type to leave all the responsibilities of the estate to a manager."

She was right, and it made Saffron's heart hurt for her cousin's family. Uprooting Suzette and Benjamin would be hard on them all. She sighed. "Perhaps if he found someone exceptionally competent."

For some reason, color rose in her mother's cheeks. Intrigued, Saffron ventured, "Perhaps Mr. Mathers would be up to the task?"

"Oh, yes, of course," her mother said, and she busied herself with setting down her teacup and placing another few sandwiches on Saffron's plate.

"Speaking of Mr. Mathers—" Saffron began, but it was then that the door to the saloon opened, and her grandfather appeared.

When the commotion of family and servants initiated by her grandfather's arrival died down, and the older man was settled in the armchair before the fire with a thick wool blanket over his lap and a disagreeable expression, Saffron realized that Bill had crept into the room and was now *lurking*. She eyed him, nearly invisible in his perch on a chair in a corner. He silently observed Benjamin be brought forward and introduced, her grandfather gruffly greet the boy and offer his hand. The small boy dutifully replied in halting English to his questions about whether or not he was a good lad and listened to his parents and nanny.

Saffron had to give Bill credit; his spectacles were a masterful disguise. The details of his facial features faded with each flash of his lenses. Bill could have been anyone.

"Saffron!"

Her grandfather's bark interrupted her staring at Bill, hopefully before anyone noticed. She got to her feet. "Yes, Grandpapa?"

"Come here," he commanded.

She supposed it was a good sign he'd maintained his domineering manner through his illness. And as she did as he bid, she saw he did not look as ill as she'd worried. His usual ruddy face was pale, but his blue eyes were alert.

"Found your way back home in the end, I see," he commented as she came to brush a kiss on his cheek. "Knew you would. Glad to see you, my girl."

Saffron held her tongue, rather pleased at the warm greeting, however tempting it was to remind him that he all but summoned her to Ellington. She shot Alexander a look and said, "Grandpapa, may I introduce Alexander Ashton?"

"Ah," Lord Easting said, craning his neck to get a better look at Alexander as he approached. "I recall this fellow." He pushed his teacup into

Saffron's hands and braced himself on either arm of his chair, hoisting himself to his feet with a grunt of effort.

"Hush now," he muttered when Violet and Lady Easting made noises of protest. "Got to meet the fellow eye to eye, don't I?" He gave Alexander a jaundiced look and barked a laugh. "Or at least attempt to. Tall, isn't he?" He stuck his hand out to Alexander.

He shook it. "How do you do?"

Lord Easting's response was more of a hum than actual words, but he at least didn't announce he was tossing Alexander, or them both, out on their ears. When he finally let Alexander's hand drop, he looked at Saffron. She was surprised to see emotion there, though it was gone before she could name it.

Benjamin chose that moment to be adorable, drawing the attention of the entire party once again. Lord Easting attempted to communicate in his mother tongue with him, amusing the boy with his very poor accent.

The weight of the argument with her grandmother lightened somewhat as Saffron watched her grandfather and Benjamin. Out of all of them, she'd expect her grandfather to be the least pleasant.

She blew out a breath and looked about for her teacup. Her mother offered her a fresh one filled with steaming tea.

"Thank you."

"That went rather well, all things considered," Violet murmured.

"Yes," she replied, sipping the tea. "I suppose it's foolish to hope for anything resembling interest in Alexander."

Her mother gave her a sad smile. "At this moment, perhaps. But your grandfather is a reasonable man. He respects intelligence and hard work. Alexander will win his approval in short order."

Her words were meant to be encouraging, of course, but they only stoked Saffron's anxiety. Yes, she and Alexander's relationship was quite serious, and yes, sometimes she did become distracted with daydreams about what their future could be, anything from adventuring together on an expedition to marriage and domestic bliss. But they were daydreams, far off and slightly blurry in her mind's eye. Their implications were never closely examined. She'd been too busy with her work, her classes for her master's degree at the U, and enjoying Alexander's company to worry about more than a few months in the future.

She glanced at Alexander, now speaking to Suzette and John across the room. The sun had given up its last watery attempts at illumination, leaving him bathed in golden light from the lamps and fire. As she watched, he chuckled at something John said, and she could practically feel its low rumble.

Violet touched her arm, and when Saffron refocused on her, she was smiling. "Any man who is able to put that look on your face is disposed to quickly earn my approval, too." She squeezed her arm gently.

Saffron swallowed the lump in her throat. "Thank you for saying that, Mama." As much as she hated to ruin the tender moment, this was her chance. "I want to be able to share with him about our family as much as possible while we're here. Since it was so important to Papa, I wanted to show him the greenhouse, but I forgot to retrieve the key before we went there earlier. Do you know where it is? I should like to see inside myself, especially if Grandpapa means to tear it down."

"Oh," her mother said, lashes fluttering in surprise. "No. That is, I don't know where the key is. But . . ." She glanced at Lord Easting, who was now speaking to Bill. "I wouldn't go asking for the key, Saffron. With your grandfather's health so delicate, upsetting him really isn't wise. We ought to do all we can to bolster his health."

Mention of Lord Easting's health drew Saffron's attention back to Bill. He sipped tea, watching her family without expression.

Violet clasped Saffron's hands. "I know your being here now will do just that."

"Alexander would love to see some of the older microscopes Papa collected," Saffron pressed. "And I spent so much time in Papa's study as a girl. If even just for a moment, I would like to show Alexander the room."

Violet started. "I . . . I don't think that would be appropriate. I'm sorry, my dear."

Saffron let the matter drop, feeling just as ill at ease as her mother looked as she rose and busied herself at the tea tray.

She would have to find a way to get Bill's answers another way, or at least give the impression of it. She certainly would not be handing over whatever she found.

She shot Bill a glare. She wasn't going to let him take anything else from her.

CHAPTER 13

The rest of the day passed in a predictable yet uneasy way. Dinner was a quiet affair, the mood somewhat dampened by Lord Easting's absence. Lady Easting gave no explanation or acknowledgment, and John muttered into Saffron's ear later that he suspected their grandfather was already heartily sick of them all. It was meant to be a joke, but Saffron couldn't take it as such. Without access to her grandfather, she had no way of discovering if his health was improving or declining, nor would she have the chance to tell him that Bill needed to be dismissed.

Saffron continued to make subtle inquiries regarding the greenhouse key the next day, looking over her shoulder all the while, expecting Bill to jump out of every dark corner. She and Alexander spent time in the library, their noses in books. No one questioned it; the weather had grown even more unpleasant with an iron-gray sky that spit a mixture of snow, ice, and rain.

That afternoon, Elizabeth threw herself down into an armchair across from where Saffron and Alexander sat together on one of the blue couches in the library. It was just after tea, which she had missed, and her cheeks and nose were flushed pink.

"Well," she said, "you shall never guess what I've been up to."

Considering Saffron had believed Elizabeth to be in her room for most of the day, ignoring the novels and tidbits of food Saffron had brought to her door as little apologies, she'd been rather worried her friend might have actually left Ellington as she'd suggested.

"I went to my parents' house," she said, "fully intending to confront Madame Martin. I was told she wasn't available. Some rot about spending her days in deep meditation. My mother thought I was there to apologize for what happened at the séance." She rolled her eyes. "Apologize! When I told her I was there to kick that phony out of their house, do you know what she said? That I must"—her voice turned airy and high-pitched—" 'open my heart and mind to the workings of the universe,' so I might 'hear Wesley speak through the extraordinary talents of Madame Martin.' " Her voice dropped to her usual alto. "I nearly keeled over right then and there. It was simply too much. So, I did what any sensible person would do and snuck away to snoop in Madame's room."

Saffron blinked. "You searched Madame Martin's bedroom? Why?"

"*My* room, actually." Elizabeth sat up, and with

131

the aura of a gossip with news to share, explained, "My parents have put her up in my old bedroom. To my immense disappointment, the room did not reveal a stash of cheesecloth ectoplasm or gramophone records of ghostly moans. I had only a minute to poke around before I heard a pair of maids coming down the hall and had to breeze. But what I did find was significant. Or rather, what I did *not* find."

She looked around the room and asked, "Saff, darling, do pull the bell. I know I've missed tea, but I'm famished."

Saffron couldn't be irritated that she was leaving them in suspense when it seemed she'd recovered her spirit so thoroughly. When she returned to her seat at Alexander's side, Elizabeth continued.

"Most importantly, I saw no vials of drugs she'd dripped into our coffee cups. Nothing to make us see things that weren't there. So, she is cleverer than I hoped. Had she just left it out for me to find, I could have taken it to my parents and they would have had to kick her out then and there." She paused, artfully thin brows gathered in thought. "But I suppose that is expecting too much sense from them. Also, there were no signs of old letters or journals she'd pillaged for information about Wesley and the rest of my family. She's convinced them she's in contact with Wesley, so she must have some source of information. As my parents never paid us any mind as children apart from harassing us to behave, I doubt they've provided many details. I had a little think and decided to go on a jaunt into Goldington. The walk was damnably wet, but worth it. I discovered something rather fascinating in the pawn shop, and it wasn't that the furniture my parents sold off years ago is still sitting there, gathering dust. The books were in the pawn shop!"

She paused, as if waiting for exclamations of shock at her reveal.

"The penny dreadfuls, you mean?" asked Alexander.

Elizabeth granted him a smile. "I'm so glad you caught that little detail, darling. Yes, the silly gothic novels Wesley and I used to read, the ones Madame Martin mentioned. They were just sitting there in the back corner, available for perusal for anyone popping into the shop. My dear late brother saw fit to inscribe his name into them as a boy. And I, in turn, saw fit to scratch his name out and add my own, for the bounder was always stealing them away from me. Therefore"—she raised her brow as if awaiting Saffron and Alexander arriving at a stunning revelation—"Madame could have easily discovered that Wesley and I read penny dreadfuls as children and incorporated that into her act."

Elizabeth said it with such relish that Saffron didn't want to point out that this was not the sort of significant discovery she thought it to be. The arrival of the tea cart forestalled her response. Once the maid had arranged it for them and departed, Elizabeth leaned forward to fix herself a cup and said, "While in Goldington, I went down the pub. The Black Swan is just as dismal a place as ever, but that old Hubert Rawlings is a still dear. Gave me my first taste of gin, you know." She winked at Alexander. "I enjoyed one or two tall pours as he regaled me of tales of Madame Martin in the village. Madame has apparently channeled the dead no less than four times, each time charging *three pounds* for her services."

Saffron's mouth fell open. Three pounds was likely the budget of many families in the village to feed their families for a week or more.

Elizabeth gave her a dark look. "She's a heartless witch to be preying on those for whom that much money is dear, and who have lost their loved ones. I told Rawlings to warn the villagers away from her, lest they waste more of their money and hope, but you know that won't be enough. I'm wanting only enough evidence of her phony divination to convince my parents to send her packing. There is certainly proof, I need only to find it."

Alexander cleared his throat. "If we're speaking

of evidence, I may have some. Though with the rain, it is no doubt already gone."

"Do tell," Elizabeth said, and popped a jam tart into her mouth.

"Footprints," he said, "outside the window of your bedroom."

"The soldier!" Saffron exclaimed. "That's what you were looking for when we went to the greenhouse! It wasn't a vision—it was a real person." Her relief that the man she'd seen was real and not a hallucination was short-lived.

Outrage colored Elizabeth's face. "You saw the soldier outside my window? How could you—" She inhaled sharply, holding a palm up at Saffron, eyes pinched closed. "I will not berate you for yet another egregious oversight now, there is too much to do." To Alexander, she said, "You're certain you saw footprints under my window?"

"I did," he replied. "A man's boots, walking from the south side of the house to the front."

"Good. One does hate to think one's mind is running amuck," she said firmly. She began loading a plate with sandwiches and cakes. "I theorize it was Mr. Fischer playing soldier. He must have a uniform for such theatrics. With their clientele, he must often have a need to go haunting in that hideous mask. We can search his room, too. I will arrange for an invitation. Shouldn't be hard; my mother has been singularly forceful about my welcomeness in their home."

"An invitation to what?" Saffron asked.

Elizabeth lifted her teacup in Saffron's direction. "To tea, of course. We'll go over, and while I'm distracting the fraud and my mother, you'll poke around in Madame's and Mr. Fischer's room."

"Why am I the one to do it?" Saffron protested. She certainly hadn't been angling for her own involvement in Elizabeth's vendetta.

Elizabeth frowned. "I've already looked around, haven't I? And you've done this sort of thing many times before. You know what to look for." She got to her feet, and balancing her teacup and full plate, said, "I'll let you know when we're going over, darling. See you at dinner."

CHAPTER 14

I really don't think this is a good idea," Saffron murmured to Elizabeth.

"It can hardly be a bad one," Elizabeth said. "Any opportunity to learn more about Madame is valuable. But damn my mother for managing to turn things around and invite herself over here for tea."

They paused at the top of the stairs. Mrs. Hale's voice trilled from the drawing room. Mrs. Hale, in a violently green dress and matching coat and hat, and Madame Martin, draped in heavy black serge, had arrived five minutes earlier, followed by the Harvey sisters wrapped in moth-eaten furs.

Hours of looking through books in the library earlier that day had gotten Saffron and Alexander nowhere. She'd come no closer to finding the greenhouse key. Her grandfather had been downstairs for luncheon, but Bill had dined with them, and they'd disappeared together for a "treatment" before Saffron could approach Lord Easting privately. No progress had been made in getting rid of Bill, and a break could hardly hurt.

"My dearest girl!" exclaimed Mrs. Hale, coming forward to smack a kiss on Elizabeth's cheek as soon as they entered the drawing room. Her eyes fairly sparkled as she took Elizabeth's hands to hold her away from her, as one might do to a child to take their measure. "How chic your time away has made you. You shall have to direct me to your dressmaker when next I visit town." She beamed at her daughter, and when her eyes flickered to Saffron, her smile went flat. "And Saffron. How nice to see you again."

"Mrs. Hale," she replied politely, "we're so happy you were able to join us for tea. And Madame Martin."

Madame Martin looked less abstracted than she had before, her dark eyes clear as she nodded. Her lips parted as if to speak, but her eyes locked on something over Saffron's shoulder, forestalling her.

Saffron turned to see her mother had come into the room. "Mama, do come and meet Madame Martin."

When Violet came forward, a hand extended in greeting, Madame hesitated just long enough for it to be noticeable but not offensive. "Madame Everleigh," she said with feeling, "it is a pleasure to make your acquaintance."

Fluttering about the tea service took up a good deal of time, and then the next half hour was spent in discussion of the comings and goings of those in the village and surrounding area. John and Lord Easting were meeting with a tenant, and

Alexander was not inclined to be the sole male at tea.

The conversation eventually turned away from local news when Miss Eloise asked that Madame Martin describe Paris for them again. "Went there once, as a girl," she said in her wispy voice, "and have never forgotten its magic. How does it fair, after the war?"

"She is bruised, my city, but she is strong. Rather like the ancient tree after the worst storm. Her branches are bare, but she remains. Everyone must visit Paris in their lifetime," Madame said fervently. Saffron rather thought she sounded like an actual person for the first time instead of a poorly-drawn character from a gothic novel. "The food, the people. It is the best place in the world. *C'est stupéfiant*, no, Mademoiselle Hale?"

Elizabeth blinked slowly at her. "Oh, indeed."

Madam's lips turned up in the corners as if amused by Elizabeth's lukewarm response. "Ah, but I am inconsiderate," she murmured, dark eyes flickering to Violet. "Tell me of the beautiful grounds here at Ellington, Madame Everleigh."

Violet did, and Saffron had to wonder how long it had been since Violet had read a book in the sunshine on the lake's dock, or enjoyed the scent of the roses Thomas Everleigh had planted to twine on the arbor in the formal gardens. When had she last set foot in one of the fields to seek out a perfect buttercup?

The ladies broke apart into smaller clusters of conversation after that. Saffron and Elizabeth were approached by the Misses Harvey, who wanted to hear about their life in London. Mrs. Hale saw fit to engage Lady Easting in conversation, loud enough that it carried across the drawing room and thoroughly distracted Saffron from Elizabeth's explanation of her secretarial work.

"What a challenge it is," Mrs. Hale tittered, "to staff a house these days. We've taken on quite a few new people and have found all of them lacking. They expect too much, you know. Entire days off! An Electrolux *and* a washing machine. A washing machine! They cannot genuinely think to repay the kindness of providing employment in a good house, far from the toxic fumes of those dreadful factories, by demanding expensive devices. They are labor-saving, they say, but I pay them to do labor, do I not?"

"I consider it best practice to have the latest technology available to my servants," was Lady Easting's blithe reply. "I expect the best, I hire the best, and I provide the best. And so, I am always satisfied. You might consider hiring an agency to undertake the hiring process on your behalf. It saves one the time and labor of doing it by oneself."

She said it without censure nor emphasis, but no one overhearing them could have missed the rebuke in her reply. Elizabeth, equally distracted from the Harvey sisters, covered her grin with her teacup.

At the drawing room door, the young woman Suzette had referred to as Nanny Badeaux paused half inside, looking torn about coming all the way within. Suzette broke away from her conversation with Madame Martin to go to her, and they exchanged a few words before Suzette beckoned for Violet.

Saffron's mother conferred with the nanny and Suzette, and the two younger women appeared to decide something before they both disappeared into the hall. Violet stood at the door a moment longer before following them.

Miss Lillian seemed to hardly notice Saffron and Elizabeth's lack of attention to their conversation. "And what do you make of London society, Miss Saffron?"

"Oh," Saffron said, straining to recall what had led them to this topic, "I don't make much of it, I'm afraid. I haven't seen much of my prior acquaintances recently." That was by design, for she'd been as bored of their insular world as they'd been of her scientific talk.

"Of course," Miss Eloise said, her feeble voice trailing off so the rest of her thought was inaudible.

Saffron bent closer, catching a whiff of her powdery scent. "Beg pardon?"

"You must speak up, sister," Miss Lillian said in strident tones.

"Must miss the boy," her sister said slightly louder. "Hard to enjoy society with a broken heart."

Saffron's lips parted in surprise. "Er—"

"Oh, certainly," Elizabeth said. "Dearest Saffron's heart still aches for my brother. It is such a comfort to know he's been in touch with my parents through the talents of Madame Martin."

The sisters nodded, looking rather like a pair of turtles slowly bobbing their heads.

"Indeed," Miss Eloise managed. "Such a comfort."

"We have always known of the powers of the Great Beyond," said her sister enthusiastically. "How extraordinary to have it confirmed."

"Madame has summoned someone from your past as well?" Saffron asked, for that was clearly what Elizabeth was angling for.

"Another meeting," Miss Eloise said. "Soon."

"Last we met with Madame, she disclosed that there were many spirits within Goldington House that ached for contact with the living," Miss Lillian explained. She leaned around Saffron, sending the overlong fringes of her shawl wriggling. "We must insist she comes again to give them some relief. Madame must be in the powder room. We shall ask her in a moment. Come have another bonbon, sister."

The sisters drifted back toward the tea cart, Elizabeth following in their wake, asking Miss Lillian to describe the spirits Madame had summoned at Goldington Hall.

Saffron's fingers drummed against her thigh as her eyes moved from face to face. Her grandmother was ignoring Mrs. Hale near the fire. Elizabeth stood with the sisters at the tea cart. Suzette, just returning from whatever errand the nanny had summoned her for, found a chair, apparently savoring a quiet moment. Madame was gone from the room.

For some reason, her absence unnerved Saffron. She drifted to the door and peered into the entrance hall, but saw no one. She glanced back at the women clustered around the room, and realized why she felt so uneasy with Madame being gone: her mother had not come back, either.

CHAPTER 15

Saffron heard the faint echo of voices after only a few steps onto the polished stone floor of the entry. Following it to the reception room, she recognized the lilt of Madame Martin's voice and all but pressed her ear to the cool wood of the door to listen.

"I wished to offer my services to you in private," Madame Martin said, voice so low it was hard to hear through the door.

A warm pressure touched her arm. Saffron stifled a gasp and lurched away.

Elizabeth gave her an incredulous look and mouthed, *What is the matter with you?* She pointed to the door. *Who is in there?*

Madame and my mother, Saffron mouthed back, returning her ear to the door. Elizabeth copied her, pressing her own ear against the door so they were nearly nose to nose.

"The sensibilities of the lady of the house are not in favor of my capacities," Madame was saying. "But I could not leave your home, a home so filled with melancholy, without begging that I be allowed to ease the pain you bear."

"Oh," Violet said. "Well, I—"

"The moment I set foot in the door—no, on

the land itself—I felt the draw to those souls lingering here. There is one, he is so strong, so desperate to speak." A weak murmur of response, then Madame declared, "Do not feel you must answer now, Madame. Allow your heart to consider its needs. I will come to you when you are ready."

There was a pause in which Elizabeth shifted and Saffron elbowed her to stay quiet, lest she miss her mother's answer.

And if she'd moved again, she might have missed Madame's last words: "We might walk out those doors together, Madame Everleigh. You might sit under the rose arbor again . . ."

Elizabeth had the foresight to scramble out of the way and around the corner just as the door to the reception room opened, taking Saffron by the arm just in time. They stood side by side, tucked up under the stairs such that all Saffron saw was dark wood paneling.

Sounds of fabric swishing and heels clicking on stone soon faded, leaving Saffron wondering which woman had walked away. Madame, confident that her snare had been laid attractively, or her mother, dismissing it?

A dry voice made Saffron jump.

"I feel as if I've been transported back in time," Violet said, peering into the alcove. "I believe I caught the pair of you eavesdropping in just this spot before."

Elizabeth blinked innocent eyes. "Eavesdropping, us? Never, Mrs. E."

No one would ever believe that, least of all her mother.

"We were just—" Saffron began.

"—Admiring the lack of cobwebs in such an out of the way spot of the house," Elizabeth said, waving her hand to the corners of the alcove. "Nary a spider. Most impressive. Lady Easting is clearly well within her rights to proclaim her staff among the very best."

Violet's eyes twinkled. "I shall pass on the compliment."

"I'll tell her myself," Elizabeth said brightly and hurried back to the drawing room.

There was little point in perpetuating Elizabeth's flimsy charade, so Saffron asked, "What did Madame Martin want?"

"To offer her services." Violet gave a half-hearted shrug, one that spoke to indifference her eyes did not show. She set an arm around Saffron, drawing her to her side, and guided them back to the drawing room. "Let's return to our guests."

It was very quiet, and it surprised Alexander how uncomfortable he found it. In London, it felt as if he was always seeking out respite from motorcar engines and horns, the clop of a horse cart, the thunks and clangs of construction. Now, surrounded by miles of peaceful countryside, he felt he might crawl out of his skin from how quiet it was.

He had retreated with a pile of books to his bedroom when Saffron told him that she and the other women would be having tea in the drawing room, too close to the library for comfort or concentration. The layers of expensive heirloom furniture and decor only chafed at his already prickled senses.

Rather than attempt to push past it and inevitably fail, Alexander shed his jacket, waistcoat, oxfords, and socks to settle cross-legged on the floor before the hearth.

He sat that way, delving deeper into his own consciousness until he found the cold, clear depths of undisturbed concentration, until a knock sounded at the door. He knew immediately it was not Saffron, for it was nothing like the bright two-beat rap of her knuckles. It was also not a servant, at least not the one who'd crept into his room at dawn to tend the fire.

He was not, therefore, very surprised to find John on the other side of his door.

"What, ho, Ashton!" he said cheerfully before looking quizzically down at Alexander's bare feet. "Caught you in the middle of a nap, have I? What do you say to a game of skittles?"

"It's raining, isn't it?"

"Indoors, of course. The nursery has a little set that Saffron and I used to torment the hallway walls with when we were children. Well, she was a child, and I was a poorly mannered youth." John's ever-present smile was soft with nostalgia. "What do you say? Shall I introduce you to a Everleigh family tradition?"

A few minutes later, Alexander was already questioning his agreement to the game. The portrait-covered length of wall along which they played the game was open to the entry, and though the thick carpet underfoot did much to dampen the sound, each *crack* of the little wooden ball as it sent the matching pins scattering echoed in the vast, empty air. John and Benjamin's laughter only added to the noise. Ironically, it was not the sort of noise Alexander had been missing, for it only made him wonder if they would get into trouble for making a ruckus.

Benjamin scuttled forward to reset the skittles, his giggles filling the entry.

John came to stand next to Alexander. "How is Saffron?"

Surprised, Alexander glanced at him. John's expression gave nothing away. "She's well. Pleased to be with her family."

"Seems she's distracted," John said casually, nudging the ball with his foot so it rolled down the hall toward his son. "Things at the U going all right? No more of that nonsense about that fellow she sent to prison?"

"I've not heard her mention anyone bringing

up Berking for some time," Alexander said. With their relationship now being public knowledge, Saffron seemed less likely to be directly harassed by their coworkers, and Alexander more likely. He was glad for the change, though he worried what their colleagues said behind raised hands. They'd done their best to keep things professional at the U. Occasionally temptation proved too great, but they'd managed to keep that mostly behind closed doors.

He left his answer at that, deciding not to address John's first question. Saffron's work was going well, as far as he knew, but he got the sense she was not enjoying her first solo study as much as she'd anticipated. It was her choice to let John know that, just as it would be her choice to reveal Bill's true intentions. He'd tried to take choices like that away from her before, and he would try not to do it again.

John's brows furrowed. "Saffron's worried, isn't she?"

Another direct question he had no business answering. He accepted the ball from Benjamin with a smile and took his turn.

It seemed John didn't require a response. "I knew it." He blew out a breath. "She's worried about the state of things here. My grandfather has only been ill for a short time, but she knows how quickly things can go south. She must see something I don't. That's what she was looking for in Mathers's office, wasn't it! Does she believe Mathers might be taking advantage? But he's been gone longer than my grandfather has been ill. And Aunt Violet has been managing quite well, if the books are anything to go by . . ."

He trailed away as he jogged after the ball to take his turn.

"I see why Saffron finds you indispensable during her investigations," John said as he took the bowling position. "You've got the singular ability to set one's mind at ease."

His arm swung back, and he released his ball at such a speed that the skittles crashed into the railing and the wall. Alexander winced. Benjamin cheered.

John dashed after the skittles, scooping them up in his arms. He turned back to Benjamin, grinning, but the smile fell immediately.

The thump of a cane on carpet announced the reason a moment later.

Lord Easting stood at the end of the gallery. "This is the reason you left our meeting early?"

John's free hand found Benjamin's shoulder. "Good afternoon, my lord." His tone suggested this was anything but a polite pleasantry.

Lord Easting tapped his cane against the floor again. "You left the meeting, the only one we will manage with your short time at Ellington, to play a child's game?"

Alexander glanced between the two men, on

either end of the gallery with matching expressions of impatient frustration. He caught movement out of the corner of his eye; Saffron and her mother, walking across the tile below, heads bent together in inaudible conversation. A moment later, a shadow emerged from the corner of the landing over them. Alexander's stomach turned. Bill ghosted up the remaining steps.

"I left the meeting," John ground out, "because the fellow we spoke to had nothing to say except repeating his concerns that your demise would send Ellington off a cliff. I'd rather spend my time with my son, ensuring he has some happy memories of this place."

Bill arrived at Lord Easting's side just as the old man looked to be on the brink of an explosion of temper.

"Come, my lord," Bill murmured. "It is time for your next treatment."

Lord Easting bristled, glaring at John, before turning away. Bill's lip curled into a minute smile just for Alexander as he followed Lord Easting down the hall and out of sight.

CHAPTER 16

When tea concluded and the guests had departed with promises of another visit soon, John requested Saffron show him and his little family around the conservatory, to, in his words, "show us which plants will kill us straight away, and which ones will simply keep us in the lavatory for a day or two." Suzette did not find this amusing, but her scolding was cut off by Benjamin asking her why he was calling his father a sausage. Watching her and John struggle to explain that *andouille* could be both a food and an insult—"But why would you call Papa a mean word?" Benjamin wanted to know—was enough to have Saffron and Elizabeth in fits of giggles.

The conservatory was far more beautiful in full daylight, but Saffron was happy to visit it, even as she felt the pressure to find answers. After two days at Ellington, she felt she hadn't even managed one step in the right direction.

The long glass room felt far larger in the dark, almost like a small jungle with its layers of fanning leaves. Most private conservatories Saffron had visited were nothing more than hothouses to grow pretty flowers for arrangements or places for potted fruit trees. Ellington's might have been like that, but her father had nurtured it into an impressive collection of exotic plants. She was pleased to see they were thriving despite the cold weather.

A pair of coal stoves kept the place toasty, so much so that Elizabeth let out a pleasured groan when they stepped inside.

"I forgot how bloody cold these enormous houses get in winter," she said, making for one of the stoves immediately. "It's so much easier to keep the flat warm."

A brief tour for the others demonstrated that the plants were all in good health. Several challenging orchids were putting up new stems, and a number of plants Saffron recognized as cuttings from her mentor, Dr. Maxwell, were flowering.

"Why am I not surprised you know every single one of these plants by their Latin name?" Alexander asked.

Saffron shrugged, momentarily happy. Benjamin was already tearing down the simple gravel path that cut through the center of the space, squealing with delight as John chased him. "Some things you don't forget." She slipped her hand into his.

Her sense of peace didn't last long. Breathing in the thick air scented with verdure and soil only reminded her of Madame's appalling attempt to entice Violet. Referencing the rose arbor was a clever, heartless thing to do. Her father had proposed marriage under that arbor, and she wondered if Madame had known that, or simply picked up on the way her mother's eyes had grown misty while describing it. Her mother's heart was still so broken. Would she be tempted to invite the medium to channel the spirit of Thomas? Thus far her family, save for John, had been safe from Madame Martin and her séances. If Madame took up a serious campaign to win her mother's patronage, her mother, and possibly the rest of her family, would be vulnerable to the substance Madame used to muddle her clients' minds. That, combined with Bill's presence, was too much to bear.

Elizabeth wandered over. "All right, lovebirds, where are we in the ousting of Madame 'The Fraud' Martin? My bid for searching Madame's room was abysmally unsuccessful." She reached out to a small fruit hanging from a nearby tree, then paused with her fingertips an inch away. She looked over her shoulder at Saffron. "Is this one safe?"

Saffron eyed the *Jatropha curcas*, a likely gift from Dr. Maxwell, and shook her head. "I wouldn't."

She sighed and dropped her hand. "Shall I angle for a dinner invitation for us, then?"

"It would be more expeditious to request a séance at your parents' house," Alexander said, "to secure access to Madame's room."

"And Mr. Fischer's," Saffron added. "I want to know if he's the ghost soldier."

"About the ghost soldier," Alexander said. "I had a thought. Could you describe him for me?"

"He stood in a haze of gray fog," Elizabeth began, hazel eyes sparkling. "The scant light from the solitary candle glinted off the glass of his mask's eyes, as if the only thing animating him were the presence of another."

Having only just somewhat made up, Saffron made every effort to withhold a jibe about Elizabeth's poetic and extremely unhelpful description. "He wore a basic army uniform, the tunic jacket and pants with puttees wrapped up the legs, but the mist covered his feet. The gas mask, of course, and a helmet. It makes it impossible to tell who, exactly, is playing the part."

"I suppose you were too far away to decipher any insignia he had."

"He did have something," Elizabeth said slowly. "On his left shoulder. It glimmered."

"Did it glimmer in any particular shape or color?"

Rather than acknowledge Alexander's dry question, she frowned and said, "He was missing his kit."

Saffron tried to revisit the soldier's image in her mind's eye. She'd not noted it before, too distracted by the mask's ghastly face. "No webbing, no gun holster. Only the box respirator hanging from his neck on his chest."

"And no bloody holes anywhere on his person." Elizabeth shrugged when Saffron gave her an incredulous look. "He was pristine, our ghost soldier. No dirt, no blood. As much as I would prefer never to think of it, that surely isn't what Wesley likely looked like when he died."

Her words made Saffron's stomach turn, but Alexander nodded thoughtfully.

"What does it matter?" Elizabeth asked him. "It's probably Fischer, maybe even in his own uniform."

"Just something to think on."

That apparently settled for now, Elizabeth said, "Another séance it is, then."

"That'll give us the chance to observe them and learn how the drug is administered," Saffron said.

Elizabeth snorted. "It's the incense, of course."

"It could have been added to the food."

"Then why weren't we seeing ghosts float around during coffee?" Elizabeth countered.

Alexander had his answer ready. "Food is digested at a different rate from individual to individual, not to mention people eat varying quantities of the same dish, or none at all. They couldn't risk the effects beginning too early. And not all the guests were present for the séance, which they also couldn't risk. Lady Easting and the vicar would have hallucinated on the way back to Ellington."

She wasn't sure how Alexander could be cool

156

as a cucumber as they spoke about something that had unnerved him greatly only two days ago. "The coffee then, and the drinks the men were served," she suggested.

"I drank neither," Alexander said.

Saffron bit her lip, thinking. "Very well. The incense is the most likely culprit, then."

"I'm so glad we've come to the conclusion I mentioned a minute ago," Elizabeth said with an eye roll. "Now to come up with the excuse for Saffron to absent herself so she can search. What do we do to give you enough time to search both rooms? You'll need at least ten minutes for each room, I would think."

"I'll search, too," Alexander said.

Saffron matched Elizabeth's doubtful look they turned to him.

Elizabeth began, "That's quite nice of you to offer—"

"—but it's not necessary," Saffron finished. They'd managed to avoid conflict over such matters in recent months, and they were unified in their efforts to get rid of Bill. She didn't want him to be compelled into investigating he didn't want to do.

Alexander managed to cross his arms in a singularly superior way. "Your mother is likely to be suspicious of you, Elizabeth, and therefore Saffron, too. She might disappear for ten minutes without suspicion, but any longer would be conspicuous. I am a stranger, one that is not particularly well regarded, I gather, and so it is conceivable that I could be lost in a grand house, or merely considered a rude guest snooping around."

Saffron felt rather like a feather could have knocked her over. "But then we'll both be missing."

Alexander nodded. "We need a believable reason to both be absent for a few minutes. Elizabeth has made it plain she doesn't believe in Madame Martin's powers, yet we need another séance." Saffron's heart dropped with sudden understanding. Alexander's smile turned sympathetic. "Are you any good at playacting?"

CHAPTER 17

I f you will all gather around, please."
Anticipation hushed the room as Mr. Fischer raised a hand in invitation to the table. The servants had just finished moving the heavy grate into place before the hearth and lighting the dozen candles at various points around the room, and Mr. Fischer awaited them at the table he'd meticulously cleaned before placing the brass brazier in its center. Madame Martin, clad again in her bizarrely out of fashion black dress, leaned over to open the heavily ornamented top. She struck a match and dipped it inside, and as she settled in her seat, smoke began to whisper from within.

It was time to see if Saffron could manage a convincing performance.

She didn't feel particularly confident, mostly because she thought the premise Alexander and Elizabeth had come up with was absolutely ghastly. Elizabeth had taken the initiative to tell her mother that Saffron wished to speak to Wesley in order to ask for his forgiveness and approval for her current romantic relationship.

Mrs. Hale, Saffron was sure, only agreed because she was sure Wesley would tell her off rather than give his approval. She'd made this abundantly clear during the meal preceding the séance. She went to the trouble of detailing a dozen incidents of Saffron and Wesley's shared childhood and concluded with a description of their parting when Wesley left home to join his army unit. It was a touching scene, with sunbeams in a meadow and soft, sweet words, that was nonetheless entirely fictitious. The Harvey sisters laughed and cooed and dabbed their napkins to their eyes at the conclusion of Mrs. Hale's tale of Wesley asking his mother and father to look after Saffron while he was gone—which brought Saffron quite close to calling the whole thing off, being so appallingly disingenuous.

Elizabeth had decided her role was that of supportive sister, adding her own saccharine, albeit factual, recollections. Alexander remained in character by masterfully ignoring or sidestepping Mrs. Hale's pointed jabs and the way the Harvey sisters occasionally glared at him.

Saffron was mortified. She could not imagine a better way to make herself ridiculous. She was only glad that her grandmother had decided to stay at home.

As the group settled around the table, John shot her a wink. He had delighted in playing his self-appointed role in what he termed "a Saffron caper," while his wife was oblivious. Suzette had engaged Madame in conversation unrelated to mysticism for most of dinner, from what Saffron could make out of their rapid-fire speech.

"Place your palms on the table, touching the hands of the persons next to you, please," Madame Martin instructed, her words softened by her gentle accent. The group did so. "This evening, we ask that the spirit of a beloved come forth. Wesley, return to us once more."

The muffled crackle of the fire was the only response. Saffron's efforts to breathe sparingly, lest she become overwhelmed by whatever toxins clouded the air, served only to make her dizzy. Shadows wobbled on the edges of her vision.

Mr. Fischer had not commanded them to close their eyes, and she found he was watching her. When their eyes met, he quirked his lips into a devilish smile that caught her off guard. She could feel heat rising in her cheeks. How idiotic she must look to him, after she'd all but called them opportunistic frauds when last they met!

She swallowed, her throat dry. "Wesley," she said, forcing her eyes to flutter closed. "Are you there?"

Her voice was thready and anxious to her own ears. She hoped it came off as hopeful or even eager to the others. At her side, Alexander shifted slightly. She resisted the urge to peer at him through her lashes.

Instead, she screwed up her face in faux concentration. She had to make this convincing.

She pushed her anxiety into her voice, making it plaintive. "Wesley, I know I have done you wrong. But, please, won't you come and speak to me?"

Alexander stirred at her side. She wanted to open her eyes, to look at him for reassurance, but that wouldn't be in character. "Wesley, please. Won't you come"—she forced herself to form the words—"from the Great Beyond and speak with me?"

Face screwed up in mock concentration, she waited for Madame Martin to answer. She'd "summoned" Wesley right away last time, but she was taking ages now, no doubt to increase the drama and likely torture Saffron a little. As if pretending to believe in this mumbo-jumbo mysticism wasn't torture enough! She hoped word never got back to the university that she'd participated in this nonsense.

At long last, Madame Martin stirred. Her voice came out in a rasping English accent. "Saff?"

Her eyes flew open to see something like longing tightening the medium's features.

Sharp inhalations came from around the table. Several eyes, which had been closed, fluttered open and looked to Saffron, then Alexander. He didn't provide a reaction, but Saffron did. She gasped dramatically, leaning forward. Unfortunately, that put her face even closer to the smoke, and it made her eyes burn.

"I've missed you," came the boyish voice again.

Saffron teetered on the edge of laughing at the ridiculousness of it all. But this had to be done. "I missed you, too, Wes."

There was an awkward beat, almost as if this was an actual conversation. Madame as Wesley asked hesitantly, "Where have you been?"

She found herself staring at Madame Martin, and she could almost imagine Wesley standing behind her with his crooked grin fading as he awaited the answer to his question. Where had she been?

In London, doing exactly what she'd told him she'd dreamed of doing. Attending university, practicing science. Falling in love with another man.

Alexander nudged his hand against hers in encouragement. Saffron swallowed, her throat dry. "London," she managed. "At the university."

"Where your father taught," "Wesley" said.

"Yes." Across the table, Elizabeth was staring at her. When their eyes met, she widened hers with obvious impatience. Saffron was supposed to be guiding this conversation more firmly. She cleared her sticky throat and added, "The University of London."

Madame's face tensed. She swayed to the right, toward Mr. Fischer, who looked alarmed. Worried, he began, "Madame—"

"Saffron," "Wesley" said, and Madame sounded pained. "Not a lot of time. I feel the call."

Irritation swept through Saffron at this blatant redirection; if Madame had agreed that Saffron studied and worked at the wrong university, that would have been a strike against her. Madame or Mr. Fischer must have gotten the correct name at some point.

Elizabeth didn't hide her displeasure and scoffed. Mrs. Hale glared at her and hissed, "Hush!"

Saffron wetted her lips. She needed to take control of the conversation and get to the point. "I've met someone, Wesley," she said haltingly. "And I wanted to ask for your blessing. A sign, that you understand and can let me go."

Madame's face contorted with pain. "Can't, Saff. Won't. Never. We promised."

"It's been almost ten years—"

Madame's voice took on a harsh edge. "Forever. You said you'd love me forever."

It wasn't as if Saffron hadn't expected exactly this from Madame; of course, "Wesley" was hurt and angry and would paint her as the heartless women scorning his pure, youthful love, and it made Alexander the villain, stealing her away. It was absolutely unfair, yes, but it ought not to have upset her since she knew, in her heart of hearts, that this was all hogwash. Yet it did.

Heat roiled in Saffron's chest, made of too many emotions to identify. Yes, they had loved each other, and yes, promises had been made, but he had died. Wesley had been too good a person to ever have held her living her life against her.

Was this the tact that Madame Martin and Mr. Fischer employed? Guilting their clients during their spiritual conversations, pushing them to purchase their services again and again until they'd earned forgiveness from the dead? Had this woman no scruples? No sense of morality at all?

"But I don't—" Saffron broke off, too choked with anger and humiliation and the wretched smoke to form a coherent thought. But she had to say something. "I don't love him as I did you, Wesley. It's different."

A sharp inhalation from next to her had her turning to Alexander. Shadows twisted his severe expression. She blinked hard, but they didn't go away. "Alexander?"

He stood up, roughly pushing his chair back with a scrape over the bare floor. "Excuse me."

She reached for him, catching his hand. His skin was hot, burning just like she was. Did he feel as wretched as she did? She whispered, "I'm sorry, Alexander. I—"

"I comprehend perfectly." He glanced around the table, and she realized eager, shadowed faces watched their tableau. Saffron shuddered, clutching his sleeve.

Alexander cleared his throat and repeated, "Excuse me." Then he walked out of the room.

CHAPTER 18

To leave the parlor was a relief. Alexander had to force himself to continue striding down the hall rather than stop and wait for Saffron to hurry out after him. There was a footman milling about, so he took in great gulps of blissfully clear air as he strode down the hall to the lavatory. He waited inside a few minutes, glad for the chance to rebalance himself. His eyes burned when he shut them as he leaned his head against the wall. He hadn't been dizzy the last time. Perhaps the repeat exposure to the smoke was worsening his symptoms. It was incredibly reckless to drug unsuspecting people like this, when a severe reaction might occur. If he hadn't been motivated to help before, this only further encouraged him to help Elizabeth foil the medium.

When his head no longer felt hot and clouded, he reviewed Elizabeth's instructions for getting to Mr. Fischer's room and took off down the hall.

For all their show of having many servants, the Hales certainly had few around. He strained his ears for a sign of Saffron's search in Madame's room, but heard nothing. Fischer's door was locked, but not for long. When Alexander stepped into the room, he was immediately taken aback by the smell.

166

To his knowledge, Fischer didn't have a repellant scent about him, yet it hung in the air nearly as thickly as the incense in the room below. It was an unctuous smell, somewhat nutty and deeply unpleasant. Alexander saw no source immediately available. One of his goals was to locate the incense with the hope of identifying the drug affecting them, and as the incense certainly smelled nothing like that, he attempted to ignore the unpleasant odor as he searched.

The wardrobe demonstrated what Alexander already knew: Fischer's clothing was uninteresting, French and cut stylishly. That suggested Fisher made a decent living doing what he did for Madame Martin. There was no uniform hanging next to the shirts, not that Alexander had expected it.

His hand was poised to delve into the pockets of the nearest jacket when a pang of guilt hit him. It was easily brushed away. Saffron had sounded genuinely upset back in the drawing room, though they all knew that the whole thing was an act, on Madame's part and their own. She knew he wasn't truly upset by what she had said; they were all playing their roles. She might have meant some of what she'd said, but even so, he knew what she'd meant, especially about loving Alexander differently. They had spoken of Wesley a number of times, especially immediately following their dealings with the other Hale brother. Wesley had been nothing like Nick, according to Saffron. A fun-loving, mischievous boy with a heart of gold. He would have likely grown into a man worth being jealous of, but to envy Saffron's memory of her first love would be juvenile and petty.

For a moment in there, Alexander wondered if Saffron wished she really could commune with Wesley. Before the war, he would have laughed at anyone paying to talk to a ghost, but after the things he'd seen, he had more compassion for those seeking connection with their lost loved ones. He certainly believed that the men who'd lost their lives deserved any comfort from the living they could get, if only it was possible. And that was precisely how Madame and Fischer made their living, conning grieving people. He'd not allow himself to feel bad for putting an end to it. Not to mention he'd volunteered to help search Fischer's room in order to determine whether he or Madame was involved with Bill. He needed to know if they'd need to battle him across multiple fronts.

It wasn't until Alexander reached the bed, where the rancid, oily smell became inexplicably stronger, that he saw anything of interest. As he knelt to search under the bed, a tiny object on the carpet caught his attention. The room was not particularly clean, not like Ellington where even rooms that were rarely used were spotless.

Dust and stray particles were seen throughout the room, but this was no fluff of dust, but a black dot. He picked it up, squinting at the hard, carapace-like surface. It reminded him of a lentil, a tiny flat circle pressed between his forefinger and thumb. It was out of place here, like Fischer might have tracked it into the house after a walk. If that was the case, perhaps it was important. He'd show it to Saffron and see if she knew where a plant shedding black seeds like this grew.

A peek under the bed and bedclothes did not reveal the origin of the offensive odor, nor any indication if Bill was involved with the medium or her assistant. There was no desk, but one of the drawers of the dresser was dedicated to correspondence. There were letters from creditors, a sister, and clients, both former and prospective. Most were in French, but a handful were in other European languages and English. Some were addressed to a Mr. Samuel Cartwright, most likely an alternate identity. Doubtless, Fischer had many for when his grifting brought unpleasant consequences upon him.

Most interesting, however, were the newspapers. There were the usual major papers, *The Daily Mail* and *The Sun*, mostly the business sections, some articles underlined or marked with circles, but also a stack of local papers, dating back two months. Alexander perused them briefly, looking for any reason Fischer might have such a stash of the *Bedfordshire Standard*, the *Bedfordshire Times*, and the *Bedfordshire Daily Circular*, but awareness of the time weighed on him, and he moved on.

Fischer's toilette implements were arrayed on the dresser. Several scent bottles, ointments, and tonics stood neatly in a row. From a faint ring of wood free of light dust, Alexander guessed one had recently been used up. He glanced around for a dustbin to see if the missing one had been discarded, but his eyes caught on the timepiece sitting next to the closed razor. His right hand twitched at his side as his other picked the watch up.

Bold white numbers on a bare black face, the six replaced by a minute dial with a tiny hand racing along its path. Black hands outlined with faint green, sometimes all one could see in the unrelieved blackness of night.

Carefully, Alexander set the watch back down. He exhaled slowly.

It was the same timepiece that hung from his brother's watch chain. He had seen it dozens of times; Adrian liked to tap on its face to tease him about Alexander's precise punctuality. It shouldn't have affected him to see that Fischer had flown during the war just as his brother had.

Yet it did affect him, knowing that Fischer had likely looked down at his watch a thousand times with uncertainty, fear, boredom, longing—

just as Adrian had during countless flights, just as Alexander had watched the slender hands tick past luminescent numbers of his own watch as he sat in a trench. It made it harder to hate the man.

The watch said it had been approximately ten minutes since his dramatic exit from the drawing room. It was time to return. Alexander gave the room one final scan, and left.

The lights made hazy stars all around Saffron's head. It was terribly distracting when she knew she was meant to be searching Madame Martin's room.

When she found the room, blessedly unlocked, she allowed herself a moment to sit on a chair just inside the door to refocus. Though the light was low, she didn't feel the need for more. There was enough to see that what she'd expected, the familiar room decorated with lacy curtains and heavy furniture in the mode of Eastlake, which Elizabeth had always hated for its heavy, straight angles, was not what she'd walked into.

She crept over to the window to ascertain that this room had the familiar view of the little garden below. It was the same room, but the hours she and Elizabeth spent playing and reading and chattering away felt as if they'd been cleaned out, replaced by something bland, like a room at a hotel.

Madame was present in the black shawl draped

over the dressing table's chair and a tiny bottle of scent next to a toilette kit. With shaking hands, Saffron lifted the bottle and cautiously sniffed at the cork, only to find it was an unremarkable rose perfume.

The cloying scent of the rose and jasmine incense clung to all of Madame's clothing, especially strong on the other Victorian-style gown in the closet. Surprisingly, the closet contained a number of modern clothing items, none of them high quality, but respectable.

In the trunk at the foot of the bed Saffron was disappointed to find not a store of hallucinogenics or stolen goods from the neighbors, but an unmarked package of incense. She slipped one dark stick from the package and wrapped it into her handkerchief. It pleased her to find the incense, but there were so many steps between her and the knowledge of what drug was imbued in the charcoal that she felt no thrill of success.

Her search of the trunk turned up something else. From what little Saffron could make out of the four pocket-sized journals, they detailed Madame's communications with those beyond *le mince voile de la mort*. The handwriting, its spidery elegance stretched and blotched by feeling, combined with the rose-scented hush that filled the room, made it difficult to dismiss Madame's reflections, however trite. They spoke of lost loves and disappointments, regrets and finding release in *le grand ciel*. She flipped to the most recent pages, dated only a few days before, and found agitated writing dotted with the names of the Hale family, and her own. It was all but indecipherable, save for a few words here and there: *prediction, reprise, reuni*. It made her shiver, though she was far from cold.

Just as she was tucking the journals back in the trunk, she belatedly heard footsteps in the hall beyond. She staggered behind the changing screen in the corner of the room just as the door opened and two sets of feet entered. Their tread was dainty to match the voices that began when the door was shut.

"Can't I go do Mr. Fischer's room?" one girlish voice said. "It's creepy in here."

"Fine by me," the other said with a more mature, huskier voice. "You go build his fire, and I'll do this one. I'd rather not breathe in that wretched stink if I can help it."

"It smells like them smoke sticks in here," the girl whispered, dropping her voice low. "How do you know there's not a spirit hanging about?"

There was a revealing pause before the other said, "Don't be silly, Maisie. Madame would have to be here, wouldn't she?"

Behind the screen, Saffron shifted from foot to foot. She really didn't want to be stuck in this room for much longer. It was so warm her face was flushed, though the fire had not been lit, for that's what the maids were arguing over. She rather thought she would crawl out of her skin, now she had no search to distract her. It seemed to be getting worse, not better, being away from the smoke of the séance.

"I don't know," whispered the younger girl. "This house is different now. You weren't here before Madame Martin came."

Inspiration struck Saffron, as the maid continued, "And after that last spirit summoning, I could have sworn I saw—"

A horrid screech pierced the room, and a whole-body shudder wracked Saffron, punishment for dragging her fingernail against the cold window-pane.

The maids squawked. The older gasped, "Father help us!"

Saffron rattled the screen, and that was all it took for the maids to careen out of the room, screaming. Saffron followed, a little unsteady on her feet, and swiftly made her way back downstairs.

Golden light poured from Ellington. Saffron squinted at it through the window of the motor-car, wondering idly why light seemed to be flowing through the windows rather than shining. It seemed viscous, like honey. She'd once seen honey shimmer like that, slicking the blade of a knife she'd placed into a sunbeam during breakfast, inexplicably lovely.

She sighed, pressing her overwarm cheek to the cold windowpane. The motorcar bumped and swayed, almost rocking her to sleep. She was powerfully tempted. Her eyes were dry, their lids heavy. She longed for sleep, especially as the nearer Ellington came, the brighter the lights seemed.

By the time she exited the vehicle, it looked like broad daylight.

"Are you all right?" Alexander murmured to her.

She blinked up at him. He was pressing her hand into his arm. When had he threaded their arms together?

"No," she said slowly.

His expression darkened, so harsh in the lights from the house. She didn't like it, so she looked away.

He escorted her inside, holding her rather firmly. It was a good thing; her body was not quite her own. Her head was too heavy, and her legs too light. It was a good idea to wait until they'd made it back to the house to tell Alexander what she'd found in Madame's room. She'd likely make no sense and he would be even more concerned.

John, Suzette, and Elizabeth had agreed to cram together in the one motorcar, and they'd already reached the top steps. Kirby awaited them inside, and he wasn't alone.

Saffron reared back. Alexander pulled her tight against his side, perhaps not as immediately repulsed by the shadows crawling across Bill's face. She blinked hard and they were gone a moment later.

Ahead of her, Suzette exclaimed. Bill was speaking to her, to John, too. Their voices rose in consternation, fear. Suzette darted up the stairs, John on her heels.

"What's wrong?" Her voice sounded strange to her ears.

Before Elizabeth or Alexander could answer, Bill turned his cool expression on her. "The little boy, Benjamin, took a tumble. He fell down the stairs earlier this evening."

Cold trickled over her, building to a torrent that raced over her skin until she was filled with it, head to toe. Her lips were numb as she asked, "He is all right? What happened?"

"A minor accident," he said smoothly.

Her vision swam in relief, but the cold didn't cease. "He's all right?"

His glasses flashed. "Just a little bruised. And frightened."

Shivers overtook her, and Alexander, still holding her arm, looked down at her with worry creasing his brow.

"What can I do?" he asked. "Can I get you something? Tea, or brandy?"

She felt so strange, so out of sorts that panic

176

threatened. She nodded jerkily. "The drawing room." Were her lips even moving?

Alexander left her at the door to the drawing room and strode to the liquor cabinet.

Elizabeth sighed. "Poor boy. I'm sure that's the last we'll see of John and Suzette this evening. I could certainly use a lie-down. Talk later, darling." She winked meaningfully and blew Saffron a kiss that she swore she could see move through the air, swirling in Elizabeth's wake as she trailed up the stairs.

She closed her eyes for a moment, willing the floor to stop swimming beneath her feet.

"Miss Everleigh."

The words brushed over the nape of her neck. Saffron held herself rigid, not daring to even breathe.

"It is unfortunate," Bill whispered, "that so little time and effort has gone into fulfilling my request. You can see that with very little effort of my own, I can make you regret your lack of focus."

She gasped. Across the room, Alexander jerked his head to her. He slammed a glass down and started for her, thunder in his face. She could feel Bill's presence melt away behind her, leaving her cold and shaking and more sure than anything in her life that she'd made a terrible mistake, one that she had no idea how to remedy.

CHAPTER 19

Morning dawned gray and dismal. Saffron watched its slow approach from the little window seat in her room. As the fog-cloaked grounds lightened by degrees, her fingers curled around the edges of her notebook. She'd spent long hours there as a girl, reading and drawing and dreaming. She'd spent the last two hours there, writing down all she knew or could guess about the situation she'd thrown herself and her family into.

After Alexander had pushed her into Elizabeth's arms with strict instructions she was not to be left alone in her condition—that was, drugged and terrified out of her mind that Bill would murder them all—Saffron had paced and cried while whatever was in Madame Martin's incense worked its way out of her body. At two thirty in the morning, the soldier appeared at her window.

A thoroughly disgruntled Elizabeth had hid behind the curtain while Saffron, shaking badly but aware that her part in Elizabeth's melodrama was not finished, managed to place her hand against the cold windowpane and look pitiful. Without the misty rain, Fischer looked less ghostly in his getup, though the mask and its baleful eyes were still rather horrible. He stood perfectly still save for one slow shake of his helmeted head. "Wesley's" blessing was not given.

Elizabeth had snapped the curtains shut and muttered, "How much extra do you reckon my parents paid for that?" before stomping off to her bedroom.

Exhausted, Saffron fell into a fitful sleep, broken by visions of Benjamin's broken body at the bottom of stairs, and at the top loomed a soldier in a gas mask.

What she knew of Bill Wyatt was written in her notebook:

In his late thirties or early forties, has a scar below his ear, and can effectively change his appearance with very little effort.

Involved in anarchy—for what else could it be called when one bought and sold secrets indiscriminately?—*and has access to my life and that of those I am closest to.*

She frowned at her summary, her pen tapping at her bottom lip. She'd revisited his words a dozen times since that day in her flat when he'd masqueraded as a policeman. *"I know about the flowers and vines you draw in your notebooks. I know the shop where Elizabeth prefers to buy her wine. I know what Alexander's shaving soap is scented with."* The recollection no longer made her shudder, perhaps because she'd realized something important. He hadn't actually

179

demonstrated that he knew any of those intimate details about Elizabeth or Alexander. He could have simply stated he did to rattle her.

As for the flowers in her notebooks . . . Dr. Maxwell had left his office at the university unlocked more often than not, leaving their possessions unprotected for hours at a time. Bill could have slipped in there anytime during the year Saffron had worked for Dr. Maxwell and peered into her notebooks.

That in mind, she added a question mark to indicate that the point had yet to be confirmed. The next items on her list were equally questionable:

Claims to have earned the title of doctor.

Knows enough about my father to know he'd been working on something valuable, something that no one else was aware of.

The final point had, without a doubt, been proven:

No compunction against harming children.

The last angered her as much as it frightened her. Her ability to fight against him was severely handicapped now she knew exactly how far he would go for her father's research. But the question remained: What the *devil* did Bill believe Thomas Everleigh had discovered?

Someone quietly knocked, not waiting for her reply before entering. Alarm froze her, only to melt with embarrassed heat when a maid tiptoed inside. The maid was equally startled, however, for when she caught sight of Saffron sitting on the windowsill, she let out a yelp.

"Beg your pardon, miss," Martha said, pressing her hand over her heart. "I was that frightened!"

"I confess, I was, too," Saffron said.

"Can't blame you," Martha said, moving swiftly to tend the fire. She gave the hearth a rueful look when she saw Saffron had already built it back up. Even scared out of her mind, Saffron refused to pass the night in a freezing room. "You attended a séance at the Hale house, didn't you? I'd be scared by my own reflection after that!"

"Yes, the séance was perturbing," Saffron replied.

Martha moved to the bed and tidied the bed-clothes. "There's talk that woman is a witch."

"I'm inclined to believe it's nothing more than a bit of smoke and guesswork," Saffron said firmly.

Eyes like dinner plates, Martha paused where she leaned over the bed. "Oh no, miss. I know it's real. My sister works for Mr. Hale, you see. She saw the spirits herself!"

Surprise stilled her tongue, where a correction lay ready. "She *saw* a ghost?"

"She did, a great shadow, black as night. She had to keep to her bed for a whole day to recover from the shock of it."

That was unexpected, but not improbable. The

incense smoke would affect whoever breathed it in, including the maids. "The housekeeper must not have been pleased," Saffron said to prevent the girl from falling silent.

"No, indeed, miss. Threatened to give her duties to someone else. Told her plenty of girls in the villages want to tend to fine ladies and gentlemen rather than be worked to the bone in the factories."

That was another statement Saffron rather doubted, if the stories Elizabeth mentioned from the newspapers about factory girls were to be believed, but that faded as she realized what the girl had said. "Your sister tends to the guests?"

Martha canted her head, perhaps perplexed by the unwarranted urgency of Saffron's tone. "No, miss. She's a chambermaid but wants to be a lady's maid. That's me, too," she added shyly. "I've received an offer, actually. I'll be moving on, soon enough." Her proud smile faltered. "If you please, miss, please don't mention it to anyone. Miss Sharnbrook wouldn't like it. Will you be needing anything before breakfast?"

"No, thank you," Saffron said, and the maid left.

Breakfast would be served in the next half hour. She didn't know what she would do if she had to sit across the table from Bill and make polite conversation. She wandered back to the window. The fog had cleared slightly, allowing for a tenuous sun to peer over the horizon. A figure moving through the fog made her heart stutter, until she recognized the tall man as Alexander. He was headed in the direction of the lake.

He'd threatened to take her rowing on the Thames, his preferred exercise, on more than one occasion. Doing so in the dead of winter was unappealing, but she suddenly felt like fresh air might do her some good.

Her eyes dropped to her notebook once again, lingering on her fourth point. The crux of all this mess was her father's research. She needed to find it, even if doing so would risk more than her grandparents' ire.

Alexander emerged from the boathouse ravenous. Rowing, even if it was a dozen lengths across the small lake on Ellington's property, always stoked his appetite. He'd been unable to resist his usual exercise despite not sleeping more than an hour for worry—for Saffron, for her family, especially for little Benjamin, and for a question that had wormed its way into its brain ever since he saw Fischer's watch. He could, at least, remember the events of the previous evening, and his arms now shook from exhaustion rather than anxiety.

He paused just outside the door of the boat-house, his hand fumbling for his cufflink. The tremor in his right hand was worse for a few hours after exercise, and he could barely do up the buttons of his shirt. It wouldn't be the done thing to go into the house in just his knit shirt. The thing didn't have sleeves, and considering Saffron's grandparents' already low opinion of him . . .

He exhaled in frustration as his cufflink slipped from his fingers and fell into the frosty grass at his feet. He muttered a curse and dropped to find it. When he looked up again, cufflink in his left hand this time, Saffron was coming down the steps leading from the conservatory.

"Good morning," she said brightly, crossing the lawn.

As she grew near, he saw she looked like her normal self, albeit tired. The lingering worry twisting his insides eased. "Good morning."

She took a deep breath, her smile hardening into determination as she took his hand in hers. "I have an idea, and I need your help."

She explained how a game of cricket might help solve their problem. When she was finished, she stepped back and said, "There."

He blinked, then looked down where their hands were still clasped together. She'd done up his shirtsleeve. He hadn't even noticed she'd slipped the cufflink from his hands. Powerful emotion swept through him, leaving his throat tight and his heart thudding as he lifted his eyes back to hers. A soft smile was on her lips, one that told him she knew his trouble and would help him carry it without question or judgment.

Knowing full well that the fog had faded enough that they were perfectly visible from the house, Alexander pulled her so they were chest to chest, and kissed her.

She came away with roses in her cheeks and eyes brightened. "Well, then."

He wove their arms together and began back toward the house. "When is this cricket match to happen?" He cast her a sideways glance. "And if you mean me to lose to make nice with your cousin, I'm afraid I can't do that."

"Why not?"

"I have grown in many ways since I was a young lad bowling in the streets with my own cousins, but that particular personality quirk will never change. I don't lose."

Saffron looked at him incredulously. "You don't lose? You sound like the most appalling meathead."

His eyebrows shot to his hairline, and he laughed. "*Meathead?* Is that some Shakespearean insult I missed in school?"

Saffron shrugged. "Elizabeth came home from one of her poetry clubs saying it one day. I think it fits perfectly." She lowered her voice an octave. " 'I don't lose.' What rot!"

She spent the rest of the walk to the house and most of breakfast poking fun at him. He could easily forgive her for the excessive joking, especially because it seemed both her cousin and his wife seemed in poor spirits.

Suzette assured them when they entered the breakfast room that Benjamin was fine after his tumble down the stairs. Saffron visibly relaxed after that, but it seemed John and Suzette were dancing around the topic of the medium's peformance. When it became clear that the medium's channeling of "Wesley" and their supposed spat after was a thing of the past, John and Suzette both looked rather relieved. Soon Saffron had them agreeing to the cricket game later that day.

It was not enough to defeat Bill, but it was a start. And Alexander knew what he had to do next.

CHAPTER 20

Its dark burgundy brick face was covered by a mass of ivy studded with barred windows. The interior reminded Alexander of the King's Cross police station. The similar jumble of cluttered desks and dark-uniformed officers milling around put him on edge.

When he was at last invited to speak to one of the officers on duty, he sat alongside a desk across from an older man who was round and florid with a patchy head of graying hair. His tired eyes never left the form his pen was poised to complete. "Your name?"

Alexander provided it, his address, and his business in the area before the officer, sounding beleaguered, asked, "What brings you to the police station, Mr. Ashton?"

Alexander sketched out the barest details: Bill Wyatt had followed Saffron, making her feel unsafe, only to find him in her family home posing as a doctor.

The officer's torpor lifted by degrees until, at the end of the brief explanation, he stared at Alexander. "You mean to say that there is some sort of . . . confidence man at Ellington Manor?"

Alexander nodded, not liking the man's suspicious tone.

The officer heaved to his feet. "I'd best tell my superior about this."

Five interminable minutes later, a man in his early forties, stocky and wearing a suit slightly too small for him, strode up to the desk at which Alexander waited. He introduced himself as Chief Constable Hackett. "I understand you're here with a complaint?"

Alexander repeated his concerns. The chief constable stood with hands in his pockets, nodding after each statement. When Alexander finished, he asked, "Miss Elizabeth Hale is also staying at Ellington Manor, is she not?"

"Yes, she is," Alexander replied.

The chief constable exchanged a look with the older officer, who'd returned to linger at his side. "I understand Miss Hale's family is hosting a few guests from out of town. A Frenchwoman who claims to speak to the dead. You've been . . . entertained by her?"

"I've attended a séance she performed at the Hales' house," Alexander answered.

The chief constable sighed, lifting his eyes skyward. "A fraud, I hope you know. One doesn't like to hear someone like that is in the area, taking advantage of grieving families. A plague on our community."

"Indeed," Alexander said slowly, "but I fail to see how that affects the situation in question."

"Don't you?" The chief constable's tone turned

syrupy with condescension. "You're suggesting there are two confidence men—er, people, what with the Frenchwoman being female and all—not only in the neighborhood, but right next door to each other? That seems very unlikely. Don't you think, Dunley?"

The older officer nodded. "Seems unlikely, Chief Constable, very unlikely indeed."

Annoyed, Alexander said, "Simply because something seems unlikely doesn't make it impossible."

"We have limited resources here in our little town," Chief Constable Hackett said in a tone so oppressively reasonable, it grated on Alexander's nerves. "We're not the Met, are we?" Dunley shook his head. "And we have a number of complaints coming in about the Frenchwoman, in fact. In the last few days alone, we've had five different people come in or telephone from Goldington to complain they've been targeted by this fraud."

At least Elizabeth's efforts to oust Madame Martin from the village were productive. "I'm glad that the victims of her ploy are coming forward. But I don't understand—"

"I understand your confusion, Mr. Ashton," the chief constable interrupted in a patronizing tone, "as we do things a bit differently around here. We haven't got the manpower to run off after every reported would-be criminal. Especially one that has been invited into the home of the Everleigh family. They're well respected in these parts, you know."

"Very well respected," Dunley echoed.

Far from being soothed, Alexander narrowed his eyes. "Have you met Dr. Wyatt, Chief Constable?"

There was a telling flicker in Chief Constable Hackett's eyes, an answer to the real, unspoken question.

Alexander stood abruptly. "I see my concerns will not be taken seriously here. I do hope that nothing unfortunate precipitates from this situation, Chief Constable." He gave the man a hard look. "Lord and Lady Easting give me the impression of being stalwart servants of the people. I hope they continue to support you as the man in charge of their nearest police force after this matter is put to rest."

With that, he left the police station, leaving the chief constable and Dunley staring after him.

Upon returning from his failed venture, Alexander found himself trooping down the steps with half the Everleigh clan.

John had Benjamin on his shoulders, wearing only shirtsleeves though the temperature could be no warmer than forty degrees. Suzette was bundled up, protesting that Benjamin ought to be, too, when the boy immediately shed his coat upon being set down on the lawn. He seemed no worse for wear after his fall down the stairs. Alexander watched his antics with a strange combination of gratitude and lingering unease. They were all at risk with Bill around, more so now Alexander guessed that, at the least, Chief Constable Hackett was in his pocket. The boy was singularly vulnerable.

Saffron looked on with an affectionate smile that reflected none of the negative feelings he knew she bore. She was disappointed her mother had declined to come outside to watch the match, both because she wanted to see her mother was capable of leaving the house, even to step onto the terrace overlooking the lawn, and because it would have made Saffron's goal much easier.

John tucked Saffron under his arm, drawling, "Fetch us the cricket equipment, Saffron, be a good girl."

Saffron elbowed him. "*You* can go pick through that dusty old shed, thank you very much."

"You dreadful girl." John sighed, releasing a white cloud that quickly dissipated in the chill air. "Right-o. You make sure Benjamin doesn't escape my wife and end up in the lake." The boy was, indeed, edging closer and closer to the water. "Ashton, lend a hand?"

Alexander followed John down the slight slope and into the boathouse. It was, indeed, a dusty old shed. The only somewhat clean thing in the building was the canoe and oars Alexander had taken out that morning.

"Uncle Thomas was rumored to have gifted me these each birthday," John said, nodding to the shelf of dust-coated equipment. "The lawn tennis, the darts, the bocce balls . . . The cricket set was for my first birthday. He wanted boasting rights of having introduced me to the game." He snorted. "He was a mean bowler. Never let me off easy, even when I was a boy. I think I was Benjamin's age when I first went up against him. It took me until I was eight to actually hit anything, of course. But did we ever have some matches! One game went on so long that even Saffron and my father gave up on us. They went in for supper and left us outside in the dark."

Alexander couldn't help but return John's smile. His fond memories were contagious. "I believe there was a time or two my brother and I were sent to bed without supper after refusing to abandon a game." Granted that had taken place amid London street traffic, but that was beside the point.

"Ah," John muttered, sticking his arm between dusty cases on a shelf. "Here it is." He hefted out a cricket bat. "This was Saffron's. She was a good sport and always played. We wouldn't have even teams, otherwise. I think Uncle Thomas imagined this set would expand, you know. But we Everleighs are not particularly prolific." His perpetual smile faded. "Not many of us kicking around these days."

Beyond the boathouse, Saffron called for John impatiently. She was uneasy being so near the water with Benjamin, Alexander guessed. He didn't blame her; the boy was a handful. An enjoyable one, but it seemed Saffron had little experience with children. He wondered if she'd imagined having a small family, like her own, or if she'd dreamed of children enough for a whole cricket team.

He helped John collect the rest of the cricket gear and they left the musty air of the boathouse for the cold humidity of the lawn. Setting up the game took a moment, with John explaining to his squirming three-year-old how he was meant to play.

When Saffron finally had her chance to bat, and though he knew the entire game was a ruse, he couldn't help but grimace at her terrible technique. It couldn't matter less, but it rankled to learn that the woman he loved was a hack at cricket.

She swung low and hard, twisting at the ankles and missing the ball entirely, and had he not known better, he would have been taken in by the way her face spasmed in pain.

"By gad, Saffron!" groaned John as he abandoned the imaginary bowling crease and jogged over.

"It's just a sprain," she said, shooting Alexander a look over John's head as he bent to look at her ankle needlessly. "I ought to see if I can get ice for it before it swells."

"I suppose you won't ask that doctor fellow about it, will you? No, ice would be best, though I think Aunt Violet mentioned Grandpapa had that old ice cellar blocked up," John said absently, looking up at the house. He waved, and Alexander peered around him to see a pale silhouette in the window of what he figured was the saloon. Mrs. Everleigh, watching as Saffron had predicted. "If no ice is available, you ought to just stick your foot in the lake. It's cold enough, I'd wager." He sighed dramatically as he hefted her to her feet. "Very well, ruin our game, why don't you?"

"I'm quite sure Alexander will give you and Benjamin more game than you can handle. I'll come back when I'm sure I can walk tomorrow. No, no, I can manage myself. Keep the blood pumping, and all that."

She made a good show of hobbling up the lawn, taking care to go around the conservatory so her mother wouldn't be able to see her limping. When she'd rounded the terrace, John shot him a smile. "Well, Ashton, let's have this game Saffron promised."

Alexander managed to toe the line between a good showing in the cricket game and not shaming John in front of his son when Alexander won. Benjamin ran about most of the time, putting Suzette through her paces, but the boy did show himself to have a future on the pitch when he swung the bat with great enthusiasm.

Suzette approached him with a tired smile at the end of the game. John was chasing Benjamin from the lake, and Suzette knelt to pick up the stumps and bails from where John had last knocked them over.

She said, "You are very good at this game. A point in your favor, I think."

Alexander shot her a smile, taking the wooden pieces from her. "It's nice to know I wasn't wasting my time with cricket as my father warned." He collected the bat that John had tossed to the ground when he went off after Benjamin, and redonned his jacket. It was cold now he was no longer jogging across the lawn, and chill moisture flecked his face. They walked together toward the boathouse.

"I wish someone tutored me in English before I came," she said rather suddenly. "I had no reason to practice much before. I am at a great disadvantage here." She sighed. "You are lucky. You have no position, but you make up for in *anglicité*."

Alexander understood her to mean that what he lacked in nobility, he made up for by being English in the eyes of the Everleighs. "My father is English, but my mother is not. English is not my first language, either."

She turned to him in surprise. "You sound as English as my husband."

He stepped into the boathouse and hefted the cricket equipment onto the shelf. It gave him a moment to decide what he wanted to share with Suzette considering it would get back to John, likely within the hour. He ducked back outside, and decided honesty, even openness, was the best choice.

"My mother is Greek," he said. "I did not learn English properly until I was four years old."

When Adrian started school, he'd brought home enough English to fill in Alexander's gaps in understanding and vocabulary. Their father's distant style of communication meant that most of Alexander's English consisted of "no," "be quiet," and "ask your mother."

Suzette's lips formed an "o." "I had no idea. Perhaps there is hope for me, then," she said with a little laugh. "But I dread it for Benjamin. When we move here, he will no doubt lose his lovely little voice. He will ruin his mother tongue and break my heart."

"If you continue to speak with him and nurture his love of the language, he will be as masterful as you, Mrs. Everleigh. My mother regularly tells me my Greek surpasses her own."

Suzette tutted, waving a hand. "A mother's love

blinds her to most things. You likely speak like a child."

Alexander laughed aloud at the unexpected remark. Suzette had been so guarded in conversation with the Everleighs that he'd never expect something so irreverent from her.

John jogged over to them with Benjamin on his shoulders, already grinning in anticipation of the joke. He didn't seem to notice the mud Benjamin's boots smeared on his lapels. "What's so funny?"

Suzette and Alexander shared an amused look as they began across the lawn, and Alexander said, "Suzette is worried your son's accent will be corrupted."

"Nonsense! How can his accent be corrupted from just a few weeks among *l'Anglais*?" John jostled the boy with a hop that had him shrieking and tugging on his hair. "Away from these naysayers!" He galloped up the hill toward the house.

Suzette watched them go with a tremulous smile. When she realized Alexander was looking at her, she cast her gaze to the ground, blinking rapidly. "I am no fool," she murmured. "We leave this place in a few weeks, but we will return. Benjamin will pass most of his life here, learning to be . . ." She looked up at the manor, which from their lowered position on the lawn, looked imposing with its dark windows and roof padded by clouds. "This."

She said it with such resignation that Alexander felt pity for her. He had no idea what to say, and so he said nothing as he accompanied her up the hill.

Suzette slipped inside the conservatory door, and Alexander would have followed, but a flicker of movement caught his eye.

He turned to the right to see a woman in black disappearing into the trees that lined the drive. A flush of alarm rushed through him, followed by determination. He knew that was no phantom. He took off in that direction, keen to make sure of it.

CHAPTER 21

It was during one of the first university lectures Saffron attended that she'd first heard of a sinkhole. Dr. Maxwell's colorful tale of venturing into the southern Mexican rainforest to investigate a massive hole in the ground for its botanical treasures seemed like something out of one of Jules Verne's unlikely tales. But Maxwell had provided proof in the form of a photograph: massive, empty blackness bordered on all sides by lush jungle. Though time had softened its jagged edges with plant life, it seemed impossible that the earth could create such things in sudden, violent rushes: the ground suddenly falling away into nothingness, leaving gaping chasms behind.

Saffron felt as if a sinkhole had opened inside her.

She stood at the threshold of her father's study, or what had once been his study. The room was all but empty. All his scientific equipment, books, and files were gone. Only his desk and bare bookshelves remained.

Anger rose to fill the hole in her chest. Anger first that she'd broken her mother's trust by entering her rooms and sneaking into this one and it was for nothing; anger that this room, like the defunct greenhouse, was nothing more than an empty shell where the memory of her father dwelled.

"Ah."

Saffron flinched, wheeling around to see Bill not three feet away from her in the middle of her mother's parlor. He looked less like retiring Dr. Wyatt without his spectacles shielding the sharpness of his gaze.

"I thought you were more intelligent than this, Saffron," he said softly. "How disappointing to learn you aren't." His posh tones had been replaced by his nebulous Continental accent. "Did you think I'd not exhausted every possibility myself?" He gestured to the room at her back. "Did you really think the most obvious places hadn't been thoroughly examined? These amateur schemes are below your ability, or so I thought. I do not need you to play at your games of sneaking about. I need you go to where I cannot."

Moments before, she'd assumed this was one such place. It felt terribly wrong to see Bill, menacing now with impatience darkening his usually placid face, in her mother's domain, her safe place in a cruel world that had harmed her.

Saffron wanted him out, and it sharpened her tongue against her better judgment. "Have you no respect for the dead? For any sense of family duty or affection? You're speaking of my father, Bill."

He shrugged. "We all have fathers. Some better than others. Some worse. Some alive, some dead."

She'd never thought to plead with him, but her next words came out imploring. "What of patriotism? My father was a soldier, and I would wager you were as well. What about respect for him, or my family and what they lost?"

"I have no respect for soldiers or those who command them. Considering my profession, that ought to have been obvious." His nostrils flared with a deep breath, and Saffron rather thought she had touched a nerve.

His thin lips curled. "Perhaps you believe that if you stall long enough, your detective will come to your rescue or that I will lose interest. Or that you might find a way to frighten me away. Let me assure you, Saffron, those are incorrect assumptions. Dangerous ones, even. Again, a disappointment to find your intelligence wanting."

"But if it's not here, the papers or files or whatever it is you want, where am I meant to look?"

"That is for you to discover," he said easily. "If, for example, you might need to search outside of Ellington, I could not fault you."

"What do you mean?"

He smiled. "Recall my words: I need you to go places I cannot. I'll not limit your imagination with suggestions. But I must tell you that my client and I grow impatient. You have already caused one of my sales to fall through; you'll not delay another without consequences. You have until the end of the week to get me something."

He'd come so close that she might have reached out to touch him. As if someone had turned a valve, malice poured off him in an almost tangible way. It was not a physical thing; he was no beast, towering and threatening, and neither was he a viper, winding up to attack. He was something else altogether, something unnatural.

He leaned still closer, bringing his face close enough to hers that she could finally see directly into his eyes. They were a hazy gray, no longer simmering with quiet amusement or impatience, but steady with a calm certainty that frightened her far more. "If you need it spelled out for you, here it is: you will give me what I am asking for, because if I am forced to take it, I will take it and far more than you are willing to part with."

The clouds seemed to drop lower and lower as the afternoon wore on, leaving Alexander with the impression that he was exploring a cloud forest like the ones he'd read about in a zoological journal once. There were no noteworthy reptiles lurking in these trees, however, only a woman in black floating across Ellington's grounds. He had no doubt who it was: Madame Martin, on some errand he didn't doubt was nefarious. Meeting with Bill, perhaps, or at the very least plotting some further mischief against the Hales or Everleighs.

She flickered in and out of sight as she made quick progress through the trees. He followed her until the cover gave way to a misty field. Now he was closer, the woman cloaked in black was too tall to be Madame Martin. He hurried after her regardless, unsure if his aim was to catch her, or simply follow.

The choice was made for him, however, as the woman slowed when the shadow of a building appeared. The spire peeking from the clouds identified it as a church. He squinted around the grounds, but the woman had disappeared in the seconds he'd spent observing the building. He crept along the damp stone wall, preparing to peer around the corner for her.

A hand lashed out and grabbed his arm. He wheeled around, jerking away, only to find Elizabeth glaring at him from beneath a black cloak that closely resembled a black bear fur, stepping halfway out of the shadow of a willow tree.

"What are you doing, following me?" she hissed.

"What are *you* doing, creeping about dressed like that?" he hissed back.

"Well, I couldn't very well creep about in my

usual coat, could I?" she whispered as if it was obvious.

It was, though Alexander had to strain to recall why. Her coat was a rusty shade of red, he recalled, and would have been easily spotted. He nodded in acknowledgment of her point. "What are you doing?"

Her eyes glittered. "Following Fischer! I saw him out my window, crossing the drive. I rushed after him and just snatched this from the cloakroom. Vile, isn't it?" She swished the cloak, releasing the scent of dust and cedar.

"And Fischer came to the church?" Alexander asked. That was not particularly remarkable.

"See for yourself." Elizabeth pointed in the direction Alexander had intended to go.

Alexander took a few steps and looked around the corner. Wisps of mist wrapped around blocky shapes standing at intervals. He could feel Elizabeth's presence behind him. "A graveyard?"

She hummed confirmation, and peered around his shoulder. "Just the sort of thing a medium would do, isn't it, lurking in a graveyard?"

"Then why is Fischer doing it?"

Elizabeth eased back, a hand on his shoulder. He turned to face her. "That is exactly my question. Fischer claims to believe in all that claptrap, but that doesn't explain why *he* is here, and not Madame Martin. She should be the one communing with the dead or whatever rot she claims."

Alexander turned back to watch Fischer. His shape, the mist and his hat not quite obscuring the brilliant red of his hair, made progress along the edge of the graveyard, his back to them. His slow pace and the subtle movement of his arms reminded Alexander of Saffron documenting the progress of her Amazonian specimens when they visited them in the greenhouses.

"He's taking notes," he told Elizabeth.

She let out a too-loud "Ah!" She slapped her hands over her mouth and froze, but Alexander heard nothing from the graveyard to suggest Fischer had heard her. After a minute of stillness, he risked a glance around the corner. Fischer had moved away, now drifting down another row of gravestones.

He signaled to Elizabeth to move, and they retreated from the church.

"How do you like that!" Elizabeth muttered as they made their way across the field and back toward the darkened line of trees. The light was fading fast though it was only mid-afternoon.

"He's looking at the gravestones for information for Madame," Alexander guessed.

"What else would he be doing there? He'll use whatever little tidbits he finds to fuel Madame's business. She'll sit in the pub and spin some nonsense about dead uncles promising hidden treasures or something to get the villagers to hire her. That wretched witch." The look on her face was severe, but not quite murderous.

"Further evidence you can use against her."

"That's right." Her frown turned pensive, and they didn't speak again until they reached the side of the drive. Since their shoes were soaked and muddy, Elizabeth marched them around to the servants' entrance. The moment they set foot onto the hard-packed dirt of the courtyard, Alexander could hear the clangs and conversations of the staff preparing for tea and dinner.

Just as they were to walk in, Elizabeth abruptly turned to Alexander. "Saffron is all right, isn't she?"

Nonplussed, Alexander managed, "Er—yes."

Elizabeth's eyes narrowed on his, looking serious rather than suspicious. "She was quite upset about her grandmother saying ridiculous things about the pair of you." She looked as though she wanted to say more, but she stepped inside the door.

Only to come right back out and say, "I hope you appreciate how hard this is for her. Coming back here. It was a privileged life she led here, yes, but it wasn't easy." Her eyes fixed over his shoulder. "People who are meant to love you telling you that your dreams are worthless is wounding no matter how gently they say it, and leaving those people doesn't always heal the harm it leaves behind."

Alexander caught her eye and said quietly, "I understand the challenge of returning to a place where one was once someone very different from who one is now."

Emotion flashed across Elizabeth's face. She mashed her lips together and nodded curtly. "Good. I'm glad you understand." She waved a hand at the door. "Go on, in you go."

It took Saffron a long time to regain her nerve after Bill departed, but she managed to search her father's rooms and most of her mother's before she heard the patter of Benjamin's footsteps returning to the nursery. Suzette's admonishments to discard his boots before he coated the carpets in mud trailed after him.

The sweetness of their simple interaction drew Saffron from her frenzied search, but did not change the fact she had, yet again, been unsuccessful. Her father's desk and shelves had held nothing but dust, an indication that her mother did not allow even the maids into her father's space. His bedroom was still fully furnished, but none of his belongings remained. The wardrobe was empty, as was the bedside table and dresser. Saffron only realized as she replaced the white dust covers that she hadn't been bothered by their eerie presence. It seemed these new fears of failure and Bill had overtaken her past ones.

She was a sweaty, dusty mess by the time she ducked out of her mother's room and fled to her own. She hurried to the window, but the men were no longer playing. The clouds had darkened dangerously.

While searching, Bill's reminder scratched at the back of her mind. *I need you to go to the places I cannot.* She'd assumed that's why she was needed at Ellington to investigate, but Bill hadn't summoned her here, had he? Her grandfather's illness had. It was possible that Bill had orchestrated that—any number of substances could induce heart attacks—but she couldn't know either way. He didn't need her to look through her father's old rooms. Where could she go that he could not?

Her mind skipped to Madame Martin and her spirits, and contemplated briefly, desperately, asking the medium to ask her father about the research.

She pushed away that foolishness and began to pace the room. The university was the only place she had access to somewhat private information. But was it a place Bill could not infiltrate? He'd gotten his people into a government-run laboratory, hadn't he?

She shook her head. Too many questions with no hope of answering.

The door connecting hers and Elizabeth's rooms swung open, revealing Elizabeth, who swanned into the room with cheeks flushed. "I know I ought to treat you with kid gloves after the wretched incense got to you last night, but truly, darling, I would really appreciate a little tipple before tea."

Saffron sighed. "It's in my luggage."

Elizabeth retrieved her little flask from the wardrobe and winked at her as she took a sip of whatever liquor she'd refilled it with. "You look like you could use something to put some steel in your spine. Lady E giving you a hard time again?"

It was as good an excuse to seem unsettled as any, since Elizabeth still didn't know about Bill. "Yes," she said, though the lie felt slimy on her tongue. "She repeated her accusations about Alexander and I . . . being incautious."

Elizabeth laid across the end of Saffron's bed, propping herself up with an elbow. "Your granny knows nothing about you if she thinks you'd risk an unplanned child without a ring on your finger."

Surprised by her vehemence, Saffron said, "You can't know that for sure."

"Effectively ending your career? Yes, darling, I am confident you wouldn't do such a thing. And I would know if *that* particular event had transpired. You would want to analyze the whole thing and likely make some very amusing biological observations I would tease you about for years." She took a thoughtful sip from her flask. "I am most impressed by your self-control. If I was so often in mortal peril and in love, I'm sure that bridge would have been crossed ages ago."

"It's not so much my self-control as his, I think. Before we can get anywhere, he suggests we go on a walk, or have a cup of tea, or says he should go."

"That's very gentlemanly of him."

"I wouldn't mind if he'd be a little less gentlemanly sometimes," Saffron said, heaving a sigh.

"Well, dear, whenever it does come up, just be sure that it's what you want. Don't be convinced unless you want to be."

Saffron saw the momentary pain on her face before it smoothed into a smile. "Eliza . . ."

"I don't want to talk about it, Saff. It's done and in the past. I've got bigger fish to fry." She heaved to her feet.

Saffron bit her lip. "Don't you think this fixation on Madame Martin is an attempt to settle your feelings about what happened with Colin? A way to get some closure, since you never got to, ah—"

"Exact my revenge on him?" She laughed bitterly. "It doesn't take someone with your keen deductive powers to see that's exactly what this is about. I'm not able to punish Colin myself for being a selfish, manipulative user, but I certainly can do so to Madame, even if my parents deserve it."

"Right," Saffron said, dragging out the word. "As long as you understand what this is about."

With a smirk, Elizabeth raised the flask to her mouth once more, only to pause with it nearly at her lips. "Why don't you care?"

"About Madame Martin? Of course I care. She's drugged us and might be targeting my mother. Alexander and I searched Madame and Fischer's rooms for you."

"You didn't volunteer. You haven't done any sneaking around or questioning without me forcing you into it."

Saffron raised her hands in surrender. "I have helped! I put on that awful display last night—"

"You are nowhere near as interested in Madame Martin and foiling her scheme as you ought to be. Why?"

Saffron swallowed nervously. "I'm concerned about my grandfather, of course."

"Had you truly been so worried, you would use foiling fraud as a distraction."

Saffron folded her arms over her chest. That was a very unflattering truth. "Alexander is meeting my family for the first time, Eliza, and you know it isn't going well."

"Bollocks," declared Elizabeth. "John plainly likes Alexander, and your mother adores him already. Lord Easting was quite nearly civil to him. Your grandmother is the only one with the problem and if she *didn't* have a problem with you falling in love with a plebian, I would be deeply concerned about her well-being. Now, Saffron Everleigh"—she poked Saffron's shoulder with each word—"you will tell me what you are hiding!"

And so Saffron confessed all. When she was finished explaining her conviction that she needed to return to London to visit the university, Elizabeth had murder in her eyes.

"Don't do anything stupid, Eliza, please," Saffron said.

"Let's put aside the fact that this entire mess is the *essence* of stupidity," Elizabeth snapped. She paced before rounding on her, hands propped on her hips. "Let's ignore the fact of you keeping this all from me is the *definition* of stupid. You said this man taunted you with stalking us, both of us, and you didn't bother to tell me?"

"I *chose* not to tell you. After Colin—"

"After Colin was the exact right time to tell me! After Colin, I ought to have known that there was still more danger. Do you know how careless I've been, Saffron? Getting drunk at all hours and allowing my friends to ply me with anything they promise will mend a broken heart?"

Saffron's mouth dropped open, not the least because she'd known nothing of Elizabeth's disreputable friends' attempts to help her. "A broken heart? For Colin?"

"Thank you very much for completely missing my point," Elizabeth ground out, and guilt squeezed Saffron's chest. Exaggerated patience made Elizabeth's tone syrupy. "The heartbreak was for me. I was an idiot about Colin, and my heart breaks for my past self for being such a fool." She strode toward her door, saying, "Speaking of which . . ."

She disappeared into the passage, and for a moment Saffron imagined that was Elizabeth's way of telling her to go hang. But she reappeared a moment later, and Saffron nearly swallowed her tongue at what she was holding.

"What," she gasped, "are you doing with a gun?"

Elizabeth smirked down at the little pistol. It was a tiny thing with a glossy silver and mother-of-pearl handle. "I bought it a few days after we were abducted. I'm not ever going to let something like that happen to me again. But if you're worried I might do something foolish, you ought to take it."

"Why on earth would I take it?" Saffron asked, holding her hands up to reject the proffered pistol. "I don't know how to shoot it. You don't know how to shoot it!"

"Don't be silly." Elizabeth's hands swiftly swept the safety off and she sighted the sconce on the far wall, one eye pinched shut. "I made sure to choose one that I could handle easily. The man at the shop said there was nothing to it when I went to test them out, and he was quite right."

"You tested pistols out?" Saffron's head was spinning. "When? You barely left the flat save to go to work the last few months!"

"You have been preoccupied, darling. Of course, I tested it out; I refuse to be the idiot who doesn't know how to shoot her own gun." She wiggled the pistol at her again. "Take it, Saffron. Out in the world, there are few repercussions for Bill or his evil henchmen should they try to harm you. Who's to say he won't order them to nab you off the street and stash you somewhere?"

"He needs me to find the research, remember?"

She shrugged. "Alexander could find it for him."

"Then give the pistol to him."

Elizabeth lowered her hand holding the gun. "Lee might have mentioned Alexander does not respond well to guns."

Saffron blinked. "When did you speak to Lee about Alexander?"

Another shrug, less casual and more avoidant. "He telephoned for you, just after the business with the lab was finished, and we got to talking. After I explained what had happened, he insisted I needed something stronger than wine. We went out together, once or twice."

The vice of guilt around Saffron's lungs tightened. She'd missed so much of Elizabeth's comings and goings in the last few months, even when she'd believed she'd done well to care for her. "I'm sorry. I'm sorry for all of it. Colin and Alfie and—"

Elizabeth stopped her with a hand on her shoulder and a deathly serious gleam in her eye. "I appreciate that, darling. Make it up to me by taking the gun."

Weakly, Saffron said, "You're in danger here, too."

Elizabeth wrapped her fingers over hers, pressing the warmed metal into her hand. "I feel quite safe here, and better knowing you've got this. Besides, I know where the gun room is."

CHAPTER 22

London was another world, one both welcoming and jarring. Saffron stepped off the train and took a deep, grounding breath, only to regret inhaling the acrid, smoggy air.

Alexander took her arm and guided her through the bustling crowd of St. Pacras. She'd not planned on asking him to come, but upon explaining her plan to go back to the city for the day, he'd had too many good reasons to accompany her for her to argue.

Their plan was two-fold, and they enacted it the moment they set foot on campus. University College London spread through the neighborhood of Fitzrovia, but at its core was the U-shaped building that formed the Quad off Gower Street. The library, Saffron's home away from home, occupied the top floors of the Wilkins Building, topped with a stately dome. The South Wing extended on one side from the Wilkins Building, and the North Wing, where Saffron and Alexander worked, lay on the other. Saffron made for the black door in the center of the North Wing's gray facade. She was headed for her department head's office, and Alexander for the administrative offices in the South Wing.

Though it was the middle of the semester and early in the day, Saffron found the halls were fairly quiet. This pleased her; less people to run into to question why she'd returned from family leave so early.

Mr. Ferrand was at his desk when she knocked and entered. The personal secretary of her boss, Dr. Aster, Ferrand was a suave, gentlemanly sort with stylishly cut salt-and-pepper hair and a charming little mustache. He stood when he recognized her.

"Ah, *mon ami*," he said, offering her his hands. Though it wasn't typical to allow one's work colleagues to kiss the air next to one's face, Ferrand's demeanor had always been strictly avuncular. She squeezed his hands in reply.

"How do you do, Mr. Ferrand?" she asked with a genuine smile. "I'm afraid I must speak with Dr. Aster rather urgently."

"For you, I would rearrange *le lizard's* schedule, even if he would flay me alive with those icy eyes of his, but he is not here," Ferrand said.

The weight of the entire mad situation collapsed on her all at once. She didn't want to speak to Aster. From abandoning an important government study, to skipping work to investigate the Harpenden Path Lab and then requesting family leave, she'd already pushed his limits of tolerance several times. He'd told her flat out that her father's work was not up for discussion, and that was precisely what she had to pry out of him. But now it was not even possible.

"Your Dr. Maxwell convinced him to take a long lunch away from campus."

Dr. Maxwell being at the U rather than in his place of retirement in Dover was the best news she could imagine. Just as he'd mentored her during her school days and employment, Maxwell had mentored her father when he'd first begun teaching. He would be able to answer her questions better than Aster, and he was a kind man whereas Aster's off-putting manner had inspired Ferrand's nickname for him. "Where are they? When will they return?"

"I do not know," he said apologetically, "but Dr. Maxwell mentioned something about Kew Gardens."

"But—" Her hope deflated with an ache in her chest. If the professors had gone to Kew, they'd be gone all day. Kew Gardens was only about an hour away by train, but it was Kew. No botanist could simply stop by. It was their Mecca in England, and she did not doubt that Maxwell and Aster could spend hours discussing the first display garden they came across, even in winter.

"It is very essential you speak to Dr. Aster today?" Ferrand asked gently.

Her throat had gone tight. She nodded.

"My dear Miss Everleigh." He gestured for her to take the seat opposite his own, and she did.

218

"What is the matter?" Ferrand asked. She looked up to see him offering her a handkerchief, and she flushed when she realized tears had leaked from the corners of her eyes. "How can I help?"

"You're too kind," she mumbled, patting her eyes with the soft linen. "It is merely a . . . a family matter. Dr. Aster and Dr. Maxwell knew my father, you see, and there have been some questions . . ."

"Ah," he said, nodding. "A crisis in the family can unearth certain things, can it not?"

"It has, yes." She glanced up at him, and found him watching her with sad eyes. "When did you begin here at the U?"

"1918," he replied. "When it became clear returning to my previous position at the *Université* Grenoble would not be possible for some time, I came here."

"My father worked here for eight years before the war," she said. "Have you . . . have you ever seen his name in any records or anything?"

"But of course," Ferrand said, his brows knitting. "I put together the file for *le lizard*, did I not?"

Tears forgotten, Saffron straightened up. "What file?"

"Last year, when you began the study with the charming doctor," Ferrand said. "When I'd just started in this position, you recall. *Pardonne-moi,* but did Dr. Aster not show you the file? I thought he requested the information for your benefit."

"He did not show it to me. Do you still have it?"

"I do." He rose from his chair to access the filing cabinet. "I gathered all the information available, but you understand some things are not always filled correctly."

He turned around and offered her a fat file filled with papers. She hugged it to her chest. "Thank you, Mr. Ferrand. May I borrow this for a while? When I return to work, I'll bring it back."

"*Bon.* I am happy to be of assistance. But keep it to yourself, eh? Can't have *le lizard* knowing I'm passing his files around."

"Of course." Saffron got to her feet. She would need privacy to see what was hidden in this file. "*Merci infiniment.*"

Saffron's office was freezing, but she was sure she wouldn't be there long enough to bother with the radiator. She needed to collect Alexander and go to Kew for Dr. Maxwell, but first, she needed to go through the file about her father.

She set her handbag and the file down on her desk and opened the blinds, letting in the weak morning light.

Settling at her desk, she opened the file.

She looked for references to Bill or poisonous plants or the research Thomas Everleigh had supposedly been doing into breeding plants. If there was only more time, she would go on to Harpenden and return to the Plant Pathology Lab to ask Dr. Calderbrook to tell her about what he'd wanted her father to do at his laboratory. She'd had the information within her grasp, but Colin Smith—and her own cowardice, she owned—had prevented her from delving into it. In order to make it back to Ellington in time for dinner, and avoid awkward questions about disappearing with Alexander for the day, they needed to leave the U as soon as possible if they were to go to Kew in search of Maxwell. Dr. Calderbrook would have to be a backup plan should Maxwell prove unhelpful.

Maxwell's name came up often in the pages of the file. He and Thomas Everleigh had not often worked together, as their areas of expertise were not especially complementary, but they collaborated on behalf of the department often, connecting faculty with researchers at other universities, research stations, and botanical institutions around the country and the world.

Other familiar names flitted past, mentions of journals which had published Thomas Everleigh's papers. She even found class schedules and semester budgets. It seemed Ferrand had gathered anything with "T. Everleigh" on it, even bits of scrap paper that looked like the litter one might find at the bottom of a long-used desk's drawers.

A knock on her door caused her to jump. "Miss Everleigh?"

It was a feminine voice, one that was familiar. Saffron rose and opened the door.

"Why, Savita," Saffron said with a surprised smile. She didn't know the young chemist well, but she was pleased to see her. Their paths had crossed on campus a few times since they'd met in November when she'd asked Savita and her cousin for help amassing some information for the Path Lab case.

"I figured it out!" Savita exclaimed. Her short cap of black waves curled unevenly around her head and her round spectacles were slightly crooked on her nose, and Saffron had never seen her look happier. "I've looked for you for days to tell you!"

"That's marvelous," Saffron said, grinning back at her. "Figured out what?"

Savita shoved her glasses back up her nose and offered Saffron a book, her thumb nudging it open to the page it marked. "That plant sample you gave me ages ago. You asked for its chemical composition—which I did manage as well, by the way—but it wasn't enough. What good would a collection of chemicals be?"

Saffron didn't mention that a collection of chemicals was exactly what had been needed at the time to discount the plant as a murder weapon.

"So I kept looking and cross-referenced it with some of the phytotoxicology texts I'd seen on your shelves here," she continued, then tapped the page excitedly, "and found this!"

Saffron peered down at the page. Teucrium chamaedrys, *known colloquially as wall germander, is a species of plant found in the Mediterranean regions of Europe. Characterized by its scalloped, opposite leaves and tubular flowers in shades of pink and fuchsia . . .*

Saffron's mouth fell open. "You are a marvel, Savita! That plant was practically unidentifiable."

"You might want to find a sample of a living plant to desiccate to ensure it's a visual match to the sample, but I'm quite certain I'm correct." She looked abundantly pleased. "And now you'll be able to finally move forward with your case!"

"Ah." She didn't want to tell her that the germander's relevance was long passed. Then she recalled another item that would benefit from Savita's unexpected doggedness. "I have another challenge for you if you're up for it." She went to her handbag and withdrew the envelopes containing the incense from Madame Martin's room and the little seed Alexander had given her from Mr. Fischer's room. After breaking the incense in half, she passed it to Savita. "I need to know what this contains."

Savita seemed disappointed when she lifted the stick to wave before her nose. "Rose and jasmine." She raised a thick eyebrow. "I assume you know this is an incense stick, meant to burn and produce fragrant smoke. The Hindu faith utilizes them for cleansing rituals and prayer, as does the Buddhist faith. Not this sort, though. None of the rituals call for rose or jasmine."

"I see," Saffron said. She hadn't considered that the incense might not be of Eastern origin. Was that relevant? "I believe this contains something more than floral extracts. My friends and I believe it is being used to drug those who inhale its smoke."

Savita dropped the stick back into the envelope but didn't look frightened by the possibility, only determined. "I will analyze it as soon as possible."

Saffron couldn't help but smile at her solemnity. "I appreciate it. One day you will have to teach me how to do it myself."

"I like doing it. And it gives me a good reason to work in Romesh's laboratory. He can't kick me out if I'm working on police business, can he?"

Guilt touched Saffron. "This isn't a police matter. It's personal."

The girl looked disappointed but rallied immediately. "It sounds important, regardless. Now I've done the germander, I think this will be easier. I'll let you know when I've completed the analysis." She nodded to the other envelope. "What else?"

"That's something I need to look up myself," Saffron said. She picked up the envelope and opened it so Savita could take a peek. "A seed of some sort. I'm not sure if it's important or coincidental."

Savita glanced between her and the seed, a small smile forming on her lips. "Has a crime of a personal nature been committed in Whitechapel or Tooting?"

"What do you mean?"

"Those are the neighborhoods in which this can be easily procured." Savita dipped her finger into the envelope and a black dot of a seed stuck to its tip. "This is *kalo jeere*. A black caraway seed. It's a spice."

"Caraway," Saffron said slowly, trying to recall anything she knew of the plant and its use as a food or medicinal.

"Oh yes," Savita said. "My mother uses it in her *garam masala* and for stomach ailments. Though this one must have gone bad; the smell is off." Her nose wrinkled as she scraped the seed off her fingertip to fall back into the envelope. "I feel as if your criminal must have traveled to the East. Perhaps they served in a place like Calcutta or Baghdad."

That was possible; Fischer was likely to have been in the military, and who knew where Madame Martin had traveled before France and England.

Saffron thanked Savita, and the girl left with the envelope containing the incense and renewed enthusiasm for a fresh challenge.

The bell at the nearby church rang, signaling the noon hour. Saffron gathered up her things.

She stepped out of her office, locked the door, and set out in search of Alexander.

CHAPTER 23

"What do you mean, I can't get the file myself?"

Alexander looked up from his stack of files at the small desk, immediately registering the brash male voice before catching sight of its owner. Down the low-ceilinged aisle of filing cabinets came a man nearly as wide as the row itself, with shoulders like the mountains he was famous in academic quarters for climbing, and a manner just as brutal as the landscapes he traversed in the course of his anthropological studies.

Under normal circumstances, Alexander wouldn't be likely to tolerate that sort of man, let alone like him. But Alexander had seen a change in Dr. Lawrence Henry in the months since he and Saffron had helped solve the crime of his wife's near-fatal poisoning. He was still abrupt and demanding, but his womanizing ways were long gone. He even managed to amend his condescending attitude, though that continued to prove a challenge as evidenced by his next words.

"I'll get any file I want," Henry said, striding forward. His blue eyes flashed with impatience as he glared around at the filing cabinets.

The young clerk scurried after the professor. "But Dr. Henry—"

"You just point me in the right section." He caught sight of Alexander where he sat at the end of the row. "Ashton, what the devil are you doing down in this hole!"

Alexander got to his feet and accepted Henry's bruising grip in a handshake. "Dr. Henry. I was asked to take on some administrative work for Cunningham."

Henry scoffed, accepting the lie easily. "Grunt work? How many publications does it take to prove yourself in Biology, eh?" He crossed his arms over his chest, a move that tested the endurance of his gray suit's seams. "Man like you ought to be where the real work is. Jump ship and join me in History! We'll get you your doctorate and a tenured position within three years, I guarantee it." He leaned forward, planting a heavy hand on Alexander's shoulder. "I'm close to getting this university the anthropology department it needs. Our next expedition will cinch it, I swear."

A familiar shimmer of interest lit in Alexander's mind. For all he prized organization and routine, he did love getting out in the field. Expeditions provided the intellectual stimulation he'd come to enjoy and the tests of his mettle he craved. "Where to?"

"There's an agora in Smyrna that has proven

interesting," Henry replied, his swagger shifting to business. "Turkey, you know. Now things have settled down over there, the possibilities for further excavation are significant."

Disappointment hit him hard. There was little cause for a microbiologist at an archaeological dig. "It's already dug up, then?"

"It was abandoned, thanks to the Ottomans relinquishing their hold on the region, so much the better for us! Saved us a lot of work and money. Not to mention the site is so close to the city, no camping would be required."

"Sounds appealing." Alexander glanced at his watch, noting he only had half an hour before he was meant to meet Saffron in the Flax-man Gallery and he'd found nothing in the university's records about anyone named Bill Wyatt or variations of that name.

"It is," Henry said, rocking back on his heels. His eyes glittered as he added, "Not just for my people, either. Stores in the agora's ruins have been found to contain preserved goods from the Roman period. I don't suppose you'd be interested in examining samples from such a stash?"

"I would," he said automatically, surprised Henry had bothered to remember one of his areas of interest. The bacteria involved in food preservation was outside his current sphere of study, but he could certainly make an exception.

"I want you as a team leader, Ashton," Henry said, surprising him. "You did good work in Brazil. Calm, when the rest of the crew were losing their heads over a little sweat and a few maggots." Alexander withheld a grimace at the memory of fat white bodies wriggling in places they were *not* meant to be. "I need a cool head in a place like Turkey. That's you."

"Thank you," Alexander said, "but I—"

Henry lifted a broad hand. "Don't answer yet. Applications open in a few weeks and decisions won't be made until May. We'll have the summer to make arrangements, then leave before the fall semester begins."

The plan laid out, visions of travel to a place that closely resembled his mother's homeland stirred in his mind. It was not the same, of course, and his mother's side of the family would be aggrieved to know he'd even contemplated similarities between Greece and what was now Turkey . . . But perhaps the air would taste the same. And into the vision of a rugged, golden coastline walked Saffron, pink-cheeked from the Mediterranean sun, delighted to catalog unfamiliar plants of a new region.

"Would the crew include other members of Biology?" he asked.

"Of course," Henry said. "And you'd have input, should you agree to join the leadership of the crew."

"If there are preserved foodstuffs, I imagine other subdepartments might have an interest. Botany, for one. I know Miss Everleigh would be keen."

"Miss—Miss Everleigh. Ah." Henry opened his mouth to speak, then snapped it shut again. His unease was plain.

Dr. Henry was not the first staff member to have a negative reaction toward Saffron, nor would he be the last, but it was irritating all the same. Considering Saffron's actions had exonerated Henry in the case of his wife's poisoning, which eventually led to their reconciliation, he owed her a great deal. Alexander had no problem reminding Henry of it. Evenly, he asked, "What's wrong with including Miss Everleigh?"

Henry's expression turned peevish. "Nothing at all. You know I like the girl. The missus still asks about her, you know." He cleared his throat. "But you know how these trips are, Ashton. The long hours hauling equipment over rough terrain—"

"The site was in the city, you said."

"And you know the sort of lads who opt to go on expeditions are a rowdy sort—"

"You mentioned you were looking for cool heads," Alexander said, raising a brow.

"Yes, but even the coolest of heads might find it challenging . . ." Henry's bluster increased to cover up the strain of not immediately dismissing the idea of including a woman in the crew.

Alexander decided to stop tormenting him when he was trying, in his way, to be considerate.

"I will think on it," Alexander told him, stopping him midway through a long-winded sentence about the weather. "And you will think on including Miss Everleigh. It would make a bold statement regarding your dedication to modernizing the university." He offered him a conspiratorial smile. "I imagine Mrs. Henry would be thrilled to hear that you'd be willing to champion a woman to the selection committee."

Dr. Henry's hard face turned thoughtful. "Indeed, indeed. Later, then, Ashton."

He walked back the way he'd come, apparently forgetting whatever file he'd been harassing the clerk over.

Alone again, Alexander combed a hand through his hair as he replayed the conversation in his head. He didn't know if he'd done right, suggesting Saffron for the expedition. They'd often spoken about his experiences in the field, and she'd said herself that she would love to travel abroad for work, but saying one had an interest in doing something and actually being willing to make it happen was not the same thing. It would be an uphill climb every step of the way, and one she would need to make mostly by herself. It was hard enough that most of the department knew they were together now; he couldn't be perceived to be helping her or giving her preferential treatment, for both their sakes. Should she choose to apply to join the crew, her application and study proposal would have to be flawless.

His wristwatch told him he needed to make his way to the upper levels. He tucked his things away in his bag and replaced the files in the bin to be replaced by the clerk before heading up the stairs to the ground floor.

His feet did not immediately turn toward the North Wing and Saffron, but guided him to a stretch of hall that he usually avoided.

The lunch hour had the ground floor of the South Wing swarming with students. With his eyes fixed on his query, Alexander waded through the young men in loud ties and young women with their faces shadowed by hat brims. He found shelter from the buffeting currents of students in the lee of a column and leaned against it to study the rows of black-and-white faces in the photographs just visible through the crowd.

The images took up the length of the wall. Faces too young to have belonged to men now several years dead and gone looked down on him. Shame and grief had prevented him from facing them, his fellow students and faculty who'd lost their lives in the war. Alexander's life had been haunted by such shadows after the war. Memories of pain and fear blended with future terrors until life had become unbearable and Alexander desperate. He'd beat back the shadows, and Saffron's arrival in his life had reduced them to nothing more than flimsy cobwebs.

He found he could look at the faces of the dead with resignation, and maybe a little bit of peace.

The initial flood of students slowed, and Alexander approached to take a closer look at the plaques beneath each photograph, scanning names, dates of birth and death, and units.

"I would say you didn't have to come in search of me," a quiet voice said at his side, "but I don't believe you did come to find me."

"I did, but I remembered another query that required a little more research," Alexander told Saffron.

Her chin lifted, blue eyes on the portraits. "In my more maudlin moments I've wondered how things might have turned out differently. In another life, I walk into this hall and look up at this wall and see your photograph. A handsome face representing a man I would have never known." She tucked her arm into his, drawing close enough he could feel her sigh. "It makes me terribly sad. I've taken to avoiding this hall just as you usually do. What brings you here now?"

He patted her hand. "I had a thought about your ghostly soldier."

She tutted. "Fischer, you mean."

"Most likely. But in his bedroom, I found a watch very much like the one Adrian was issued." She turned to him, frowning. "The sort distributed by the Royal Air Force."

"Fischer was a pilot!"

"And not in the army."

"So the uniform—"

"—isn't his," Alexander finished.

"But what does it mean?" Saffron asked.

"I don't know," he admitted. "It is also worth noting that Wesley would not have had a respirator mask. They weren't issued until well after his death." He turned back to the photographs. "Do you see anything that matches what Fischer wore that night?"

Teeth sinking into her lower lip, Saffron's eyes flew over the photographs. They were now nearly alone in the hall, save for the beadle the university kept on duty to honor the dead servicemen. He stood at attention on the other side of the hall, gazing steadily forward.

Saffron took a few cautious steps, pausing at a few photos before lifting her finger to point to the portrait of a stocky man with his service cap set at a jaunty angle. "This fellow. His tunic, and his belt. And his trousers. They've got a detail on the, er, inseam."

"The corduroy patches. They served as reinforcement for a calvary rider." His eyes skated over the man's rank and unit. "Calvary officer. A lieutenant, two stars."

"Like my father, though he had only one star.

Second lieutenant," she said, a soft smile on her face. "He's just over there."

He followed her nod a few feet away to a portrait of a man he instantly recognized as Thomas Everleigh wearing an officer's uniform and a solemn expression quite unlike the cheerful smile Alexander remembered. Alexander had taken one of Professor Everleigh's classes, an introduction course to botany, long before he'd set eyes on his daughter.

Had Thomas Everleigh survived, would Alexander have ever met Saffron? Would he have approved of their relationship, thought a man like Alexander worthy of his daughter?

In the end, it was Saffron who would decide if he was worthy or not, and it seemed it was time to offer her the choice. "I need to make a stop in my office before we go back to Bedford."

Saffron's wistful smile faded. "Not Bedford. We need to make a detour."

CHAPTER 24

It had been years since Saffron had visited Kew Gardens. Her memories of the walk through the town of Kew were vague, eclipsed by the powerfully clear recollections she had of the gardens themselves. Each street and garden gate might have been familiar or just as easily unknown, like the hint of a familiar face in the corner of one's eye, only to see upon closer inspection it was the face of a stranger.

The garden gate loomed ahead, a striking, ornate black gate bookended by massive stone posts. Gold filigree shone from circular crests at the center of each panel of black wrought iron. Beyond the gate, the garden stretched brown, dark green, and muted gold.

Arm in arm under Alexander's umbrella, they followed the broad path toward the places Saffron believed it most likely she could find Dr. Maxwell and Dr. Aster. At the roundabout, they turned south, which allowed them a peek of the orangery through the pines. It had been half a century since that building, with its tall ceilings and massive panes of windows, had actually housed any citrus. It wasn't long after its construction that the gardeners realized the fruit trees didn't receive enough light, and its original purpose had been abandoned.

Next came the boardwalk, a long stretch that would take them to the center of the grounds, lined with bare garden beds. A picture, clear as a photograph, appeared in her mind of purple spikes of veronica and tall, lush columns of hollyhock and foxglove sitting over spills of phlox. She found herself taking a deep draught of the cool, damp air, as if to catch the rich layers of fragrance. Each area of the garden was dedicated to different climates and types of plants, with each planting more exotic and impressive than the last. The boardwalk, by contrast, exemplified the best of English gardening, and she'd always loved it. As a child, it had delighted her to race along the path in a place world renowned for its botanical accomplishments and see it lined with the same flowers she'd grown up with at Ellington.

"I can feel your effort to withhold interesting facts about this place," Alexander murmured. "You've been doing it since we stepped through the gate."

"Don't be silly. This isn't the time for trivia." She cringed at the highness of her voice giving away her feelings.

"You can tell me if you would like."

His tone was too light. Saffron shot him a look. His face was neutral under the brim of his

238

dark fedora, but the corners of his eyes crinkled with humor. For some reason, that irritated her enough to blurt out, "But it's all wrong, isn't it? Coming here, like this. This place is one of my favorite places in the world, and we've come to chase down information, the source of which isn't even guaranteed to be here. We don't have time to explore the best sections of the garden, and we'll have to skip Kew Palace entirely, and there's no time to show you the Japanese pagoda, and—and it's *February!*" She'd stopped walking. Alexander's serious expression wavered, and she scowled at him. "It's the worst possible time to come to a garden. You've never been here, and you're seeing it all for the first time like this." She waved a hand at the uninspiring brown landscape peering out of the gloom. "We'll never get to do this again, come here together for the first time." She exhaled, suddenly feeling quite silly to be upset about a visit to a garden when so many more important things hung in the balance. But Bill and his threats had already ruined Alexander meeting her family; it seemed grossly unfair that he should take away the pleasure of visiting Kew, too.

Alexander considered her for a long moment, and then he placed her arm around his once more and guided her to continue down the boardwalk. "It seems we've got a long walk yet. I would like to hear your Kew trivia on the way."

• • •

If there was a place more fascinating, more glorious, more soul-filling in the world, Saffron had yet to find it.

Even full of anxieties and frustrations, the sight of Kew's Palm House was enough to bring a smile back to Saffron's face. Her feet picked up their pace the moment its massive glass hull came into view.

She paused only to detail the contents of the small water lily house when they passed by it. She regretted that they didn't have the time to explore the murky pond and observe the alien plants that inhabited the smaller glass house. Alexander likely would have recognized a few of the specimens housed there after his adventure in the Amazon.

The massive metal and glass door creaked as it slowly swung open to reveal the interior of the Palm House. Alexander held it for her, and she entered, holding her breath until the wintery air had dissipated into the fragrant, silent warmth of the glasshouse.

"I see why you like this place," Alexander said.

Saffron couldn't imagine anyone not liking it. Even for one with her scientific bent, it was magical.

Two stories of green fanned over their heads, sculptural shapes slicing the humid air. Pockets of shadow interspersed sporadic, wild bursts of color. It was exuberant, elegant chaos, a church of verdure complete with the hush customarily found in sacred places. The only sounds were the slight vibration of softly rustling leaves and drips of moisture from leaf tips, or condensation from the iron arches overhead. For the first time in far too long, Saffron's mind quieted.

"I like this better than the rainforest," Alexander said, interrupting that peace with a smirk. "Fewer insects."

They set off down a path, eyes peeled for the professors. Plants familiar and unknown sprawled, spread, climbed, and dangled all around, creating green walls of infinite detail. The workday and gloomy weather worked in concert to make the house dim and largely vacant. The long pathways between plots were empty save for the occasional figure glimpsed in passing. By the time they'd wound through the entire massive glasshouse, they'd seen only three other people, none of them their queries.

"Where next?" Alexander asked.

"Dr. Maxwell's specialty is Polypodiales," Saffron said. "It's an order that includes many sorts of fern. We've passed by half a dozen he's studied, including the one he donated. This was my first guess of where he would go. I suppose we ought to check the Temperate House."

Cold air slapped their cheeks as they departed the Palm House. The walk to the Temperate

House was not an enjoyable one, with the rain picking up and slicing against Saffron's legs where her long wool skirt left a few inches of leg exposed. She anticipated the Temperate House's warmth, but just as the glasshouse came into view, she saw two men halfway down the perpendicular path, moving in the opposite direction.

"That must be them," Saffron told Alexander, pointing to the two bent shapes under their umbrellas.

They forwent the promise of the Temperate House's dry warmth and began after Maxwell and Aster. They made for the end of the path, to a quaint two-story building with a veranda wrapped around its front, reaching it just as the old men prepared to climb the dozen stairs leading to the front door.

"Dr. Maxwell," Saffron called to the white-haired, stooped figure.

He turned and his face, ruddy from the cold, creased with confusion before brightening with a smile of recognition.

"Everleigh!" Maxwell said with a dry laugh. "Fancy meeting you here!"

At his side, Dr. Aster looked on with neutral curiosity. He was Maxwell's opposite, apart from their similarly advanced age; he was the sharp lines of a palm, while Maxwell was the familiar softness of Irish moss. Aster was neat as a pin in his dark coat and perfectly brushed derby hat. Even though his black wool coat was buttoned to his throat, Maxwell managed to look rumpled, with his white flyaway hair clouding under his shabby hat and his spectacles dotted with moisture.

Affection for her mentor welled in her chest, and Saffron came forward to press a kiss to his cheek. He smiled at her, pale blue eyes sparkling. "How do you do, Professor?"

"Ah." Maxwell's fuzzy white brows lifted. "Funny you mention that—"

"May I suggest we actually enter the gallery?" Aster asked crisply. "It's quite disagreeable weather."

It wasn't much warmer inside the gallery, but without the rain and wind, it felt cozy.

It was a dizzying space. The walls bristled with hundreds of frames filled with Marianne North's vibrant botanical illustrations. These were not anemic figures on white backgrounds, but full renderings of specimens in their natural environments, as exotic and unique as the plants they featured. Vertical wood panels lined the wall below the paintings, each a different sample the artist had collected in her extensive travels. Even the tiled floor was a riot of color, with geometric patterns of rust, cream, and black stretching across the floor. Today, with the windows of the mezzanine barely illuminated, it was hard to make out the details of the pictures in the upper rows.

Once their umbrellas were placed into the stand at the door, Dr. Maxwell turned to Saffron and asked, "How did you come to find us here?"

Aster's gray eyes sharpened on Saffron as if he, too, wanted to hear the answer to that question, though he seemed to anticipate her response with far less delight than his friend.

Saffron swallowed and offered the answer she'd prepared. "I don't know if Dr. Aster mentioned it, but my grandfather is unwell. I've been in Bedfordshire these last few days tending him. But, ah . . . Things have come up, during my visit. Things about my father." She darted an uneasy look at Aster, worrying over his reaction. As usual, he gave nothing away. "I went to the university in search of answers and Mr. Ferrand mentioned you had been there, then came here. Since I didn't want to venture all the way to Devon to speak to you, or wait until your sabbatical finished, I came here in search of you."

Maxwell nodded, his eyes flickering to Alexander. "Good fortune that I happened to be at the university, then." He let out a dry cough, and nodded toward the large open door to the next room. "Let us see if I may answer these questions, then. If you'll excuse us, Aster, Ashton."

Saffron cast a curious look over her shoulder to

Alexander as she followed Maxwell into the next room. He watched her go with the slightest smile. If anyone could handle a disgruntled Dr. Aster, it was Alexander.

CHAPTER 25

Questions about your father," Maxwell began as soon as they passed through the doorway into the next room. They ambled past more walls plastered with colorful paintings and drawings. "What do you want to know that I've yet to tell you?"

Saffron smiled despite her nerves; Maxwell had told her story after story about her father's time at the university. Thomas Everleigh's years as a professor had provided many amusing tales that Maxwell had expertly wielded to encourage and distract Saffron in times of distress. In the first years of her education, there had been many.

"You have told me a great deal about his experiences teaching," Saffron said, "but I've recently learned there was more to his time at the U than I'd known. His work, for example, was more expansive than I'd realized."

"What do you mean?" Maxwell asked.

"It seems he was invested in a good deal more than just his published works," Saffron said carefully. Considering how stringent Aster's refusal to discuss her father's work was, she didn't want to push Maxwell into a similar reaction.

A wheezing laugh was her answer. "Of course,

his work extended beyond what he published! Publication is the goal for many of us academics, but you know the reality. Not everyone attempts to publish every study, and fewer manage to publish all they write."

"That is true," Saffron said, and let silence fall between them as they restarted their slow turn about the gallery. Images of flowering cacti and tangles of vines slipped past like a reel of a film rotated too slowly.

"What is bothering you?" Maxwell asked when they reached the door into the next and final room. "What did you come across at Ellington?"

"Nothing." Saffron sighed. "That's the problem. It's all gone. His rooms, his private greenhouse . . . I can't find anything. I looked forward to learning more about the intricacies of his work."

"Ah," Maxwell said, the furrows on his brow smoothing out. "Searching for inspiration, were you?"

"Er, yes," Saffron said. That was a better excuse than what she'd been able to come up with.

"You were always one of the most focused of my students, and I was very pleased to hear of your promotion to full researcher," he said. "I wondered when Aster said you were struggling. It didn't seem in character."

Aster had told him she was struggling? It was true that some things were not going as well as she'd like, but how galling that Aster had noticed, let alone told Maxwell! "Things have been difficult."

"Taking on a full schedule of master's classes while doing research would be challenging for anyone." He fixed her with the serious look that he'd given her when she'd contemplated quitting school. It hadn't been often, but there had been days when the struggle to be taken seriously became too much. "Especially with so little support from your colleagues."

That, at least, was no surprise. Maxwell had always been a gossip; of course he'd heard she was still unpopular within the botany department from two hundred miles away.

"Looking to your father's work for inspiration is a wise move, considering his success," Maxwell continued. "But I'm sure you've considered it'll be hard to make a name for yourself if you decide to follow in his footsteps. Which leads me to a topic I fear you will find indelicate."

"What is it?"

"I couldn't help but notice you're in the company of Alexander Ashton."

Heat crept into her face, and she turned to look at the nearest painting. She got only the impression of cool greens and vibrant fuchsia. "We've been stepping out for some time. He wished to accompany me today."

"Yes. Well, I, er . . . That is to say, Saffron"—

he cleared his throat, his face pink—"I have no right to speak on such personal matters, but I—" He cut off, reaching into his jacket pocket for a handkerchief he used to polish the lenses of his spectacles.

"Professor, you don't need to say anything." She was nearly as uncomfortable as he was, but she didn't resent his bumbling attempt at questioning her. He had always had her best interest at heart. "We have a good deal in common. We get on very well. Mr. Ashton is a good man." They were bland words, but she could hardly tell him the full truth of her feelings for Alexander. If Maxwell was blushing already, he might have an apoplexy should she be more detailed.

He coughed lightly into his handkerchief, avoiding her eyes. "Yes, my dear, I know. I had my doubts, when first you and he worked together, but after I learned of his role in Berking's arrest and his comportment on the Amazonian expedition, my views have changed. He's accomplished some impressive feats in his research in the last few years, as well."

"Then what is the problem?"

"I've no objection to the man himself," Maxwell said, "only that a serious attachment between the two of you will not go unnoticed." He winced as Saffron let out a frustrated sigh. "The gossip mill is alive and well in the North Wing, my dear."

"That is not news to me, unfortunately."

"I understand the pressures of constant observation. We live in something of a glasshouse ourselves at the university, don't we?" He smiled weakly.

He had no idea how right he was. Since Bill's introduction, she'd spent the last few months bouncing between denial of his claims and feeling as if her every movement was being watched.

"We have been careful in our behavior toward one another in public." Perhaps not *flawlessly* careful, but—

"I don't refer to that issue alone." His eyes strayed over her shoulder.

With a thrill of fear, Saffron turned, but saw only Alexander and Aster through the doorway, standing side by side before one of the walls of framed art. Alexander seemed to be speaking.

"If you attach yourself to Mr. Ashton, or indeed anyone, I worry your work will suffer for it."

Saffron jerked back, stung by the implication. "I would never abandon my work, Professor. You just said I had the focus—"

Maxwell huffed, shifting in a restless, agitated manner. "I don't mean you will become distracted, my dear, though I must say that I would hope that should love come into your life, you *would* become a little distracted. Mrs. Maxwell has kept me from my work on more than one occasion." He chuckled, and Saffron sent him a severe look in an attempt to encourage him to get to the point.

He looked sufficiently chastised. "I mean this: What will happen when you marry? Should you take on a new name, even one respected like Mr. Ashton's, what will become of your career, the one you've built on your name? You'll have to start over, in some ways. A new name on your work will take away some of the credit you've earned as S. Everleigh. And many will expect you to move out of the academic sphere and into the, er, domestic one. If you catch my meaning."

Saffron did, and it returned the color to her cheeks. She didn't know which was worse, speaking to her mentor about the possibility of childbearing or being accused of being in the process by her grandmother. "I think you're being rather hasty in your concerns, Professor."

"It must be considered," Maxwell said heavily. "It is the course of nature. I say it only because I would hate to see the work you've put into getting where you are, and the opportunities you've been offered, go to waste." He forced a smile. "Let us return to why you tracked me down here."

"What can you tell me about the unpublished work my father did?" She held her breath for his reaction.

In answer, Maxwell wandered to the nearest

bench and gestured for Saffron to join him. She did, and he cleared his throat. "Well, when he first began at the university—that was in 1906, or perhaps 1907—he was interested in a pathogen he'd run across. I believe he first noted it in the fields near Ellington land, I believe . . ."

Alexander knew enough of Dr. Maxwell, mostly through Saffron's stories, to know that when he and Saffron settled on the bench in the adjacent room, it meant that their conversation would be a long one. He returned his attention to the picture before him, an arid landscape. It reminded him of Dr. Henry's invitation to join him on the expedition to Turkey.

Dr. Aster was at his side, perhaps attempting courtesy by accompanying him on his very slow circle about the room. "Has Dr. Henry mentioned anything to you or the other department heads about his proposed expedition to Turkey?" Alexander asked him.

Aster took a moment to respond, ostensibly completing his observation of a fluffy pink flower depicted in the frame before him. "He has brought it up to the various committees and boards responsible for such things, yes."

"Do you think it likely that Botany will approve any researchers for the crew?"

Aster's thin lips disappeared as he fixed Alexander with a sour look. "Considering applications have not even been announced, it would be inappropriate to comment."

"Of course." He mulled over his next words. "Dr. Henry has asked me to lead one of the teams. He mentioned that responsibility came with approval over the members of that team."

Alexander had no doubt that Dr. Aster read between the lines: he wanted to know if Saffron would get approval from her department head should she want to go. It would be embarrassing for her should she apply and Aster, the one who promoted her to researcher, be the one to deny her. Department politics were dull, but their necessity had never been keener now that he was involved with Saffron. A wrong move could damage his career and sink hers entirely.

Aster said nothing, however, merely taking a measured step toward the next section of wall and lifting his cold eyes to gaze at the pictures.

"What would it take?"

"I find it unlikely," Aster said, drawing his words out, "that any department head would approve a young, unmarried woman, one who has found herself in trouble a number of times, to be sent a foreign land under the care of a known philanderer and her . . . beau." He looked like the word tasted unpleasant.

A glance over Alexander's shoulder showed that Saffron and Maxwell were still deep in conversation. Saffron's expression was rapt, but it was not enthusiastic. That look of anxious attention had been on her face too often for his liking lately. First with worry over Bill and Elizabeth, then over her family. It burned that he had no idea how to fix it.

That frustration climbed his throat, bursting out in the form of questions he knew better than to ask. "Why do you support her at the university at all? Why promote her, if only to dismiss her ambitions?"

"I support any ambition of my staff as far as they benefit the standing of our department and our university within local and global spheres. Innovation and progress never come without a cost." Aster turned back to the painting, and muttered, "My patience, in this case."

The clack of Saffron's heels signaled her conversation with Dr. Maxwell was at an end. Determination was plain on her face as she and the older man approached. Whatever Maxwell had told her, she had a plan.

"Dr. Aster," she said, nodding to him, "I will see you in the North Wing next week as scheduled." To Alexander, she said, "We've one more stop to make."

He nodded, and began toward the umbrella stand. Behind him, he heard Aster say, "How good to know that you plan to be where you say. That is rather a departure from the last two times you've requested time away from the university."

"I daresay Everleigh has had good reason to alter her plans, Aster," Maxwell said.

"Indeed," Aster said crisply as they approached the door. "I suppose interrupting a family emergency to visit a garden is sensible."

Maxwell cleared his throat. Saffron's expression tightened. "I can explain—"

"I would prefer there be no cause for explanations," Aster snapped.

Saffron opened her mouth to speak, but Maxwell scowled at Aster and said, "There is no need to be unpleasant. Miss Everleigh came to Kew at your assistant's suggestion because she knew this would be one of the few opportunities for us to meet now I've decided not to return to teaching after my sabbatical." Next to him, Saffron's eyes flared with surprise, giving away Maxwell's lie. She hadn't known at all, and they all knew it.

Aster didn't seem inclined to argue, however. He merely retrieved his umbrella and nodded curtly to them. "Good day."

Maxwell huffed as Aster left the gallery, and Saffron's face crumpled. Alarmed, Alexander reached for her, but Maxwell got there first.

He held her hands in his. "I did not intend to tell you this way. I am sorry for the shock." Saffron nodded, not meeting his eye as she blinked furiously. A pang rocked Alexander, and he dug into his pocket for a handkerchief.

She accepted it and turned away to dab at her eyes for the briefest moment before turning back to Maxwell with a starched smile. "You've decided to officially retire, then. That's wonderful, Professor, truly. After such a career, you deserve the chance to relax. But I shall miss you very much on campus."

"And I, you, my dear."

They spent a few moments making promises to visit and telephone, and then they stepped outside together.

Saffron watched Dr. Maxwell's slow progress in the direction of the clouded structure of the Temperate House. "I am happy for him." She sounded rather like she was trying to convince herself of it. "It won't be that much of a change, since he hasn't been at the U for a long time. And it is good he is retiring before his health fails him." She exhaled, releasing a cloud of white. "I'm not sure if I'll ever see him again. The world is an uncertain place, you know."

Alexander wrapped an arm around her shoulder and pulled her to his side. "Some things are certain. I believe you will see him again."

CHAPTER 26

Jodrell Laboratory wasn't where Saffron expected to go when she'd impulsively decided to chase down Maxwell at Kew, but it should have been one of the places she'd considered looking for information regarding her father. The laboratory was on the grounds of the garden, a squat little building tucked back near the fence close to where they'd entered. Thomas Everleigh had never worked there, but he had been invited to. Perhaps the reason for that invitation was related to Bill's demands.

Maxwell's long reminiscence of Thomas Everleigh's time at the university had reminded Saffron of several things. First, that she ought to have asked Maxwell specific questions rather than allow him to ramble, and second, that what her father worked on wouldn't have necessarily been a secret. Maxwell told her of Thomas's large correspondence that stretched across oceans and continents. He could have shared his projects and ideas with his colleagues, such as Dr. Calderbrook, who'd taken over the Jodrell Lab and its successor, the Harpenden Path Lab. Just because the work Bill was interested in wasn't published didn't mean Thomas Everleigh hadn't *tried* to have it published.

In a whirlwind of introductions, Saffron soon found herself and Alexander seated across from the assistant keeper of the Curator Office with cups of tea. The Curator Office maintained all the records of the Jodrell Lab and the journal that Kew published, the *Kew Bulletin*.

With the assistant keeper, a pleasant man in late middle age with a shining bald pate, they exchanged pleasantries and caught up on the news of the university and laboratories, including the Path Lab. The assistant keeper knew a good deal about its activities, including that Saffron had briefly worked there. Calderbrook and the government agency in charge of the investigation into the stolen research Bill had been after had concocted a story to cover what had actually happened, but Saffron had never imagined she'd be a part of that story.

It took only a gentle request to the assistant keeper to be given access to the correspondence filed under her father's name. He then gave her and Alexander use of his office, and they once more delved into a stack of papers in the hope that they would reveal answers at last.

"I don't understand," Saffron said, not for the first time. She'd said as much at least four times since first reading the paper in the assistant keeper's office, and no further understanding had dawned since she'd boarded the train back to Bedford and had the chance to pick through the reports again. She'd slipped the relevant ones into her pocket without compunction, needing longer than a few moments to analyze their contents.

She ran a finger over her father's energetic script. "How could I never have known my father had any sort of connection to Demian Petrov? I investigated his death. I sat at his chair at the Path Lab! We broke into his flat! I . . ." She shook her head, swallowing another useless refrain. "But I suppose it does answer the question of how Bill knew anything about my father."

Alexander nodded, not looking up from the papers he held. "He must have found evidence of their partnership."

"But where? We searched Petrov's flat ourselves. And if this was the information Bill said I had access to that he did not, he hasn't seen these papers."

"Bill could have tracked down all of your father's or Petrov's publications and found some footnote. He could have had someone in the Jodrell Lab, reporting on interesting findings. He could have even spoken to Petrov about it. For all that he makes it seem it's a mystery, their partnership on these projects"—he held up the papers—"was not a secret."

Mulling that over, Saffron gazed out the window.

It had taken two hours to make nice with the assistant keeper, look through the papers, and rush back to the train station. The sun had set on their walk back to the station, and now they were scheduled to reach Bedford just before it would be time to dress for dinner. Her hopes of their absence not being noticed were diminishing with each second of deepening darkness.

Thomas Everleigh, professor of plant disease and heir to a viscountcy. Demian Petrov, a Russian émigré who'd supposedly fled instability and offered his expertise in horticulture to the British government. Bill, a mysterious anarchist in search of secrets to sell. How did they relate?

Thomas and Petrov had worked on a cure for a phytopathogen. The paper detailing their work in routing a strain of bacteria victimizing potatoes had been submitted to the *Kew Bulletin*. It had not been accepted for publication, thus why Saffron had never known of it. It also was not undertaken through University College London, and that was Saffron's explanation for why Aster had refused to disclose it. He was obsessed with bolstering his department's reputation; it must have been a thorn in his side that he couldn't encourage her to pursue that line of research, since it had no basis at the university.

Alexander turned the last sheet of paper from the journal article and settled back in his seat. "I believe work of a similar nature was being done on that strain of bacteria at that time. Your father and Petrov were likely not the only ones pushing for publication at the time. This is not what Bill was searching for, then," Alexander said with a frown. "If he knew your father worked with Petrov, why not simply tell you?"

"He's casting a wide net," Saffron said bitterly. "Likely wants to see what other valuable fish I'll bring in."

They fell into silence as the train rattled on through darkness. Her mind wandered through the clues all the way back to the Harpenden Path Lab.

"Nick told me I ought to work at a place like Jodrell or the Path Lab," she said. "Before he offered me work through his specific branch of the government. He said I ought not to settle for the university."

"You would be excellent in a more independent laboratory," Alexander said. "Fewer politics to cope with, less chance of your father's reputation hanging over your head. And nobody would bring up Berking, most likely."

Saffron grimaced. People still muttered about her getting the former botany department head arrested for attempted murder and fraud.

She blew out a breath and leaned back into her seat, meeting Alexander's shoulder. The train car was drafty, and she snuggled closer. "Aster told Maxwell I'm struggling."

"Are you?" he asked.

Her eyes gazed at the empty seats across from them, tracing the faded pattern of the upholstery. "I didn't think so. The last few months have gone well, even after my classes began. I've no concerns about missing them for a week. The pigmentation study is nearly finished, my Amazonian samples are progressing nicely, and . . ." She wasn't sure what else to say. It was true that she'd been dragging her feet on writing up more study proposals. It was perhaps that short-sightedness about her future she'd been wondering about before. Did she truly have no vision for the rest of her life? "Well, what do you want to do after your current study is complete? I'm sure you've stashed away a catalog of perfect proposals."

He chuckled. "A catalog of perfect proposals. If only."

She glanced at him, and found his eyes on her with the sort of expression that made her insides melt like butter. She poked his side, unwilling to be sidestepped. "What is your plan? For next year, the year after? I suppose you have it all mapped out."

"I don't, actually." He picked up one of her hands and fiddled with the tips of her gloved fingers. "I have ideas of what I'd like to do, of course. Complete my current projects, travel more. I don't know if I would want to stay at the university forever. I don't see myself becoming a professor."

"Where would you go?"

"Another university, perhaps. I can't envision going to work for a company like Burroughs Wellcome & Company. No opportunities to travel apart from back and forth from America." His fingers paused in their exploration of her hand. "Would that be something you're interested in?"

"Traveling to America? Of course," she said automatically.

"Specifically?"

She considered it. "No, not specifically. Anywhere would do, really. One day I'll pack up and venture off to some corner of the world. But who knows when that will have the chance to happen?"

Alexander resumed his tracing of her hand, though not the conversation, leaving Saffron momentarily distracted from her present troubles and worrying over the future instead.

CHAPTER 27

The dinner gong had not quite rung when Saffron and Alexander snuck into the house through the kitchens. The chaos of dinner preparation covered their entrance, and they dashed up the stairs and into their respective rooms to dress.

Saffron scampered down the stairs a few minutes later, still tucking a short lock of her dark hair into a glittering barrette. She froze on the landing.

Exactly opposite her on the other landing stood Bill.

Their eyes locked. He did not wear his glasses, so his gaze bore into hers. The stillness stretched taut, leaving Saffron feeling like a deer caught in the sights of a hunter.

A laugh erupted from the drawing room, jolting Saffron. She hurried down the rest of the stairs, her shoulders itching with Bill's gaze all the while.

The family was in the drawing room, and they were noisier than Saffron would have expected for a handful of people. A quick glance behind her showed Bill had not followed, but then, he hadn't been dressed for dinner.

The reason for the extra noise was made apparent as she entered the room. John guffawed loudly alongside another fellow who was vaguely familiar to Saffron. Upon her entrance, the man's eyes shot to her, and he grinned. Recognition struck her, and along with it came a hot burst of annoyance.

She did her best to hide it as he approached. "Justin Thorgoode," she said, offering her hand.

He bowed over it, his overlong dark blond hair flopping onto his forehead. He straightened up. "It's Whitley now, I'm afraid."

"Oh," Saffron said, her eyes questing to John's. He shrugged, still grinning.

"No need to be sorry, the old Baron Whitley was some distant relation who had the misfortune of dying with only me as heir," Justin said.

Considering Saffron had made mud pies with Justin as a young girl before he and his family had moved away, she couldn't refer to him in her own mind with his new title. Two years her senior, he was still boyish and blond and had a bright, lopsided smile that brightened his rather heavy features. A quick survey of his person indicated he'd not suffered any significant bodily losses in the war.

"It is good to see you after all this time," she ventured.

"Indeed," he said, beaming. "You've quite grown up! Nice to replace memories of a muddy little thing with something as dazzling as this." He nodded down her body.

That was an exceedingly clumsy compliment—or a very forward proposition, considering they stood surrounded by her family. She ignored it. "Have you moved back to Bedford?"

"Gads, no." He guffawed, and John smirked. She shot him a repressive glare, and he only wiggled his eyebrows as he took another drink. "I was passing through, staying with some friends, and was summoned here." He winked at her. "I suppose Lady Easting caught wind of me nearby. I couldn't very well say no! Now I'm quite glad I didn't attempt to. The Everleighs were always some of my favorite people."

"More like we serve some of your favorite booze," John muttered, earning a humorous look from Justin.

They stifled their laughter as Lady Easting approached. She wore a gracious expression and cast Justin a warm look before saying to Saffron, "I'm glad you've finally made it down to greet your old friend. How pleasant it is, Whitley, to welcome you back to Ellington."

Justin bowed to her. "Very pleased to be back, my lady."

Lady Easting dropped her voice somewhat. "We are about to go in to dinner. If you wouldn't mind escorting my Saffron, that would be much appreciated. I know John wishes to spend some time with his aunt since he is visiting for such a short time."

This looked to be news to John, but both men agreed readily. Saffron scanned the room, attempting to tally their numbers. Suzette spoke to Father Leavenworth, whom Saffron guessed was there to make up numbers. Lord Easting sat next to the fire with Saffron's mother. He and Violet weren't speaking, but they looked companionable. Elizabeth and Alexander stood together in a corner, and from their serious expressions, Saffron guessed they were discussing what they'd uncovered.

Kirby stepped into the room a moment later to announce dinner, and Justin offered Saffron his arm and escorted her from the room.

The dining room was replete with soft golden light and the warmth of the massive hearth that lined one side of the green-papered room. She settled next to Justin, who was next to her grandmother at the foot of the table, certainly not the usual arrangement, since Justin was now titled and was therefore a guest of some standing.

It took only a moment to see why Lady Easting had arranged the table in that way, however, as a moment after Saffron had settled into her chair, Alexander sat across from Justin, and on her grandmother's other side.

Her beau, a childhood acquaintance who happened to be recently elevated to the peerage, and her grandmother. What could go wrong?

• • •

The soup course began with a pleasant surprise: Justin inquired after her studies with all appearances of genuine interest.

Saffron responded with a general sketch of her work at the university, all too aware of her grandmother sitting on his other side, speaking with Alexander.

"You are employed by University College London, I understand," her grandmother was saying.

"Yes, your ladyship," Alexander replied.

"And what do you do there?"

"I research bacteria," was Alexander's succinct reply.

Would Lady Easting prefer that sort of reply, the kind that did not elaborate on a topic most would consider inappropriate for mealtime conversation? Or would she perceive it as rude, that he did not offer a meatier response?

"My granddaughter mentioned you have collaborated. Is there some connection between bacteria and plants? I'm afraid my education in the sciences was very limited, Mr. Ashton."

Saffron stilled. Elizabeth, on Alexander's other side, shot her a significant look. They knew that comment for the trap that it was. Lady Easting's son had been a plant pathologist, whose main concern was diseases and their harmful effects on plants. Though Saffron had rarely heard Thomas

268

discuss his work with the lord and lady of the house, it would have been foolish to assume Lady Easting knew nothing of it.

Alexander was slow to respond, but his thoughtful frown at least made it clear the delay was a contemplative one. "I'm not sure what you mean, Lady Easting."

Saffron glanced past Justin to her grandmother. She was frowning. Displeased her question was not understood, or displeased Alexander was sidestepping her trap?

"I seek only to discover how a bacteriologist—that is the correct term, I hope?—has had reason to collaborate with my granddaughter. I am given to understand that she studies plants of tropical origin." She set her spoon down, her eyes flicking down the table. Saffron hurriedly took a sip of her wine to disguise her eavesdropping. "Perhaps there is an overlap that a greater understanding of the sciences would make plain."

The wine caught in Saffron's throat. She pressed her napkin to her mouth and managed not to choke.

Alexander's reply came after another circumspect pause. "I'm fortunate to have a degree of latitude with my work, your ladyship. During a recent expedition to the Amazonian rainforest, I was tasked with collecting some botanical samples, and upon my return to England, I had the opportunity to learn more thanks to Miss

Everleigh." He nodded in Saffron's direction.

She looked quickly away so her grandmother wouldn't notice her watching him. She heard the rest of his reply, however, his low voice still perfectly clear.

"With scientific discoveries being made day by day, there are new connections between fields of knowledge being discovered and investigated constantly. Even those at the heart of an academic community often find their knowledge obsolete within a few years."

She could not have designed a better response. Humble but acknowledging his ability, praising Saffron without being sappy, and refuting Lady Easting's claim of lack of knowledge with finesse. Saffron could have kissed him, and, in fact, made a mental note to do so later.

Lady Easting's expression was blank as she nodded to Kirby, and the footmen began to clear the dishes for the next course.

CHAPTER 28

With the fish and the shift of conversation partners came Lady Easting's next volley.

"And how is the timber mill coming along, Whitley?" Lady Easting asked rather more loudly than necessary.

Saffron paused with her forkful of haddock halfway to her mouth, curious despite herself.

It was then that Father Leavenworth seemed to recall he was meant to be speaking to her. In his scratchy voice, he said, "It's been a very long time since I've seen you at the church, Miss Saffron."

On her other side, Justin said, "How kind of you to ask after the development of my recently inherited land, my lady. The mill should be ready come summer for the first harvest of wood."

"I encourage you to consult Lord Easting regarding the latest in market strategies. Saffron is not the only one keen on the agricultural world, you know."

Unable to resist, Saffron shot her grandmother an incredulous look.

Lady Easting patted her mouth with her napkin and offered Saffron a serene smile. To Justin, she added, "Though Saffron's education would likely

271

add much to the conversation. She has been so dedicated to her studies. If your schedule allows for it, perhaps tomorrow the three of you might discuss your plans for your land."

"It is terribly important," the vicar continued, unbothered by Saffron's lack of response, "to one's everlasting soul that one attends regular services to receive the edification that the good book offers. Do you not agree?"

In the corner of her eye, Justin bobbled his head in an eager nod to Lady Easting's suggestion.

"Miss Saffron?" Father Leavenworth set his fork down and peered at her. "Do you not agree?"

"Oh, absolutely," she said immediately, unclear what, precisely, she was agreeing to.

"In this day and age," Lady Easting said, her voice the tiniest bit louder so it carried down the table, "one cannot be too circumspect with one's responsibilities. You've inherited a wealth of rich land, and a stalwart title steeped in history. But you now also bear the duty to bring the management of that land into the present to benefit your tenants and their families. Duty and innovation in one. Very admirable, indeed."

"Then I will see you on Sunday," the vicar told Saffron, resuming his meal with satisfaction.

When it came Alexander's turn once more for Lady Easting's attention, she said, "Baron Whitley comes from an old Bedfordshire family, much like the Everleighs. His grandmother and I were good friends, and Mrs. Everleigh spent a good deal of time with Mrs. Thorgoode, especially when their children were young. He and Saffron were constant companions for many years."

Elizabeth saw fit to interject, "The Thorgoodes were always good fun. It was very sad when Justin—beg pardon, *Baron Whitley*—moved away at the age of seven. It was a loss to the neighborhood, I assure you."

Saffron momentarily wondered if this was a comment borne of wine consumption, belatedly remembering to watch for her friend overimbibing, but found Elizabeth's glass of Sauvignon Blanc almost untouched before her.

Alexander's response was brief. "Loss of a childhood friend is always difficult."

Justin leaned toward Saffron, his voice low. "I heard there's a bit of a fuss over a spiritualist in residence over at the Hale house. Conjured up all sorts of spirits, has she?"

Across the table, Elizabeth snorted. Justin was easy to overhear, it seemed. "The only thing the woman has conjured up is trouble for the villagers. She's got her assistant roaming the village cemetery, goading the villagers into paying her to summon the spirits of the people he finds under the dirt."

Wine, it seemed, was not necessary for Elizabeth to make outrageous statements. On the other side of John, Violet blanched.

It might have also been the increasing fervor of the conversation between John and Lord Easting that had upset her.

John looked like he held onto his temper by his fingernails. His lips were stretched into a strained smile. "Come now, Grandfather, one can't be expected to make journeys all over with a small child in tow," he was saying.

"Leave him here, then, for a few years," Lord Easting said, not removing his attention from his meal. "The boy needs to develop an understanding of the place he's one day to inherit."

John sent a wary look across the table to Suzette. Saffron wished she could see her reaction.

"You lived here months at a time, didn't you? Much good it did you," Lord Easting went on. "Some have a care for family duty. I'm sure it's possible the boy will, even if his father doesn't."

John colored. "One doesn't have to be at Ellington constantly to understand the business of it."

"It certainly helps. We spent more time yesterday discussing business than we have in a year's worth of letters. You're allowed to travel about without your wife and child. Some prefer it."

Violet said, "It can be a burden to leave one's family."

Lord Easting scoffed, but Violet continued, "Thomas often complained when he was far from Ellington when he was teaching."

"He could have easily remedied that," Lord Easting said irritably. "And that was different. Thomas spent most of his time here. John hasn't set foot in England since 1915. Much good it has done him."

Even from halfway down the table, Saffron could see how John's jaw worked. "A wife and children are plenty good enough for me. Not to mention a successful career."

"Career," repeated Lord Easting disdainfully.

"Yes, a career," John snapped.

By now, the rest of the table had quieted.

"A career which I built myself," John continued. "One that is meaningful and serves the people."

"You think feeding people isn't important?" Lord Easting's color rose, staining his pale cheeks red. "Providing arable land and machines and employment for a hundred people isn't enough for you?" He jabbed a finger onto the tabletop. "And the village? I suppose you think sustaining an entire community—"

"Have you learned nothing from the last ten years?" John interrupted. "Inheritance and family name mean nothing when half the male population has been wiped out, not to mention owning farmland is more like a millstone hanging about one's neck!" He nodded down the table. "You think Whitley is reveling in his new title? He's been saddled with failing lands and debt up to his ears."

"Oh, I say," Justin stammered as attention swung around to him. "Quite uncalled for. The timber mill will fix us up in a hurry."

"Times have changed," John said. No trace of his usual humor was left. "Things are different now. We're better off with our *careers* than we would be stuck managing a place like this. Twenty years from now—"

He cut off with a strange movement, almost as if he were reaching out toward Lord Easting. The flush building in Lord Easting's complexion had drained away. His hands were gripping the end of the table, his hands so white Saffron could see them from where she sat.

Lady Easting stood abruptly. All eyes flew to her. "I believe it is time for coffee."

The meal was barely half-finished, but no one saw fit to disagree.

CHAPTER 29

The dinner party broke up soon after the coffee cart was rolled into the parlor. The coffee, brewed hastily and nearly tasteless, had not been bad enough to dissolve the party, but the tense atmosphere was, despite the good humor put forth by Justin and Elizabeth. John and Suzette had disappeared between the dining room and the drawing room. Lady Easting spoke in undertones to Violet, and both slipped from the room.

When the guests had departed, Justin with promises to call the next day that Saffron didn't bother to discourage, Saffron told Alexander and Elizabeth that she would meet them bright and early to discuss what to do next regarding the search for Bill's information. Her head was aching, but she felt she had to check on her grandfather considering Bill was no doubt tending him.

She knocked on her grandfather's door. Her grandmother answered, and after staring at her for a full second, she directed her to her own rooms instead.

"I wanted to ask after Grandpapa," Saffron whispered when Lady Easting opened the door and Saffron stepped inside.

The room was very warm, with a blazing fire

in the hearth and an electric radiator near the window. The delicate floral patterns on the cream walls and silk brocade furniture were unchanged from last Saffron remembered being invited into this room. She used to be summoned there to account for her misbehavior as a girl, and then when she'd been away at school, to report on her accomplishments and failings.

"It was so good to see Justin Thorgoode again, was it not?" Lady Easting asked as she settled on the settee opposite Saffron. "He has grown into such an agreeable young man. And one with such prospects."

"It was good to see him." Saffron glanced between her grandmother and the door Saffron knew connected her grandmother's rooms to her grandfather's. "Can I not peek in and tell Grand-papa goodnight? I know he was feeling poorly at dinner."

"No. He has been upset quite enough this evening."

"I haven't done anything to upset him." Even to her own ears, she sounded petulant. "I promise I won't mention anything about John."

"Why would you?" Lady Easting asked dis-missively.

"Well, because he's right," Saffron said. "Times have changed. And it's quite within John's right to decide where he prefers to raise his child and how he wants to make a living."

"He doesn't have to make a living. He has one. I cannot understand why you and your cousin refuse the boon you have been given."

Saffron refused to go near that land mine of a comment. "I would like to see Grandpapa."

"You will be better served by getting a full night's rest after your busy day," her grandmother replied. "What were you doing today?"

Saffron sipped her tea. She hadn't had the chance to ask what exactly Elizabeth had said about her and Alexander's absence. "I was mostly in the library."

Lady Easting tutted. "Do you not have enough of books in London?"

"No," Saffron said flatly. "Did you not praise my education earlier this evening? Or is it only acceptable when a man might be interested in my particular brand of knowledge?"

"Don't be crass, Saffron."

"It was crass, Grandmama," she said, her temper flaring like kindling catching, fast and hot. "It was painfully obvious what you were doing, inviting Justin Thorgoode here. You know that Alexander and I are a couple, yet you brought in my 'old childhood friend' who just happened to have recently inherited a title? You might as well have invited Mr. Roddingham so you might humiliate Elizabeth, too!"

"Roddingham died last year."

Saffron jumped. Her grandfather stood in the

doorway. His dinner jacket was gone, as was his collar, and he was wrapped in a heavy dressing gown of quilted silk. His color had improved, but he looked cross.

"Well, I—I didn't know that, obviously," she said lamely.

Her grandfather walked into the room and sank into the armchair between her and her grandmother. She was glad he was well enough to be up and moving, but that only encouraged her to speak her mind to the both of them.

"I don't understand why you invited Justin when I have told you, quite plainly in word and action, that I have no interest in returning to this sort of life. And Justin doesn't even live in Bedford!" She leaned forward, trying to catch either of her grandparents' eyes. "I have a life, a good one, in London. I have meaningful employment, friends, and—"

Lady Easting's lips twisted. "If you include Mr. Ashton on that list—"

"I do," Saffron burst out, face hot.

"—then you do *not* understand why I asked Baron Whitley here. You are still looking through the world with the eyes of a child. An idealistic child, one who refuses to see anything beyond what she finds diverting for the moment. The reality is that you are aging past the ability to make a good match—"

Saffron was on her feet before she realized it.

"I do not want a good match. I do not want a match that is safe and satisfactory for all families involved. I want—" She shook her head, unable to articulate all it was that Alexander offered her. How could they understand the value of his determination to better himself, or the subtle, endearing affection he showed her? She did think they might appreciate his keen mind and calm competence, but she didn't believe they deserved any further explanation.

She drew herself up, determined to finish this conversation with composure. "I don't see why you bothered to summon me home if you were only going to insult my choices and try to rope me into a life I have made clear I do not want."

Her grandparents' matching frowns deepened in concert with each other. Lady Easting said, "No one summoned you here. Word simply came that you were coming."

"Word came—?"

"I have no interest in belaboring topics that don't deserve the attention," Lady Easting said. "You are welcome to take your leave, if you are unsatisfied with your reception here."

With the rancor glaring at her from her grandmother's eyes, it was powerfully tempting to do just that. "I can't."

Lady Easting's nostrils flared. "And may I ask why not?"

"You know why not," Saffron said. She

addressed her grandfather. "I do not trust Dr. Wyatt, and I feel I must stay here while he is caring for you."

"I told you not to upset your grandfather with this nonsense," Lady Easting snapped.

Lord Easting glared at his wife. "I'm not some delicate flower, Evelyn! Saffron, you tell me what you're on about."

"The doctor is an impostor," Saffron said. "My friend Dr. Michael Lee is familiar with him and told me before I came here that he ought to be turned out of the house. Dr. Wyatt is not who he says he is."

Her grandfather harrumphed. "Nonsense. Dr. Wyatt is a physician from Oxford. He comes highly recommended." He squinted at her, then at her grandmother. "Enough of this now, this *managing*. I'm not on my deathbed, nor am I a boy! I don't need protection, not the least from women."

The look on Lady Easting's face put a chill in Saffron's bones, but for once she was quite glad to see it, considering the women in her family were running his estate while he was ill.

Somewhat desperate now, she said, "Grandpapa, Dr. Wyatt is a fraud, same as that woman the Hales have hired pretending to channel spirits."

"Then why has he not asked for money? If he were a confidence trickster, wouldn't he ask for money upfront and then disappear? Or sneak the silver out each night at dinner?"

"He wants something other than money."

Her grandmother asked, "Such as?"

Saffron swallowed. "Just . . . something else. I don't trust him." She wished that would be enough.

It wasn't, of course. Her grandparents exchanged a look that told her this was an exercise in frustration.

She straightened up, pressing her hands to her middle where emotion raged in tidal waves. Her attempts to mend bridges and protect her family were a failure.

"If you will not trust me about this, then I hope you will at least take precautions. Summon another doctor to confirm Dr. Wyatt's course of treatment. Despite our differences, Grandpapa, I want nothing but a swift recovery for you." His stony features blurred as some of the upheaved emotions crashed against her eyes. "Goodnight."

CHAPTER 30

Saffron's head throbbed as she carefully pressed shut the door to her grandmother's rooms. She wasn't going to slam the door, no matter how much she would like to. Her hands remained pressed against the cool wood for a long moment, her head bowed and chest aching with each tight breath. She'd failed so many times today.

But there was still so much to do. Bill wouldn't care her evening had been an utter disaster. She had to find what he was after and manage to keep it from him.

All the papers she'd collected were in her bedroom, and she'd work into the night to discover what she could. There had to be something buried in the layers of correspondence and record-keeping.

A maid startled her as she rounded the corner to the family hall. Both she and the girl jumped.

Saffron pressed a hand to her pounding heart. "I'm sorry, I didn't see you there."

"Beg pardon, miss," the girl said, face to the floor as she bobbed a curtsy.

"Since you're here," Saffron said, "would you search me out a headache powder? I'm sure Mrs. Sharnbrook has some."

The maid nodded and scurried off. At least a headache was a problem that could be solved easily.

Ten minutes later, she'd replaced her gown and heels with a dressing gown and slippers and drunk the powder in cool water from the pitcher the maid brought in. All the papers were spread out on her bed. She had her notebook and pen ready.

And the moment she picked up one of the papers, an overwhelming sense of impossibility overtook her. What if these papers didn't hold any answers, but more questions? What if she'd wasted a precious day of her dwindling deadline?

Her breath became hot and tight, her lungs not quite working properly. She couldn't do this, not by herself. She needed help.

Saffron knocked on Alexander's door, counting slowly to ten, when she would give up and return to her own room. After all that had transpired that evening, it was downright foolish to go to his door, but her head was in such a jumble and the pressure of Bill's deadline only sent her thoughts into further chaos. She needed Alexander's brilliance to help her get through the papers with all speed, and she needed his steadiness to get her through the night without losing her mind.

The door cracked open a few inches, then

swung back on silent hinges. Alexander blinked at her. "Saffron . . . You should go back to your room."

"We need to talk," she whispered.

"It's late," he said, "and need I mention you're in your pajamas?"

She ought to have changed out of her colorful paisley dressing gown, but she'd been too frazzled. "I'm also standing in the hallway. May I come in?" Alexander hesitated for long enough that she was hurt. Her face flamed. "I'm sorry, I've interrupted you. Goodnight."

He stepped forward as she turned to leave. "No . . . Come in, then."

She took a few steps inside the room, unsurprised that it looked all but vacant. The only sign of Alexander's occupation was the slight dent in the bed's coverlet from where he'd likely been sitting.

He closed the door with a quiet snick, and she turned back to him to explain they needed to reexamine the papers now.

He'd removed his jacket and tie and left his shirt open a few buttons, revealing the strong column of his throat. His features were perfectly suited for the dim glow of the lamps; it made his olive skin gold and his eyes depthless. She didn't realize she was staring until he cleared his throat meaningfully.

"With everything going on, I felt it was better

we speak privately, with less possibility of being overheard." She glanced around the room. The fire was banked already, and there was no chair before it to sit in anyway. She perched on the foot of the bed.

"Saffron."

She jumped at the harsh crack of his low voice. "What is it?"

"I don't . . ." He blew out a frustrated breath. "As much as I would like to *speak privately,* this is not the right time."

Something about the way he said it was different than his usual straightforward tone. "But I—"

Alexander ran a hand through his hair, then over his face. "This is not the time. Not for you to be in here."

"Fine, then come back to my room."

Incredulity swept over his face, leaving his mouth hanging open for a moment before he hissed, "Go back to your bedroom with you? Are you mad?"

"I want to figure out—"

"I have no interest in ruining my chances with you over a few exciting moments together." Ruddy color bloomed across his cheekbones. "You may think we are not a perfect match, but I think we are. I intend to do things with you the right way."

She stared at him, too surprised and perplexed

to do more for several heartbeats. His dark gaze didn't waver, and, after far too long, she finally realized what he meant. "You overheard my argument with my grandparents."

"They invited another man here, intending for him to capture your interest. I cannot ignore that." He exhaled, nostrils flaring as he looked away. "You told them you didn't want a perfect match. I am no longer too proud to admit it upsets me. We are not compatible in the ways your family might want, but—"

"We are." She stood, feeling a little unsteady. He didn't move away when she approached him. "We are compatible in every way that matters. I don't care for *their* idea of a perfect match, Alexander. I want this one. Us."

She lifted her mouth to his and, to her relief, he responded with fervor. The kiss was a continuation of the argument Alexander was trying to have. One of his hands fisted in her hair, another gathered her to him. It was a very good thing he held her so tightly, for she felt like she was melting. Light-headed, she sighed when his mouth left hers and trailed to the particular spot behind her ear he'd all but declared his own.

She tried to cling to him, for she felt like she'd be a puddle on the floor in a moment, but his lips on her skin made her weak all over. In a world of chaos and danger, even in the midst of what was clearly a misunderstanding on his part of why she'd come to his door, Alexander made her feel right, safe.

It was that feeling that cradled her as all thought and sensation faded from her mind.

CHAPTER 31

Alexander was being a hypocrite again. He'd told Saffron to leave, told her this wasn't the time or place for this. Not with her family just down the hall and jealousy darkening his emotions, not with his newly accelerated plans, but damn it all if she didn't *enflame* him so easily—

He paused, nose buried in the dark curls just behind her ear. Her arms had gone slack about his neck. He whispered her name, but she was silent, completely pliant in his arms.

He tipped her back, still cradling her head in one hand. Her eyes were closed, rosy lips parted. He was no expert, but he was quite sure his attentions weren't so boring as to put Saffron to sleep. Nonplussed, he whispered her name again.

She didn't respond. Alarmed, he carefully walked her backward to the bed and laid her down. He leaned over her, patting her cheek, first softly and then a light slap. "Saffron!"

She didn't stir. His head spun. One moment she was fine, responding with her usual enthusiasm. The next she was asleep. He tried patting her cheek again, lifting her eyelids, and even lifting her against his chest so she was upright. She was lifeless but for the faint tickle of her breath on his cheek. What was wrong with her?

He needed help, and perhaps equally importantly, he needed to get her help not in his bedroom.

Alexander lifted Saffron in his arms and went to the door, opening it half an inch and peering outside into the darkness. He saw nothing but a circle of lamplight where the guest wing met the gallery. He couldn't hear anything but his heartbeat loud in his ears.

When he felt he could wait no longer, he nudged the door open. When he saw no one, he took off down the hall. He managed near silence without his shoes, for which he was abundantly grateful when he passed through the gallery and next to the master suite where Lord and Lady Easting were hopefully asleep. Saffron's door was blessedly unlocked.

He arrowed for the bed. There were papers scattered across the surface, and he swept them aside to make room for her. And when he lay her down on the canopied four poster, he felt he could breathe again. Saffron's scent permeated the air, flowers and old books, uniquely hers and perfect.

He took another steadying breath, only to catch a whiff of something distinctly not Saffron, and distinctly alarming.

A quick search of the hearth and sources of light around the room revealed nothing. The offensive odor grew stronger as he neared a door with light shining under it. Heart in his throat, Alexander grabbed the door handle and pushed.

Alexander hadn't expected the door to open, and nearly fell into the next room.

"Well, hello there."

He recovered his stumble and swung around to where Elizabeth sat at the fire in a dim room that mirrored the one he'd just left, a short taper of incense in her hand. Swirls of smoke twirled through the air next to her face, which was delighted. "If you're looking for your beloved, you've come to the wrong room, darling."

"What are you doing with that incense?" Alexander demanded.

"Found it in Saffron's things, thought I'd test it out," Elizabeth said, waving the thing around.

"Put it out."

She narrowed her eyes. "No."

"Damn it, Elizabeth, put it out," he ground out, hands fisting at his sides. "Saffron just collapsed in my bedroom."

"Oh, my." She dunked the incense in a tumbler of half-melted ice and followed him into Saffron's bedroom. "When exactly did she collapse?"

"Five minutes ago."

She shot him a suspicious look as she

approached the bed. "Why did you wait so long to bring her in here?"

"I had to ensure no one saw me carrying the unconscious daughter of the house from my bedroom," he said tightly.

"Fair enough." Elizabeth crawled onto the bed and prodded at Saffron, who didn't stir, not even when she lifted her eyelids. "She's breathing, at least."

She sat frowning at Saffron for a moment before saying, "Well, it wasn't the incense."

"You can't know that for certain," he said.

"I can, mostly because I only lit the stick about a minute ago."

"Why exactly would you do that? What if the smoke had infiltrated the whole house? What if Benjamin inhaled it?" His insides, which had relaxed somewhat after settling Saffron in her own room, wound up tighter as more questions spilled from his lips. "What good would it do to inhale the stuff again yourself? As someone who once used dangerous substances to dull pain, it will not help you. It is reckless, especially when you know the danger we all face here."

Further stoking his ire, Elizabeth rolled her eyes. "Oh, do shut up, Alexander. You fell in love with a girl who poisoned herself practically the third time you spoke to her. You pretend at being this serious, studious dullard, Alexander Ashton, but you crave adventure. You *long* for it. Why else would you go off on all those expeditions? Why else would you put up with Saffron and her manic desire to help solve crimes?" Her amusement faded. "And do not pretend that you understand what I have been through. Our hurts are not the same, even if we tried a similar bandage to heal them.

"And besides all that"—she sniffed, then grimaced at the too-sweet smell that had invaded the room—"this smoke did nothing more than irritate my sinuses. We're both still wholly ourselves, are we not? The incense is not the source of whatever Madame Martin uses to drug her clients." Her eyes lit on something across the room. "Nor do I think that's what has gotten Saff this way."

She strode to the dressing table, where a pitcher of water sat next to an empty glass speckled with water droplets. A paper wrapper sat next to it.

Elizabeth dabbed her finger onto the wrapper and tasted it. She grimaced. "That is Askit. Saffron did look rather poorly before she came up to bed." She smelled the pitcher, then splashed some into the glass and sipped. She looked thoughtfully at it, then held it up for Alexander. He took it and sniffed.

"Veronal." He looked at Saffron's supine form, then back at Elizabeth. "She doesn't take it, does she?"

"Never," she confirmed.

"Someone drugged her water."

"Madame Martin had no reason to, nor any opportunity. It's clearly not the same thing she uses anyway."

"No, not Madame. This is most certainly Bill." He looked around the room, straining to come up with why Bill would drug Saffron now. His eyes lit on the mass of papers he'd shoved to the far side of the bed.

Now he looked at them, he recognized them as the contents of Ferrand's file and the papers Saffron had taken from Kew.

Guilt and regret gnarled together in his chest. *That* was why Saffron wanted him in her bedroom, to go through the papers again. He'd known Lady Easting's game from the moment he caught sight of Baron Whitley in the drawing room, but he'd allowed his temper to be roused, nonetheless. He shuffled the papers together into some sort of order, thinking furiously.

"Bill wanted to find out what we'd learned while we were out," he said. "That's why he drugged her. To get a chance to see if we'd returned with his information."

"Did you learn anything in London?" Elizabeth asked.

"Not nearly enough. But these papers are a start." He told her about Petrov and the unpublished paper he'd written with Thomas Everleigh.

"Will you take some of the papers to look through?" Alexander asked her.

Her thin brows arched. "Me?"

"Yes," he said. "Anything related to Petrov, anything that sounds like it could be dangerous. Saffron was planning to go through them tonight." Before she was drugged and he shouted at her for doing nothing more than asking for help. "We'll share anything noteworthy in the morning. We have to figure this out. There's only a few days left before Bill's deadline."

For the first time since meeting Elizabeth, her cloak of self-assurance slipped away, leaving her looking earnest and a little frightened. "I'll go through them now. Can't be any duller than listening to my mother natter on about the wonders of Madame yet again." She attempted a smile. "Don't worry, I'll keep an eye on Saffron."

He nodded, but he knew his expression was bleak.

Elizabeth put a hand on his shoulder and squeezed. "It will be all right, Alexander. If I know anything about Saffron, it's that she had an uncanny ability to survive the unexpected. A little Veronal won't keep her down for long. And neither will Bill."

CHAPTER 32

Alexander rose from his perch on the bed and stretched. He caught sight of his reflection in the wardrobe mirror and frowned at the scruffy and disordered version of himself. It was probably time to sleep.

It was nearly two in the morning, and Saffron needed him to be focused and aware tomorrow since she likely would not be. He had used sleeping aides like chloral hydrate and barbiturates like Veronal when he'd suffered insomnia after the war, and they always left him foggy the next day. He'd already be dulled with exhaustion tomorrow after spending the last four hours combing through Thomas Everleigh's correspondence.

Equipment request forms and recommendation letters for students swam in his head as he discarded his clothing. He settled on the floor for meditation and began to release his concerns one by one with each breath. There were an awful lot today.

He'd just let go of the image of Bill looming behind Lord Easting when a vibration in the floor under him caught his attention. Footsteps?

It was far too late for anyone to reasonably be

up and moving through the hallway. Alexander immediately rose to his feet and tugged his shirt and trousers back on. He dimmed his solitary lamp and opened the door silently. He slipped through the doorway and began walking noiselessly down the hall in the direction of the footsteps.

Movement ahead of him made him freeze. He stepped swiftly to the side of the hall, eyes trained ahead.

A maid in a neat black uniform with a white apron, her light hair partially covered in a cap, came to a halt outside Saffron's door. Her back was to Alexander, and the darkness made it impossible to see much else. She paused before raising her hand to the handle and trying to open the door. She carefully brought a set of keys from her apron pocket and selected one, slipping it into the lock. The door appeared to be immovable, however. The maid pushed against the door with increasing agitation to no avail. A moment later, she turned from the door and continued down the hall and around the corner, out of sight.

Alexander waited several minutes before moving to ensure the maid wouldn't return. He gently tapped on Elizabeth's door, then when she didn't answer, Saffron's door, calling to Elizabeth as quietly as possible.

"Alexander?" came Elizabeth's voice from the other side.

"Yes," he breathed.

"Go back to my room," Elizabeth directed.

"Wait, relock the door first."

When he heard the lock click back into place, he moved a few paces back down the hall to Elizabeth's door, which she cracked open slightly and peered out.

"Oh, good, it is you," she said with a sigh. She stepped back and Alexander stepped inside the room just enough for her to shut the door behind her. "What's going on? Surely that wasn't you trying to get in just now?"

"It was a maid."

Elizabeth's unmade-up face frowned. The effect was lessened by her lack of eyebrows. "A maid at this hour? Highly unlikely. Please tell me it was Bill in a maid's uniform!"

Alexander smiled wryly. "I don't think so. All I could see was a uniform and fair hair from where I was."

"How unfortunate. I suppose we can't even trust the servants now." Elizabeth looked thoughtful. "I don't know how he could pull any of this off without them, actually. He must have some source of information within the house, someone to tell him the comings and goings of everyone. A maid could have easily drugged the water; Saffron wouldn't think twice about the pitcher left on her desk. I wouldn't have. And the maid could have a reason to come into her room in the middle of the night. She could pretend Saffron rung for her."

"She must have come for the papers. Dinner concluded well before it normally would have and Bill must have missed his chance to look them over."

"I'll stash the papers somewhere safe, just in case they attempt to snoop again. You do the same." She tapped her long red fingernails on the door. "Now, back to bed before anyone catches us and thinks we're cavorting."

Alexander turned to leave, then paused. "What did you do to the door? The maid couldn't make it budge."

Elizabeth grinned. "I mastered a technique of jamming little wedges of wood along the bottom of the door to keep my brothers and parents out of my room when I was an adolescent. I was forever in need of more privacy. I found the ones I gave Saffron in a drawer."

Alexander bade her goodnight and returned to his room. He paced the dark room for a long time before settling before the banked fire to attempt his meditation again. Even as he sought to push thought and feeling from his body with each breath, he doubted that anything he did could settle his mind tonight.

Waking was like pushing upward as if out of deep water. Saffron's head was ten pounds too heavy. Her bleary eyes blinked against a vague, too-bright light.

A strident voice prodded her into fuller consciousness. "Come now, darling, it's been hours. You've slept it off by now."

"Eliza . . ." She swallowed against a dry throat. "Why do I feel as if I've eaten a bucket of belladonna berries?"

Elizabeth's face came into focus, illuminated by painfully bright light from between the open drapes. "Bill had a maid drug your water last night. You've been asleep for hours."

"Oh, but the papers!" She sat up suddenly, her head revolting against that brash decision. When her head stopped spinning, she gazed around.

"Alexander took some to read over, and I've got the rest." Elizabeth ducked into her room. A moment later, she returned with a stack of papers. "Dreadfully boring stuff. But I did find something interesting, though I think you ought to have some coffee or something before I tell you."

She rang the bell and stuffed the papers under a pillow before sitting back down in her chair.

"By the way, darling, I'm afraid Bill not only ruined your reading plans, but something that looked remarkably like a seduction. Alexander looked rather put out that you'd fallen asleep."

Saffron looked up from the tangle of bedclothes she was trying to remove herself from. "What are you talking about?"

301

"You, in your dressing gown, apparently in his bedroom?" Her lascivious grin faded. "You ought to ask him about it, if you don't remember. Might be important. It's almost lunchtime, by the way, so get a wriggle on dressing while the coffee comes and we'll go down. I'm starving."

Half an hour, a dose of cold water, and a pot of coffee later, Saffron was feeling as awake as ever.

"I suppose sleeping for fourteen hours will do that to you," Saffron said as she and Elizabeth walked down the stairs. "What did you tell them I was doing?"

"Well, you missed Justin calling on you. I told your mother you were indisposed when she came to see if you'd see him. She recommended a warm bath and offered a tisane of motherwort, which, quite frankly, sounds dreadful. I imagine Lady E is rather peeved you missed the baron's visit."

Motherwort reminded Saffron of all the hours she'd spent researching folk remedies in order to discover what herbs Petrov had been taking. "It's been used as an herbal remedy for centuries," Saffron said absently. Something tickled her mind.

Motherwort was a mint, if memory served. Many herbs were included in that family, including germander, the species Savita had identified from Petrov's flat. There was something there, something just elusive enough to be maddening.

Saffron and Elizabeth reached the bottom of the stairs at the same time that Alexander emerged from the reception room.

"How are you feeling?" he asked Saffron.

"Well enough," she replied. "Were you using the telephone?"

"I was. Let's talk."

Alexander led them to the conservatory. The glass panes showed a sky filled with heavy clouds that promised more precipitation, but within it was warm and colorful. Saffron opened the little receptacle containing gardening implements and donned a pair of gloves. Tending to the plants would help soothe her nerves, which Alexander's serious expression promised would be further agitated.

"I telephoned Inspector Green," he began.

"What did you tell him? What did he say?" Saffron asked.

"In November, I asked him if he could find any information regarding Bill. He said he would look into it, but last I checked in with him, he had yet to hear back from one of his sources. The inspector got word yesterday. There is a record of a William Wyatt at Oxford's medical school within the reasonable range of time we could expect Bill to have attended."

Saffron's mouth fell open. "Do you mean to say Bill is actually a physician?"

"It is possible," Alexander allowed. "But when

Inspector Green followed up on the information in the registration records, he found they had been mostly falsified. The parish he provided as the place of his birth had no record of a William Wyatt."

"Did he attend Oxford before or after the war?" asked Elizabeth.

"Before."

Elizabeth's thin brows arched. "If that man is actually called William Wyatt, I'll eat my left shoe."

Saffron and Alexander looked at her in question.

She waved a hand. "You're in a muddy, bloody trench. There is an attack. Chaos ensues. Bodies are dropping left and right."

Next to her, Alexander tensed. Saffron linked her fingers through his and squeezed until he squeezed back.

"My apologies, Alexander, dear, but you know what I'm getting at. How thorough could the recordkeeping truly be in the heat of battle? My guess is this fellow snagged someone else's identification discs and came out of the war with a new name."

"That is possible, but I don't see how it helps us much."

Elizabeth tutted. "It reminds us he is a man, same as anyone else. He's done his best to seem otherwise in order to frighten you."

Unnerved, Saffron knelt and inspected the base of the *Adiantum raddianum* at her side, looking for signs of dryness at the tips of its delicate green fronds. It was perfectly healthy, she found.

"Going through the papers didn't tell me much more than we'd already discovered," Alexander said. "I set a few interesting articles aside, but I don't know how relevant they are."

"I had some luck," Elizabeth reported, "or at least I think so, based on my scant knowledge of botany. Buried in the piles of dreadfully dull stuff were a few sheets of paper scrawled with notes. It looked to be scratch paper one might keep at one's side when typing something on the fly. You know, jotting something down to see if it sounds right, or to double-check your spelling. I'm guessing from the wording that it was about a study proposal—I've read enough drafts of yours to recognize the language, Saff—and there was mention of some word I don't want to venture to pronounce, but it was something like Artemisia, or Aristotle, which made no sense to me in context, of course—"

A light went on in Saffron's head. She jerked upright. "What did you just say?"

"Aristotle, darling," Elizabeth repeated. "Makes no sense to me."

"*Aristolochia*," Saffron breathed. "My father was writing about *Aristolochia*."

CHAPTER 33

S affron pulled book after book from the shelf, anything she could guess would contain any information about the genus *Aristolochia.* The library was silent, apart from the rustling of pages as Elizabeth and Alexander rifled through the books she'd gathered.

The moment her mind had made sense of Elizabeth's attempt at the pronunciation, Saffron heard Bill's voice lamenting Petrov's death: *"I think it a great pity he never found a solution to his* Aristolochia *problem."*

She'd worried so much about all the other things Bill had said that day that she'd never thought about it. But what if he was testing to see if she would react to the mention of the genus to see if she already knew something about it? What if this was what Bill was after?

Saffron knew a little about the family in general—it contained a wealth of interesting plants, including a number that Maxwell had noted in his journals detailing his explorations of Central America in his early days as a botanist. She'd meticulously read through those journals not a year ago, when she'd sought to exonerate him for a poisoning.

Journals. She paused, the cold floor biting her knees where she knelt. Her father's journals were essential. They weren't in his old rooms, but they had to be somewhere. Her family wouldn't have thrown them away. She should have looked for them rather than haring off to London.

Alexander craned his neck around to call to her, "Found it."

Laid open before him was a massive, hand-painted guide that had been a favorite of Saffron's as a child. The book was an exploration of the taxonomy of the Plantae kingdom, and it had taught Saffron the basics of taxonomy and plant identification as a girl. It was several decades out of date at this point, but its colorful images were as vibrant as ever.

They gathered around the book to see a spread of meticulous illustrations detailing pipe-shaped flowers.

"I certainly hope this has no bearing on the present issue." Elizabeth's long fingernail tapped a description nestled among the flowers and leaves. "'*Aristolochia* owes its name to the unique flower shape, said to resemble a birth canal.'"

"*Aristos* means 'best,'" Alexander murmured, his brows knitting, "and the rest . . . My Greek vocabulary regarding this area is limited, but *lochia* refers to childbirth."

"Plants were often named for what the ancients

believed their use was." Saffron stood and began pacing slowly.

Her thoughts went to her mother. She knew that her parents had had an interest in more children. She had no memories of her mother pregnant, but looking back . . . It was possible, likely, even, that Violet had lost at least one child. Had her father been looking for a solution within his area of expertise?

Her insides squirmed with some indefinable emotion. She returned to Elizabeth and Alexander, who were muttering over the *Aristolochia* page.

"I'm rather shocked at the audacity of the author," Elizabeth was saying, scrutinizing the veined folds of the plant's calyx. "I'm all for a naughty metaphor, but my, isn't it a bit vulgar?"

"I think I need to speak to my mother," Saffron said.

They looked up at her, and she attempted a confident smile. "We'll need to see my father's journals, and she's likely the one to know where they are."

She'd already had a terrible row with her grandparents, so what had she to lose?

Violet welcomed Saffron into her parlor with a sympathetic smile.

"Shall I ring for tea?" she asked as she guided Saffron to the couch and settled next to her. She patted her hand. "Your grandmother mentioned the, er, conversation you had last night. It sounded like a difficult one."

"It was not a good talk." As much as she wanted to tell her mother about it and hopefully receive some support, she had to get down to business. "I need to see Papa's journals."

Violet blinked. "But why?"

Perhaps if she was to explain the specific thing she wanted, Violet would be able to tell her which journal to search through. "It's important for my work. Dr. Aster has not been pleased for my ideas for research, and he suggested—"

She withdrew her hand from Saffron's. "I don't—No."

Nonplussed, Saffron repeated, "No?"

"No, the journals are not available. I'm sorry, my darling."

"What do you mean, they're not available?"

"They simply aren't available." Her mother stood, her hands clutching together before her. "Shall we see if Benjamin and Suzette are in the nursery? I know Suzette is disappointed you've been so busy; she was looking forward to spending time with you."

"I will see her later. I need the journals, Mama," Saffron said. "Where are they? Even if they're in the attic, I don't mind a few cobwebs—"

"I—" Her mother's face had gone pale. "I destroyed them."

Though she was sitting still, the world tilted beneath Saffron. "You destroyed them? You— what do you mean, you destroyed them?"

"I burned them," Violet whispered through bloodless lips.

Saffron was on her feet before she knew what she was doing. "You *burned* them?" Her mother looked at her helplessly. Anger flooded her in a dizzying rush. "You burned my father's journals? Where he wrote all his ideas and discoveries? Why on earth would you do that?"

Violet swallowed, looking away. "It seemed like the right thing to do at the time."

The right thing for Violet was the *worst* possible thing for their family. "How could you do that? Now I'll—" She broke off, her lungs so locked up she had no breath to speak.

"You don't need your father's research to be successful," Violet said softly. "You are as brilliant as your father. Moreso, I think."

"There is more value to the journals than that. It is his legacy, Mama. All he was is written into those journals. His passions, and—and obser- vations, his ideas and his research." Her hands flew up in frustration. "I wanted to see those journals for myself, too. Why did you never ask me if I wanted them?"

"It was just after his death; I couldn't ask you something like that."

"Of course, you could have," Saffron said,

dumbfounded. "I would not have fallen apart."

Some color returned to Violet's face. "As I did."

Saffron hung her head. She did not wish to hurt her mother, but at that moment, the desire for answers outweighed her desire to protect her feelings. "You make me feel cruel for even asking to see Papa's old things, things you know he would have wanted me to explore."

"That is not true." Violet immediately looked like she regretted it, for she looked away, eyes glittering with unshed tears. "I have to believe that I am doing what Thomas would have wanted."

Something like a dam inside her burst, and hot frustration poured out. "Papa would not have wanted you trapped here!"

Violet's head jerked back in surprise. "I am not trapped."

"Aren't you? Why else will you not leave the house? Why else have you never come to see me?"

Her mother looked stricken. "Oh, Saffron," she began, but Saffron couldn't bear to discuss her infantile hurt over missing her mother when so much was at stake.

"Lord and Lady Easting lost both of their sons in rapid succession," Violet said softly. "Would you prefer I abandoned them in their grief?"

Anger surged again at the excuse her mother

had created for her grandparents' unfeeling behavior.

Violet held up a hand. "They do not show it in the way that you would prefer. They can be sharp and unforgiving with you and John, and even me. It comes from fear and regret. I believe they think that had they taken Thomas in hand about his studies and his career sooner, they could have convinced him to stay in England. They blame themselves for his loss, and that of your uncle." Her hands twisted in her lap, and she was silent for the long moment during which Saffron tried to assimilate what she'd told her.

"John did not come back from France. You left for London. Neither departure was painless. I suppose you have never considered that I stay at Ellington for them, to give them someone to care for. And care for them in return." There was heartbreak in Violet's voice. "I lost both of my parents just after I married your father. I was nineteen. I had no one else after they died. Your grandmother took me under her wing and taught me all she believed I would one day need to know as her successor. And though she shows it differently than I would have wished, she came to care for me. Both of them did, when they saw I made your father happy." Her voice had thinned to a whisper. "A few months after word came of . . . what happened to Thomas, I began making inquiries in the town nearest your school. Your grandfather told me I ought to stay here." She gave her a wan smile. "Had your grandmother asked, I might have said no to show I'd developed the backbone she'd always insisted I have. But Lord Easting asked me, very kindly, if I would consider staying so they might see you. I couldn't say no. I didn't want to. They have become my own parents, in a way. Ellington is my home. I am not trapped here. I am useful here. As they have aged, Lord and Lady Easting have passed on responsibilities to me. I wonder if they realize they are doing so, sometimes. Mr. Mathers has been gone some months now, and it is I who have been attending to his duties. The ones that can be managed from within the house, that is."

Violet stood and walked to where Saffron was rooted to the ground. Her mother stopped just before her, her gray eyes searching Saffron's. "I won't deny that I face difficulty getting myself through the door, and the prospect of spending my life as your grandmother's sole companion can be unappealing at times. I understand why you must despise my remaining at Ellington. But I do not judge your choices, Saffron, though I sometimes disagree with them. I would ask you to give me the same kindness."

Saffron departed her mother's rooms with burning, ringing ears. Violet was right. She'd long harbored judgment and hurt about her mother's circumstances. Unfortunately, airing that frustration and hearing her mother's explanation did not resolve them, and nor did it solve her problem.

She didn't believe for a moment her mother had destroyed the journals. Her mother had loved Thomas and valued his work as a scientist. She'd often watched him work, even helped him in the greenhouse or in the field, just as Saffron had.

She didn't want Saffron to go through his things. She wanted to keep Thomas Everleigh's memory at rest because it was easier than dealing with her mess of feelings about his death. It was beyond frustrating that her mother's lingering grief prevented her from seeing that.

Saffron went into her bedroom and made for the closet. As she dug through the contents, she made a list of the places the journals could be stashed.

Thomas's old rooms? Checked.

His old offices at the university, his old flat in London—both were occupied by others now, and had been for years.

An old jumper passed through her hands.

Her mother's rooms? She'd seen no sign of journals or instruments or files. She doubted her mother would keep them in a place she would see every day, anyway.

She flung dresses aside.

The library, checked. The steward's office, checked.

She finally found what she was looking for, and tossed the pile on the bed before she tugged off her jumper, dress, and stockings. Her old gardening clothes, a pair of patched, stained trousers and threadbare green jumper, would be perfect for digging around in quite a different place. She was off to the attic.

CHAPTER 34

It had been nearly a decade since Saffron had rooted through the dust-laden wares of the attic. It had been a favorite place to play on rainy days. Its shadows had been full of mystery, the various trunks and armoires and covered paintings promising adventure and treasure.

Saffron stared around the cavernous, dark space, wondering if this could be the same place. There was no promise of anything but becoming filthy.

Lamp lit and in hand, she picked her way across the room, snatching dustcloths off as she went. She didn't want to jump every time furniture dressed as angular ghosts loomed in the corner of her eye.

The search revealed a number of familiar items, like the wardrobe filled with the moth-eaten clothes she and Elizabeth had worn for dress-up games and several items that had once been in her father's old flat in London. He had lived in a flat across from Regent Square while working at the university. Saffron had never been there; it had been let out soon after her father's death.

After opening all the drawers of the flat's

furniture and investigating all the nooks and crannies, she'd found nothing but broken pen tips and a cheap letter opener.

She blew out a breath and propped her hands on her hips to consider the room. Why could there not be a convenient sign indicating the hiding place of her quandary?

A trunk in the farthest corner of the attic caught her eye, large enough for a man's body to fit inside. She dismissed her gruesome imagination as she settled on her knees before it, feeling a strange sense of unreality as she stared down at its worn surface.

It was her father's army trunk. She'd stood atop it to press a kiss to her father's cheek before he left for training.

Scuffed, rusted metal bracketed the corners and was nailed into the edges. The top was curiously not coated in dust. She untucked a few pins from her hair to set to work on the lock, but found it was already unlocked.

A chill ghosted over her skin. She swung the lid open, and though she would not have been able to put to words her suspicion, she knew what she would find within. Or not find.

It took barely a minute to sort through the dozen objects haphazardly strewn through the nearly empty trunk: a creaking leather bandolier with half a dozen pockets, a matching holster with the weapon inside, a ration tin of crumbling cigarettes, a discolored pack of field dressing—

There was no uniform in her father's trunk.

Down three sets of stairs Saffron went, each step matching the determined drumbeat of her heart. Below stairs, servants blinked in surprise as she marched down the narrow passage leading to the warm, cavernous kitchen.

When she emerged into the kitchen, she found the usual swirl of activity had been interrupted. Several people idled, watching the handful of servants clustered together in one corner.

As Saffron drew closer and was able to make out a few words couched in violent sobs, the indignant anger that had fueled her march down into the kitchens faded with each sniffle and wail.

"And I wouldn't—I couldn't—stay in that house one more minute! Not with that w-witch in there with her ghosts and d-devils!"

"You did right, Maisie," said one of the surrounding maids, and Saffron recognized it as the girl who tended the fire in her bedroom, Martha. This must have been her sister. "Come on then, up you get. Let's have a cuppa and we can figure out what to do—"

"What is all this?" asked a sharp voice.

Saffron, and the others in the kitchen, looked around to see a pinch-faced woman, coming down the stairs with pursed lips. Her chatelain jingled with each step. The housekeeper, Saffron guessed.

"It's my sister, Mrs. Sharnbrook!" Martha cried. "That cruel Mrs. Hale tossed her out, dismissed her without recommendation all because she wouldn't clean that witch's room!"

"I can't!" wailed Maisie, eliciting a chorus of sympathetic sounds from the maids, who patted her shoulders. Saffron could see her face was buried in a handkerchief.

Mrs. Sharnbrook's beady eyes didn't soften. "As much as I'm sure you all would like to hear about the dreadful ghosts over at the Hale house and their cruel mistress, we have work to do. Martha, go to find Miss Saffron. His lordship wants to see her in his study."

The servants who had taken note of Saffron's presence swung their eyes around to her. She smiled sheepishly as she raised her hand. "I'm here, Mrs. Sharnbrook."

The housekeeper stared at her. "Whatever are you doing down here, miss?"

"I came in search of you, actually. May I have a word?"

Once seated in Mrs. Sharnbrook's cozy little office, Saffron asked, "Who among the household staff has access to the attic?"

Mrs. Sharnbrook blinked. "You wish to know who has access to the attic?"

"Yes."

With coal-black hair and a pointed beak of a nose, Mrs. Sharnbrook looked as if she'd never done anything without the starch expected of a housekeeper to the upper classes. With stiff dignity, she said, "I have access, though I have never had reason to go up there myself in five years of service at Ellington. Mr. Kirby, of course, has access to every room in the house."

Since Kirby had to be close to seventy years old, not to mention had worked for the Everleigh family since he was a boy, Saffron was confident he was not the one who had stolen her father's army uniform. Mrs. Sharnbrook could be responsible, though a housekeeping position for a lord in a well-funded house would be a foolish thing to risk. Her going up into the attic would be noticed, but she could have easily sent a maid or footman on the errand, sworn to silence by a reward or the promise of punishment. But was it even the right conclusion to draw, that one of the servants had taken her father's uniform for Fischer's use? Did it even matter, really?

This was a poorly thought-out venture, questioning the housekeeper. Still, she was here, and Mrs. Sharnbrook was looking at her with composed expectation. Changing tack, Saffron asked, "What can you tell me about Dr. Wyatt?"

"He is a quiet man who keeps to himself."

Rather as Saffron suspected, really. If the drugged water was anything to go by, Bill had also meddled with Ellington staff. It was likely to be someone he didn't need to seek out, since that would only draw attention. "Has he any regular requests? A fire lit at an unusual time?"

"No, Miss Saffron."

"Any visitors? Telephone calls?"

"Not that I am aware of."

"Who cleans his room?"

With a decidedly patient tone, Mrs. Sharnbrook asked, "May I ask the reason for these questions, Miss Saffron? I assure you all our practices are aboveboard. Lady Easting keeps the highest of standards for the household, ones I am only too happy to uphold."

Instinct told her that the imperturbable Mrs. Sharnbrook was not working for Bill or Fischer. It wouldn't be a bad thing if the housekeeper was aware of her suspicions. "To be honest, Mrs. Sharnbrook, I do not trust Dr. Wyatt. He is not at all respected in London. And . . ." She leaned forward, widening her eyes and dropping her voice. "And I noticed something is amiss in the attic. My father's army trunk has been tampered with."

It was admirable how effectively Mrs. Sharnbrook withheld her surprise. The barest flutter of her lashes was all that gave away her dismay. "You suspect the doctor?"

That was a good enough explanation. "He has been known to bribe the staff to do his bidding."

Mrs. Sharnbrook's nostrils flared. "I see. I will inform Mr. Kirby, and together we will ensure that the staff are reminded where their loyalties lie." She rose with a jangle of keys as if she were setting off to do just that. "May I ask if you have informed his lordship or her ladyship of this doctor's habits?"

Again, she saw no reason to lie. "Lady Easting is aware of my concerns. I'm sure it's not my place to ask, but Martha's sister—is there a possibility of hiring her on here? I know it's a considerable blow to be let go without a recommendation."

Mrs. Sharnbrook cleared her throat. "I'm sure your concern is appreciated, but I daresay one Garrett girl is quite enough for Ellington. If that is all, I should remind you that Lord Easting wished to see you."

"Thank you, Mrs. Sharnbrook. I appreciate your time."

The housekeeper opened the door and made an awkward sort of sound that drew Saffron's attention. "If I may make a suggestion, Miss Saffron," she said, looking pained. "A change of clothes may be in order before you attend to his lordship."

A glance down her front demonstrated Mrs. Sharnbrook was right; her battered gardening clothes were filthy. Saffron took herself off upstairs to find Elizabeth and tell her that she now had another source of information about Madame Martin, and to see her grandfather. If only someone would materialize with a source of information to help her solve her own difficulties.

"Why on earth are you so dirty?"

Elizabeth stood in the threshold of their separating door, nose scrunched as she took in Saffron's appearance.

"I was searching the attic for my father's journals." Saffron pulled her jumper off, sending a cascade of dusty bits over her head.

"Well," Elizabeth said, coming forward to pluck more particles from Saffron's hair, "thanks for not including me in that venture."

"You need to go below stairs to talk to my maid's sister," Saffron said, quickly explaining the dismissed maid's situation as she finished undressing.

Elizabeth's eyes lit up. "This is perfect! Inside information. I've let myself get rather sidetracked with this Bill business." She handed Saffron her hairbrush. "Speaking of Bill, if I'm to go below stairs, I'll look out for that maid Alexander mentioned."

Saffron retrieved a fresh pair of stockings from a drawer and sat on her bed to roll them up. "The one who tried to get into my room? Good. You might ask who brought me that pitcher of water, too. I didn't manage to ask who it was, but I don't think I saw a blonde girl when I was in the kitchen earlier." Irritation at herself and the whole situation had her roughly pulling the stocking up, and a tingling tearing sound made her swear as she glared down at the rip.

"I'm guessing it isn't the maid's drugged water that has you so irate," Elizabeth said. "Did you and Alexander talk?"

"No," she replied absently, forcing herself to slowly unroll the ruined stocking so she'd only have one tear to mend later.

Elizabeth handed her a new stocking from the drawer. "Your grandmother again?"

"I . . ." Saffron broke off, shaking her head. "My mother said she destroyed my father's journals. She made it sound almost like she'd done me a favor, removing them so I couldn't be hurt by them. I'm not the one who would look at my father's things and be heartbroken. She knows I am a scientist, and the reason for that is my father's influence. Why would she imagine I wouldn't want to see his work? I can't understand it." She went to the wardrobe for a dress.

"Can't you?" Elizabeth sounded truly puzzled. "You're angry with your mother for doing something remarkably similar to what you did to me. And her, actually. Withholding information out of the desire to protect delicate feelings. You didn't tell me about Bill. You also haven't told your mother what you've been doing with your research, let alone how you've assisted with catching murderers and spies. You haven't told her about Bill's true identity."

Surprised, Saffron turned away from her reflection to face her. "That isn't the same at all! My mother *is* delicate, Eliza. She can't leave the house. Imagine how it would torment her to know I was going after killers, that one is in the house."

"Just so you know what this is really about," Elizabeth said loftily, plainly enjoying echoing Saffron's words back to her.

But it wasn't the same, she thought as she buckled her shoes and left the room. Saffron's temperament was sturdier than her mother's, and not compromised by a betrayal like Elizabeth's.

She found her grandfather was alone in his study. She expected him to be sitting near the fire as he had each time he'd been out of his rooms the past few days, but he sat at his desk instead, a sheaf of papers before him. The room was precisely as one might expect the study of a seventy-year-old peer to look. Dark leather and polished wood occupied every surface of the room, with burgundy velvet curtains closed against the chill of the damp day.

"Come," he told her. "Sit."

Saffron did so. They stared at each other.

Lord Easting looked like the ghost of himself, pale and slightly shrunken in his oversized leather chair. His eyes, a lighter shade than her own cornflower blue ones, bore into her with steady pressure.

"How are you feeling, Grandpapa?" she asked, breaking the silence. She'd rather him shout at her again instead of continuing to look at each other.

"I've been better," he said gruffly.

Grief struck her in the chest. It had been a long time since her grandfather—and even longer for her grandmother—had been people she felt safe confiding in. She mourned that loss, even as her grandfather sat before her. Mourned the loss of the closeness she might have shared with some of the few family members she had left.

A realization welled up, replacing that regret and grief with sharp guilt. She had done this. She'd been the one to put distance between herself and her family. She'd physically moved, yes, but she'd kept things from them. She'd lied. She'd backed herself into a dangerous corner, and now couldn't reach out for help because doing so would only further endanger them.

She stood suddenly, unable to bear her grandfather's silence any longer. "Grandpapa, I understand that we have had our differences." She found he was looking at her steadily, the same grief she felt plain on his lined, pale face. "I understand that I may not be invited back to Ellington for some time. And I wanted you to know that I am sorry for it. Not for making the choices I've made about my schooling and work, but I . . . I am sorry that it has caused you and my grandmother and mother pain." Lord Easting said nothing, and she rushed on. "Before I go, I wanted to go through some of my father's things. My mother doesn't know where his things were stored after his study was cleared out. Do you know where his journals and things are?"

He shook his head. "I don't know anything about Thomas's belongings." He met her gaze, and though his tone remained the same, she felt he truly meant it when he said, "I'm sorry."

Saffron nodded, clenching her teeth. She turned to go, and her grandfather's curt voice said, "Ask Kirby. He ought to know."

Surprised, she turned to thank him, but he'd already gone back to the papers on his desk.

CHAPTER 35

Dinner that evening was a somber affair. Lord Easting was not present, nor was Suzette, and Lady Easting said very little. No additional guests were present, so John took it upon himself to provide much of the conversation, but by the end of the meal, even he had gone quiet. When it came time to separate for drinks and coffee, Alexander thought John might suggest they simply go with the women into the drawing room. Alexander would have preferred it; Saffron had looked like she was sitting on hot coals all through dinner. She'd learned something after disappearing that afternoon, he was sure of it.

Instead, when the ladies had left the dining room, John cocked his head to the door. "What do you say we go have a game of billiards, rather than sit around in here?"

Alexander agreed. Even a game as inane as billiards would put his mind off the sensation of ants crawling beneath his skin that he'd been coping with all day.

The smoking room was cold and dark. A pair of footmen hustled inside after them to light a fire and illuminate the room. Soon, Alexander found himself alone with John.

The other man looked pensive as he set up the table for play.

"Friendly wager?" he suggested as he took up a cue.

"No, if you don't mind," Alexander replied. For all he didn't care for the game, he was good at it. It wouldn't be polite to take Saffron's cousin's money.

They played half a match mostly in silence. John drifted to the drinks cabinet and poured himself a brandy, offering Alexander one. He declined that, too.

At the end of the match, Alexander reset the table. John watched him.

"I suppose I ought to be grateful you've no obvious vices," he commented after losing the lag. He stepped back so Alexander could take his first shot. "You don't gamble, you don't drink. Saffron would notice if you were a criminal of some sort, so I doubt you're lifting handbags from old ladies on the street, either."

"Targeting old women wouldn't be sporting," Alexander said dryly.

"I wonder what my grandmother would do if someone nabbed her handbag. Probably breathe fire on them."

Alexander ducked his head to hide his smile. "She is a formidable woman."

"Thinks me an ungrateful lout." His cue slipped, missing the cue ball.

"I wonder if Lady Easting is aware of the great deal of work it is to study and practice law, especially in a new country." Alexander took his turn, choosing to shoot just a hair to the left of what would guarantee him a winning hazard. "My father is a lawyer. I began my studies with a focus on the law, and changed to biology later."

John's brows rose. "Does your father have any notable clients?"

"Not that I'm aware of."

He sighed. "Pity. Might have helped your cause with the lord and lady."

Another few plays passed. John finished his drink and poured another. "I don't mean to be nosy, of course. But you understand that Saffron's got only her mother and our grandparents to watch out for her, and I'm quite sure at this point they'd rather see her sink than swim, if you know what I'm getting at."

"I understand." Though he would rather be with Saffron, this was an important conversation. He reset the table. "How did you come to practice law in France? I gather you stayed there after the war, but that would have been after Thomas Everleigh died and you knew you would succeed your grandfather."

"When I met Suzette and married her—another despicable choice, by the way," he added, shooting a grin at Alexander over his cue, "I was never meant to have Ellington at all. My now wife nursed me back to health after a skirmish left me bleeding rather dramatically. I was in hospital for a week and asked her to marry me by the end of it." He seemed to deflate slightly. "My uncle was still alive then. My father hadn't yet become the heir."

He was quiet for a long moment, draining the last of his drink before saying, "I'm afraid my father was a rather underwhelming sort of fellow. The classic second son, overshadowed by the first. Thomas was a bright, enterprising fellow. Struck out on his own sort of adventure, following his love of plants to the university. My father, meanwhile, did whatever my grandfather told him. Married a wealthy woman, produced a child. He never had any aspirations of his own."

It seemed John had abandoned the game, for he set his cue against the sideboard in favor of a cigarette. "He followed my uncle into war, and I'm afraid he came out of it rather badly. I know we all say that, but it changed him. I wasn't here; I didn't come back to England after Suzette and I married. We don't . . . The family don't speak of it—won't, really—but my father ended his own life. I never learned why."

That was perhaps why Thomas Everleigh was mentioned frequently while John's father was not. Alexander wondered what that was like, being pushed into an important position in a family that neglected the memory of his father.

John's eyes were unfocused, gazing across the room. "He died only four months after Uncle Thomas did and I found myself suddenly not just heir presumptive, but the heir. A rather unpleasant surprise, to be honest." He recalled his cigarette and tipped ash into a glass dish on the sideboard. "I love Ellington, but I had planned to live out my days in some nice little French town with my wife and whatever children came along. Maybe stop by once every couple of years to impress the children with Papa's important relations. Suzette didn't even know about any of this until my father died and I had to tell her. Now look what I've done! Suzette will have to live somewhere she hates and poor Benjamin will be stuck with the same nonsense for his whole life."

The look in John's eyes as he turned to Alexander was wary yet hopeful, as if he was waiting to see if Alexander would believe him. Who among John's friends believed him that he wasn't pleased to inherit a title, wealth, and property? Had he not experienced Saffron's same indifference to her family's wealth, Alexander wasn't sure he would have believed it himself.

"I don't pretend to have any idea about how things work in the peerage, but perhaps you could be a viscount from a distance," Alexander said.

John replied with a rueful smile. "You must think me an ass for acting like a martyr."

Alexander's outspoken brother, Adrian, would have felt right at home in this conversation. He was good with these sorts of conversations, not Alexander. "Not everyone is happy with the life their family has provided them, even if it's a comfortable one."

"Very diplomatic," John said. "Saffron would fall into that category, I think."

"So she says," Alexander said, more to himself than to his companion.

"There's a reason she's stayed in London all this time. I'm not saying it's not because she loves her work," he added hastily. "She loves all things green and growing, but escaping Ellington and the life that comes with it . . ." He mashed his cigarette into the tray with a significant look. "Let's just say that Baron Whitley's surprise visit was the barest taste of what Saffron's late adolescence was like. The moment the war was over, it was a veritable parade of men, young and old."

Alexander didn't particularly want to think about Whitley or any that came before him. "I see."

John added another splash of brandy into his glass. "I don't mean to put you off, quite the opposite. I think you're good for Saffron. A sensible, stable sort of fellow. She needs someone like that, I think."

The last week had left Alexander feeling

anything but sensible or stable. He merely nodded in acknowledgment, and John declared it time to rejoin the ladies.

Upon entering the drawing room, Alexander saw only Elizabeth, sitting in the window seat, facing the darkness.

Behind him, John asked, "The snow is falling fast, isn't it?"

Elizabeth jumped and glared at them. Her hands gripped the edges of her wrap.

John sauntered over with a lazy smile. "Saffron off to bed already?"

"I wonder if we'll be snowed in tomorrow." Elizabeth burrowed deeper into her wrap. "Does Benjamin like snow?"

They chatted for a few moments, and Alexander considered sneaking up to see what Saffron had learned from her searches that afternoon. They also needed to discuss what had happened last night. He hadn't had the chance to properly apologize.

Elizabeth's head twitched yet again as she looked out the window. White flecks fluttered beyond. If he remembered correctly, Elizabeth didn't particularly like the cold. It was strange, then, that she'd chosen to sit in the coldest possible place in the room. What was she watching out the window?

John bit off a yawn, saying, "'Spose I'll be going up myself. Quiet in the country, isn't it?"

He drifted away through the open drawing room door.

Alexander already knew the answer, but he asked, "Where is she?"

Elizabeth turned and blinked slowly at him. "Who?"

He took his time walking across the room. She watched him approach warily. "It's freezing over here."

"I find it quite comfortable."

"You're shivering."

"I am not."

"And now you're being difficult."

"Oh, *now* I'm being difficult."

Alexander crossed his arms. "We have the same goal, Elizabeth. Keep Saffron safe. Is she safe?"

Her hand slipped from the cover of her shawl and made a lazy circle in the air. "Safe is such an abstract concept. What does it mean to be safe? How shall we define it? Are we talking about the physical state of being in a secure loca—"

She froze, arrested by something out the window. Alexander leaned over, his heart stilling as he made sense of what the wintery landscape revealed.

A light drifted across the white ground, moving in the direction of a single stationary dot of light far in the distance.

Elizabeth's husky voice was a croak. "No, I don't think Saffron is safe."

CHAPTER 36

S affron fitted the key into the rusted lock. It required some exertion, but it gave, turning with a forceful jerk of her wrist. She pushed open the door to the greenhouse. The hinges let out a mournful creak, and she took a step inside.

Her feet crunched. She looked down and the lamplight revealed nothing more than scant patches of snow and blackened leaf debris. Though the temperature had dropped, allowing the week of rain to frost the ground, the sound was likely glass from the broken panes rather than ice. When Kirby had given her the greenhouse key and cautioned her to be careful, she doubted he'd known just how hazardous the place truly was.

She took another wary step forward, lifting the lamp and daring to turn the handle to increase its light.

Any softness of the snowy sky's lavender lambency was lost in the starkness of the lamp light; it cast harsh shadows of limp vines and fractured panels. Light reflected oddly in the glass and ice beginning to form where rainwater lingered.

Snow and ice clung to rotted wood lining garden beds. The air tasted like musty decay and smoky winter, at once familiar, invigorating, and disturbing.

Her strongest memories of this place were of sunshine and misery. She'd hidden here when she'd learned her father was gone, using it as a refuge when grief seemed to expand to fill every inch of the too-quiet house. She'd watered her father's specimens with her own tears that summer.

The greenhouse had continued to be a special place when she'd returned to Ellington during school holidays. There'd been signs of neglect as time went on, in the chipped white paint on the elegant ironwork, cracked panes that hadn't been replaced. The garden beds had been a bit overgrown, and some plants had withered while weeds sprouted and thrived. But this was more than neglect; this was abandonment.

It made her terribly sad.

The greenhouse had been a gift from her grandparents, a show of approval and pride in her father's scientific efforts when he was a young man, a decade before Thomas's love for his work divided the household. The Victorian design was based on some of the most beautiful conservatories in the world, a glittering, hidden treasure. It had once been filled with exotic species and common ones alike. Her father had *created* here, lived most vibrantly here. Images clear as day flashed before her eyes—spotless panes gleaming in the sun, moisture-dotted verdure, her parents grinning at each other's dirt-covered hands—before fading to the lonely, fallow view before her.

Her breath clouded before her. Where to start?

The east wall was where the work table had once stood. It knelt now, one leg broken and the others entwined with frost-blackened vines from a sprawling plant that emerged like a kraken from the sea from the nearest bed.

She tugged at the drawer of the work table. The sounds of her movements were far too loud in the quiet of the falling snow, fluttering down in disparate columns where the broken glass gave it entry. She worked the drawer out until she could see there was nothing inside. The next drawer revealed something, however: a family of mice huddled in what looked to be a discarded handkerchief and long pieces of grass. She gently shut the drawer on the squeaking creatures, feeling bad for startling them.

Shelving was built into this side of the greenhouse, and she examined each shelf, wondering what, if anything, could be left in this wrecked place. It wasn't much: stacks of cracked terracotta pots, rusted shears, and a ball of twine that looked like the mice had nibbled on it a time or two. Not so much as a seed packet, however.

She blew out a breath, feeling stupid and sad. What had she expected, really? This place had been open to the elements for some time. Even if something like a journal had been left behind, it would likely be illegible.

She turned away, but as she moved, her boot caught on something. Her hands and knees slammed into the ground. Pain lanced her left knee, and she carefully rolled over to find that a shard of glass had embedded itself in the soft space between the bones. Wincing, she peeled off her gloves then pulled the shard out. She flung the wedge of glass away, only to look up sharply when it pinged against something metal.

From her position on the ground, the view of raised beds was different. She could see beneath the drooping cover of blackened weeds. And she could see what the bloodstained glass had struck.

A metal box was secreted underneath one fall of dead vines.

She rushed forward, shoving the wilted plant aside and dragging the heavy metal case forward. It was a toolbox of some kind, not brand new but new enough that the freezing metal hadn't rusted. It was locked, which she rapidly remedied with trembling hands.

She flinched away from the vacant eyes glaring up at her from the depths of the toolbox. The canvas skin was cold and stiff beneath her fingers as she lifted the mask. She carefully set it aside, face down, with the eerie feeling that she should cover it up so it wouldn't watch her.

A hastily folded army tunic was beneath, and under that lay a pair of khaki trousers. Her fingers briefly traced the fabric of the trousers where the thick cotton gave way to ribbed corduroy. Calvary riders wore breeches like this, Alexander had said. The tunic bore a number of small pinholes where badges should have been.

This was her father's uniform. It was clear why it was hidden here, where no one would think to look for it. It was also plain to see why Fischer needed it: his own uniform, if he still had it, was that of a pilot. Wesley Hale had not been a calvary officer, but deprived of its badges of unit and rank and at a distance in the dark, this uniform looked like it could have belonged to an infantryman.

The mask was not her father's. She picked it up and set it on top of the uniform.

No, Thomas Everleigh was never issued a respirator box. He'd died before they were even invented, died from the very thing the masks were meant to protect against. The first use of chlorine gas, a victory of scientific warfare, had been her father's, and thousands of others', undoing.

Fischer wearing this mask with her father's uniform was a mockery of his death.

She slammed the lid on the mask and shoved the toolbox away.

She shot to her feet, uncaring about the sharp ache in her knee, ready to cross the snowy fields and march right up to Madame Martin and tell her to go to hell.

"I'm not surprised to find you here, chasing down Madame Martin's little tricks."

With a violent gasp, Saffron jerked around. Bill Wyatt stepped into the circle of her lamp's light, expanding it with the glow from his own lantern.

"I'm not here for Madame's tricks," Saffron said. Her voice shook, caught between fear and fury.

"You forget," Bill said softly, dangerously, "that I know you, Saffron. I know you find puzzles like the ones Madame Martin presents irresistible. What confuses me is that *my* puzzle has gone unstudied, unsolved."

He wasn't wearing his Dr. Wyatt spectacles. His eyes speared her like minutien pins on a mounting board, and he observed her with the mild interest of a collector.

A beat passed, of him watching her, of her watching him.

"I was so sure," Bill said softly, "so *sure* that you would turn up something useful on your little jaunt into London. I was frustrated when I didn't get to see exactly what you'd found. At first I thought you were stalling, attempting to coordinate something with your Detective Inspector Green, or even Nicholas Hale."

Snow fell on his shoulders, only emphasizing his utter, disquieting stillness.

"But surely someone who holds her family so dear would want me gone as soon as possible. Then I thought you sought to sabotage the information before handing it over, but you know better than to test me in that way. And now? I think I am angrier with myself than with you." He raised his arms, gesturing to the dead vines threaded through broken panes and the snow-dusted debris on the ground. "You are like a glasshouse, aren't you? The foggy panes obscure the contents of the grand structure, and when you open the door, you see the truth: lackluster, common plants, drooping over the sides of their beds." His face twisted into a smile, a departure from the easy smiles he'd used to lure everyone into a false sense of security. This was bitter and seething, the smile of one who'd been disappointed but not for long.

She was too afraid to be struck by the insult. "I'm looking. I'm looking for what you want. I've discovered my father was working with Demian Petrov, studying *Aristolochia*."

Bill's eyes flared. "Things I could have told you myself, and, in fact, did so. This is wasting my time. You are wasting my time, Saffron."

"You have to give me a chance—"

"I've watched you bungle every opportunity you've had to recover my information. It seems you care more about ingratiating Alexander to your family or helping Elizabeth with her foolish mission to foil Madame Martin." His bitter smile melted away, leaving him looking innocently thoughtful. Saffron shuddered even before he said idly, "But perhaps it would be better to remove these distractions so you might better focus on the simple task I've set for you."

Panic flared. "If you touch them, you'll never get what you want from me."

"Don't wager that which you're not willing to lose," he chided. His hand dipped into his jacket pocket, and it emerged with a small object that he flicked with his thumb. A short blade swung out, catching the light with a flash. Her stomach bottomed out. "I did that once." He lifted the blade across his neck and rested it on the angry raised flesh of the scar beneath his ear. "And I learned my lesson. Be grateful I'm more patient than my captors were."

He closed the blade and slipped it back into his pocket. Eyes not leaving hers, Bill backed away, lamp light leaching from his face. "You have until tomorrow night."

CHAPTER 37

Alexander had had enough.

He strode down the hall and knocked on Bill's door. He was angry enough that he might have thrown the door open rather than bother with the nicety of knocking. Saffron's bloodless mask of a face when he'd retrieved her from the greenhouse had destroyed what was left of his composure.

The door cracked open, then swung wide. Bill stood at the threshold, a small smile nearly hidden in his neat beard. He still wore his coat, and it was damp at the shoulders. He must have come in after Saffron had, for Alexander had packed her off to her bedroom half an hour ago and paced his bedroom since.

"You need to leave," Alexander said, voice low.

"Perhaps it is you who need to leave," Bill countered easily.

Alexander tensed when Bill reached into his pocket, but he merely withdrew his glasses wrapped in a handkerchief. He rubbed the lenses idly before setting the spectacles on his nose.

The events of the past twenty-four hours had eroded every last bit of Alexander's patience. Saffron was terrified, Elizabeth wasn't helping, the Everleighs were oblivious, and he had no

344

ideas left for how to solve this problem but one.

Alexander lunged for Bill's shirtfront, but before he was aware he'd missed, Bill was at his side, one hand on Alexander's arm and the other on his neck. Both of his thumbs dug into Alexander's flesh, and rather than eliciting pain, the pressure drove an electric numbness into his bones. It took all his willpower not to thrash against Bill's grip. He didn't know what damage it would do.

"I'm an old hand at divining useful information from medical records," Bill hissed. He drove his thumb deeper, sending the cords of Alexander's taut muscles thrumming. "Like exactly which of your cervical vertebrae were fractured during the war. How you still experience twinges and numbness in your right arm."

Alexander said nothing, and after a moment, Bill let go of him. Bill smirked, easing around him to return to his bedroom. "Don't challenge me, Alexander. I know how you hate to lose."

He closed the door in Alexander's face.

He didn't know how he came to be back in his bedroom, but sometime later, when his temper had settled, Alexander found he was staring out the window. Snow was piled high on the ledge outside, and beyond that, fog crept over the grounds. If he telephoned Inspector Green in the morning, would he be able to manage the roads, or a train? Would he even come?

Things were spiraling out of control faster than he could grab onto the strings, and after seeing how Bill could immobilize him with so little effort, he realized that he had never had the strings to begin with.

It had been hours, and Saffron's mind had not stopped spinning. It churned with possibilities, and their consequences, again and again, a rough sea crashing against the rocky shore. Her ideas were the waves, and the lack of sorely needed information the rocks.

Saffron had already written down everything she knew about Thomas Everleigh, Demian Petrov, *Aristolochia*, and Bill. She'd reviewed every detail from the papers, ran through every conversation with Bill. It wasn't enough. She didn't know enough, and had no way of learning more.

Exhausted, she sank onto the floor before the fire, which she'd kept blazing to chase away the lingering chill. Her notebook in hand, she stared at her notes until her eyes blurred.

His captors. His *captors*. That was a clue. Bill had been imprisoned, but who called their jailors captors? He'd been abducted, kidnapped, then? That had been personal information, perhaps shared unintentionally out of frustration with her lack of progress. What did it mean? Did it matter?

She groaned, pressing her fingers to her temples, and the cycle of questions restarted.

She flipped back several pages to begin again, and her eyes caught on the page where she'd listed all the possible locations of information. She reread them, agonizing that she'd managed to search each one and turned up *nothing*—

Regent Square. Her father's flat.

She stared at the scrawled words, her heart suddenly thudding. That was the only place she had not been. Mr. Feyzi, the family lawyer, had given her some papers the tenants had found. The papers had seemed innocuous enough, but they were worth revisiting now she knew what to look for. To get into the flat would be even better. If one set of papers had been stashed away, there could be more.

She would go there in the morning. She'd go to her flat and retrieve the letters and get the key from Mr. Feyzi and—

A soft knock on the door followed closely by its opening had her reeling back with a yelp.

"Miss?" Martha poked her head into the room.

"What is it?" Saffron asked. "What's the matter?"

"Oh, er, nothing," Martha stammered, frowning. "Do you want me to come back later? Only I've brought your tea, and the fire . . . Well, you've been tending it, I see."

"Tea?"

"Er, yes? Did you not want morning tea?"

Saffron gawked at her. It was the morning? She rose unsteadily and pulled the curtains aside, only to see a wall of fog pressing on the window. It was charcoal gray, a sure sign of dawn.

It was time to get ready, then. She had twelve hours to find whatever it was Bill wanted.

Ten minutes later, she was in the entry downstairs, pulling her gloves on as she waited for Perry to pull the motorcar around. Footsteps sounded on the stairs, and she turned to see Alexander.

"Where are you going?" he asked.

She braced herself for the confrontation she'd hoped to avoid. "I have to go to London. My father kept a flat there. It's the only place left to look."

His voice was low and carefully patient. "Were you going to tell me you were leaving?"

"No," she admitted. His nostrils flared. She put her hand on his arm, leaning closer. "I knew you would want to come with me."

"Of course I'm coming with you. I'm not going to let you go to London alone when Bill—"

"He made it very clear last night that my time is almost finished. If I can't find what he wants, he is going to hurt my family." She slipped her hand into his and squeezed. "Please, stay. I can't do this knowing that I left my family alone with Bill when he's so angry. I'll go straight to the police station when I get to London, and I'll ask for an escort. I just . . . I don't know what else to do," she finished on a ragged breath.

She could see the conflict in his eyes. "Please," she whispered again, squeezing his hand so hard it hurt.

He nodded.

"Thank you."

The grinding noises of the motorcar announced its arrival. Saffron went on tiptoes to press a kiss to Alexander's cheek, whispering, "I love you. Thank you," before she slipped through the doors.

CHAPTER 38

The moment the motorcar returned from dropping Saffron off at the train station, Alexander asked Perry to turn around and drive right back into town.

He had one goal in mind and little hope of achieving it. But something had to be done before Saffron's time ran out.

Chief Constable Hackett was not available, Alexander was told, but Constable Dunley was. Alexander accepted this as his only opportunity, and sat down once more with Dunley.

"He was following her in London," Alexander ground out after explaining about Bill again. "He's placed himself in Lord Easting's household and is now threatening them with violence."

"We looked into this Dr. Wyatt after your last visit here," Dunley said in his slow, plodding manner. "If this Dr. Wyatt is not a doctor as you claim, how do you account for Lady Easting hiring him out of all the doctors in England?"

Alexander balled his fists under the desk. He had to have help, and since he wasn't believed, he'd use the only thing these men seemed interested in. "Very well. There is another matter—"

"Lookee here, son," Dunley said, frowning,

350

"I don't have time to bother about every bit of whining from a bloke from out of town, do I? There's real work to be done."

"Exactly. Miss Hale said she's discovered how to catch the Frenchwoman, the phony medium. She's put together a plan, and she's worried things might go sideways. She asked me to request a police officer or two to be present at Ellington Manor later today."

It took a moment, but Dunley's eyes lit up. "Aye, now that's more like it. Chief Constable Hackett will certainly want to send a couple of fellows over. What time?"

Regent Square was a ten-minute walk from the U's campus. The buildings were elegant but modest, clustered around a small park. Few people were out on the street, even fewer in the park, but Saffron felt dogged every step of the way. She was glad to get inside the building and up the stairs to her father's flat.

Saffron fit the key into the lock and swung the door open with the slightest creak. She paused, her ears pricking at a noise behind her.

Heart in her throat, she turned quickly but saw nothing behind her but the empty landing.

She was being paranoid. Bill would not attack her now, nor send someone to attack her, surely. If he'd wanted to harm her, he'd had plenty of opportunities in far less obvious and public places. Even her own flat, which she'd visited to retrieve the letters found in this flat, was on a much quieter street and would have been a better place. She ought to have done as she said she would and gone to the police station to request an escort.

She shook herself and firmly turned her back to the stairwell. The open door yawned before her.

The family solicitor, Mr. Feyzi, had been out when she stopped by his office. His secretary had mentioned the couple who'd rented the flat had recently left town after receiving a job offer in Edinburgh. When he'd implied Saffron wanted to check the flat over on behalf of her family, she hadn't corrected him and accepted the key.

All she could see within was gray shadows. A hundred thoughts cascaded through her mind, but the loudest one was that this felt more wrong than invading her parents' private spaces at Ellington. Her father had never brought her here when she'd come to visit him at the university. She felt awkward, stepping into this place where Thomas Everleigh could have been anyone, a stranger.

The church at the corner's bell rung, loudly announcing the noon hour and making her jump. She went inside.

It was much the same as the attic at Ellington. White sheets covered the remaining furniture, rolled carpets were pushed to the side of the sitting room and a bedroom. No photographs or paintings remained on the walls; frames were stacked in one corner of the parlor. She could ignore all the furniture, at least, as it belonged to the couple moving out.

A subtle creak echoed through the silent flat.

An electric current of fear ran down her spine. The door to the flat had been open. Why hadn't she locked it?

Looking about her quickly, she lunged for the lamp sitting on a sideboard. From behind the door into the parlor, she set her handbag down and raised the heavy lamp above her head, ready to bring it down upon whoever had followed her into the flat.

The door silently swung inward. There was a pause during which she was sure the invader scrutinized the white-shrouded furniture, looking for her. Fear coalesced in her chest, icy and sharp.

They took a step into the room. Saffron smashed the lamp against the back of their head.

A loud swear accompanied the man falling to the ground. Saffron leaped over the man's legs and was a step into the hall before the sound of a familiar voice stopped her dead.

"That was bloody uncalled for, Everleigh!"

Saffron went from terrified to outraged in a moment. She stomped back into the room. "What the devil are you doing here, Lee?"

CHAPTER 39

Michael Lee sat up, legs splayed on the dusty floor, and touched the back of his head gingerly.

Though Saffron was furious he'd scared her half to death, she knelt next to him and reached into the pocket of his jacket where she knew he kept his handkerchief. She drew it out and gave it to him, alarmed that the hand that accepted it was bloody.

"Oh, goodness," she said. "That lamp was rather effective, wasn't it?"

"Yes, it bloody well was." Lee winced as he held the handkerchief to his head. "What inspired that act of violence? We haven't argued in months. I can't have offended you from afar."

Considering she'd bashed him on the head with a lamp, Saffron felt he was owed an explanation. "There is a man who has been troubling me . . ."

At the end of the story, Lee was staring at her with green eyes narrowed with pain, his lips parted. He blinked a few times. "I suppose I can forgive you, then. Sounds quite serious." He made to stand up.

Saffron pressed a hand on his shoulder. "Shouldn't you stay still?"

"I don't think your hit was strong enough to do more than knock me over. Well done, though, you would have easily made it back into the hallway." He looked about the sitting room and said, "Find me a chair, won't you? I'd rather bleed in comfort, if you don't mind."

Saffron found what turned out to be a nice chintz armchair on the other side of the room and Lee sunk into it, still holding his handkerchief to his head. He looked up, a mischievous smile in place. "Any chance of a drink around here?"

"Do try to be serious."

"Not to drink, to clean the great gaping wound on my head." When she opened her mouth to apologize, he waved it off. "Where are we, by the way? Whose flat have you broken into?"

"This is my father's old flat. He stayed here during the semester when he taught."

She fell silent, looking around. Even with another person there, the place felt dead and empty. She looked back at Lee, who was studying her with a frown.

His lips quirked. "I know we've been rather out of touch, Everleigh, but you really should have told me. I could have helped."

It was true, they had been out of touch. She and Alexander had run into him at a play in January. Despite the lingering tension of a past romantic entanglement that hadn't quite come to fruition and the jealousy it had inspired, it had managed not to be awkward between the three of them. But Saffron hadn't seen Lee since.

"You've been in touch with Elizabeth," Saffron said.

He shrugged. "She needed someone to talk to."

She lifted an eyebrow. "There's nothing more to it than that?"

Lee's brows dipped in confusion, then he snorted. "No, old thing, not a chance. Speaking of romance, why isn't Alexander with you? I'm surprised he let you out of his sight if this Bill fellow has been skulking. Unless you haven't told him?"

Saffron cleared her throat, uncomfortable with the subtle hope in his eye. "He's at Ellington with my family, actually."

Lee nodded thoughtfully. "And you're here."

"Looking for information." She explained about the *Aristolochia*. "I'm at my wit's end, Lee. There's just . . . nothing. No real information, apart from some notes here and there."

"How do you know there's even anything to find?" Lee asked. "What if Bill is just a sort of madman?"

"He might be," Saffron replied, turning to look around the room. "But he's a determined one. He wants me to turn something up, so I have to try."

"Well," he said, getting to his feet, "I'm here, I'll help."

"Speaking of, why are you here?" Saffron asked as she peered behind a door. It proved to be a closet, and she set to work checking the floor and wall for hiding spots. The previous tenants had evidently found her father's papers while searching for a rodent, so it was likely that if there were more, they'd be tucked away somewhere.

"My father asked me to drop something off for him at the women's medical school," Lee said. "It's just there on the corner, you know. I was coming out and saw you walking furtively into this building, so I followed you."

Saffron made a face at him as she emerged from the closet. "I was not being furtive. I was being inconspicuous." She tried knocking the door frame, feeling ridiculous.

"Of course you were, Everleigh."

Giving up on the windows, Saffron moved to the floor, carefully examining the seams in the parquet floors. Lee described his task at the women's medical school, which led to a series of stories about his recent work that lasted the length and breadth of the room.

"Did I miss anywhere?" she asked, getting to her feet and brushing dust from her clothing. "I suppose I can't climb into the chimney, can I?"

Lee discouraged the idea. He followed her into the bathroom, where he sighed upon seeing there was no iodine or alcohol to clean his cut. "It's stopped bleeding, at least," he muttered.

In the kitchen, where they pulled open each drawer in turn, he said casually, "Alexander and Elizabeth ended up at Ellington, then. How does Alexander like it?"

She didn't miss the question within the question. "You could just ask, Lee."

"Well, I'd like to think I'd receive a proper notification if there was happy news," he said, poking around an empty cutlery drawer.

She ignored him and went back to feeling along the back of the dusty cabinet she was inspecting.

They moved on to the bedroom. When they opened the closet, Saffron's dwindling hope finally evaporated. It was empty.

"Well," she said, fighting the tightening of her throat, "thanks for helping me search."

Lee patted her shoulder. "Don't be so pessimistic, old thing. Let's give it a once over."

They did so, squeezing inside the tiny room together.

"What's this now!"

Saffron struggled to turn around. Lee was running a hand along a seam in the wall. "Are there other seams like this?"

Saffron frowned; she hadn't noticed that. She shuffled around to examine the other walls, but there was nothing. "No, that's the only one."

"What can we use to smash the wall a bit?"

358

She blinked. "Smash the wall?"

"Yes, let's smash something apart from my head." His eyes lit up. "Just a moment."

He slipped out of the closet, and a moment later, she heard the front door slam. She blew out a breath, hoping whatever he was up to would be useful.

Her gloves were coated in grime, as was the lower half of her coat. She peeled the ruined gloves from her hands and shoved them into her pocket.

The door opened. Lee declared himself then strolled into the bedroom a moment later, happily twirling a meat mallet in his hand.

"The woman across the hall was kind enough to lend us this useful kitchen implement. She's not entirely all there, I think, but very generous." He removed his jacket and rolled up his shirt sleeves. "Come out here, will you? Only one of us should be hurt at a time."

Saffron removed herself to the outside of the closet and watched Lee smartly hit the seamed wall. After a few strikes, he'd managed to break through the wall and Saffron rushed forward to help him clear away the pieces.

He peered into the space he'd revealed, then arched back to reach down inside.

Saffron grabbed his other arm. "You can't just reach down in there!"

"Whyever not?"

"You might touch anything inside. There could be an angry rat, or a dangerous mold, or—"

"A dangerous mold?" Lee drawled.

"Touching certain molds can be dangerous," she sniped. "You ought to know that! We studied half a dozen plants that shouldn't be touched, and mold can be just as dangerous. It could give you trouble breathing, or a rash, or even—" She stopped. Her brain sprinted forward, and when it arrived at its destination, she breathed, "Or even give you hallucinations." She gasped. "I've got to telephone Elizabeth!"

Lee's arm was still swallowed up by the wall. "Wouldn't you like to know if I found anything in the wall first?"

That stopped Saffron short. "What did you find?"

He rolled his eyes, easing his arm from the hole in the wall. His hand came away empty. "Nothing, but I might have found something useful and you'd already be halfway down the street."

Saffron groaned. She wanted to stomp her foot like a child. "Why can I find nothing relevant!"

Lee wiped his hands on his bloodstained handkerchief. "Perhaps there's nothing to find, old thing."

Saffron gave the flat one last hopeless look before she and Lee returned to the landing and she locked the door. Lee took off down the hall to the next flat.

"Mrs. Davidson, thank you very much for the loan of this handy little device," he said, presenting the meat mallet back to the frail-looking woman who answered the door.

Mrs. Davidson's lined face gave her an abstracted look, and she slowly reached out for the mallet. "You are . . . welcome," she said uncertainly. Her gaze strayed over Lee's shoulder to Saffron, and her eyes lit up. "Violet, dear, it has been an age!"

Uncertain what to say, Saffron ventured, "Violet is my mother. I'm Saffron Everleigh, Thomas Everleigh's daughter."

"Oh, Thomas is a good lad," Mrs. Davidson said in a warm, though creaking, voice. "I must remember to invite him and his lovely wife over for tea. That girl always tidies up after for me, the dear."

Lee shot Saffron a look, and registering her confusion, asked, "Do you see Violet Everleigh often?"

Mrs. Davidson smiled, then frowned. "Yes, but not for some time. I made Violet a cake with sugared violets—for her name, of course—but she never came to collect it." Her eyes grew damp. "She forgot it."

"I will remind her," Saffron said, unaccountably teary herself. "I will remind her, when next I see her."

"Oh, thank you." Mrs. Davidson was clutching

the mallet to her chest. She seemed to brace herself, and nodded at them, saying in a brisker voice, "Now, if you will excuse me . . ." She closed the door.

Lee turned to Saffron. "What was all that about?"

"She knew my parents."

"You look like you've seen a ghost! You said you father lived here off and on for years. Why does that shock you so?"

"Well, I . . ." She drew in a breath, and exhaled slowly, trying to discern why it was surprising. "My mother had some difficulty after my father's passing. She doesn't leave Ellington. The house, I mean. I suppose I'm surprised to hear she was here, even before his death. I was away at school. I never knew she came here, and often enough to make a friend of the neighbor."

Lee looped their arms together and tugged her toward the stairs. "I count myself grateful not to know of my parents' comings and goings. There are certain things one's children ought not to know about their parents, I believe. Some secrets are better kept."

He led her to the street, where he opened his umbrella to shelter them from the fine mist. She was grateful for his lack of chatter; her mind was churning. She didn't know why it bothered her so, learning her mother had visited her father in London often.

362

Lee walked her to King's Cross Station. When they were inside, under the arching beams swirling with steam and smoke, he asked, "Should I accompany you on the train?"

She shook her head. "I need you to go to the police station and speak to Inspector Green. Alexander said the local police are likely on Bill's payroll and can't be trusted to help. The inspector already knows some of the situation, but I need you to explain that we need help now, tonight. Ask him to get in touch with someone in the area who can help. And telephone Ellington, if you can. Tell anyone in the family not to touch anything of Madame Martin's or Mr. Fischer's, should they see them before I return."

Lee agreed, and after squeezing her hand tightly with a reassuring smile, disappeared into the crowd.

When Saffron had settled on the last remaining seat in the crowded train carriage, she tugged a bunch of rolled-up papers from her handbag. She hadn't read the letters between her parents included in the papers from her father's flat, not wanting to look into their private matters. But things were different now. She had to see if she had missed something essential. Careful to avoid dampening them with her coat, she sorted through the papers and found her mother's handwriting. She began to read.

Just as the gray, angular cityscape slid out of

view, Saffron realized she'd made a horrible mistake—the same error in judgment that had been made against her for years. She'd underestimated a woman, and that woman was her mother.

CHAPTER 40

"Well, I certainly hadn't imagined this turn of events," Elizabeth said, staring down at the toolbox.

It stood open on a table in the library, baring to the coffered ceiling its unlikely contents.

Elizabeth looked down on the gas mask thoughtfully. "It is certainly bold of them, isn't it?"

"That isn't the word I would choose," Alexander said flatly. The news that Fischer had not only burgled Thomas Everleigh's uniform but had stashed it in his old greenhouse was so offensive it was beyond his comprehension.

Elizabeth tapped a finger to her chin. Since he'd summoned her into the library a few minutes ago, she'd been oddly circumspect, even after he'd announced that the police would be arriving with the expectation of arresting Madame Martin in a matter of hours. "We need to leverage this somehow. It's the perfect thing to take them off guard, that we've found the uniform. And it provides a very nice distraction for the dire doctor, doesn't it? The house in uproar over a dramatic séance. The question is, how are we to do that? With you and me on unfriendly terms with Madame Martin and Saffron gone, we haven't anyone to invite her."

John would likely enjoy being in on the scheme. Suzette had showed interest in Madame, so it wouldn't be unlikely, but would that be enough to draw Madame here today, now? "Would Mrs. Everleigh do it?" he asked.

"Would I do what?"

Alexander's eyes closed as he braced himself to address Saffron's mother. When he turned toward her voice, he found her smiling at the library door, looking as if she'd just stepped inside. "Good afternoon, Mrs. Everleigh."

"Hi, Mrs. E," Elizabeth said brightly, easing a few inches to the left to obscure the toolbox.

Alexander followed suit, realizing his mistake when Mrs. Everleigh's soft gray eyes sharpened, her lips quirking to one side in a dry expression he'd seen his own mother wear after catching Adrian and him in the middle of making mischief. "What am I likely to do, Eliza?" She stepped forward and peered between them.

Far from looking chagrined, Elizabeth looked thoughtful as she took a deliberate step away from the table.

Mrs. Everleigh's gasp was sharp, hand flying to her mouth as if to stifle it.

"This is Professor Everleigh's uniform," Elizabeth said softly.

Shocked, Alexander's eyes flew to hers, but she

was looking hard at Mrs. Everleigh as she stared down into the box in horror.

"Madame Martin stole this from Mr. Everleigh's army trunk," Elizabeth said quietly. "She's been sending her assistant out onto the grounds of my parents' house and Ellington. He's been wearing this uniform and mask, hiding his face, pretending to be Wesley. I've seen him outside my window. Saffron has seen him, too."

Mrs. Everleigh was pale now, and her lips stuttered around her words. "Where—where is Saffron?"

"She had to go into London," Elizabeth said. "I hope she'll return soon. I need your help, Mrs. E. I have to show my parents that Madame Martin is a fraud. She and her assistant have got to go. If they're doing things like this to us, they've done this to others." She leaned closer to Mrs. Everleigh, touching her shoulder gently. "They've schemed and playacted and worst of all, used other lost brothers, husbands, and fathers to squeeze money out of grieving families. We need your help to drive them out of here for good."

Mrs. Everleigh closed her eyes, shaking her head. Considering the shock this must have been and knowing how delicate Saffron believed Violet Everleigh to be, Alexander was not surprised by her answer, but he found himself disappointed, nonetheless.

Elizabeth's hopeful expression disappeared, not

to be replaced with anger or disappointment, but with the most kindness Alexander had ever seen on her face.

Mrs. Everleigh stepped away from the table, her hands clasping together before leaping apart and fluttering to the toolbox and the uniform within. Her fingers rested on the edge of the box.

With trepidation shaking her voice and filling her eyes, she turned to face Alexander and Elizabeth. "What"—she gulped—"what do you need me to do?"

A muffled ring of the telephone interrupted Elizabeth explaining her idea. Alexander immediately quit the library to answer it. Uneasiness swept over him like a cold breeze when he considered it might be Saffron on the other end of the line with some new danger at her heels. With conditions worsening outside, the only news he expected was bad.

A trill of laughter reached his ears just as Alexander opened the door to the reception room. Inside, a woman in gray stood at the window, receiver in hand. Nanny Badeaux glanced over her shoulder at him in surprise as she murmured into the telephone. "*Oui, mon homme?*" she asked him.

It was such an unusual thing to say that it took Alexander aback long enough to realize this was clearly a private telephone call and not one meant for him, given the vivacious laugh he'd heard. He waved awkwardly and closed the door.

He returned to the library, where he bent his head together with Elizabeth and Mrs. Everleigh to make their plan.

Fog blocked out everything but a few feet of road ahead of the motorcar. It felt as if Saffron and Perry were driving into gray nothingness. Saffron spent the entire drive from the train station fearing a blinded driver would strike the motorcar, so much so that she'd nearly forgotten about the reason she'd hurried back to Bedford in the first place.

It all came rushing back to her, however, when Perry pulled to a stop at the front of Ellington. She practically fell out of the vehicle, thanking her lucky stars that she'd made it back.

Kirby stood just inside the door. "Miss Saffron," he intoned as a maid took her hat, coat, and gloves, "Miss Hale wished me to inform you that the séance has already begun, if you would be so kind as to wait until the end to enter the drawing room."

Saffron's stomach turned. "What séance?"

Kirby opened his mouth to explain, but Saffron didn't wait. Having her companions affected by the hallucinogen just now would be very bad. She needed Elizabeth, Alexander, and especially her mother fully functional if she was to work out the last pieces of Bill's puzzle. She strode to the drawing room and pushed the doors open.

"Stop!" Saffron declared.

The thick scent of the incense and the dimness of the banked fire and closed curtains served to make the atmosphere within nearly as impenetrable as outside. She flicked on the nearest lamp. Those around the card table, which had been moved to the center of the room, squinted as they turned to face her. She was relieved to see that they were still standing, and no hands were pressed on the bare tabletop.

Madame Martin stood opposite Violet, Suzette, and, shocking Saffron entirely, Lady Easting. Mr. Fischer and John looked quizzical, while Mr. Hale glared at her and Mrs. Hale gasped dramatically at her arrival before pressing her handkerchief to her mouth.

"Do not touch anything," Saffron said firmly. Elizabeth gave her a wide-eyed look of irritation that Saffron ignored in favor of turning to the man to her left. "Turn out your pockets, Mr. Fischer."

Mr. Fischer frowned at her. "Miss Everleigh, interrupting Madame just as she begins to channel the spirits is a terribly dangerous thing to do. Should she be possessed of the wrong spirit, horrible consequences may befall her, befall all of us."

"Horrible consequences?" Saffron repeated, suddenly quite angry. "Something like being unable to remember stretches of time? Or experiencing fear and pain at seeing the ghost of a lost loved one appear at your window?"

Saffron could see Mr. Fischer's concern for Madame flicker as he registered what she was getting at. Even in the dim light of the single lamp, she could see color rising in his face. "Every participant is informed of the potential ill effects of communion with the dead."

"And the potential ill effects of the substance you use to inspire that communion?"

Mrs. Hale spoke up, voice shrill. "What are you talking about? Madame Martin will be overtaken by some evil spirit!"

Mr. Fischer straightened, his chest swelling with indignation. "What you imply is insulting to both myself and Madame Martin. She is an earnest servant of the dead and living."

"Prove it, then. Let's see how genuine you and Madame truly are." Saffron lifted a doubtful brow. "Turn out your pockets, Mr. Fischer."

Mr. Fischer opened his mouth to deny her again, but Lady Easting spoke in a dry, cutting voice. "Considering you've convinced my daughter-in-law to hire you, at great expense I might add, I am curious to see their contents myself."

The table went still at her words. Mr. Fischer looked ready to explode. Slowly, he drew from his pants pocket a small notebook with pencil in its crease and a folded handkerchief.

"The rest?" John prompted. "Your jacket."

With a withering glare at John, Mr. Fischer said, "I have nothing in my jacket pockets."

In a flash of speed Saffron wouldn't have thought him capable of, Mr. Hale snatched Fischer's notebook from the table. He squinted at it, grunted in frustration, then stood to march to the lamp. He flipped through a few pages and let out a strangled roar. "Fischer! What the devil is the meaning of this!" He shook the notebook in one fist.

"That is—" Fischer cleared his throat, glancing at Madame, who watched him without expression. "Those are messages from the spirits, not yet decoded by Madame—"

"The devil they are!" barked Mr. Hale. He strode to the table and slammed the notebook down before Fischer. "These are the stocks!"

Though the light made the writing all but illegible, Saffron could see there were lines of numbers and letters written in Fischer's notebook.

"Of course." Fischer affected a soothing tone. "The stocks the spirits advised Madame to encourage you to acquire."

"The spirits didn't tell me *the prices* of the stocks!" He shoved an accusatory finger into Fischer's face. "You've been in my papers! How else would you know the share prices?" He swung around to Saffron, who, despite herself, flinched when he shouted, "What have they been doing to us?"

"That is what we need to discover," Saffron told him. "I believe they've been drugging us during the séances."

Mr. Hale looked to be nearing apoplexy. He rounded on Fischer. "Turn out your pockets, boy, before I turn you upside down and shake their contents out!"

Tight-lipped, Mr. Fischer dipped into his jacket and produced a small glass bottle of what appeared to be scent.

Saffron took it and carefully unscrewed the top. Her head jerked back the moment a rancid smell invaded her nose.

She quickly recapped the bottle and set it down next to Fischer's handkerchief. The two next to each other formed a connection in her mind and Saffron knew exactly how Fischer and Madame had administered their drug.

"A wise choice, the incense," Saffron said, nodding to the brass pot in the center of the table, still roiling with smoke. "The strong scent covers up the awful smell of the substance you wipe onto the table before each séance. You dab it onto your handkerchief and wipe it on the place where your target sits, ensuring they make contact with the drug so they can absorb it through their skin. What is it made from? Mandrake, or perhaps angel's trumpet or jimson weed? I know it isn't belladonna, that has a far more pleasant scent."

Fischer stared at her in seemingly genuine shock.

"Whatever it is, it's highly potent. To intoxicate your victims with just the amount they might absorb in a few minutes . . ." She shook her head, taking a moment to truly appreciate the genius of the plan. The effects were subtle enough that most would attribute it to the mystique of the séance. Its effects varied from person to person, depending on how long they spent in contact with the substance on the surface of the table, their metabolism, and how it interacted with other chemicals in their bodies such as medication and alcohol. And it kept Fischer and Madame entirely in control of their own exposure. All they had to do was avoid wiping the essence on the parts of the table they would touch.

"This is outrageous!" Mrs. Hale cried. "But of course, this isn't true. Mr. Fischer has not been *drugging* us. Madame is no fraud. She foretold Elizabeth's return, did she not? And along with it, the return of our fortunes!"

"What?" Elizabeth cried.

Mrs. Hale plowed on, "Both of which have happened. Elizabeth is back and we've made tens of thousands! How can you accuse her—"

"You told me," Mr. Hale growled at Fischer, "that a reunion with my child would bring about a reunion with my fortune." Fischer rose to his feet, backing away. Hale jabbed a finger at the notebook. "First it was my son, then when she showed up, my daughter. You fed me these ideas while I was half off my rocker from that poison you've been feeding us, damn you!"

Fischer's hands came up in a placating gesture. "Let's not be hasty, now. This is not a poison; it is a solution proven to deepen the spiritual susceptibilities of participants—"

"Susceptible to what?" barked Mr. Hale as he stalked Fischer across the room.

Fischer inched backward in the opposite direction. "Congress with the spirits," he said weakly.

"You lying bastard." Mr. Hale jabbed a finger in the direction of Madame Martin. "You lying bitch!"

Madame finally looked affected by the events unfolding around her. For a moment, she looked lost, maybe even afraid. Saffron almost felt sorry for her.

"I want it back," Mr. Hale said. "I want it all back. All the promissory notes, all the stocks."

"The stocks they told you to buy?" Elizabeth asked.

"The stocks I gave these frauds in payment for their 'services,'" growled Mr. Hale. "Fischer said he would accept them in lieu of cash. Madame's predictions have paid off. The stocks have doubled in worth since I handed them over."

The group turned as one back to Mr. Fischer.

Sweat gleamed on his forehead. He seemed to be fighting an internal battle, and after a beat of silence, he bolted for the nearest door.

Moments before his hands touched the handle to the conservatory, it opened.

The masked ghost soldier stood framed in a white halo.

Fischer yelled, arms wheeling as he stumbled back.

Cries of alarm and fear, including one long, high-pitched shriek from Mrs. Hale, filled the room. The ghost soldier stepped forward and grabbed Fischer by the arm. Fischer fought the soldier bodily, screaming, "No! No! I'm sorry! I'm sorry! Please—"

His screams cut off abruptly when the soldier tore off his mask, revealing Alexander scowling down at Fischer.

That was when the drawing room doors burst open. Nanny Badeaux stumbled through the door, disheveled and panicked. She jabbered in French so rapid that Saffron could only make out half of what she said. John and Suzette raced to her side, and after a moment, had calmed her enough for the rest of the room to understand what had alarmed her so.

Benjamin was gone.

CHAPTER 41

Between hiccups and sips of brandy, a tearful Nanny Badeaux explained that she'd noticed the boy was missing about an hour ago, when the guests for the séance had arrived. In the midst of her search for him, she had been hit over the head and her wrists had been bound.

Saffron listened to the nanny with her hands pressed to her middle and her mouth clamped shut. Any less controlled position and she was sure her tumultuous insides would spill out onto the floor.

Lady Easting listened with a mask of composure. Saffron could see that her hands twisted a handkerchief in her lap. "Who was this person, the one who tied your hands? Was it a man or a woman?"

"A man," the nanny said, nodding firmly. "It was definitely a man."

Saffron was only half-listening at this point, her mind racing around Ellington's property even as she was aware that John, Suzette, and Elizabeth—along with a dozen servants—were already doing so.

Mr. Hale, who'd been pacing before Mr. Fischer with a red face and clenched fists, said,

"Ask that one!" He jabbed a finger at Alexander. "Ask that"—here he used an offensive and inaccurate insult to Alexander's origins—"about what he's been doing, running around in masks, impersonating my son!"

With the current state of unrest, Alexander hadn't had the chance to explain why, exactly, he was wearing Thomas Everleigh's uniform jacket and cap, apart from muttering to Saffron that it had been Elizabeth's idea.

Incensed by Mr. Hale's insult, Saffron began, "That is *quite*—"

"Mr. Hale," snapped Lady Easting, "if you interrupt to speak such nonsense again, I will be forced to ask you to leave."

Mr. Hale sputtered, "Surely you must see—"

"I see that you are in great distress over the realization of your folly in hiring these people," Lady Easting said with a disdainful look at the still-trembling Mr. Fischer and Madame Martin. "But even you can see that the abduction of my grandson is more important than avenging your bruised ego."

Mr. Hale did not speak again after that save for disheartened rumbles.

The medium, oddly enough, had remained in the drawing room with no attempt to flee. She had quietly announced she would consult the spirits for Benjamin's location, to which Lady Easting had said, "Do what you must, but you are not to leave this room until the police have been summoned."

Alexander, who'd remained behind to hear the details of the nanny's story and prevent Mr. Fischer from attempting another escape, had shared that the police should already be on their way but had likely been delayed by the poor visibility and slick roads.

It was a good thing he'd thought to send for them, too, for it had quickly been discovered that the telephone line had been cut.

As it was, should someone wish to disappear, it would be easy. White fog coated the grounds, and the temperature dropped further every moment. Saffron's only comfort was that whether by motorcar or cart, it would be difficult for Benjamin's kidnapper to get away. If they could find them before the fog cleared . . .

"He came upon me quickly, just as my back was turned to check beneath the bed," the nanny said, recalling the group's attention, "but from his heavy steps, I am sure it was a man. A large man."

Saffron turned away from the window and studied the woman. She'd only ever seen the nanny composed as she directed her charge about the house, but now she saw her flushed and tearful, she looked very young. Definitely younger than Saffron's twenty-four years.

But she seemed so mature, especially in the

manner of her expression. She was fearful, to be sure, but her story came out in the correct order, and she did not repeat herself. Saffron had never been able to piece her accounts of her adventures so succinctly, especially not after being hit on the head.

She'd only ever heard the woman speak French, but her French-accented English was essentially perfect. Hadn't John mentioned Suzette and the nanny shared a lack of proficiency in English?

Slowly, she moved to where Alexander stood not far from Mr. Fischer. "The nanny," she whispered. "Have you spoken to her? I don't recall her English being so good."

"It is rather good. And . . ." He gave Saffron a sidelong glance that spoke volumes. "Her hair is blonde."

Saffron's eye was drawn to the library door, where Elizabeth sidled into the room, worry clouding her face. She made her way to Saffron's side, and said in a low voice, "There's no sign of Benjamin outdoors."

Saffron's chest grew tighter. Now she'd heard the nanny's tale, she ought to go out and help John and the others search. She knew Ellington better than anyone and might be able to find something helpful.

Elizabeth's thin brows drew down as she peered around Saffron to get a better look at Nanny Badeaux. "She looks so . . . familiar."

"How?" Alexander murmured.

Elizabeth turned her head to get a better look at the girl, who'd suddenly broken into loud sobs into her handkerchief again. "I've never really gotten a good look at her until now, I suppose. She just . . ." She went still, her eyes going wide with a sharp breath. "The maid from the Path Lab, Saff. The little mouse of a cookmaid. I spoke to her when I rounded up all the staff."

As much as she wished to look on the youthful face of Nanny Badeaux and recognize her, Saffron couldn't. She traced her soft features, currently half-hidden by lace fringe, and saw nothing remarkable. Amelia Gresham's words from months ago floated through her mind: *"It is shocking, isn't it, how easily overlooked a messenger is, a maid, a nurse."*

As the bitter words swirled in her head like suds going down a drain, a hot wave of nausea washed over her. If this woman had worked in the Path Lab, she was working with Bill. Which meant that Bill had Benjamin.

"What do you want to do?" Alexander asked.

If-then scenarios whipped through Saffron's mind. If Bill had Benjamin, he would be alive, wouldn't he? And he would have to be nearby if Bill wanted his information. Why had he not waited to confirm she'd missed his deadline before taking Benjamin? If she gave him all she'd assembled, then he would give Benjamin back, wouldn't he? And if he didn't, then would she have to tell Bill the truth about her mother?

Alexander cleared his throat. "If I may?"

Saffron nodded, and she and Elizabeth followed him to where Nanny Badeaux sat quietly sobbing into her handkerchief.

In French, Alexander asked, "What is your full name, Nanny Badeaux?"

"Nadine Louise Badeaux," she said, pausing her tears to pat her eyes. From this distance, Saffron could see that the redness of her eyes and her tears were real, if not genuine.

Cadence smooth, Alexander asked, "And where are you from originally?"

"I was born in Eauze," she replied, slower this time, looking from Alexander to the others in the room as if suddenly aware that it was odd that he, of all people, was asking her questions.

The Hales eyed him unpleasantly, while Lady Easting gazed into the fire, mouth pressed into a line. "It is a small commune in the south, not so far from Toulouse."

"You have traveled much, then," Alexander said.

"Why do you say so, *monsieur*?"

"Your English is very good." He smiled a little. "Far better than my French."

Nadine's lashes fluttered. "Thank you, *monsieur*," she said in English.

At her side, Elizabeth softly scoffed. She'd

clearly caught how Nadine's accent was suddenly much thicker. Saffron wondered if she also noticed how Nadine's pleased expression dropped when she bashfully ducked her head.

"It must be very hard, having your charge being stolen away," Alexander said, returning to French. "And to be restrained in such a manner, too. How did you escape?"

Nadine repeated in now halting English what she had told them, that she had come to after the dark figure of a man hit her on the head and her hands were bound by rope. She'd struggled for quite some time, she guessed twenty minutes, before she managed to pull her hands free.

Alexander made a sympathetic noise in his throat before extending a hand to Nadine. She looked at him cautiously, and gave him her hand. "I am sorry you had to suffer through that. I have been tied up with ropes before. It is painful, to be bound so tightly. I dislocated my shoulder attempting to free myself from them. And they left marks."

Nadine's eyes flashed, and she jerked her hand away. Alexander was too fast for her. His hand locked around her arm.

"I'm going to examine your wrist now," he said.

By now, the rest of the room was riveted on them. Saffron was half-surprised that her grandmother did not interrupt, but her attention was rapt on him as Alexander said, "The buttons, Saffron."

She undid the trio of tiny white buttons at Nadine's wrist and pulled the sleeve back. She and Alexander's eyes met over Nadine's perfectly smooth white skin.

"Where is Benjamin?" Saffron asked Nadine.

The girl had gone still, her gaze distant. In response, she pressed her lips together.

Lady Easting got to her feet and stood before the girl. "Young woman, you will tell us where my grandson is now."

Nadine said nothing.

"If you help us recover him safely, I will do what I can to lessen the consequences for you." When the girl continued in her silence, Lady Easting's even expression soured. "And if you refuse cooperation, I will guarantee you shall never see the light of day again. Where is my grandchild?"

In the corner, the clock chimed four o'clock. Nadine turned to Saffron. A bitter smile touched her lips as she hissed, "Your time is up."

It was then that Saffron remembered the gun that Elizabeth had given her, tucked in an interior pocket of her jacket. She was grateful she hadn't remembered it at her father's flat, else Lee might have ended up shot instead of bruised.

Her fingers trembled as she reached for it, and a hideous sense of falling rose within her as she drew Elizabeth's pistol out and leveled it at Nadine. "Answer the question. Now."

Nadine froze, her eyes flickering from the gun to Saffron's face to the pair of French doors Mr. Fischer had meant to go through. Saffron's grip tightened on the pistol.

Lady Easting demanded, "Why in heaven's name do you have a pistol?"

Saffron swallowed. Voice remarkably calm, she replied, "I think it's appropriate considering the situation, Grandmama."

The drawing room door burst open once more, making them all flinch. Nadine leaped up, but Alexander was there, gripping her arm and forcing her back into the chair.

Fischer had the same idea, but Mr. Hale roared, "Oh, no you don't!" and slammed him into his chair with such force that the chair creaked forebodingly.

"What is happening here?" Lord Easting wheezed from the door.

They no doubt presented a bizarre tableau: Lord Easting's neighbor all but sitting on his own houseguest, and his granddaughter standing at the center of the room, aiming a pistol at a servant being restrained by the granddaughter's unwelcome boyfriend. He blinked, then cleared his throat. "We'll need to secure the girl, will we, Ashton?"

Nadine bared her teeth and struggled against

Alexander's grip. He was unfazed. "Yes, my lord."

In short order, Nadine Badeaux was tied to her chair with a curtain tie, along with Mr. Fischer. He'd made a further attempt to flee, after which he was determined to be at too great a risk of escaping. Mr. Hale likely would have continued nearly sitting on him, but Alexander made quick work of binding Fischer to his chair, as well.

"Listen here, you miscreants," Lord Easting growled. He leaned heavily on his cane as he stood before Nadine, Fischer, and Madame, who had made no move from her place at the round card table. "My grandson is missing, and I want to know where he is."

"I've got nothing to do with the boy!" Fischer protested.

"It's Dr. Wyatt," Saffron said, stepping forward.

Lady Easting's displeasure iced over her voice. "I cannot believe you would use this as an opportunity to air your nonsensical fixation—"

"I am trying to help find Benjamin," Saffron interrupted. "Why would I be insisting on something unless I thought it would help? I *told* you." Now her voice shook. "I told you that he wasn't to be trusted, that he was dangerous—"

"But you neglected to mention the severity of the situation," spat Lady Easting. "If you believed the man capable of abducting a child from our home, you should have said so."

John entered the room, his eyes wild and face ruddy. Suzette followed, clinging to Violet, as Violet helped her into the nearest seat. They were both pale.

"We've found nothing," John said. His voice sounded like his throat had been through a meat grinder. "There's not even tire tracks on the drive apart from the ones on Perry's motorcar."

"He's kept him here," Saffron said to Alexander and Elizabeth. "We've got to search the grounds—"

"We just did," John said, hands pushing into his hair to tug at it. "There's nothing. Damn it all, there's no clue! Why would he take my son?"

Lord and Lady Easting swung around to stare at Saffron.

"Well?" Lady Easting asked. "You claim to have some insight into this—this person. Why would he take Benjamin?"

Saffron squared her shoulders. It was well past the time for honesty. "Dr. Wyatt took up a position here to blackmail me into finding information about a study my father was working on before his death. He believes it is valuable information he can sell. Nadine is working for him, and we don't know who else he might have fooled or threatened. I know him as Bill."

"And he simply showed up here expecting he

would find Thomas's research?" Lord Easting asked incredulously.

"He has been following me, in London. He likely knew that you would send for me if Grandpapa was very ill," Saffron said.

Lady Easting stiffened, her eyes looking away in a singularly avoidant manner.

"Grandmama?" Saffron prompted.

But it was Violet who spoke. "I sent for you," she said apologetically. "Not your grandparents, Saffron."

"I—I see," she said. That her grandmother had not summoned her home when she worried Lord Easting was very ill, possibly deathly so, was a blow she would have to reckon with another time. "There is no time to waste. Bill must be found, and hopefully with him, Benjamin. Grandpapa, send someone you trust to the police to tell them what's happened. We can't know if the officers Alexander mustered will actually come. Then everyone must be locked up together. We don't know who else might be under Bill's thumb." Lord Easting did not respond, so she added, "Alexander and I will go in search of Benjamin."

"Don't be ridiculous," her grandmother said. "You're not going after a mad criminal!"

"I've already explained—"

Her ladyship was undeterred and grew louder. "Be quiet, girl. You will not be running all over waving a gun about like you're in the Wild West. This is my house and you will not—"

Saffron walked out of the room.

There was no one about, but she could hear feet rushing around upstairs and gravel crunching in the drive. The servants, searching for Benjamin.

She paused. Finding Benjamin was paramount, but would Bill release him if she didn't have anything concrete to give him?

She needed her mother. Her head fell forward with a regretful sigh that she'd have to go right back into the drawing room, but the soft clatter of heels on the tile floor drew her attention.

Alexander and Violet came to where she stood in the middle of the cold entry.

"Mama," Saffron began, and her mother's face crumpled. "You know what Bill wants?"

Violet covered her face with her hands. "Yes." She gulped a breath. When her hands fell away, her eyes were haunted. "It's me. I'm what he wants."

CHAPTER 42

Tell me everything." Saffron stared at her mother, willing her to respond. Even an angry denial would be better than the far-off, sorrowful look her mother wore. "I know about the research. I know you and Papa worked on something together, something with Demian Petrov."

Life came back to her mother's expression with a look of shock. "How do you know about Demian?"

"That explanation will have to wait. Bill wants the research, Mama. He's taken Benjamin to ensure he gets it. Where is it?"

Violet looked about somewhat helplessly before taking Saffron's arm and leading her down the hall. "We need privacy."

When they were ensconced in the saloon, Saffron asked, "Well?"

Violet's hands flexed with nervous energy before her. She took a few steps toward the couch, then turned sharply and took a few paces away. "I thought this was over and done. I never considered that I would ever have to explain it."

"Mama," Saffron said sharply.

"It started in Brighton," Violet said. "Your father was presenting a talk at the Booth Museum.

390

I went along. After the talk was through, Thomas was approached by an older man who wanted to discuss a particular comment he made in regard to chemical analysis."

"Demian Petrov?" Saffron asked.

She nodded. "He and your father spent hours speaking together that evening, and much of the week we spent in Brighton. Demian had come to the sea to see if it improved his health, you see. It was failing, and he was desperate to see if he could find a solution." Violet settled herself on a couch and looked at Saffron expectantly.

Saffron didn't want to sit and listen to a story, not with worry eating at her, but she did.

"I asked him, some years later, why he was so passionate about finding the cure to his ailments. He was not a joyful fellow. In truth, he was rather dour and pessimistic. He cared only for his work but never seemed to take pleasure in it. So I asked him why he worked so hard, and hounded Thomas so relentlessly, to find a cure. He told me it was because it was not just him that was affected. He came from a small rural town not far from Odessa. Many in the town took ill over his lifetime with similar complaints."

She remembered his autopsy report. "His kidneys and liver."

Her mother's lips parted in surprise, but she gave her head a little shake and continued. "Demian wanted to find the solution for the illness affecting him and his people. He wanted to discover its cause and find a cure."

"But why work with Papa?" Saffron asked. "He was a plant pathologist, not a medical doctor."

"Demian had been working on this problem before he was forced to leave Russia when the revolution began. He'd narrowed it down to diet and had fled the country with samples of his region's common plants, intending to continue his work wherever he found refuge. Our government hired him, but they had no interest in that particular project, he said. He was quite bitter about it."

"How did you know him so well?"

"I was his main correspondent. He wrote something like twice a week for . . ." She blew out a breath, thinking. "Seven years. Since this was a private project, Thomas grew the samples Demian had given him here, in his greenhouse. Your father believed that breeding the plants for potency would make it easier to isolate the chemicals that might have caused the illness. I took care of the specimens while your father was away at the university, and I gave Demian updates." She smiled slightly. "I eventually took over all responsibility for communication between Thomas and Demian. I advised him on medicinal plants that might ease his symptoms. He told me things about his life, his work before fleeing Russia. I cannot say he and I became friends, but we were in continuous contact."

"And when Papa died, that ended?" Saffron guessed.

"No," Violet said slowly, "not exactly. We'd made progress, good progress. Through Thomas's experimentation, we narrowed it down to a single plant responsible for Demian's illness." Her gray eyes went distant. "We'd just made plans for the next step, finding the counter to the poison, when the war began."

Questions welled like collecting raindrops on Saffron's tongue, but her mother continued.

"Just before Thomas left for the war, the government had approached him. It happened in London, so I don't know the precise details, but I know Demian's nationality and allegiance were a topic of some interest. Your father felt they didn't believe they were working on something so innocent as identifying and countering an illness. They told him to turn over all the research, all the samples. He refused, of course. He sent me a telegraph telling me to burn it all. And I did."

Saffron's mouth went slack. "But . . . That was years of research—research that could have helped hundreds, maybe thousands of people. What about Petrov?"

Her mother was nodding. "It was under Petrov's orders that I destroyed everything. We thought he was paranoid when he told us of the importance of the research. But he was sure that if it was discovered the effects of consuming birthwort—"

"*Aristolochia clematitis*," Alexander said.

Saffron and Violet flinched in unison. They had both forgotten he'd followed them into the saloon, not to mention it was terribly disconcerting to see him wearing an army uniform. Unlike Fischer, he wore the accessories, including a pistol holstered at his waist.

Violet nodded, now a little unsure, as if being recalled back to the present had daunted her. "Yes. That was the plant they'd narrowed it down to. Innocuous, but deadly if chronically consumed. Demian was convinced that sort of information would be dangerous, should it be widely known. Something about his experiences as a government scientist made him wary of it. After what happened to Thomas, the gas . . . I will never again doubt it."

Saffron didn't know what to say. All her life, her mother had been a quiet woman, supportive of her interests from a distance, and her father was enshrined in her memory as her educator, her guide and inspiration in adventure and intellect. To learn her mother had some of the same skills and knowledge and could have been a companion to her in her studies and struggles . . . It hurt. It hurt to know her mother had never shared that with her. Would she ever have brought it up, had this not happened?

But there was no time for that.

"And you truly destroyed the research?" she asked her mother. "I have nothing to give to Bill in exchange for Benjamin?"

There was a commotion outside, muted by the closed door. Alexander stepped over to it and opened it swiftly.

Two young women tumbled inside, one in a maid's uniform and the other in simple garb. They scrambled to their feet, speaking over each other in increasingly loud, desperate voices.

Martha, the maid, and her sister—Maisie, Saffron recalled—were near identical images of each other, right down to the red flush of their cheeks and the tears glittering in their eyes.

Martha addressed Violet. "Please, please, Mrs. Everleigh, we didn't know—"

"—the boy would be taken!" her sister finished. "We would never have helped if we'd known!"

Their hands rung in twin motions at their waists. Martha said, "He told us he would take us to London with him if we went along with his schemes."

Saffron's heart sank. These two had been wrapped up in Bill's plot, and now had not only put Benjamin in danger, but their own lives would be ruined.

"But why wait to tell us until now that you knew something?" Violet asked.

Maisie's eyes pleaded with her. "We only just heard what's happened, that he was here!"

Saffron and Alexander looked at each other. Alexander said, "Dr. Wyatt has been here at Ellington the entire time."

It was the twins' turn to share a confused look. "Not Dr. Wyatt—" Martha began.

Maisie spoke over her. "Mr. *Fischer*."

It was nearly painful to take the sobbing maids to the drawing room. Their story was ready to be unraveled, but Saffron had no time for it. Her mother's tale had already taken up far too much time, with nothing to show for it.

They reached the drawing room, which Saffron was glad to find locked.

"Eliza," she called, "it's me and Alexander and my mother. Let us in, please."

Elizabeth's voice called through the door, "What color are my toenails?"

"What—?" Saffron shook her head. "They are red."

"What shade?"

"What on earth for?"

"Answer the question."

"Old Rose," Saffron said impatiently. "Now let us in."

At last inside, Elizabeth waved away Saffron's disgruntled questions. "Had to be sure it was you, darling. I've discovered a rather interesting thing about dear Nanny Badeaux."

The maids' tears dried up the moment they

caught sight of Fischer and Nadine tied to their chairs.

Elizabeth pointed at the nanny and said, "This one has quite a mouth on her. Not only did she take credit for drugging your water the other night, but she is a rather talented mimic. Apparently, when my beau telephoned, she pretended to be Suzette."

"Your beau?" Saffron asked.

"Lee," Elizabeth said, rolling her eyes. "Bill's information gathering about us has proven faulty in at least one regard."

"I'm happy to hear it," Saffron murmured, eyeing the nanny. She was glaring at them in a way that made her look like a petulant twelve-year-old. "That explains why you all went ahead with the séance; you didn't get my warning."

Ignoring the rest of the group, who watched with a mixture of disdain (her grandmother), hope (Suzette), and avid curiosity (her neighbors), Saffron marched up to Nadine and said, "Where is Bill?"

"Bill was right," she sneered, her French accent gone, replaced by an undistinguished English one, "you are simple. These people have asked me that a dozen times already. What makes you think I'll tell you?"

"The water."

All eyes swung around to Madame Martin.

She'd risen to her feet, and her dark eyes were wide and focused on something far away.

"What are you blathering about now!" Mr. Hale growled.

"Don't let her speak," Mrs. Hale chimed in, clutching her husband's arm. "She will only draw us back into her lies!"

"He took the boy to the water," Madame said. "I have seen it."

Mr. Hale groaned. "For the love of—"

Madame raised one pale hand, a finger extended, to the window. "I know this. The doctor, he took the boy to the lake."

Lady Easting deigned to turn in the medium's direction. Her face was so white as to resemble paper. "Madame Martin," she said with deceptive civility, "if you say one further word capitalizing on the disappearance of my grandson, I will ensure—"

"Believe what you will about me and my abilities, my morals." Madame enunciated each word, her waving hand like a brush painting the room with censure, "but I would never confer a child to danger. I have seen the doctor with the boy." She pointed to the window again.

Saffron dashed to the window. Through a gap in the curtain, she could see a short stretch of dark water as the fog shifted. She turned back to Madame.

Madame Martin regarded her with dark eyes

bright with something Saffron didn't quite understand. Intelligence, defiance, trepidation. Whatever it was, Saffron had no other clues as to where Bill had gone.

She pushed through the doors of the conservatory. She could hear the protests of her family, but she ignored them as she strode down the gloomy path to the doors leading to the formal gardens. She shoved aside a palm's leaves and attempted to open the door.

"Allow me," Alexander said behind her.

She stepped aside and he wrenched the doors open. Freezing fog flooded the room and Saffron launched herself into it.

Swirling white obscured everything save what was directly before them: the solemn columns of cypress trees appearing like cloaked figures and bare branches of the ornamental fruit trees reaching out with gnarled fingers. Occasional breaths of wind revealed and then disappeared the landscape like a magician.

"What are we going to do?" Saffron said, gasping for breath as they ran for the lake.

Alexander didn't break pace. "I don't know."

As they broke through the garden onto the lawn, Saffron stumbled and cursed under her breath, and quite nearly fell over again when a voice hissed her name.

Dumbfounded, Saffron turned. "Mama?"

Her mother emerged from the white-cloaked

garden, wild-eyed and panting. "It's me he wants. I'll go."

She felt as if her lungs were going to shrivel up. "Mama, *no*—"

Alexander said quickly, "We're all going. Three is better than one."

CHAPTER 43

The wavering edge where grass met water appeared before them, then the posts of the dock and its worn planks, then at last, Bill's shadowy figure standing at the end, a small skiff eerily still in the water next to him. With the water reflecting the fog, it looked as if the dock and the boat were suspended in clouds. Saffron, Alexander, and Violet slowly walked toward him, stopping just when Bill's face became clear. It was just as calm as ever. He held Benjamin in his arms. The boy's eyes were closed, rosy lips parted slightly. There was no way he was sleeping peacefully with a stranger outside in the cold; he was doubtless drugged just as Saffron had been.

"What an assemblage," Bill said blandly, his eyes moving face to face to rest on Saffron's.

"Is Benjamin all right?" Violet asked, voice trembling.

Bill's eyes moved back to hers with a little smile. "Of course."

Saffron's fingernails dug into her clammy palms. "Why have you taken him?"

"I'd planned on taking little Benjamin here

with me to ensure continued cooperation in a different venue. A change of scenery can be so refreshing."

He turned his bland smile on Violet. "But you were so good to bring me the person who has the information I want." Benjamin whimpered and shifted against him, and Bill murmured something to him, not taking his eyes from Violet. "I should have seen it from the beginning, the moment I learned it's been you keeping the conservatory so full of green all these years. The woman so dedicated to her husband's memory *must* know something about his work. I do admire your bravery, Violet, in overcoming your fears to come to Benjamin's aid. You shall come with me now."

Saffron stepped forward, Alexander following her. "My mother doesn't need to go with you anywhere. I have new information for you."

"I gave you too much leeway and not enough motivation. This little project has taken quite long enough. My client grows impatient, as do I. I'm not going to be snapping your leash any longer." He shifted Benjamin to rest on his other arm. "Violet will come with me, assured that the safety of her family will depend on her honesty and efficiency."

Saffron's mouth went dry. "Bill, please—"

"Or," Bill said quietly, "we can provide some motivation right now." He moved slightly toward the side of the dock. "The cold water will wake him up . . . hopefully."

Saffron stepped forward. "Please—"

"Stop," Violet called. "I'll come. I'll tell you everything." She put a hand on Saffron's arm. It was not reassuring; Violet's entire body quaked. "It will be all right."

"Very good," murmured Bill, more to Benjamin's sleeping form than Violet.

Saffron looked fearfully at Alexander. His eyes met hers, and she hoped behind his unfathomable gaze a plan was forming.

"Come here, Saffron," Bill said.

Though she could practically feel the opposite pull of Alexander and her mother's thoughts, she stepped toward Bill. Her heart hammered in her chest.

When she stood three feet from him, arms outstretched to take Benjamin, he murmured, "Turn around."

"Why?"

His voice was silky and quiet. "You're questioning me when I have still your cousin's son in my arms? Do it."

She swallowed and turned around.

"Now bring your wrists together behind your back."

"What—?" The question died in her throat as metal cinched around her wrists with a click. Her eyes locked on Alexander's. She tried to look brave, but the addition of handcuffs without explanation made that impossible.

"Now, Violet," said Bill slowly, easing around Saffron. "You are coming with me, and we shall see if you've entrusted your daughter to the right man." And he pushed Saffron off the dock.

CHAPTER 44

A lexander watched Saffron fall into the water with steely resolve. He was annoyed by this tactic; it was stupid and time-wasting. Saffron could swim, even with her hands bound, to the nearby shore.

The moment Saffron hit the water, Mrs. Everleigh had stepped forward and cried out, ignorant of the gun Alexander slipped into her jacket pocket. Thomas Everleigh's army-issued Webley had been Alexander's addition to Fischer's costume, and Bill locking Saffron into the handcuffs had given him just long enough time to take the revolver from the holster and tuck it into Mrs. Everleigh's jacket pocket. He hoped it would be more useful to her than it had been thus far to him. Even if he'd been certain he could manage to maintain control over himself holding the gun, he wouldn't attempt a shot at Bill with the boy in his arms.

Bill hurried past him with a smug smile. His pleasure at having out-maneuvered Alexander was clear. With Saffron in the water and a drugged child in his arms at risk of being thrown into the lake as well, there was little Alexander could do.

In the year-long handful of seconds he'd

experienced between Saffron going into the lake and Bill forcing Mrs. Everleigh forward onto land, he waited for the splash of Saffron swimming to shore, but it never came. Instinct took over, and he dove into the water.

The water was frigid but not impossibly so, and it broke easily before him as he dove after Saffron. His eyes blinked against the murk, searching for Saffron in the cloudy water. His breath ran out and his head broke the surface.

A gasp somewhere several yards away said, "Ben," before bubbles gurgled through the mist. The resolve Alexander felt broke apart into panic in a second. He took a stroke forward toward the sound.

"Alex—" Saffron's voice came again, scared and breathless, before succumbing to the water.

He swam forward. Her pale forehead broke the surface, followed by her terrified eyes.

He caught Saffron's shoulder as her head slipped back under. He tried to jerk her head above water, but she didn't come up farther than her lips, which gasped and began to cry out before water flooded her mouth again.

He dove down, feeling the weight of her flooded coat and layers of wool and cotton. His hands ran from her hips to her legs until he came upon a tree branch had hooked the ties of her boots. He unhooked her foot and pushed her toward the surface.

Heart pounding, he took a long breath once he was in the biting cold of open air. "Are you all right?"

Saffron was swimming on her back, kicking wildly toward the shore. "Get Benjamin!"

"Bill took him with your mother—"

She made a choked sound, shaking her head in violent jerks that made her swallow water. "By the shore. In the water."

Alexander tore off through the water, diving with hands outstretched and eyes open. His hands caught on reeds and he found he could stand. He paused, ears strained for any sound apart from his own body disturbing the water and Saffron's splashing.

"Stop kicking," he called. "I can't hear."

Yards away, the splashing stopped.

The boy would have been in the water only a minute or two, no more. There was still time.

That thought echoed in his ears as seconds ticked by. The flat white of the fog that now bore down on him was suffocating, a physical reminder of his panic. He slopped his way out of the water and dashed up and over the dock, looking frantically about him. There was nothing but ripples of water.

A dark shape came into focus and Alexander dove. He grabbed at it, hands closing around wet wool. Benjamin was motionless, his face starkly white. Alexander scooped him into his arms and began forcefully patting his back.

"I have him!" he called.

"Is he—" Saffron's voice cut off.

Dread seeped into his heart like the cold into his bones. "I'm coming to shore."

Alexander set Benjamin along the wet grass at the water's edge. How did one help a drowning victim, a small child? His chest wasn't moving at all.

Alexander pressed gingerly on his belly, causing a small spurt of liquid to come from his mouth. He pressed several more times with less hesitation and laughed aloud when Benjamin coughed and sputtered and began to cry. He gathered him up and held him tightly to his chest, speaking words of comfort as best he could in French.

"He's alive!" Saffron cried, stumbling forward and collapsing next to where Alexander knelt. Her white face was plastered with hair so dark it was black. Her eyes glittered with tears.

He brought Saffron to her feet with difficulty, her hands still trapped behind her back by the handcuffs. His limbs were weak with relief and cold, but they weren't safe yet. Slowly, they made their way up the slope of the lawn toward the house.

CHAPTER 45

Through chattering teeth and blue-tinged lips, Saffron repeated, "I couldn't care less about becoming ill! Bill has my mother!"

Lord Easting, who watched Suzette weep over her son with a pained look, shook his head. "The police will be here any moment. John went to retrieve them, and they can manage."

"I'm not letting my mother be taken away by the man who tossed a three-year-old child into a lake!" Saffron turned to Alexander for support. He barely looked ruffled, though he, too, was dripping steadily onto the Axminster before the fire in the drawing room.

"In this fog, we're losing them moment by moment," he said. "If we can't find them in an hour, we'll return."

Lord Easting cast a surreptitious look at Lady Easting, who sat with a rather blank look next to Suzette. It was odd that she wasn't the one arguing with Saffron, but her grandmother looked shell-shocked by what had transpired.

Saffron clutched her blanket about herself tighter, the bracelets of the cut handcuffs jingling slightly at her wrists. The bewildered groom, armed with a hoof clipper, hadn't known how to do more than cut the chain when he was summoned to get the things off her.

Saffron rounded on Nadine. "Where did he take my mother?"

Nadine laughed coldly, attempting to toss her hair but unable to do so, bound as she was to the chair. "Why should I tell you?"

It was hard to sound cool through her chattering teeth. "Because you have a shred of decency."

"Try again," said Nadine. Her impassivity was not as perfect as Bill's; Saffron saw a hint of something like doubt in her eyes.

"You are going to prison no matter what else happens today, but that experience might be less unpleasant if you assist us now," Alexander said.

Nadine scoffed, but Saffron sensed her tension. She had no idea if her grandparents would be willing to say anything in support of Nadine, but if she found her mother safe, she'd be perfectly willing to tell the police that Nadine had cooperated. Saffron counted down in her mind; every moment Nadine wasted was time given to Bill to secret away Saffron's mother.

"Time's up," Saffron said. She tugged Alexander's hand toward the door. "Good luck."

She stopped just a few steps into the hall, her body suddenly shaking uncontrollably. Alexander wrapped her in his arms, and though he was just as wet and clammy as she was, she pressed into him. "I don't know what to do," she mumbled into his chest.

"We search for them. You said you had some ideas of where he would have taken Benjamin. We'll start there."

"Miss!"

Saffron and Alexander turned as one to the drawing room. Martha stood with one foot on the threshold, looking torn.

"What is it?" Saffron asked, wiping her tears away.

"The boot boy!"

Saffron frowned. "Er, what about him?"

"I've heard Harry, the boot boy, complaining," Martha said, "about the doctor's shoes. Every day, Harry's been asking how a fancy doctor mucks up his shoes when all he had to do was sit about in the house. I thought it was strange. A man like Dr. Wyatt, with a motorcar and horses and all at his service. I reckon it means that doctor fellow has a place 'round here to hide out. Harry whines about how the clay is dreadful to get off."

Saffron jerked out of Alexander's embrace. "Thank you, Martha." She spun around to Alexander. "I know where Bill is."

CHAPTER 46

The ice cellar was halfway between the main house and the road that went along Ellington's western and northern border. It had been dug into the side of a hill, and that hill was barely distinguishable from the rest of the land, given the tall, matted grasses that covered it. But this hill was unique, made taller by layers of the hard clay from the southern reach of the property where the lake had been dug out a century and a half ago. It made for claggy dirt perfect for insulating hundreds of pounds of ice. In wet weather, like the sort they'd experienced for the past week, the whole area became slippery with it.

Saffron guided Alexander around the base of the hill in search of the gated opening. She came up short when a curious sound floated through the mist.

The raspy clicking didn't register until Alexander touched her arm and whispered, "A lighter."

A moment later, the pungent scent of a cigarette floated by. Someone was standing just before the entrance to the ice cellar.

"A guard?" Saffron whispered. She ought to

have known; Bill was too smart to assume that he could control the situation with only one young woman in his employ.

Alexander narrowed his eyes, attempting to see through the haze.

Saffron did the same. She could see the outline of the hill, abruptly edged by the angular frame of the stone entry. She could imagine it better than she saw it: a wrought-iron gate, practical rather than decorative, covering the cavernous entrance. The smoker, whoever it was, was likely outside so as not to pollute the air within the cellar.

That was confirmed a moment later when the soft swish of footfalls on vegetation indicated the smoker was walking. Back and forth they went, coating the whiteness with the stink of cigarette smoke.

Carefully, Saffron drew herself and Alexander away toward the tree line.

"Do you think this is it?" Alexander asked when they'd settled their shoulders against an old oak, facing one another.

"I think it must be. Who else would be holed up in the ice cellar?" She swallowed, imagining the dank darkness of the cellar. Nobody would willingly linger there. "The gate might be locked."

"We have ways of dealing with that," Alexander said.

She attempted a smile, but her face was

frozen and not just from the cold. Fear, dark and squirming, filled her insides. "If we attack the guard, the noise will alarm Bill. He might hurt my mother."

"You don't need to attack anyone," Alexander replied. "I'm capable of dealing with one man standing guard. However, that is a good point. I can't guarantee a quiet fight."

Saffron considered the pistol in her pocket. It was useless, having been in the water, and she wasn't sure she was willing to use it now anyway. Not when there was an alternative, even if it was an alternative that made her insides feel like a slurry of churning ice. "There is another way into the cellar."

"Where is it?"

Saffron forced herself to say the words. "There's a short passage into the pit on the west side of the hill, an alternative place to push the ice through when the store was low and they didn't want the blocks to be smashed by falling from the hole in the ceiling." He was nodding. "You can't use it. You can't fit."

He was quiet for a beat. "But you can."

Fear welled inside her, making her lungs tight and her eyes wet. "I can get in that way. But I doubt my mother and I could come out that way again."

Doing it once would be enough to put her right over the edge into utter panic. Not to mention she didn't know what state her mother would be in. No, they would need faster egress.

"You'll need to subdue the guard and have the gate unlocked and ready," she told Alexander.

"I will," he said firmly, his eyes not leaving hers. "As soon as I put the guard down and get the gate unlocked, I'll tap three times on the bars to signal I'm ready. Then we'll deal with Bill together."

Saffron nodded jerkily and straightened off the tree trunk. The walk had warmed and distracted her from how cold she was, but she felt it anew now. Her whole body quaked.

Alexander didn't let her stand there shivering. He wrapped himself around her, one hand in her hair, pressing her head against his heart, and the other slipping under her coat to warm her back. They stood like that, suspended in fog and grounded only to each other.

He stepped back, hands sweeping down her sides before pressing a kiss to her lips. "We will get her," he murmured. His eyes were so calm, so certain. "Wait for my signal, and then we'll do this together."

CHAPTER 47

The ice cellar had once been used to store ice from the River Ouse, but never in Saffron's lifetime. The underground pit and rooms had been a place Saffron, Elizabeth, and other children in the neighborhood had been warned never to go but had frequented, nonetheless.

Saffron had never liked it. One might imagine that some traumatic event in the underground structure had caused her aversion to all things subterranean, but years of contemplating her fear of small, underground spaces and prodding at her mind to discover its roots had left her with no real explanation.

Looking now at the dark indentation in the hill's overlong dead grass, it was perhaps less of a mystery. How could anyone want to climb into something so closely resembling their own grave?

Or maybe not her grave, but her mother's.

Saffron pushed aside that horrid thought as she pushed aside the grass. She needed to keep her mind far away from the dark, tight space she was about to crawl into.

Had Wesley not nearly broken his leg on this hill after stepping into this hole one sunny afternoon, they would have never known the passage existed. She'd never crawled through it before, though she knew it could be done because Wesley had when they realized where exactly it went.

She stared at the hole. Perhaps three feet in diameter, it was wide enough for her to crawl into. But just barely. It was a short tunnel, though not short enough she would be able to simply push herself through all at once. She would have to crawl.

And she would have to do it now. Alexander would give her a head start, but if things went wrong and disabling the guard alarmed Bill, she wanted to be ready.

Her hands reached inside the hole and felt cold, hard earth. Head ducked and eyes squinting, she could just make out the tiniest of lights on the other side. Someone had lit a torch or lantern inside.

She straightened up, then filled and emptied her lungs a few times. She crouched down, and wriggled her way into the tunnel, hands first.

The smell of cold earth filled her nostrils. Loamy dirt, rich and fertile, mixed with mineral clay left undisturbed, out of sight of the sun.

She clenched her teeth and wriggled forward. Her hands had not yet found the opening and her feet had not yet entered the tunnel.

She pushed and pulled, digging her hands into

the earth, dragging herself forward. Every breath tasted of dirt. Cold soil pressed into the tender flesh beneath her fingernails. Particles rained on her face, and she wished she could brush them away, but her hands were stuck in front of her. They dug into the dirt. She was entirely encased now, and that knowledge made her dizzy.

She thrashed against it, nearly rolling over with the strain of trying to move. Her muscles burned. Her head was hot. Her lungs screamed as she struggled to fill them, but stopping for even a moment to catch her breath was impossible. Ceasing moving would feel like acceptance of this place, this tomb. She clawed at it, ripping her fingernails. She would not be staying here and she would not leave her mother in this place, either.

Her hands met open air. She choked on a light-headed sob. She leveraged her palms against the rough stone and pulled. Her arms burned, her lungs burned, her eyes burned, but she emerged from the tunnel.

Slowly, she extricated herself. Clinging to the wall and the tunnel's edges, she held still, breathing deeply, until she no longer felt the terror of the tunnel pressing down on her.

When she stood straight, back pressed to the wall along the shallow ledge, she wished she'd found another way inside.

Yawning, gaping blackness filled the space

between her and the softly lit stone passage on the other side.

It had frightened her as a child. She'd never even contemplated doing what she'd been dared to do half a dozen times, what she would have to do now. She was going to walk the ledge to the other side.

Being half the size of an adult made the pit seem twice as large, but the ledge that much more possible to traverse. As it was, she had only a foot between her and what appeared to be an endless fall into darkness.

Her rational mind knew that this was not true; the pit where the ice used to be kept was only about thirty feet down from the ledge. She'd seen the bottom before, on days when full sunlight shone down through the opened hatch at the peak of the egg-shaped roof. She'd tossed stones and sticks and any number of objects into the pit for the sheer pleasure of hearing the terrific echo of them landing at the bottom.

Her less rational mind, however, saw unrelieved darkness and imagined she'd have plenty of time to regret her decisions as she fell.

She exhaled slowly, locking her eyes on the passage on the other side. She started to move.

Inching her way along the ledge made her thankful she'd chosen to wear her short boots. It also made her marvel once again at Wesley, who'd frequently dared to circumambulate the pit along the edge during their childish raids on the place. He'd never fallen in—none of them had, somehow—but there had been close calls. Elizabeth had tripped on a loose stone once, and they'd had to haul her up—

Saffron's foot slipped. Her hands, already thrown wide against the wall, twisted desperately, searching for something to cling to.

Time spun out into darkness—

And her balance returned.

She gulped for air. After her heart restarted its rhythm, she realized she'd likely been far too loud between the jangling of her cut handcuffs, soft pings of falling stone into the pit, and her hysterical panting. But nothing stirred through the opening to the passage. She resolved to stop remembering past adventures and focus on this one.

The passage grew closer as she slowly traversed the ledge, moving with the same steady rotation as the moon around the earth and seeming to take just as long to reach her destination.

She was a handful of feet from the break in the sloping wall of the pit when it occurred to her that she hadn't been listening for Alexander's tapping. Had she missed it? How long had it taken her to climb through the tunnel and then make the journey around? She'd told him it would take some time, anticipating panic to suck up a good piece of it, but she had no idea how long she'd been at it.

She stood at the edge of the passage's opening, straining her ears. She could hear voices that never quite coalesced into comprehensible words.

A rattle echoed down the passage. Saffron jerked in surprise, grabbing at the corner to prevent herself from falling.

Was that Alexander? She peered around the edge.

A soft golden glow illuminated the rough stone. She could just see the last stair, where a lamp sat, swathed in fog.

She bit her lip. Had that been the signal? There were too many possibilities and too many things to go wrong—hell, everything had already gone wrong.

She maneuvered herself around so one foot touched the ledge and her hand pressed against the wall. With one great heave, she launched herself around onto the ledge and into the passage.

CHAPTER 48

Rough rock steadied her as Saffron got to her feet. A lamp burned low on the bottom step of the stairs at the other end of the straight passage, the only illumination and a ghostly one at that, with tendrils of fog falling like vaporous honey around it. A scent of mildew infiltrated her nostrils, tinged with—was that smoke?

The voices had stopped, but there were only two chambers in the cellar other than the pit, so it was easy to narrow down which room was occupied. As Saffron crept closer to the twin openings on either side of the passage, she could hear the slight scratch of a pen on paper.

Her mother sat in a chair facing the far wall, her ankles tied to the legs and her arms bound behind her. A stack of books and a smattering of papers covered the small table at which she sat. The rest of the space was bone-white stone, empty and bare.

Hesitantly, Saffron stepped into the room.

Her mother turned, and Saffron saw that only one of her hands was bound as the other dropped the pen with which she'd been writing.

"Saffron, no—" her mother gasped, her eyes wide with disbelief.

"Hurry, Mama!" She rushed forward and dropped to her knees to pull at her bindings. They were too thick and tight for her already broken fingernails to manage. She would need a knife, or—

A slight scuff of footsteps on the ground outside echoed through the passage. She froze.

Turning slowly, she saw Bill, a mild look on his plain face as he stepped into the chamber. It didn't match the wicked-looking revolver he held at his chest.

"Not that I mind lively company in so unpleasant a place," he said, "but whatever do you think you are doing, Saffron?"

"I came for my mother," she replied, rising and stepping in front of Violet.

"Ah, ah." Bill wiggled the revolver's barrel, and Saffron froze. "None of that, now. There's no getting around the consequences of your failure, Saffron. You did not provide me with what I required, and now you must cope with the fact that your mother will have to do so. As you can see, finally leaving the manor has already challenged her composure."

Her mother did look deeply uncomfortable, but that was more likely the result of being held at gunpoint.

Bill's eyes gleamed with something Saffron thought was amusement. "And you, yourself, look a little worse for wear. I would ask how you managed to get inside, but from your clothing . . ." He trailed off with the suggestion of a question.

"There is an additional passage into the pit," she said stiffly.

Bill hummed. "I must say I am impressed. I chose this place as my little hideaway, hoping you'd avoid it due to your little underground phobia. I believe that is what they're calling it, these days. It is interesting, isn't it, from a scientific perspective, that both you and your mother have developed such aversions in the years since the death of Thomas Everleigh. His demise made such an impact, didn't it?"

Bill seemed content to chat, and that was to her advantage. The longer she kept him talking, the longer Alexander would have to get down here. Alexander could catch him by surprise if she distracted him sufficiently.

"Did you suffer from a significant loss, Bill?" she asked rather boldly. "Is that why you are the way you are?"

He arched a brow. "The way I am?"

"Conducting your business in this way," Saffron said, nodding to the little room. Actually, it was better not to look at the room, better not to remember where she was. "Stealing secrets, facilitating treason, killing people."

His brows rose. "Killing people? I think you ought to choose your words more carefully. You've frightened your poor mother."

Saffron didn't dare glance behind her to see if her mother was further upset by the accusation.

Bill sighed. "She is convinced I will kill her and slaughter the entire family in my wake. I assure you, that is not my intention." He smiled slightly over Saffron's shoulder at Violet. "I detest wastefulness, and loathe causing a sensation."

"That is supposed to assure us that no harm will come to our family?"

He shrugged again. "I see no reason to do so. There is little chance the police will be able to put together enough evidence to find me, let alone prosecute me after all this is over." He cleared his throat apologetically. "And it would be extremely unlikely that you would be believed, in any case. It is far-fetched, is it not?"

An indistinct noise echoed through the passage. Bill's gaze flickered to the side, but he must not have seen anything to give him pause, for he said, "Now, Saffron, if you will excuse us. Mrs. Everleigh has work to do."

Saffron didn't want to find out what Bill meant by that dismissal. "How do I know you won't simply use that gun on us and toss us into the ice pit the moment you get what you want?"

"You offend my honor," he said blandly.

"There is no honor among thieves," Saffron shot back.

"Saffron," Violet whispered, "you mustn't provoke him."

"Do listen to your mother, Saffron," Bill said, his voice so condescending it was almost a croon.

"No. If we're to be held here in some bizarre situation, I feel I ought to know my captor."

She'd chosen that word specifically to provoke Bill, since he'd used it himself to such odd effect before.

She could see that it was not lost on him. His smile hardened. "I offer you the same deal I was offered myself many years ago. Information for freedom."

"You were a prisoner in the war," Violet said softly. She was struggling to face Bill, half her face lit by the lamp and the other in shadow.

Anger cut through Bill's mask of neutrality. "A clever assumption," he said softly. "Yes, I was captured during the Great Retreat. The circumstances I was found in and the number of bars on my arm invited interrogation. I stayed true to my country and moral code for far too long." His lips twisted in that same bitter, ironic smirk he'd worn before, and to Violet said, "I won't offend your tender sensibilities, Mrs. Everleigh, by describing that experience. But I learned from it. Oh, pain is a brilliant instructor."

To Saffron's surprise, he lowered his revolver, tucking it into his belt. It was no reprieve, however. He came toward Saffron and her mother.

The urge to retreat was strong, but Saffron

resisted. She stood her ground at her mother's side.

"What have your adventures with crime solving taught you, Saffron? The motives for murder, robbery, or treason are varied though simple. Loyalty and love, greed and lust, and hatred. But fear of pain and death . . . They are *supreme*." He said the word with odd relish. "I came to live and breathe by the fear of what the Germans would do to me next. It left no room for any other motivation. No love or loyalty for the country who'd abandoned me to my fate."

Bill's gaze dropped to Violet, tracing her face in an unhurried, disinterested way that set Saffron on edge even more than if he had leered at her mother. "I felt no shame when I told them everything I knew. I believe you will feel the same, Violet. If the choice is loyalty to your late husband and your current family . . . Well."

"You said you wouldn't harm her or my family," Saffron said sharply.

"I said I would not slaughter them. I said nothing about a little . . . encouragement." From his pocket came the switchblade he'd shown Saffron before. He flicked open the blade and examined it. "We've already discussed some of the possibilities. Unfortunately, it seems she doesn't care for my suggestion that she accompany me somewhere that distractions won't be a problem."

"You'll hide her somewhere," Saffron said, "until she gives you all you believe she knows."

"It shouldn't take more than a few months for me to be convinced that there's nothing left to reveal," Bill said easily.

"That isn't necessary. I came here to propose a trade."

"Now I'm finally on the cusp of getting what I want, I highly doubt you have anything I would trade for."

"You'll trade for me."

Bill's brows rose in a graciously doubtful expression. "And why would I do that? You've proven yourself . . . inconsequential in this matter."

Saffron looked him dead in the eye. "Because today I learned exactly what my father and Demian Petrov accomplished all those years ago. And I'm quite sure I'm the only one who knows."

CHAPTER 49

These were ruined when you pushed me into the lake." Saffron reached into her pocket and tossed the wad of papers she extracted onto the floor with a wet slap that echoed in the chamber. "The final letters between Demian Petrov and Thomas Everleigh. They were found in my father's old flat and I read them on the train back to Bedford. My mother was in charge of the correspondence between Petrov and my father that was sent *here*. She never saw what my father received from Petrov in London. No one knows what was on those papers but me. She doesn't know that they had success, or how they achieved it. I do."

Bill narrowed his eyes at her, studying her as she held her breath. "Well done," he said softly.

Saffron had to force her shoulders not to slump with relief.

"Well done, indeed." He shook his head, his eyes not leaving Saffron. "Had my people not searched that flat top to bottom just last week, I would have believed you. Where do you think that sudden offer of employment in a distant city for the tenets in the Regent Place flat came from?" He smiled. "I needed them to vacate the place so I could ensure I missed nothing."

429

"Mr. Feyzi—I'm sure you're familiar with our family solicitor—gave these papers to me months ago."

Had Saffron not been inches away, she might have missed the tiny twitch in Bill's lips tensing his neutral smile. She pressed the issue. "You've no idea what was said between Petrov and my father. And you never will, if you don't let my mother go."

"A fascinating development." With a thoughtful frown, he lifted his knife and applied the tip to the soft flesh under Violet's jaw, tipping her chin up. White shone all around her irises, her nostrils flaring. "You're a brave woman, Saffron. I knew this. While I did not anticipate you overcoming your fear of being trapped beneath ground in quite so impressive a fashion, I did know you would come. And I knew you would not come alone." He readjusted his grip on the knife. Violet inhaled sharply, the sound echoing strangely in the small room. "Now, you have the opportunity to define yourself further. Are you the sort of person to rescue your mother from the hands of a trained killer?"

In a flash, the knife's blade pressed against Violet's throat. Then a sharp whistle left Bill's lips, making Violet flinch so badly that a dot of blood appeared along her throat. Bill asked, "Or are you the sort of person to ensure the man you love will survive a deadly injury?"

Saffron had been prepared to answer to the first question, but his second was so unexpected that she merely blinked at him. "What are you—"

An anguished yell rang out from beyond the tunnel. Terror wrenched at Saffron and she spun toward the doorway, half expecting to see the source of the cry.

Another grunt of pain echoed through the cellar. Bill chuckled.

She turned to stare at him. That was Alexander, Alexander being hurt. And Bill was *laughing*.

Something cold overtook her. It might have been renewed fear, or anger so hot it burned like ice. She wanted to do more than hurt Bill for what he'd done to Alexander, to her mother, to herself—she wanted to end him. End him so this would stop.

"Saffron?"

She heard her mother's whisper as if from very far away. Bill watched her avidly, his anticipation obvious.

Her mother repeated her name. When she finally tore her eyes from Bill and looked at her mother, Violet looked like she'd aged ten years in the last minute. Strain deepened every line on her face, and sad knowledge welled in her eyes along with tears.

"Go to him," she whispered. "Go to Alexander. Now. Please."

It was all Saffron could do to nod, a mechanical, jerky motion. There was no telling what state Alexander was in and how much time she had to help him. Her mother would be safe, at least until she told Bill what he wanted.

She ran through to the door and paused, looking back at her mother. There wasn't enough time to memorize her face, but she didn't want this to be the last memory she had of her mother anyway: tied to a chair, her face blank, free hand twitching where it sat on the battered table next to pen and paper.

She had no way of defeating Bill. He'd proven himself a superior opponent at every turn. She had no further tricks, no ideas left. But one.

Rounding the corner to press her back to the stone wall, out of sight, she reached for Elizabeth's pistol. She could finish this right now, rescue her mother and Alexander. The pistol was wet, but Bill didn't know that.

Her hand dug in her pocket, but nothing but damp fabric met her fingertips.

It wasn't there. Her pocket was empty.

She checked the others, but found nothing. It must have fallen from her pocket somewhere between the house and the tunnel.

She closed her eyes and clasped her hands over her mouth against the anguished noise fighting to burst from her.

It lasted only a moment. The knowledge that

Alexander was somewhere, hurt and alone, and she was the only one to help him galvanized her. She moved as fast as she could down the passage, praying those seconds hadn't cost Alexander.

CHAPTER 50

Time passed in a bizarrely stretched-out fashion as Saffron mounted the steps that led out of the ice cellar. At the top, wisps of fog had begun to fade to gray as the day dwindled. The gate was closed, but as she placed a trembling hand on it, it swung open.

There was no one outside, but Saffron could see there had been. The ground, usually covered in patchy moss, had been torn up and imprints of men's shoes were left behind.

Alexander had fought the guard. Bill must have known that would happen, and he'd ensured Alexander would be hurt as a result. Where could he be now?

She wrapped her coat tighter around herself as she leaned over to search the ground for further clues. The footprints were wide ranging, but at last she managed to pick out the deep imprints of a pair of boots going off to the east. She raced along the trail, but hadn't gone more than a dozen feet before an invisible obstacle sent her heavily to her knees. She cried out in pain and frustration.

"Saffron?" came Alexander's voice from some distance away.

With a sob, Saffron scrambled to her feet and

called to him, finally finding him propped against the trunk of a tree.

Though her heart had utterly stopped, her whole body trembled as she knelt next to him. Her hands rose of their own volition but froze just before touching Alexander's chest.

"He just caught me with a knife," he said.

"What do I do?" His shoulder and chest were soaked in dark blood, blooming from above his heart. Saffron finally looked away and to his face. He was very pale and breathing hard.

"Put pressure on the wound. If you give me something, I can hold it myself and you can get your mother." He spoke with his teeth bared, but his eyes were steady on hers.

Saffron hurriedly removed her damp coat and jumper. Cold nipped at her as she unbuttoned her blouse, hurriedly replacing her jumper over her camisole. She placed his hand over the bundled cotton on his shoulder and wove her fingers through his.

"I'm so sorry," she whispered. "This is my fault. This is all my fault—"

"It's all right," he said, voice rough. "Where is your mother?"

"She's with Bill. In the ice cellar. But he's going to move her—"

"Go." His hand moved to cover hers on his chest. "I'm not going to die. I'm not losing enough blood for that."

"You've been *stabbed in the chest*," she choked out. "I will . . . I will find my mother. Soon. He said things, things about his life. Clues. I'll use them to find him and—"

Alexander shoved her, hard. She fell away just as something hurtled into Alexander.

She rolled to her feet to find him struggling with someone. Over the sounds of their fight, she heard him shout, "Run!"

Anger and fear buzzed like a hot, angry swarm of wasps in her body. She'd tackle Bill's man herself, use her fists, her feet—

Providence saw fit for Saffron to avoid that fate, however, for just as she'd decided to enter the fray, a gun landed in front of her in the dirt with a *thunk*.

She stared at it. How the devil did Elizabeth's pistol end up there?

Alexander threw punches and received them, yet he was aware he wasn't feeling the impact of fists on flesh as he should be. A lightheaded sort of cushion separated Alexander from the world, except for the point of throbbing pain in his shoulder where he was still tethered to his body.

He was aware, however, that he was losing the fight. Bill's man had taken a thorough beating when Alexander attacked him to get into the ice cellar earlier, but Alexander hadn't been as ruthless as he ought to have been. He'd left him in a heap on the side of the little clearing before the gate, and when he was bent over the lock, the bastard had knocked him on the head. He'd come awake to the fellow patting his face as if to wake him up, only to stab him in the shoulder a moment later.

It was damned lucky he'd come to when he did. Had he not moved, the blade might have struck somewhere deadly.

But his luck was running out. He was tiring quickly. He was slow and sloppy, his adrenaline wearing off too quickly. His opponent would knock him out again, or worse, he'd put that knife back to work, and what would happen to Saffron? Would he go after her, chase her through the mist into the night?

With a surge of energy, he managed to knock the guard over and land a decent punch to the man's jaw. It served only to anger him. He growled and shoved his fist into Alexander's wounded shoulder.

A wave of nauseating pain had his eyes rolling. He was shoved to the ground, hitting his head hard enough to send his teeth rattling.

Was this it? He was too dizzy to think of much else, though regret was there, wordless and heavy on his chest. Or was that Bill's man, kneeling on him?

The pressure went away, and he could breathe. It hurt, but he took in great heaves.

"Alexander?"

He blinked, not realizing his eyes had been closed.

Saffron was standing over him, though she didn't look at him. That was a pity; he wanted to see the blue of her eyes.

"I need you to get up now." Her voice was strained. "Can you do that?"

He did, slowly. When he was upright, he realized that she was standing over someone else.

The man he'd been fighting was sitting on the ground four feet from Saffron.

He glanced at Saffron to ask what had happened, for the fellow was awake and glaring at them, but then he saw the glint of the gun in her hand. Elizabeth's gun, which he'd taken from Saffron when they embraced before she'd gone to the cellar, knowing that if it came down to it, he would do what needed to be done to make Saffron and her mother safe.

"I'll take that," Alexander told her, and reached for the gun with his right hand.

"No." She returned the guard's glare. "He's going to tell us Bill's plan. Now."

"Who is Bill?" the man asked.

"Your employer," Alexander said.

"Tell me what his escape plan is," Saffron said.

The man sneered. "You won't *shoot* me. You're no more likely to shoot me with that toy than—"

The gun cracked. Dirt sprayed from near the

man's feet, and he howled, scrambling back. The flare of shock in Saffron's eyes was quickly smothered before she redoubled her grip on the pistol.

She took a step toward the man, and with perfect confidence said, "My mother has been abducted, my boyfriend has been stabbed, and my cousin's child nearly drowned. Tell me again, what won't I do?"

The confident sneer wilted. He eyed her warily, shifting his legs slightly.

"I wouldn't," Alexander told him.

The man froze, a nasty expression twisting his face. Alexander heaved to his feet. He was light-headed, but stable enough for this. To Saffron, he said, "Give me the gun."

She did this time. Alexander took the pistol, rounded on Bill's man, and struck him in the back of the head with the pearl grip. He slumped to the ground with a groan.

Alexander sat down, hard, on the ground next to the unconscious man. He drew in a long breath, attempting to rally even as he felt the last of his energy draining away. His hand moved to his belt and struggled to undo the buckle.

Saffron fell to her knees next to him, hands fluttering around his.

"Get the buckle," he said. "We'll use it to bind his hands."

When she'd undone the belt and wrapped it

around the unconscious man's hands so tightly color bled from his wrists, Alexander handed her the pistol. "Go." He pressed the gun into her hands. "Go get your mother. Be done with this."

Fear was written into the lines of her face, but her fingers wrapped around the grip. "I'll be right back."

He managed a smile. "I'll be here."

Saffron had gone not a dozen steps away from Alexander when a shot rang out through the mist.

She froze. Her brain and body simply stopped working for a full minute.

Then, as if in a trance, she walked toward the ice cellar.

The gun in her hand weighed a hundred stone. She looked down at it, momentarily shocked by the red staining her hands, the mess at odds with the elegant designs etching the body of the weapon, the gleam of the pearl in the soft light.

The gun was a strangely beautiful thing. Deadly and beautiful. Her plants were the same, many with lush blooms and sweet fragrances that tempted the unsuspecting.

But her plants did not grow with the intention to kill. They had many uses, including saving lives. A gun had only one purpose.

She reached the gate, standing open and still. She lifted the pistol, aiming at the steps.

But no footsteps came, no one emerged. The

acrid scent of gunpowder wafted over her. She inched down the stairs. She wasn't sure she would make it down without falling from how badly her whole body trembled.

She went down the steps, one by one, until she reached the passage swirling with fog. The scent of spent gunpowder was even stronger there.

With a wavering breath, Saffron turned the corner into the chamber and lifted the pistol.

A horrible tang that Saffron recognized as blood filled the close room. Her mother sat in the chair. A gun was in her mother's hand, limp at her side. And Bill was on the floor, a dark pool growing steadily wider beneath him.

CHAPTER 51

Later, Saffron would not be able to recall what happened next. Shock sometimes had that effect, Alexander would remind her. She shouldn't strain to remember how exactly she'd gotten her mother free from her bindings, or how they'd found him again in the mist. The next she would recall was the doctor cutting away her father's bloodied uniform to examine Alexander's wound.

Saffron found that she could stomach the blood but not the sight of Alexander resisting, and then succumbing to, the pain. He'd refused morphine, but the loss of blood and the discomfort of the doctor poking around the wound and then sewing it closed proved too much and he'd lost consciousness.

John had already retrieved Goldington's crotchety country doc on foot to attend to Benjamin by the time they'd gotten back to the house. He had treated Saffron a number of times as a child and only stopped harassing her about leaving the room after Violet had quietly told him to focus on his patient rather than worry what the neighbors might say. It hadn't occurred to Saffron that others would think it inappropriate that she was present while Alexander's wounds were tended. Where else would she be?

There was nothing salacious in her watching the doctor wash away the blood that had dried to his chest, nor clean and pull at the bloody puncture with needle and thread. Rather than look at the wound, she'd focused on Alexander's other shoulder, covered in scars that she'd always wondered about. They ran from the tips of his fingers over his arm and shoulder and around to his back. The skin was still harshly contrasted, pink and mottled. This was certainly not the way she'd planned to examine them for the first time.

The doctor grumbled about modern young women after she'd returned from changing her clothing—he had, quite rightly, refused to allow her to be present for Alexander's treatment when she was covered in mud—and he bathed her hands and knees in iodine and encouraged her to down a finger of brandy. She ignored the lecture but took the advice to have a drink, barely noticing the stinging in her hands and knees or the burning in her throat.

Her mother sat with her while they waited for Alexander to wake.

Saffron didn't know what to say to her mother. It was too much to process all that had happened. All she wanted was for Alexander to wake up. He lay still, the bandage on his shoulder obscured now by the bedclothes. Saffron decided the doctor had arranged Alexander with the blankets pulled to his chin to preserve her chastity. That only served to bring attention to the bruises blooming on his face from his fight with Bill's man.

Guilt ached in her chest all the while. It was a thousand times worse than the last time she'd waited for Alexander to wake after being poisoned by the xolotl vine.

After a few hours of tense silence, Violet appeared to understand Saffron didn't want to talk and left the room.

When the door clicked closed, Saffron put her head down on the side of the bed and wept.

John nudged Saffron awake sometime later. His anxious eyes made it clear he thought she'd keeled over rather than just fallen asleep. He smiled with relief when she sat up blearily.

He brandished the tray he'd entered with. "Eat something. Got to keep up your strength."

She took a piece of buttered toast from the tray and nibbled on it. Steam rose from a cup as John poured her tea, the scent not quite powerful enough to overtake the stink of the doctor's disinfectant.

John looked about the room, eyes touching everything but Alexander in a rather determined way.

"So this . . . This is what it's usually like?" John asked awkwardly. "After your cases?"

"No, not really," said Saffron. She had no energy to explain. Her hand closed around Alexander's again. "Is Benjamin all right?"

"The doctor said no harm was done. Fed him hot beef tea until it was coming out of his nose. He's a stout little fellow, really." His lips spasmed into a tense smile. "It's Suzette I'm worried about. She's . . . We're going to have another child, you see, and the strain . . . and that damned Fischer! That damned concoction might have . . ." He pushed back his hair, leaving it standing on end. He looked exhausted.

Saffron nodded, tears in her eyes. "I'm so glad she's all right. And the baby."

"The nanny . . . That man, Bill, he was the one pulling the strings, wasn't he? He's the reason our first nanny quit, why we hired that girl. Grandmama has been right all along. I am a bloody fool."

"Oh, John," Saffron began, but he shook his head ruefully.

"Ashton will be all right, too," he said. "What did the doctor say?"

"He lost a lot of blood," Saffron said, wiping her tears away again. "But nothing vital was damaged."

Bill's words came back to her, commenting on his aversion to wasting potential.

The room fell silent. Saffron watched the steady rise and fall of Alexander's chest. Her fingers traced the knit of his blanket as they had dozens of times already.

He'd never had visitors in the hospital during the few days they'd spent there recovering from the xolotl incident. His brother, Adrian, would have come, had Alexander told him what had occurred. From what she'd gleaned about Alexander's mother, she would have been at his side in an instant. But he chose not to tell them. Would he wish he was alone when he woke? He'd likely hate that any of her family had seen him like this.

She looked up at John to ask for privacy, when Alexander's hand flexed in hers.

He blinked awake, looking at her with a hazy smile that vanished the moment he tried to move. His eyes closed in a grimace.

She carefully leaned over him, unable to resist stoking his battered face. "Don't move just yet," she whispered.

John said, "I'll just go tell Grandfather that Ashton has woken up. The old man has refused to rest this whole time, you know."

When the door closed, Alexander asked, "What happened?"

Saffron sighed, wishing they could avoid Bill's further intrusion into their lives while knowing that, if it had it been her who'd missed the last

446

few hours, that would be the first question she'd ask upon waking, too. She wished she had better news for him. "Bill is alive."

His eyes didn't leave hers as she explained that her mother had shot him, and after they'd managed to get Alexander back to the house and John and Lord Easting had gone to the ice cellar to collect both the guard and Bill, the ice cellar had been empty. Both men were gone. The police had, at last, arrived, but the subsequent search, encumbered by the failing light and the lingering fog, had turned up nothing about Bill's whereabouts.

"Nadine has been arrested, by the way," Saffron hastened to add upon seeing the somewhat murderous expression this news had inspired, "as has Mr. Fischer. They found a store of the solution he used to induce the hallucinations in my father's greenhouse, hidden in another garden bed." She'd be checking garden beds for hidden surprises for the rest of her life, she predicted.

"What was it?"

"Extract of *Datura stramonium*, of all things," she said, exasperated. "Likely from the seed you found in his room. The seeds of jimson weed contain the same alkaloids as a dozen similarly poisonous plants, most notably scopolamine."

"That's what Edwards was dosed with, wasn't it?"

She nodded, thinking back to the poison

bouquets business that concluded just a few months ago. It felt like ages, with all that had happened between then and now. "Yes. It puts one well out of one's mind. And the extract stinks."

Alexander made a soft sound of enlightenment. "That explains the reek in his room. You said Fischer was arrested. Not Madame Martin?"

Saffron shook her head. "Fischer had all the papers in his possession, all the promissory notes in his name. The drugs were on his person, in his room. Madame Martin claimed to know nothing of his scheming, and disavowed his use of the uniform to taunt us. The Hales are furious, Elizabeth first and foremost, of course, but the police said they had no means to arrest her."

Silence fell between them, and Saffron found she was back there, in the ice cellar's chamber with her mother, looking down at Bill.

Her chest went tight, unable to fill with air, but not because the whole wretched scene had taken place underground. The look on her mother's face when she looked from Bill's still and bloodied body to her . . . It had been utterly blank, as if killing someone was of no concern or interest.

"What is it?" Alexander prompted gently.

She shook her head to clear it. "He'd loosened my mother's hand, I assume to begin writing down all she knew of my father and Petrov's work. She was able to reach into her pocket and get the gun. She told the police she shot him in the stomach. They said it was possibly fatal, but we'll never know, will we?" She fought to get her trembling voice back in control. "I didn't know my mother even knew how to work a gun. She'd never accompany my father on the rare hunt here at Ellington, but I suppose she learned at some point and it would make sense that she'd arm herself when she was aware that something dangerous was happening—"

"I gave it to her," Alexander interrupted, taking her hand in his. He squeezed her fingers until she looked up at him. "I slipped it into her pocket on the dock when I realized he meant to take her away."

She nodded, but the explanation didn't comfort her much. It felt as if she'd traded uncertainty about one parent for the other. Her mother felt like a stranger now.

"We don't have to discuss it." He reached for her and gently pulled her close to kiss her. "I'm glad it's over."

She leaned her forehead to his. "Me too."

She stayed with him until he'd drank enough beef tea for him to complain, all the while wondering if and when she would actually feel that her dealings with Bill Wyatt were at an end.

CHAPTER 52

When he awoke the next morning, the pain was not surprising.

Alexander had woken a few times in the night to a maid reassuring him and providing the liquids he desperately needed to replenish his lost blood. He'd fought to return to sleep, exhaustion no match for the searing ache at the juncture of his chest and shoulder. But sleep was the only oblivion he'd allow himself; he didn't touch the morphine the doctor had left behind.

What *was* surprising when he woke to the hazy white light of morning was the presence of Lord Easting in his bedroom. He stood silhouetted at the window, a winding stream of smoke rising from a pipe apparently forgotten in his hand.

Alexander attempted to sit up and wished for a shirt when the white bedsheet fell from his torso. He attempted to retrieve it, but mistakenly put his weight onto the arm with the damaged shoulder.

Lord Easting turned at the sound of his hiss of pain. "Don't concern yourself. Scars are nothing I haven't seen before."

That was not precisely what Alexander worried about. The pink and white scars marbling his right side had ceased bothering him years ago.

He managed to sit up and swing his legs around to get out of bed and find some sort of clothing apart from his bloodstained trousers.

Lord Easting ambled over with his cane, pausing at the dressing table to retrieve Alexander's dressing gown. He handed it to Alexander without comment. He didn't watch him struggle to put it on, either, instead stumping over to stand at the window once again.

When Alexander was covered as much as the dressing gown allowed, he asked, "How can I help you, Lord Easting?"

The viscount snorted and turned back to him with a sardonic look. "What is left for you to do? You jump into a freezing lake to rescue my heir's only child, you prevent my daughter-in-law from being abducted by someone masquerading as my own damned doctor, and, if my solicitor Mr. Feyzi is to be believed, you've managed to save my granddaughter's skin at least three times." He grimaced. "So far."

"I'm glad I could be of assistance."

Lord Easting fixed him with a blue stare. "I am not too old or sick that I failed to notice not only the gun in my granddaughter's hand pointed at the nanny earlier, nor the way she ignored our commands to remain in the house. She had reason to believe that she could retrieve her mother from that man."

Though his mind was moving at a downgraded pace, Alexander knew Lord Easting wanted to know how his granddaughter had come to be so capable in such a situation. He certainly wasn't going to be the one to tell him.

Instead, he said, "I believe she was able to use her knowledge of the land and Bill Wyatt to her advantage."

The blue-eyed glare persisted. "And what of Violet? And whatever it was this Bill Wyatt wanted of Thomas's work? What did he want with either of them?"

"I couldn't say, my lord." It might make Lord Easting friendlier if he explained, but it was Saffron's choice what to disclose to her grandfather. "I hope you will ask Saffron or Mrs. Everleigh for the story. It is theirs to tell."

Lord Easting stumped over to the foot of the bed. For a man supposedly deeply unwell, he looked remarkably hearty. But he wouldn't be the first man to rise to the occasion and discard an ailment seemingly overnight when his family was under threat. Or was it that Bill hadn't been present to provide any "treatments"? That was an alarming thought, one Alexander tucked away to discuss with Saffron later.

The light from the window deepened the furrows in Lord Easting's brow and illuminated his eyes, a shocking shade of blue only matched by Saffron's. "John tells me you were in France."

"I was."

"My son died in France," Lord Easting said after a long moment. "He did his duty for his country. Thomas didn't have to serve when or where he did. He chose the hard route, to the detriment of his family." He shook his head briskly as if removing a fly. "John elected to fight, too. He is to one day take responsibility of Ellington, despite his abhorrence of the idea. He had no qualms in letting me know it is not the life he wants for himself or his wife and child. But duty and honor demand he change his plan. And so he will." He propped both hands atop his cane and leveled Alexander with a blue-eyed glare. "Saffron, too, has a duty to her family."

There it was, just as he'd expected. Alexander worked to maintain his neutral expression as he held Lord Easting's gaze. Was this pronouncement going to change anything? He still loved Saffron. He still wanted to work together at the university and help her with her investigations, if only to be the one who was stabbed or shot or kidnapped in her stead. He still wanted to share his life with her.

No, this speech from Lord Easting didn't change anything.

"I understand," said Alexander.

Lord Easting narrowed his eyes at him. "Do you?"

"I do, my lord." What he had to say needed

to be said with him on his feet, so he stood and walked a few paces to the older man. "And I also understand that Saffron would have never forgiven herself had she not acted for Benjamin, or her mother. She wants to be of value. Helping people through her work is her duty. The desire to protect her won't keep her from it." Alexander had tried that and failed.

Something glinted in Lord Easting's eyes, almost as if he'd heard those unspoken words.

He fussed about with something in his jacket pocket. He extended a gnarled hand to Alexander, dropping a little red box in his hand.

Alexander's stomach dropped.

"The constable said one of his men found that outside the ice cellar. Must have fallen out of your pocket. You're lucky it didn't fall into the lake."

Alexander, steeling himself with a deep breath, said, "Thank you, my lord."

"I took the liberty of switching out the little trinket in there for something more suitable from the Easting collection." Lord Easting glared at him, and to Alexander's amazement, he offered Alexander his hand. His grip was bruising. "You'd damned well better keep my granddaughter safe, Ashton."

At five in the evening, the Bedford train station was busy. Saffron walked arm in arm with Elizabeth as Perry trailed behind, carting Elizabeth's luggage.

Saffron had protested when Elizabeth had announced she was quitting Ellington for London earlier that day, but Elizabeth had said, "I've done what I wanted to do, darling. Now it's time for you to pick up the pieces around here."

Saffron had a hard time arguing with that, even though picking up the pieces that Bill had left shattered at Ellington was the last thing she wanted to do.

"I wish we were coming with you," Saffron told her when Elizabeth came to a stop on the chilly platform.

"I'm sure you and Alexander will be back where you ought to be, being decorous on the couch in our parlor by the end of the week," Elizabeth said with a smile. "You've got to face the music, darling. Then you can collect your man and come home."

A woman walked out onto the platform behind Elizabeth. It took Saffron a moment to recognize her, as she'd skipped the Victorian getup and wore the sort of plain traveling suit that marked her as unremarkable. Though she'd been proven a fraud, Madame Martin carried herself in a way that was simply beyond normal.

It was likely the haunted look in her bottomless eyes. Though Saffron knew for certain that she had no spiritual abilities, that look gave her the creeps.

Elizabeth caught her shift in attention and turned, letting out a laugh. "Fancy meeting you here, Madame," she called, marching toward her.

Saffron hurried after her, in part because she wanted to hear how Elizabeth would flay the fraud, but also to prevent Elizabeth tossing the woman onto the train tracks. There had been no shortage of foul feelings with language to match when the police told them that they simply hadn't the evidence to arrest Madame Martin.

Some of the haunted look faded from her gaze as Madame lifted her eyes to Elizabeth's. "Miss Hale, Miss Everleigh, how do you do?"

Instinctual good manners had Saffron nodding politely to the woman.

A train screeched to a halt. People disembarked and more boarded. When the noise had at last settled, Madame Martin said, "I am very pleased to hear that the little boy is well."

"Yes, he is," Saffron said. "Thank you for telling us where Bill took him."

Before Madame could reply, Elizabeth asked flatly, "Why did you tell us, exactly? Should Lord Easting anticipate a bill for your services?"

Madame Martin gave her a withering look.

"Perhaps your spirits told you to give away that bit of knowledge for free. But of course, there never were any spirits, special connections, or Great Beyond, were there? Just the ability to recognize weaknesses and the urge to exploit them." Elizabeth took on a mockingly impressed expression. "Well done. Very well done, having Mr. Fischer take the blame for conning my father out of his stocks. Pity you've lost all your earnings, though, isn't it?"

The shrill whistle of another impending arrival prevented Elizabeth continuing, but she seemed satisfied with her telling off. The train came to an ear-splitting stop, and she turned back to Perry and her luggage.

"It is a pity," Madame said, "that my time here has been wasted. To come away with nothing but my freedom . . ." She shrugged in an elegant, Gallic way that didn't make clear if she was disappointed or pleased. Then her lips curled into a smirk. "It seems I was right about something," she said, just loud enough for Saffron to hear. *"Celui qui était perdu est revenue, no?"*

Saffron didn't reply other than to give the woman a perfunctory smile before turning on her heel to see Elizabeth off. She did feel rather like Elizabeth had found some part of herself that was lost, but she'd certainly never let Madame Martin know she was right about that.

CHAPTER 53

You still haven't spoken to your mother?" Alexander asked.

They were in his room, alone after a footman had helped Alexander bathe and dress in pajamas and a dressing gown. The only outward signs of his injury were the bruises blackening his face and his slow, cautious movements. Saffron was sure her grandmother was itching to force her out of his room, but Saffron didn't care. Things between her and Lady Easting were as uncomfortable as they'd ever been, especially following the conversation she'd had with her family that afternoon.

After seeing Elizabeth off, she'd returned to Alexander's side, only to leave again when she realized he wouldn't attempt to sleep with her there. She'd dined with her family at lunch, seeing them all together for the first time since Bill had taken Benjamin. There had been an unpleasant sort of tension throughout the whole meal. All at once Saffron realized it was because the rest of the family awaited an explanation from her.

She had apologized for not telling them who Bill was when she arrived. This led to her rather

458

unintentionally explaining her involvement in the Path Lab, which in turn led her to the previous cases of poisonings she'd assisted with. Her grandfather, who'd likely known as much or more than her highly edited stories revealed, had frowned and grunted something like "I see." John's response had been equally brief, merely nodding before excusing himself to the nursery to see his little family.

Lady Easting had clamped her mouth shut and refused to look at her, while Violet's shocked stare didn't leave Saffron for a moment.

Saffron rounded out the blow by saying that she would be continuing her work at the university and her relationship with Alexander.

Lord Easting looked beadily at her before saying, "Very well," and Saffron could have sworn she saw something like approval in his eye. She didn't know what exactly he'd said to Alexander that morning, but she hoped it had been more than thank you.

Her grandmother and mother did not respond. Saffron suspected it would take much longer for her grandmother to accept everything if she ever did. The sight of Saffron holding a servant at gunpoint definitely hadn't been conducive to repairing what was broken between them. As for her mother . . . It felt like there was a great chasm between them, and she wasn't sure she wanted to be the first to broach it.

At Alexander's question, Saffron looked up from her notebook with a frown. "I spoke to her and the rest of them at luncheon. I told you that."

"You know that's not what I meant."

She sighed, setting her pen down. "No, I haven't."

"Why not?" The light was catching the brown in Alexander's eyes, making them appear a deep mahogany.

She'd much rather just stare into his eyes, savoring that he was alive and mostly well, than discuss her aversion to seeing her mother just now. She shrugged.

Alexander frowned. "Why not, Saffron?"

"I would rather stay in here with you, of course."

"I'm going to have to rest more in a minute, otherwise the doctor will complain."

"You hate resting."

"I hate seeing you upset." She scoffed, looking away. "You are upset. I'm fine, and so is Benjamin and your mother. Bill is likely too injured to be dangerous, and the nanny and Fischer are locked up. Nothing else could be upsetting you."

It was unfortunate that Alexander was so perceptive. "I am upset, but I doubt speaking to my mother will help that."

"Come here."

Saffron stood and went to his bedside. He

pulled her down to sit at his side, facing him. His hair curled over his forehead, partially obscuring a nasty purple blotch on his temple.

"Without what your mother did, you would still be in danger. Benjamin, John—all your family. She did what she had to do," Alexander said. "If I had had that chance, I would have done the same."

She nodded, tears filling her eyes and blurring his face. "It was my plan," she whispered. "I was prepared to do it. But it was my fault, Alexander. All of this was my fault. If I'd only seen the signs earlier, if I hadn't underestimated my mother and kept things from her, maybe she would have been open with me in return. I could have stopped it before Benjamin almost drowned and before you were hurt—" She hung her head, and he gathered her to his chest with his good arm. "She shouldn't have had to go with Bill or shoot him."

"She didn't have to," Alexander said at long last. "But she chose to. She chose to protect those she loved, and she saved herself. It's what you would have done."

As bad as she felt, the release of crying eased her, almost as much as knowing Alexander was right. If her mother felt like a stranger, at least it seemed Violet was one she'd want to know.

The clocks were chiming ten o'clock when Saffron closed the door softly behind her. Alexander was asleep, unable to stay awake any longer after she'd managed to convince him to take a small dose of morphine. He'd been helpless in the wake of the easing of his pain, and he'd drifted off within minutes. As much as she'd like to simply stretch out next to him on the bed, ready to care for him should he need something and taking comfort in his presence, she did not.

She passed through the gallery, silent on stockinged feet. The house was silent and cold. No voices came from Lord and Lady Easting's quarters. Elizabeth's departure left her room empty. Her mother's rooms were the only ones that showed any sign of life in the form of a thin line of light under the door.

She knocked softly and entered when her mother's soft voice bade her enter.

"Mama?" she asked as she stepped inside.

Violet sat in the worn armchair before the fire, a blanket on her lap and a book closed on top of it. "Hello, my darling."

Feeling awkward, she asked, "May I . . . May I sit with you, for a moment?"

"Of course." Violet looked thoroughly exhausted, the impression strengthened by her wan smile. "I'm afraid it's rather late to ask for tea or warm milk. I try not to disturb the staff so late in the evening."

"I don't need anything," Saffron said, sitting on the loveseat across from her.

The fire crackled softly, still bright and well fed. Her mother had planned on staying awake a while, she guessed. Perhaps she, too, was weary but unable to relax into sleep.

"How is Alexander?" her mother asked after a few minutes. "I suppose I should not be so familiar with his name, but after all he's done for us . . ."

"He would not mind." Saffron picked at a loose thread on her jumper's sleeve. "He's doing well. Upright and moving about."

"That's good to hear."

"Yes."

The stilted conversation stalled. Saffron didn't want to speak, to ask for an explanation when she was so weary of it all, but she wasn't sure she could walk away from Ellington tomorrow as she planned without clearing the air.

"I am sorry that I brought this on our family," she said. "It had to be terrifying to be forced away from the house. I'm sorry for it."

Her mother, watching her with concern, said, "Don't think on it a moment longer. I wish for us all to put it behind us."

Anger pierced through her guilt. "I don't want to pretend it never happened and forget it."

Her mother's brows rose. "I didn't say I wished to forget it. I wish to move past it."

Saffron stood, moving restlessly about the room. "Is there a difference?"

Her mother didn't reply. A torrent of thought rushed through her mind, and she couldn't wrangle it before it came out.

"I am so angry with you for burning Papa's things," she choked out. "I understand why you did it. I do, Mama. But . . . It isn't just because we needed it to be rid of Bill. I thought you tried to forget the pain of missing Papa. But now I know you did it to hide what you had been doing together, and that feels worse, somehow."

Violet rose and came to wrap her arms around her. Saffron realized she was crying when she allowed her mother to press her face into her shoulder.

"I cannot tell if it was a mistake or not," her mother said softly. "I did it to protect us, and I cannot be sorry for that."

Saffron allowed tears to fall, but no more of the bitter words swirling in her mind. There were still things she needed to tell her mother, truth offered and demanded in turn, but she didn't feel this was the time. Forgiveness, true and complete, was not possible when everything was still so raw.

When the storm of her feelings had somewhat passed, she straightened up and did her best to pat her face dry with the handkerchief her mother had pressed into her hand at some point. There was little left dry enough to help.

She rose, suddenly feeling too old for such an emotional display. She'd nearly made it to the door before her mother cleared her throat.

It took effort to stop walking and face her mother.

It was as if the placid lake of her emotions had been overturned, and now so much feeling churned in her eyes as she asked, "Were there ever any letters?"

Saffron blinked. "Letters?"

Her face fell. "I . . . I had hoped that the papers you taunted that man with were actually your father's letters."

"Oh," Saffron said, "they were. The tenants of the Regent Square flat found them while doing some repairs."

A trembling hand flew to Violet's mouth. After a pause in which she collected herself, she asked, "What did they say?"

Saffron contemplated for a long moment. The letters she'd read had been from her mother, not written to her. But her mother didn't need to know that.

"There was an unfinished letter dated just before his departure in 1914," she said slowly. "I don't remember the exact wording, but I will do my best." She cleared her throat, preparing for what she hoped was one final lie between them. " 'Dearest Violet . . .' "

"You don't need to walk me up," Saffron said, hovering awkwardly at the top of the steps to her building. "You ought to go straight home and rest."

With his arm in a sling beneath his greatcoat, Saffron had fluttered about like a frantic butterfly, trying to keep Alexander from lifting a finger during the short journey back to London. He hardly needed it, she knew, but she couldn't help it. He had been *stabbed.* Both the doctor and Alexander had assured her it was nowhere near the heart, but her own heart didn't care.

Rather than reassure her yet again that he was fine, Alexander merely followed her up the steps and inside. He was quiet up the stairs, his good hand tucked in his pocket as she unlocked the door when her knocks went unanswered. Elizabeth must have been out, though Saffron had told her over the telephone when she would arrive home.

Worry shot through her. She'd barely stepped through the door before she was rushing inside, calling Elizabeth's name. What if Bill had come to London after them? What if he had Elizabeth and—

Her manic thoughts came to an abrupt halt when she reached the end of the hall, where the parlor door stood open.

The rest of the flat had been dim. The parlor, however, was glowing.

A dozen candles burned throughout the room, throwing soft, wavering light onto flowers. Red roses covered every surface, in vases, bowls, and even teacups. The smell was wonderful, fresh and deep and lovely.

"I had a different plan, you know," Alexander said from behind her. She spun to look at him. He wore a sheepish smile. "Something more elaborate that I had put together myself. But my plan had to change." He glanced down at his injured shoulder. "With you, it seems, my plans always have to change."

He took her arm and gently guided her to the center of the room. It was like stepping into a fairy garden, with the candlelight flickering and reflecting, the roses filling the room with lush scent.

"Elizabeth?" Saffron managed to ask, finding it hard to breathe, let alone speak.

He smiled appreciatively at the room. "She put this together and says I now owe her a great favor." He turned his gaze on her, impenetrably dark in the candlelight.

He took her hand in his. "Do you remember last year when I helped you break into Berking's garden and we crawled around in the dirt searching for clues in the middle of the night?"

A giddy laugh escaped her. "How could I forget?"

"You asked me why I agreed to do any of it. We barely knew each other, and I said some nonsense about scientific curiosity. The truth is that you had already wrapped me up in your insatiable curiosity and determination. It's driven me mad since day one." Saffron made to duck her head in embarrassment, but he lifted her chin so their eyes met, his thumb tracing her cheekbone. "I didn't realize it then, but I had already begun to fall in love with you. Your curiosity and your compassion, your desire to learn and understand, they make you bold. They're the things that I love most about you. You make me want more out of my life. More than just being content, safe."

His hand left her cheek, and he eased back a step. Slowly, he lowered himself so he rested on one knee. With a small smile on his lips, Alexander said, "I want you, Saffron, mad ideas and all. Will you be my wife?"

Surprise flitted through her at the question, stated in a manner that was so perfectly Alexander, it filled her heart before she even contemplated the answer. The love glimmering in his eyes promised her safety and adventure in equal measure, all she could ever want or hope for. She had no other answer but the one she whispered onto his lips, light and sweet as a rose petal.

"Nothing would make me happier."

A ring was fit onto her finger, and the future was suddenly much brighter.

EPILOGUE

Four Months Later

Postmarked Munich, Germany
15 June, 1924
Miss Saffron Everleigh
9 Swan Walk, London, England

Dear Miss Everleigh,

I hope this note will not alarm you as my continued existence no doubt does. I wish you to know that I bear no ill will toward you or your family for how our last meeting concluded. I trust that neither of us will suffer any lingering effects from that dramatic parting for long.

I felt compelled to offer my belated congratulations to you and Mr. Ashton on your engagement. I have no doubts that your union will be a happy one.

I wish you the best of luck on your forthcoming adventures, in matrimony and to the East in the fall. I have no doubt your first expedition abroad will be fruitful.

As for my own future endeavors, the information I sought is now no longer the most valuable option. My client will be satisfied with another possibility I've recently learned of. You may rest assured that my pursuits are unlikely to touch you again. I have learned that Everleighs are too dangerous of creatures.

Best,
William Wyatt

AUTHOR'S NOTE

A character draped in mystique and dripping with manipulation is irresistible to a mystery writer, and I am not immune to the draw of a spiritualist and the potential for their schemes. Fortunately, history is dotted with such characters from which I can draw inspiration. The particular brand of spiritualism that inspired this book comes from the Victorians, who sought to communicate with the dead. A number of scientists we still hold in high regard today, such as Marie Curie and Alfred Russel Wallace, gave credit to their practices. From the Fox sisters and their rapping spirit friend to Helen Duncan vomiting cheesecloth ectoplasm, there were any number of methods these spiritualists used to convince their clients of their abilities. Saffron would have never credited any of the typical parlor tricks, so I wanted Madame Martin to present her with things she would have a harder time dismissing.

The effects of *Datura stramonium* do just that. The plants of the genus *Datura* are known to contain scopolamine and atropine. Readers of the Saffron Everleigh mystery series will recognize scopolamine from a previous mystery, where the villain administered it as a part of a cocktail of chemicals that made their victim "curiously biddable." Though psychology in the 1920s hadn't yet developed the concept of suggestibility, that is certainly what *Datura* plants can do to a person, along with making a person overheated, disoriented, delirious, and irritable. Curiously, it can also reduce nausea, which made it a helpful thing for poor, hungover Elizabeth. Due to the low levels absorbed by the séance participants through the skin, the effects are not so dire as to truly poison anyone, but the application is still quite diabolical. Losing trust in one's mind is a terrible thing, especially when one is helped along by a villain in a mask.

The first time I saw a WWI era gas mask in person, a true, cold to the bone shiver swept through my body. It stopped me dead as I meandered through a display at the Smithsonian National Museum of American History. I knew that anything that could cause such a reaction in me, separated by a dozen feet and a sheet of glass—not to mention a hundred years of history—must be included in this story. It is emblematic of the horrors humanity has visited upon itself. With one goal of this book being to play with gothic elements, having characters not only confronted by but embody this ghost soldier character was as irresistible as it was unsettling.

The ailment from which Demian Petrov suffered, and ultimately died as the result of complications relating to, has been affecting pockets of people in regions across Europe and Asia for a long time. Little did Petrov, Thomas, and Violet know that the origins of the disease they spent years hunting down would not be identified for nearly *one hundred more years.*

Balkan Endemic Nephropathy (BEN) is defined by a collection of symptoms including weakness, pallor, anemia, high blood pressure, and chronic kidney disease, leading to renal failure and cancer. Symptoms were only recently connected back to the consumption of *Aristolochia,* more specifically *Aristolochia clematitis.* As Saffron and her friends learned, birthwort can be used medicinally for childbirth but also for gout and even as a remedy for snakebites. In fact, the connection was not made until the friend of a medical researcher pursuing BEN suffered the same symptoms after visiting a weight-loss clinic where they were given an herbal supplement containing birthwort. What the researchers discovered, however, was that in areas where BEN is prevalent, the lovely broad leaves sheltering the tiny pipe flowers of birthwort are tucked among wheat, barely, and rye, and when the latter are harvested, the birthwort is processed along with it, contaminating the grain. If only Petrov had known to tell his people to simply pull the weeds before the harvest! But he could not have known the devastating effect of aristolochic acids, because the chemicals were only isolated and identified in 1953.

ACKNOWLEDGMENTS

Thank you to my husband, Erfawn, for encouraging and empowering me to write my books, for talking through my ideas, and making me laugh at his very silly renditions of my work.

Thanks to my kids, who sometimes make it very difficult to write but make it so very worth it. Juliet, you were with me every step of the way writing and editing this book: in my belly, sleeping on my chest, and bouncing on my lap. I'm sorry I had to remove your additions to my manuscript. Rumi, this book was the first you were able to read any piece of (not the scary parts, of course), and listening to your voice read my words is a memory I will always treasure.

Thanks to my parents for being my first readers, for helping me form my narrative and make sense of my ideas. Erin, thank you for answering my random "What would you do if . . ." texts and being the sort of friend to inspire my characters. What would I do without my own Elizabeth?

Kelsey deserves a beta reader gold star for speed reading this book in its final stages, and she deserves a hug for convincing me it was not, in fact, dreadful. My mother- and father-in-law, Audrey, Aleah, Arezou, my brothers Rob and Jack, and a host of other friends and family are owed a big thanks as well for their constant support and encouragement.

Thanks to my editor, Melissa, for chipping away at my drafts to reveal their best shape.

To the team at Crooked Lane, thank you for your work to get this book out in the world with patience and professionalism. Nicole Lecht, my cover artist, and Jodie Harris, my audiobook narrator, your exceptional work continues to bring new readers into the series, and I can't thank you enough for making my books look and sound so good.

And thank you, readers, for welcoming Saffron and her friends onto your shelves!

Center Point Large Print
600 Brooks Road / PO Box 1
Thorndike, ME 04986-0001 USA

(207) 568-3717

US & Canada:
1 800 929-9108
www.centerpointlargeprint.com